REPRODUCTION

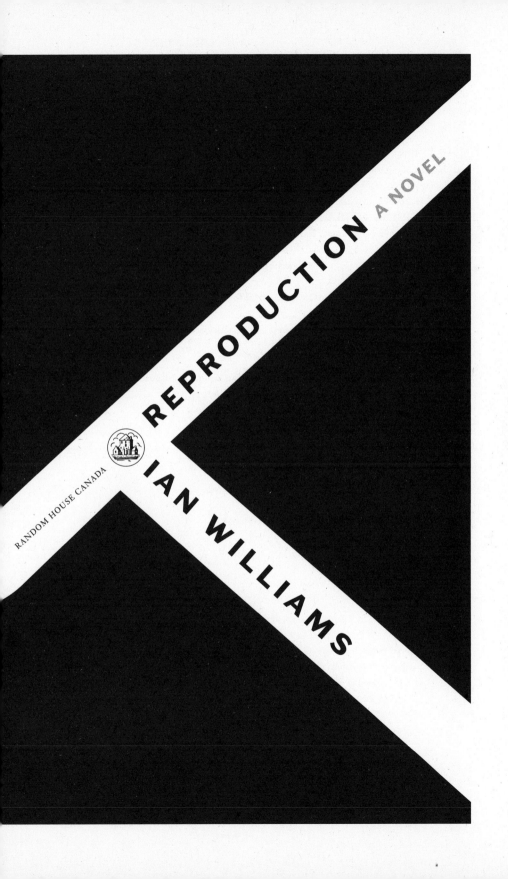

REPRODUCTION

A NOVEL

IAN WILLIAMS

RANDOM HOUSE CANADA

PUBLISHED BY RANDOM HOUSE CANADA

Copyright © 2019 Ian Williams

All rights reserved under International and Pan-American Copyright Conventions.
No part of this book may be reproduced in any form or by any electronic or mechanical means,
including information storage and retrieval systems, without permission in writing from the publisher,
except by a reviewer, who may quote brief passages in a review. Published in 2019 by
Random House Canada, a division of Penguin Random House Canada Limited, Toronto.
Distributed in Canada by Penguin Random House Canada Limited, Toronto.

www.penguinrandomhouse.ca

Random House Canada and colophon are registered trademarks.

Pages 449 and 450 constitute a continuation of the copyright page.

Library and Archives Canada Cataloguing in Publication

Williams, Ian, 1979–, author
Reproduction / Ian Williams.

Issued also in electronic format.
ISBN 978-0-7352-7405-1
eBook ISBN 978-0-7352-7407-5

I. Title.

PS8645.I4448R47 2019   C813'.6   C2018-902713-4
                                                C2018-902714-2

Book design by Lisa Jager

Cover images: (envelope) © Aha-Soft, (texture) © Jullius, both Shutterstock.com;
(palm fronds) illustration from *The Lady of the Forest* [A novel] by L.T. Meade.
London: Partridge & Co, 1889. Courtesy of The British Library.

Printed and bound in the United States of America

2 4 6 8 9 7 5 3 1

Penguin
Random House
RANDOM HOUSE CANADA

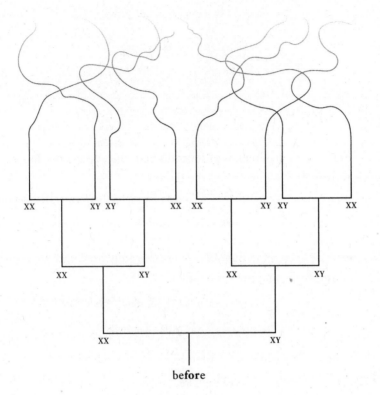

before

There is no technical means of reproduction that, up to now, has managed to surpass the mirror and the dream.

Elena Ferrante, *The Days of Abandonment*

Why does he keep returning? He keeps returning forever, keeps returning and returning and he is my father.

Adrienne Kennedy, *Funnyhouse of a Negro*

The truth is that wherever a man lies with a woman, there, whether they like it or not, a transcendental relation is set up between them which must be eternally enjoyed or eternally endured.

C. S. Lewis, *The Screwtape Letters*

If someone puts his hand here, or here, kiddies, it is sex, which you are not supposed to be having.

Lynn Coady, *Hellgoing*

On the one hand, we know today that our bodies keep a complete and faultless record of all the things we have ever experienced.

Alice Miller, *The Body Never Lies*

Now look objectively. You have to
admit the cancer cell is beautiful.
If it were a flower, you'd say, How pretty,
with its mauve centre and pink petals.

Margaret Atwood, "Cell"

Be fruitful, and multiply.

Genesis 1:28

PART 1

XX + XY

LATE SEVENTIES

XX

I.

Both of their mothers were dying in the background.

XY

I.

Both of their mothers were still alive in the background.

XX

2.

Before she died her mother was prickly. Before her mother died she was. One more time. Before her mother died she, her mother, was prickly. One more time. Before her mother died she, her mother, prickled her, Felicia.

In the days before she died, her mother flew into unpredictable rages over the littlest things. Felicia said *sardines* instead of *tuna* when passing the tin and her mother blasted her.

Why you working yourself up so? Felicia asked.

Because a tuna is a big fish and a sardines is a small fish. *A sardines*—you hear the nonsense you have me saying?

Her hands vibrated so badly she couldn't open the tin, the can, the tin.

At the next meal, Felicia didn't pour tomato sauce quickly enough into a pot, a sauce pan, thereby essentially, judging from her mother's reaction, assassinating the Archduke.

All the nutrients done gone already, her mother said. We might as well eat hair. You happy with yourself?

Later that evening, up in the room they rented from a Christian lady, a retired British-trained nurse, who stored her medical equipment in two trunks under the window, Felicia took her mother's blood pressure. It was 190 over 110.

See. You provoking me. You provoking me, man.

Two days later it was 205 over 115. Her mother said it was because she had climbed the stairs. Or it was because because because the machine was broken. But when Felicia measured her own pressure, it was 110 over 60, which, instead of confirming the sphygmomanometer's reliability, caused her mother to worry and divert the conversation to Felicia's iron levels. She demanded menstruation details, when, how long, how heavy, what colour. Where could she get good beef? West Indian beef, not from these anemic snow-eating cows. The cast iron pot—the soap Felicia used had wrecked it. Nutrients, her mother said that a lot before she turned into a seahorse and drifted off.

And then over the weekend, her pressure went down to 146 over 90. They both laughed.

I telling you I know what I doing. Don't feel I don't know.

Her mother had taken to eating two cloves of garlic at each meal.

Sunday night, after the women wrapped their hair for bed, they leaned against the headboard in their rented room in the Christian woman's house and excoriated the choir director for favouring the tenors. When her mother fell asleep, Felicia read a little *Great Expectations* for school. Three pages and she was out.

Her mother woke up and took the bus from Brampton to work in Toronto before she died. Obviously. When else would she take it?

+

Point taken. Yes, and then the office buzzed Felicia during period 4, Home Economics, and told her to bring her things with her, there had been an emergency.

But her mother was not in Emergency at St. Xavier hospital. In fact, Emergency was taped closed. Felicia imagined the worst, that her mother wasn't simply dead but that a grenade had gone off in her chest and destroyed a section of the hospital. A police officer directed Felicia and a couple with a baby to an alternate entrance.

Felicia found her mother in Palliative, sharing a room with an elderly woman. It was strange to see her mother sleeping in public. She was normally a vigilant woman with chameleon eyes that seemed to move independently from one point of suspicion to another. Now, although they were both closed, she seemed uneasy, perhaps with the fact that her bra had been removed by strangers and her breasts splayed unflatteringly sideways.

Between the two beds, a man stood holding his wrists like the Escher print of hands drawing themselves. It would become his characteristic position. From forehead to jaw, his head was the same width as his neck. From shoulders to feet, he seemed constrained in a tight magic box, ready to be sawed in two. Put together, he comprised two rectangles stacked on each other—a tall, abstract snowman. His pants were wet from the knee down. Despite that, Felicia presumed he was the doctor because he was a man, a white man, a middle-aged white man, wearing a pinstriped shirt, but it turned out he was only a man, a white man, a middle-aged white man, wearing stripes and gripping his wrists.

Unconscious, Edgar said.

Unconscious or sleeping? Felicia asked.

Unconscious, he repeated. He presented the woman in the other bed as proof of his medical expertise. My mother. She's sleeping.

His mother's mouth was open. There was brown industrial paper towel on her chest to catch the leaking saliva. She gave the impression of needing to be laced up—as if by pulling the strings of a corset one could restore her mouth, her skin, her posture, to their former attentiveness.

She's not going to make it, Edgar said. He flicked the bag of intravenous solution with his middle finger, then looked for some change to register in his mother. Seconds later, she began coughing. Her cheeks filled with thick liquid as Edgar searched for a cup, her spittoon. Felicia happened to swallow at the same time as his mother and while looking at the lump go down the woman's throat, she felt the phlegm go down her own. She pulled the collar of her coat tight around her neck.

Felicia turned back to her mother. Her mother was so careful about applying makeup and now there was no trace of it on her. Where were her earrings? Her nail polish looked more crimson than red. Felicia knocked on her knuckles.

You hearing me? Felicia leaned in. You hearing me?

She thought she saw her mother frown. She frowned. Or perhaps it was a deception of light, the passing accident of light reflected from someone's watch face.

Felicia heard the jaunty jingle of keys behind her.

So what brings your mother here on this fine autumn afternoon?

Without moving the rest of her body, Felicia twisted her cervical vertebrae to see if he was serious.

Mutter, here, couldn't breathe, he offered. It's her pneumonia. He put an odd stress on the *her* as if he were settling a dispute between feuding children: it's her doll, let her have it. They think the cancer might have spread to her other lung. We're waiting. It's not easy. The waiting. Not easy at all. Come on, get in there.

Felicia turned around fully. She hadn't seen snow since arriving in Canada.

Edgar was slouching in one of the chairs in the middle of the room, organizing his keychain. His hair was the colour of the dried oak leaves around her school.

What do you know? she said.

I'm just telling you how it goes. I've been through this once, twice, be—

No, I mean what do you know about my situation?

XY

2.

A pipe had burst on the second floor of St. Xavier and the ER was flooded. Whenever Edgar went down to smoke, he waded through water that was as deep as his knees, water so heavy he had to rotate his hips just to pull his legs through.

The hospital have more than one entrance, Felicia informed him.

Of course. We're not in West Africa, he said. But the people, who wants to deal with people?

I'm not African, she said.

Edgar looked up from his keys. Nobody said she was. Good body, useful body. Her body seemed useful to the point of being industrial, assembled out of construction machinery, the kind of body you could ask to retrieve a pen from a tight space with its claw arm. It had calculated a series of compensations for its plainness. Her chest was modest but her broad shoulders gave her shape; her backside was flat but the anterior tilt of her pelvis lifted it; her hips had little flare but her wide stance created a triangular base that balanced the inverted triangle of her torso.

He turned back to sequencing the keys by the course of his day, not just by category—house keys, car keys, office building key, office department key, office key—and explained that the hospital had stopped admitting patients around lunchtime. They diverted incoming ambulances to a nearby hospital, closed the first two floors of A wing, and transferred patients wherever they could find beds.

He finished, That's how they ended up together.

He lifted the spiral of the key ring with his thumb. What locks were these little duplicate keys for?

He finished again, That's how they ended up— And finally, That's how she ended up here.

They just pick Palliative out of a hat and throw she body in here? Felicia asked.

Edgar let the spiral snap close. That wasn't what he said. She kept misunderstanding him.

I think you scored pretty good digs, considering that some people are four to a room. I was adamant that the capacity of this room not exceed two.

There were two chairs in the middle of the room back to back, and a yellow curtain divider. Felicia's mother was on the side near the window, which overlooked a courtyard with a single leafless tree. Edgar's mother was on the side near the bathroom. Both of them were covered with cream blankets, four stripes near the legs. Next to the beds were bags of liquid, tubes, metal stands, machines with faces asking to be read or touched. There was a small tissue box on each of their side tables.

The shed key he didn't need to carry around. He said, It's the best place either of them could be right now.

In Palliative.

In Palliative, he confirmed.

The sun had gone down. Felicia hadn't yet removed her hat, which along with her coat looked unnatural on her, as if she did not choose them herself.

The boiler's working fine, Edgar said with a smile. If she were friendlier he would try to encircle the fulcrum of her waist with his hands. The girls at the office always got a kick out of that. He said, You must be burning up.

But Felicia didn't want to talk. To him. She spoke just fine to the nurse who came in to collect a medical history. Edgar learned more about her mother than he knew about his own sister-in-law. Her middle name was Eunice. She was born in March. She had a heart murmur. She was advised to leave school early because she fainted a lot as a child. But it might have been the heat. She'd had a boiled egg and porridge for breakfast. No allergies. She didn't like baked beans, canned food in general, but it wasn't an allergy. She was married. The husband was back home. The islands. No cancer in the family. No stroke. Hypertension, yes. She also had a sister who had sugar and had her foot cut off twice. Same foot twice. She had five to eight children. Three died in infancy. Felicia was the youngest. That's how she ended up in Canada. Her mother couldn't have any more children after Felicia. Something went wrong. Felicia didn't know. She didn't know.

Not everybody can have children, Edgar said. He was feeling left out because the women were talking as if he wasn't there. No, he was only coming to Felicia's rescue after the assault of questions. (He felt left out.) The woman had a heart attack. Why did he have to listen to her whole reproductive history?

Both Felicia and the nurse turned to him without seeing him, as if resting momentarily from the heat of their conversation.

Roll up those wet pants, Felicia said then led the nurse into the hallway. She doesn't take no medication except for a tablespoon of cod liver oil every morning with tea.

Edgar set the keys on Mutter's bed. He rolled up his right pant leg. Much better. Why hadn't he thought of that himself? He flexed his foot upward to admire his calves. He crossed his legs at the knee to display the muscle to its advantage when Felicia re-entered.

Edgar was deep in a cigarette when Felicia returned. His legs crossed, his socks off, the mark of the elastic smoothed somewhat but red.

She made a face and pulled the dividing curtain. Some people acted like they couldn't breathe when the thinnest whiff of smoke came their way.

Leave it open, he said.

Your mother have pneumonia, no? Felicia said through the curtain.

I can't hear you, Edgar said though he could.

I don't see how you could be in here smoking when— Felicia coughed.

Speak up.

She pushed her head through the curtain. She wore the endearing expression of a young woman who wanted to wear glasses before her time just to be taken seriously. I don't see how you could be—

I think you've forgotten how lucky you are not to be sitting downstairs in sewage right now, he said and finished his cigarette. What if he sorted his keys by size so he could find them in the dark? Lightbulbs, he had to buy one for the garage. He wouldn't find a store open before his trip to Calgary tomorrow. Did the distributor people firm up lunch?

She pulled the curtain all the way around her mother.

More doctors smoke Camel than any other brand, he said. He might as well make himself comfortable. He took off his pants and hung them on the footrail of his mother's bed to dry.

XX

3.

S he heard him removing his pants: the belt buckle clanging against itself, the zipper, the whoosh of fabric. He sang softly to himself while doing it. His mother was coughing up the trapped badger from her lungs yet Felicia could hear him singing softly in a voice so high, so nostalgic of boyhood, that she resolved to be kinder to all God's creatures.

She opened the curtain.

He was no longer smoking. He was sitting with his ankles crossed. Pants off. His dress shirt extended below his hips, covering his underwear. There were tiny, fair hairs on his legs that she wanted to blow off.

You ever been on an airplane? he asked.

How did he think she got to this country? By whale? Kinder to God's creatures. Once, she said.

I never tire of the clouds. Tomorrow I'm off to Calgary. Might go skiing while I'm out there. You'll have the room to yourself.

Thank you, Jesus. For the first time, she perceived an accent, bones in his consonants, girth in his vowels.

You ever see the Rockies?

Pictures, she said. Apparently she would have to alert him to the obvious. Your mutter's coughing.

Mooter, he corrected her pronunciation.

Mutter. That's what I said. All God's creatures. Hold it together.

The Rocky Mountains. He panned his hand across space. Last time, no, two times ago, we had some meetings in Banff. No joke, on one side of the road, a bear, on the other an elk, and us in the middle. He shook his head.

Mutter coughed shrilly. He lit another cigarette.

Oh, no, no, no. Hell no. Felicia took hold of the dividing curtain again.

She put a thousand words into her good-night-so-sorry-your-mother's-sick-help-her-with-some-water-yes-hold-the-cup-for-her-you-have-a-good-night-you-hear-such-a-shame-what-is-man-chaff-chaff-chaff-the-days-of-our-years-are-chaff-threescore-and-ten-but-don't-give-up-hope-give-her-a-sweater-cover-up-her-chest-when-the-roll-is-called-up-yonder-a-little-water-now-tsk-tsk smile.

Edgar stood up and stood in the path of the curtain, adjusting his underwear under his shirt. Felicia came right close to him. You-and-your-mutter-have-a-good-night-you-hear, announced her shoulder to his sternum.

Mutter likes to see out the window, he said. His hair was parted and swept over in a tumble to the side in a sixties hairstyle, very out of style now. But what did she know of white men's hairstyles? He looked like the father of Dick and Jane.

Felicia looked back and forth between the window and Edgar. Apart from one scraggly tree, which couldn't be seen from Mutter's angle, there wasn't anything to see. Plus it was dark.

Mutter likes to see the sky.

Then you should have put her in the bed near the window.

His mother coughed chaff-chaff-chaff-chaff-chaff.

See, he said as if his mother were coughing confirmation. He stepped around Felicia and undid the little progress she had made with the curtain.

But she's coughing, Felicia said.

I thought the cancer would take her out. But it looks like—

I can't have her coughing on my mother, Felicia said.

She's not coughing on your mother.

The last thing she need is to come down with pneumonia.

Edgar lined his forehead into a haiku:

> You've got bigger things
> to worry about, my dear,
> than a little cough.

+

She endured that cigarette.

But the next time Edgar wanted to smoke, Felicia fixed him with a look, *bad eye* they called it on her island, which he pretended not to see, but he put the cigarette back into the pack, put his pants back on, and left. Felicia took the opportunity to find the nurse on duty. The hallways were dim. From one of the rooms, she heard the choked, desperate silence of a patient recovering his breath after vomiting. There was one nurse at the station.

I don't understand why you put my mother in that room.

I did not admit your mother, the nurse said.

Can you tell me if she's— Felicia didn't know how to finish. Conscious? Better? Dreaming?

The nurse followed Felicia back to the room with a folder. She observed the monitor. She took the temperature. She looked at the colour under Felicia's mother's eyelids. But Felicia wasn't sure the nurse was capturing essential information. She pointed out the dark fingernails. She lifted her coat from her mother's feet for the nurse to touch.

She's stable, the nurse said.

She stable? She not improving?

Stable doesn't mean—

I know what *stable* means, Felicia snapped then instantly regretted it. She sanded her voice. I think you should send my mother to Emergency.

There's no Emergency.

This is an emergency.

Emergency is flooded, the nurse said slowly. Intensive Care is flooded. There are no beds in Cardiac so, given the circumstances, Miss, she's in the best place possible—above water.

You making a joke of my situation?

Would you like her floating in the ICU?

You in the wrong profession, Felicia said. I want to talk to a doctor. I here since three o'clock and no doctor come to find me yet. You tell me she in a coma when I come in here. Now you telling me she stable. You giving she oxygen. I don't see nothing hook up to she heart. I not no doctor but something need to hook up to the woman heart.

The doctor will be here in the morning.

I don't see how you could have my mother in here next to this lady who coughing coughing all the time. How you go put she next to somebody with highly contagious pneumonia?

The woman looked at the next bed. Where's her mask?

She didn't have on no mask from the time I get here.

She's supposed to.

The nurse pulled a blue mask from a box on the wall and covered Mutter's nose and mouth.

She has to keep it on, the nurse said.

The room already full of bacteria, Felicia said. I could pull this curtain?

Of course.

The man, her son, say he mother does like to see—

It's the middle of the night. Nothing to see, the nurse said and drew the curtain between the chairs, leaving Felicia on one side and herself on the other.

3.

Outside, Edgar sat high on the back of a bench, feet on the seat, smoking tobacco though his mind felt weedy. His life had been a long straight line to this point that ended with the red tip of a cigarette.

If two people travelling in a straight line meet in a hospital room, is that a vertex or an intersection? Why can't two lines be friends or form a shape of some sort? Good word, vertex. Vertex.

He noticed that his belt was unbuckled. It dangled between his legs like a—How long is a line? If line a is travelling on a plane to Calgary at 850 kilometres per hour while line b remains arrested next to a bed, how much longer will it take line a to recover from the death of its mother than line b?

He twirled the long end of his belt. He meditated long before flicking his cigarette away. Then he ducked beneath the unmanned tape of Emergency and walked through the ocean, back to the room where his mother lay dying.

+

Edgar immediately removed the mask from Mutter. She was in the middle of a rapid succession of coughs unh-unh-unh-unh-unh-unh-unh that ended with a long, high-pitched one, her windpipe trying to invert itself like a sock. She shouldn't inhale the same germs she was expelling.

He opened the curtain.

Put the mask back on her, Felicia said.

Edgar went to his chair and tapped a folded newspaper against his knee, as if he hadn't heard.

Felicia crossed the room and put the mask on his mother, *his* mutter. Edgar got up and removed it. Felicia replaced it. Mutter's coughing intensified, a thick continuous assault that left her breathless. Her eyes watered. Her mouth was full of phlegm.

Don't let her swallow it, Felicia said. This time, she was the one who lowered the mask.

Edgar took a Styrofoam cup from the side table and held it under Mutter's mouth.

Mutter spat weakly. Trails continued down the side of her mouth. Felicia found a straw and gave the woman some water then she wiped her mouth with the paper towel on her chest.

She adjusted the angle of the bed. Let that cold drain from her head, she told Edgar.

Edgar looked into the cup. The liquid was rusty. Streaks of red marbled the yellow. He tipped the cup to show Felicia, who then covered her mouth and hurried from the room. He glanced into the cup again. In English, he couldn't determine whether it was disgust or shame or tears or a vision of an impending fact that propelled her? The German word for her departure would be *Fernweh*.

+

He had the room to himself long enough to construct another word problem. If one calculated the number of hours over a period of months or years that relationships take to develop and applied them into a single, compressed meeting of heightened time, and tested that relationship years later by a reliable metric, would that relationship be as sturdy as a relationship constructed over months or years?

Before he could bring to mind personal and celebrity examples for each case, he heard Felicia in the hallway, arguing with one of the nurses. He got up to investigate.

I don't have no money for the pay phone, Felicia was saying.

I'm very sorry, the nurse said. I can't help you.

You *can* help me. Felicia's arms were expressive.

I really can't.

Edgar approached them.

You go have to live with your conscience if something happen to my mother while you upholding a policy, Felicia said.

I'm very sorry. We don't permit international calls.

Edgar jumped in. Why do you assume her call is international?

Is the sister you're calling here? the nurse asked Felicia.

Felicia didn't look at Edgar but he felt an energy pass between them like she had psychically tagged him into the fight. She nodded.

The nurse looked unconvinced.

She has people here, Edgar said.

The nurse held the receiver to Felicia while looking hard at Edgar. One call, she said. What's the number?

Felicia rattled out a local number while the nurse dialled. The conversation was too polite to be with a sister. The nurse was placing a coloured form into patient folders. She seemed satisfied listening to Felicia's acrobatics. Felicia couldn't say, Call *my* sister, if she was in fact speaking to one of her sisters. She would not need to give one sister the number of another. Handcuffed.

You run a tight prison, Edgar said to the nurse. She should be ashamed of herself, harassing an eighteen, nineteen-year-old girl like Felicia.

One local call, the nurse said. It's not a public phone.

+

When Felicia ended the call, Edgar nudged her lightly and she followed him down the hallway, around the corner, and down to the second floor. His pants were wet against his shins.

You might get lucky, he said.

They did. Immediately. They found an unattended nurse's station. Edgar lifted the phone from the desk to the raised counter.

Don't talk too loud, he said.

Edgar leaned on the counter and kept lookout while Felicia placed a call. As soon as her sister picked up, Felicia turned her back to him. Her body relaxed when she began speaking. She sounded like the younger sister. He recognized the tone—pleading, petulant, reluctantly deferential. Although his brother was only two years older, his decisions had determined the structure of Edgar's life. He studied Economics so Edgar had to. What a mess that attempt was. He worked at the head office in Germany after Vater died so Edgar had to anchor himself in Canada with Mutter.

How long it go take you to get a visa? Felicia said into the phone. Well, tell— Interrupted. Tell— Again. I know she close but she illegal. She go say she can't leave the States.

Edgar realized he was listening when Felicia glanced over her shoulder at him. He took a few steps down the hallway. Back to the first question: If two people travelling in a straight line meet in a hospital room, is that a vertex or an intersection? Solve.

Is only now I could use the phone! Felicia said. You could call the hospital or call the landlady and she go tell you what happening.

A vertex can become an intersection by extending the lines. But an intersection cannot become a vertex again.

Nobody say anything about an operation. Pause. They thinning she blood. Pause. Everything close down—Emergency, Intensive Care. She up in Palliative. Pause. I know she don't belong there but that's where they put she.

Felicia looked over her shoulder again and Edgar shot his gaze upward to study an exit sign.

I pressuring the nurses to do something but they standoffish. All I can do is wait, watch and pray. Pause. She not looking good but you remember Cling-Cling—right, clawing the casket from the inside. Pause. It don't matter. Listen, whether she get better or she get worse you go want to be here. Pause. In the morning, call the hospital and ask then I go find a way to call you and we go compare what they saying.

Felicia turned around so the telephone cord was wrapped around her body. She covered the mouthpiece and mouthed to Edgar, Excuse me. He gave her a little salute.

I don't know, I don't know, she was saying to her sister as Edgar walked toward his cigarette spot in the parkette outside Emergency. He sat on the back of a bench, feet on the seat, and smoked through his thoughts.

+

When he returned to the room, the curtain was open and Mutter's mask was off. Felicia was sitting on a chair between the two beds.

Edgar removed his wet pants and sat beside her. She took a deep breath. He gripped his wrists. They opened their mouths.

4.

T heir conversation that night was made decades later into a movie starring Ethan Hawke and a French actress.

+

Where I come from—

The islands, he clarified.

The islands, she confirmed. —everybody have they real name and the name that people does call them. Not the girls so much unless you fat or lightskin but definitely the boys.

They would call me, what, Whitey?

We already have a Whitey. Maybe Hitler.

Ignorant.

Who ignorant?

Not you. I don't mean you.

Oho.

People. Edgar conducted his hand around. Like Hitler's the only German.

You not supposed to like your name.

And even Hitler, whatever you think of him, Edgar persisted, but Felicia didn't think anything of him, the same way she didn't think anything of Genghis Khan. They were exam questions to her. Even Hitler, he got the idea for eugenics from the Americans because it was the Americans, not the Germans, who used to sterilize their people first. So people should get educated before they say Hitler this, Hitler that.

Okay, okay, she said. You can be Whitey.

+

Which Germany your mother from? East or West? Felicia asked then promptly missed Edgar's answer because she was congratulating herself on her sophisticated geopolitical question. She was not part of the ignorant, uneducated masses, despite the rejection of her high school certificate from a small unrecognized island.

Even with that Nadia Comaneci winning everything, was the next thing she heard.

Remind me, she said, which side is the good side again?

+

Felicia told him that her mother was a domestic.

Edgar beamed. We used to have one, he said. Two. One from Trinidad and the other from—

Jamaica?

No, a small island somewhere. Edgar tried again.

I not from there, she said. She told him that her mother collapsed right in the white lady's kitchen. The children called the ambulance.

How old are they?

Seven, eight. I want to know if this woman was such a concerned employer, a friend to my mother, why I didn't meet she by the bedside when I come here. Why I didn't meet anybody by the bedside?

Edgar opened his mouth.

I meet you, yes, is true but you is a practical stranger.

Edgar opened his mouth again.

You is a goldfish or what? Felicia said. And notice once my mother drop down how this woman find sheself at home to watch she own children? And my sister— Felicia touched her toque—quick to blame me for letting my mother leave the house this morning and have other people calling ambulance for she. I glad those children see she fall down. Right on the kitchen tile.

Those are smart kids, Edgar said. He had plucked the white people from the story and let the others swirl down the drain.

+

I don't mean to interrupt, Edgar said, but you really should remove your hat. He reached toward her head.

She flinched. You does just remove people clothing for them?

You're in a building.

It's not the same rule for men and women. Felicia scratched under her toque. She imagined that Edgar was overdressed as a child and forced to sit silently on a tufted settee among adults.

In this culture, Edgar began.

I could finish my story or you want to talk about a hat?

+

She told Edgar that she and her mother shared a bed in a room they rented from a Christian lady. As they were falling asleep one night, Felicia wanted to talk about what she would do if she won the Wintario, though she didn't have a ticket, seeing as gambling was prohibited, perhaps in Leviticus.

What *would* you do? Edgar interrupted.

Buy a big house and get married.

You don't need to win the lottery to get married.

You don't expect me to live in a big house by myself.

However, her mother wanted to talk about her funeral, her death, how to style her hair, who not to invite. Her mother told her to wear the black dress with the lace décolletage and ruffles at the wrist. And a hat. The brim was to be as wide as her shoulders.

If I should close my eyes, Felicia quoted her mother's euphemism.

This was a month before she was lying dying in a hospital bed in the background.

+

Paining, she told him. Her mother said her back was paining her. That was last week. She thought she might have strained herself at work creaming butter and sugar by hand. She only managed to roll half her hair into sponge curlers before lying down. But the pressure was worse when she was lying down. Felicia opened the window then continued putting in the curlers.

Felicia, girl, I wonder if this is the heart attack.

As far as Felicia knew, a heart attack was supposed to maul you between its teeth, then strut away with its cut-off tail and tailored ears, yet here it was licking her mother's back. Very much unlike Salt.

Salt? Edgar asked.

Salt down the road.

His name was Salt?

Felicia looked back unblinking, unsure what the problem was. Uncle Salt.

Of the earth? Edgar tried to clarify.

The whole village used to hear him gargling salt water every morning by the standpipe before the government bring water inside. They find him dead right there with the water on and he head crack open and blood running down the hill.

+

Yes, but then she was fine again, Felicia continued. She was leaning with her back against the headboard, saying I old enough to wear a little lipstick now and again. But not to harlot myself with too much blush. When she was my age she used to be stepping.

Edgar looked at her lips.

She ask me if I was feeling cold. The lady does turn down the heat in the night to save money.

+

I should say a prayer for her for the night, Felicia said.

Me too.

Felicia went to her mother's bed and prayed.

Edgar went to his, stood over the bed a reasonable time, then said, Does that feel better?

I not praying to feel better, Felicia said.

I was talking to Mutter. Edgar had placed his watch around her wrist. She's used to having some weight on her.

+

Felicia's mother was cold one minute and then she was hot.

I feelin' a whole picka bush through my body, quoted Felicia. Like dey beatin' me, man. Dey beatin me with picka bush. And when she touched her mother's forehead, it was slippery.

If I should close my eyes, her mother said with her eyes closed.

Nothing going to happen, Felicia said and it was like she invaded Poland.

You think I making joke, her mother snapped. I'm at the gate of death and you telling me is nothing.

Yet neither of them suggested calling an ambulance.

In Felicia's small unrecognized island, where there were only one hospital and two community health centres, ambulances were not free. They were also a leading cause of motor vehicular accidents, she told Edgar. Then she changed the subject abruptly, I don't care what the nurse say, your mother need some Vicks VapoRub to warm up she chest if you want to get rid of that cough. I go bring some for you tomorrow.

+

Felicia wanted to know who was in the bed before her mother.
Edgar told her about another woman. They had to recarnanate her.
Resuscitate, Felicia corrected.
What did I say?
Felicia stayed focused. And?
Only one person in the family spoke English.
She stayed the course. What happened to her?
Of course, she— Edgar stuck out his tongue and drew a knife across his neck, a most indelicate gesture for a man his age to make in a hospital. As I was saying, you're a better neighbour. You shovel my sidewalk too.

+

Felicia pulled her toque low over her ears. She didn't want to be looked at. Sometimes, as a woman, you don't want a man rubbing his eyes all over you in that offhand appraising way they have.

+

What do you do? she asked.
Paperplane.
Oh, Paperplane. She felt she should know what that was. He didn't seem like a mechanic. But what is it you do exactly?
I told you.
The plane company. But what do you *do?*
My title?
Right.
I don't have one. It's a family business.

+

She felt like he was trying to dress her into a category of woman the way she used to dress her doll, twisting its arms over its head and dragging outfits on and off its body.

But do you *want* to work? he asked.

How you expect me to live? she replied. But if working is all it take then every woman in my country is a feminist.

You don't have a single housewife in— He waited but she did not fill in the blank.

Well, of course, some women stay home, but they does work, bake a little sweet bread and sell it, sew uniforms, pick banana.

They have children?

Plenty.

Then no, they're not feminists.

+

He overshared. She didn't need to know that he had had a vasectomy. Or that he used to lime with some Bohemians before he cut his hair.

Like hippies, she said. He was going to call her *ignorant* again.

No, not like hippies. I mean, we didn't greet people with peace signs.

But once Vater, may he remain dead, cut him off financially and Mutter got cancer the first time, he couldn't continue driving shirtless across the continent, smoking weed, and crafting Marxist manifestos. He took the moneywhoring job his father created for him, which he couldn't leave now because he didn't finish his degree and yes he liked the money and the jets and the *Mr. Gross, could you sign here* of the secretaries in the building.

Edgar gripped his wrists as he was explaining this, his self-importance tempered by the odd self-embrace.

So I decided if they wanted to kill me then I'd make sure another Gross never walked the face of the earth.

Kill you with work, Felicia said.

Every fibre of my being.

Honest, permanent, high-paying work.

His complaint confirmed Felicia's suspicions about white people, although she now saw him as less of a white man and more as a very pitiful man, the way she pictured all men as somewhat simple and unrefined and helpless with basic things but good with abstract things like bills over fifty dollars.

Your head not on right, Felicia said.

It doesn't mean I can't have sex. It just means I can't have children.

+

She said she didn't want to hear about it anymore. But he kept talking about it.

+

I don't see why you would go and mutilate yourself, she said. She tried to recall a passage in Leviticus that prohibited the cutting of one's body. He needed the sound reproof of scripture. Weren't there Bibles in these hospital rooms? Nobody go want to marry you.

Rest assured, I'm not as hopeless as you seem to think.

And you already too old to still be a bachelor. Plain talk, bad manners. I don't know what it is you doing with your life. Then, without warning, Felicia felt herself go from critical mother to six-year-old. I'm going to have two girls and a boy, twin girls. Girls should have sisters.

And boys?

Boys too.

XY

4.

Their conversation that night was also prefigured a few years earlier aboard a flight from Boston to Toronto where a girl Felicia's age was returning to university after her father's funeral and divulged every memory to the boy next to her, Oliver, who when he first sat down appeared to be the type to close his eyes and pass gas quietly with a betraying squirm, but in fact shared a bag of chocolate almonds with her as he recounted the story of his older sister's passing (overdose) when he was eight. He never got over it although his parents later had more children. At the gate, they exchanged numbers.

+

Felicia wouldn't tell Edgar where she was from. The islands. He named the West-Indian islands he remembered from the '76 Olympics: Jamaica, Trinidad, Cuba, Haiti, Puerto Rico.

She said, I not from anywhere you know.

He thought she was flirting with him with the unrecognized island routine—twice she had mentioned it—but no, she had no intention of telling him where she was from.

I not from anywhere.

+

He told her that Mutter reverted to German as her vocabulary dried up. She used to call me—

Hitler.

Please don't call me Hitler.

Ghostface.

No.

Hansel.

No. She called me *Schatz*, Edgar cupped his elbows and rocked slightly. She called everyone that though. All the girls.

Girls?

Caregivers, day nurses, the girls who come, the girls who come when I go to work in the morning.

+

I bet you don't know why we brought all those domestics into the country.

Laziness, she said.

No, not— He was thrown off. He glimpsed into the heart of blacks and it was, as he feared, no alley for a white man to be. In the fifties, the government decided it needed to replace all the women who went to work.

And you didn't stop to think who go replace all the domestic women in their own country, Felicia said. A whole lot of women leaving their families to take care of white people children. No offence.

Edgar retreated. She came on a two-year contract?

Two years? You crazy. She here since '65.

But her initial contract was for two years, Edgar said.

Felicia gave him a long leery look. He knew too much. He didn't tell her that he had tried to get a domestic of his own to take care of Mutter a few years ago, in 1975. The domestic scheme was all over the news because the government had tried to deport seven women for sponsoring their children and all he could think was how could I get myself one of those.

Good enough to work, Felicia said. Good enough to stay.

I don't know, Edgar said. The contract said they were supposed to be single, no children, then all of a sudden they're sponsoring these mythical children.

(Mutter coughed.)

And the white women them was supposed to be out working, Felicia said. Not home smoking.

+

No, he didn't own a pair of blue jeans. Yes, he called them blue jeans. Not now, not ever. No one in his family did. Why did she ask?

+

He told her that Mutter wanted a funeral like Oma's, his grossmutter, his mutter's mutter, who had insisted on a closed casket and a portrait of her face on a table in front. Her whole life, Oma had kept up a correspondence with a married man who was not her husband and she thought that the wife might crash the funeral, squat Portuguese widow, curse-bearing thirteenth godmother, and triumphansee her dead face.

Oma died at home.

Oma died after Edgar's bath.

Mutter said the children shouldn't go in. They were too young. Vater said they should, they would, and so his brother took his hand and they walked into the bedroom where Oma, his grossmutter, his mutter's mutter, was lying with a black handkerchief over her face.

+

He told Felicia his hair was still wet.

Felicia was still wearing her toque.

As I was saying, that's how these things happen, he said. While you're doing something else—death. That's the Bard.

Felicia disagreed. Edgar wasn't sure with what.

+

She asked him if his grandmother was in an adulterous relationship with that man.

Edgar couldn't see how his oma could be in an adulterous relationship—such archaic phrasing—with a man by letter. You need to have sex, he said.

Felicia disagreed. Edgar wasn't sure with what.

Whosoever looketh on a woman to lust after her hath committed adultery with her already in his heart.

He had no Bible text in rebuttal.

Did the woman come to the funeral? Felicia asked.

I don't know.

Did the man?

He was already dead.

+

We used to share bathwater in Germany, he said as if his whole life were in that sentence.

+

He told her that apart from *Schatz*, the rest of Mutter's vocabulary consisted of varieties of pain, *der Schmerz, das Leid, der Kummer, die Qual.*
>*So starke Schmerzen.*
>And before she let those go, she dropped down to the article: *der, das, die.*
>It had been the same with his oma.

+

They didn't televise the marathon, Edgar said. Just the ending.
>I would have watch the marathon, she said. I better with the long races. The race is not for the swift, nor the battle for the strong.
>I'd be a sprinter, he said. It was time for another cigarette. And by that point, they were not speaking of the Olympics at all.

+

Felicia was at the climax of a story. They machete him and set him on fire, yes.
>What do you mean *machete him*?
>They hack him up with a machete and set him on fire. The police did bet money on whether he would live or die.
>Felicia stopped there as if she had brought the story to its natural conclusion.
>And did he?
>What do you think?
>Edgar honestly didn't know.
>Why you think I telling you this?
>He didn't know that either. All he did was ask whether she was still cold. But he nodded and feigned understanding.
>Then she finally took off her toque.

+

She tried to pry by multiplying *exactlies.*
>What is it exactly that you do exactly?
>Where are you from?
>We talking about you.
>He bit both lips and smiled *quidproquoly.*

+

Both Edgar and Felicia demonstrated a limited understanding of critical terms.

He wanted to know why her hair was shorn so aggressively. Are you some kind of feminist? he asked. But he meant lesbian.

I not no feminist.

There's nothing wrong with it. He was relieved. Do you want to work?

Not right now. She put her toque back on. I go work when I finish school.

Then you're a feminist.

He could see that she was trying on the word for sophistication, admiring her calf in its hem.

But I want to have children.

You can't, he said.

+

What he said was that he couldn't have children.

What wrong with you? Felicia asked. You have a condition?

No. A decision.

You— She made scissors of her fingers.

I— He clapped and dusted the matter from his hands.

+

He said he didn't want to talk about it anymore. But she kept asking about it.

+

He didn't have sisters.

Clearly, Felicia said. A sister would never let you do that to yourself.

His brother was like a sister, he told her. He was the one who kept him employed, as a promise to Vater, probably. Edgar had done enough to lose his job, not deliberately, but, in his words, stuff happens when you work with a bunch of idiots. Thank God for his secretary, Polly.

Felicia said, I thought you said *machete*.

Secretary, he repeated.

I coulda swear.

As they were falling asleep on chairs facing each other, backs turned to their mothers, rocking in a rowboat down the Nile, they scattered details before each other. Was his brother older or younger? Older. Married? Yes. What's his wife like? A European socialite. Did you go to the wedding? He couldn't make it. His brother—What's his name? Heinrich. Henry. Henry only told him on a Tuesday that he was getting married on the weekend. I thought you said she was a social-ite. She is. That's not how socialites do things. You didn't get a proper invitation? Maybe Mutter got it. Your hair? My hair? Your hair? My sister burn off my good good hair the night before my flight. Gasoline? Lye. You don't have hairdressers on your island? My sister does get the products cheap. Can I feel it? No. I'll feel it in the morning. No. It's growing back. I didn't think some parts would. You should have seen it—burned my scalp white. I don't think you is a good Whitey. Good. Did Mutter go to the wedding? I don't know. Yes, I think so. Does your brother have children? Two. Do you visit? No. Have you ever seen them? In pictures. Why he not here? I mean why are you here alone? Same reason you're here alone. Do you think nobody care about you and me? I don't know about you.

5.

In the morning, Felicia awoke to Edgar wiggling her foot, which was up on his chair, with his elbow. He was holding a paper bag and two cups of coffee.

I have to go, he said.

Okay.

He set a bagel on her armrest and a cup of coffee on the floor beside her, then sat down, which was the opposite of going.

Coffee not good for you, she said.

Nothing's good for you. Eat.

Felicia wasn't hungry but she unwrapped her bagel. It was still dark outside. There had been no change in her mother. His mother hadn't coughed in hours, mostly because she had been asleep for hours.

As I was saying, Edgar said, you should see downstairs. All these folders and orange pill bottles floating around. There's no way those machines are going to work after they pump out all the water.

What time is your flight?

Nine.

And you still planning to go and leave she in this condition?

Edgar stopped chewing and leaned forward.

Felicia could perceive a rebuke coming. What? she said, more challenge than question. It would be how boys in the nineties said it, opening their arms slightly and thrusting their chests forward. Plain talk, bad manners. You ever stop to think how you go feel if you on a plane to Calgary while your mother—

Of course, I have. I've been here for days, you realize. I do have obligations.

Is only one obligation you have, far as I see.

Edgar took such a fierce bite of bagel, he had to twist his head to sever the mouthful. He chewed that one mouthful until the volume in his mouth doubled and he had to swallow four times.

I not trying to be rude, she said.

Finish your bagel before I leave, he said.

He went back to eating his own, silently, leaning forward with his legs spread wide, elbows on his knees, frowning at her mother. Felicia was so impressed by this look of concentration, as if he were thinking about all of the problems of the world so she wouldn't have to, that she adopted the opposite posture: she slouched back, stretched out her legs and crossed them at the ankles, as he had done throughout the night, held the bagel just under her chin, and ate and exhaled alternately.

You're a bright girl, Felicia. He waited until her mouth was full before he added, It's too late to be fooling yourself.

She swallowed.

Edgar flicked through his wallet and gave her the business card of a funeral home. Tell Jerry I sent you.

+

Edgar left then he came back while Felicia was smoothing the grey perimeter of her mother's hair. He had forgotten his navy coat on the floor near Mutter's bed. It was far too thin for the season, she thought as she watched him put it on. He staggered in a circle to locate the armholes by touch. He searched his pockets as he walked to the door, then whirled around and stopped with a tilt of his head and an unfurling of his fingers, as if remembering his manners.

They tried to recover the politeness of strangers.

Felicia, he said, pleased to meet you.

And you, she replied. She felt a brief flare of anger under her toque. She had explicitly told her sister to relax her hair by time not by sight.

I hope that we never meet again under such morbid circumstances and that your mother regains her former strength.

I go say a prayer for Mutter.

Mooter, he pronounced.

Mutter, she repeated. What was she speaking? German?

You be a good girl, he said.

How he said that, both patronizingly and sincerely, caused Felicia to give him more penetrating attention. It pushed him backward. He was hunched and gripping his forearms over his stomach. He appeared nauseated.

Fix your coat, she told him.

He looked down helplessly so she went to him and brushed dust and wrinkles from the front.

He smiled.

She nodded then turned back to her mother. And change your pants.

Yes, mother, he said.

Then left.

A moment later, Felicia ran to the door. Your watch, she called.

She held her position in the doorway, and he squeezed by her, turning to face her with a quick haiku of his eyebrows. Mutter was lying with her arms at her side, palms down, undead. Edgar removed his watch from her wrist, let her hand drop to the bed, and left for the airport with a little tilt of the head toward Felicia, still in the door frame, but without a look at his mother.

XY

5.

After the bagels and two goodbyes and two cigarettes under a light post near the Emergency entrance and several math problems, Edgar re-entered their room in Palliative for a third time.

What you forget now? Felicia asked.

Edgar glanced at Felicia. I wanted to check—

She's fine.

No, not that. I was wondering—

Edgar was having a hard time finding the words.

Felicia leaned toward him with both arms on the armrest like grasshopper wings.

It wasn't a question so much as a feeling he'd been having for months and he needed to corroborate it somehow. He'd had a similar urge to measure his body against Henry's the summer it began to change. He had been relieved beyond explanation to discover that he was not monstrous.

Why don't you walk me out? Edgar said. I can't talk about it. In here.

Both of their mothers were sleeping in the background when they left. They walked toward the atrium then down the main stairs, all the while Felicia giving him sidelong looks. She stopped a few steps above the flood.

I not going any further.

Edgar looked at the water, then back at her as if she were making an undue fuss.

It's not deep, he said. He had waded through it so many times over the night that he barely noticed it anymore. I'll carry you.

She shook her head.

Edgar descended the final steps into the water. It came up to his knees. He reached back for her hand.

No, she said. I going back up.

It's just a little water, he said and grasped her hand as she was turning. She tottered on the stairs. He lost his balance and his grip on her tightened.

Then he found the words.

I wish she would just die and leave me the hell alone, Edgar said. Doesn't a little part of you wish—

Bite your tongue. Jesus, help me.

I didn't mean it like that, he retreated.

If you want your mother to die, that's your business, but don't come here and kill off my mother.

You don't understand. He was pulling her down the final steps into the water.

Lord Jesus, he gone and curse he own mother. She pulled her hand away.

I said forget it. Forget it. He put a cigarette in his mouth. Then he took it out to say, But of all people, I thought you might—

Is my sympathy you want?

I'm tired. That's all. She's tired too, he said. She doesn't even know she's alive.

She know plenty.

I know if it was me, I would want— He put the cigarette back in his mouth.

He took it out.

He put it back in.

He took it out.

Felicia took it from his hand and for a moment he was holding her fist.

Slowly, she said: You don't know what good for you.

He left her with the cigarette—whatever, he had a whole pack of them—and scissored his way through the water to the door.

XX

6.

Throughout the day, people visited. It was Halloween. But by then and for the next year, Felicia and Edgar would be the only two people on earth. Everyone else was background jazz.

Felicia kept a list of the day's events in the margin of the newspaper that Edgar left behind.

Her sisters called. She heard one brother in the background asking questions and kissing his teeth in exasperation.

The head elder came to visit and prayed a mighty, frowning prayer that should have raised the dead from the morgue. Her mother squeezed her hand, Felicia felt, thought, believed, wrote. After him, Sister Jazz from the choir visited and vigorously oiled her mother's extremities. Then the landlady came with investigative gusto. Felicia recorded her name and *3:45 PM* in the margin. *PM* was double underlined. They combed through the events of the morning. I saw her from the upstairs window going for her bus, the landlady said. Going in her brown coat. I telling you, said the landlady who had not returned Felicia's call from last night, I can hardly believe that's her. Sister Jazz 2 visited with some money she owed her mother. She asked the doctor why Geraldine looked so bloated. He said, It might be an infection. An infection from what? Felicia asked. Mutter's cough was less frequent, Felicia noticed. Her eyes watered like a South American statue of the Virgin Mary, an emotionless, miraculous weeping. Could be anything, the doctor said. Could even be the thrombolytic. Felicia wrote *thrombolytic,* near the date of the newspaper.

Between visitors, Felicia watched the time and urine trickle through her mother's catheter. She reread parts of the newspaper. She napped. How hard could it be to care for his own mother? If he had said, So she could be at peace or So she could remain in fair health in his memory, Felicia might, *might*, have understood. Regardless, all evening and night she had spoken too badly with Edgar, like an uneducated girl from bush country. From now on, she would bite her *th* and say *please, pardon,* and *shall.* Would you like a cup of tea?

No one visited Mutter so Felicia appended a footnote about her in the prayers of the church ladies before they could say *Amen.* Strangely, though, Mutter seemed to improve so steadily in Edgar's absence that Felicia attributed the improvement *to* his absence. She was conscious and silent, except for the coughing. He wasn't due back for days, he had told her. Mutter would be pole-vaulting by then.

6.

E dgar's daybook should have read:

8:00: Forget about Jazz, Jazz, and Jazz in Calgary.
8:30: Drive to hospital. Change mind. Drive past hospital.
9:00: ~~Flight.~~ Go home. Call Calgary. Lie. Lie down.
9:30:
10:00:
10:30:
11:00:
11:30:
12:00:
12:30:
1:00:
1:30: Wake up.
2:00: ~~Lunch with Jazz Distributors.~~ Die a little.
2:30: Rummage. Graze.
3:00: ~~Meeting with Jazz and associates.~~ Light housekeeping.
3:30:
4:00: Work on impression of smoking cat looking out window.
4:30: Take bath.
5:00:
5:30: Shrug.

6:00:
6:30:
7:00:   (Find a girl??)

7.

Both of their mothers were living or dying in the background when Felicia's lab partner visited. He was the only person from school who did. He entered the room meekly after the last church lady left, as if he were waiting in the hallway for Felicia to be alone.

My condolences, he said.

She's not dead.

Oh. He paused. I mean my sympathies.

I tell you she not dead, Felicia said. Her lab partner was a naturally effeminate boy with few friends. They had that in common. She softened. What did I miss?

Onions, onions, and more onions. He unzipped his backpack and handed her his drawings of onion cells. I skipped last period to travel up here.

By yourself?

He grinned.

She didn't thank him for the effort although she knew how difficult it was to take public transit from Brampton to Toronto. She returned the drawings to him without comment. They had shared a microscope to identify the parts of a cell. She had already completed the assignment.

He put the drawings back in his bag. Are your sisters coming to help you out?

They trying, they trying. But it's hard to leave the country.

Money?

Visas. Especially on short notice. They go find a way. God is good. Somebody must know somebody in the embassy.

How about your dad?

He doesn't travel.

This isn't a holiday.

He doesn't go anywhere by plane or boat. He doesn't drive, he doesn't like how the young boys drive taxis, and it getting hard for him to ride his bicycle up and down the hills.

Still.

You're very judgmental, Felicia said though she knew she wasn't being fair. She was touchy and more unkind to him than any of her previous visitors.

They sat in silence for a while then her lab partner unzipped his bag again and produced a banana. He offered it to her, as if he saved it from his lunch just for her. She refused it.

What's wrong with your neighbour? He pointed his elbow at Mutter.

Mutter was sleeping but without the light snore that Felicia had become accustomed to. Felicia longed for her mother to snore lightly.

She looks like my grandmother, he said when Felicia didn't answer.

She has a son. He's travelling for work.

While his mom's sick?

She's not dying.

Each of their mothers was still alive in the background.

And he had to go, Felicia said. She found herself wanting to defend Edgar. Very important business. You can't expect him to be here all the time. He was here all day yesterday and all the days before that. He help me out when the nurses was playing the fool with the phone. And this morning before he leave he buy food for me. Felicia laughed at the memory of their all night conversation. It was her first real laugh in the hospital. Oy, that man can talk.

Her lab partner put the banana in the mesh side pocket of his bag.

When I was in hospital, he began in his quiet way, they put a toe tag on me. For identification. I guess there are lots of boys like me. We're easy to mix up.

Then two orderlies came, transferred Mutter to a gurney, and wheeled her away.

XY

7.

The evening of his cancelled trip, Edgar found Felicia lying supine on his mother's vacated bed.

Did she—? He reached for his wrists.

No, Felicia said. Upstairs. B403.

He made a sound of inflation or deflation. He thought he was but he was not prepared for Mutter to die, rather, to be dead. She should die when he was thinking about her, goodsonning her. He approached Felicia's mother's bed.

You smell like smoke, Felicia said, which he understood to mean, Don't lean over my mother and breathe all over her. Go see about your own mother.

He backed away. If you want a ride later, I can come back in an hour.

It's far.

I'll take you to Brampton. It's fine.

I'm not leaving, Felicia said.

Come upstairs when you're ready. B403, you said?

Felicia didn't answer. So he left.

+

But he came back immediately, holding a business card toward her. She didn't move to take it, so he tucked it under her shoulder.

You gave me Jerry card already, she said. You getting commission or what?

No, that's mine. He wanted to restore the familiarity of the previous night, to fall on his knees beside Felicia's bed and confess that he spent the day smoking excessively, that he sat an hour in the bathtub, thinking about Oma and Salt, that he kept the radio on for company all day. Instead, he said, I took your advice.

I can see.

I put off Calgary, he said, until— and did not finish.

Felicia arched her back as she stretched. Mutter getting better.

Don't feel obliged to hope.

No. Felicia stretched again, hands in fists, then lay back. The nurse say she never should have be—never should have been in Palliative from day one.

As if he hadn't heard, Edgar sat on the bed near Felicia's feet, crossed his legs at the knee, and began to tell her a story. The price of crude, was how it began. But he realized how foolish he had been, splashing Brut on his jaw, when all Felicia wanted since yesterday was to get him and Mutter out of the room. He glimpsed a series of conflicting paths forward. Spitefully, he went on and on about tariffs and the cost of freight transportation and the OPEC dragon and shahs and did not ask about her mother.

Sometimes I feel like everybody's looking at me like I'm a kept whore, was how it ended—very far from where it began. Like if it wasn't for Vater and Heinrich, I'd be selling chocolate bars in the Moncton airport store instead of sitting in the board meeting. But I have opinions on cost efficiencies. I have *thoughts*.

No answer. Dead. Edgar slapped Felicia's foot.

I hearing you, she said.

Did you go home at all?

Felicia shook her head.

Did you eat?

She shook her head again.

Any change—he would not ask what she wanted—with the flooding?

Again she shook her head again.

You should go home. You need to leave the hospital. Come on.

I'm fine, Felicia said. What's crude?

8.

She was recounting a news story from her small unrecognized island. A man had beheaded three girls and hung their bodies like sheets over the brick fence of an elementary school, the one Felicia went to as a child. The heads only recently had been found, according to one of her sisters. Felicia's secondary school teacher used the girls as grammar, an opportunity to teach the difference between *hung* and *hanged*. If they had on their heads, the teacher said, they would be hanged.

She felt Edgar's eyes on her forehead.

What made her recall the blue pinafores of the girls' uniforms? A uniform she herself had worn. She herself. Perhaps it was because she had come apart from herself briefly and ended up here at Edgar's house without knowing how. Or rather, she knew how but did not know why. She had lost her head, so to speak, between Palliative and his poorly designed couch. Her left leg was also falling asleep because the seat of the sofa was longer than the length of her thigh and she was unable to make her knee coincide with the edge unless she slouched but she would have to slouch to the point that her neck was halfway down the back of the sofa, a position that was neither comfortable nor attractive. There were two bowls on the coffee table though she could not recall having eaten. She had never forgotten to eat, let alone forgotten having eaten. And she would not leave bowls on a wooden table like that. She leaned forward and slid a section of a newspaper beneath them.

While the beheaded girls were dying in her mouth, Edgar reached out and pressed his thumb into her forehead and with the slightest pressure rubbed small circles. It was impossible to interpret her story as erotic, yet here was Edgar, Felicia realized, trying to turn her on.

Did you see?

No.

Poor thing.

I said I didn't see.

I meant the girl, girls. He applied slightly more pressure and rubbed circles into her forehead with the pad of his finger. Are you going to put your head on my shoulder?

Despite her reclined position, she felt no alarm. Edgar was no more man than she was woman. They were benched teammates. They were children considering the hornet's nest while waiting for their mothers, one to recover, the other to die. He could have done anything to her. And who would recognize me from the back of my knees? He could have digitally penetrated her, in the Latin sense rather than the modern, a term she learned later in life while reading harassment allegations between two young people. The newspaper printed a photograph of the girls, the back of the legs, knees, socks, hanging limply over the fence. She would have gone on thinking this long strand of protein and looking at the china cabinet as he digitally penetrated her. She doubted that he could penetrate her in any other way, as flaccid as she assumed he felt, a man in his situation and of his age. By the time they found the heads, thin, mangy dogs had eaten away the flesh. The blue ribbons had been pulled off. There was still some hair though. Would it be easier to recognize a faceless head or the headless body? What would one identify against? Memory.

I want to go back to the hospital, Felicia said.

There's nothing you can do at the hospital.

She yawned.

Cut the charade, Edgar said. He pronounced it *charahd*.

What, I can't yawn?

Edgar got up. He took the bowls in one hand and adjusted his underwear through the pocket with the other while walking away toward the kitchen. She had offended him? Was that any reason to toss her head off his shoulder? She yawned again. She should buy him some jockey shorts that fit. Three in a pack from Simpsons.

I'm not taking you back to the hospital, he said from the kitchen.

XY

8.

This is a point where their stories diverge.

Her directions were poor. She might have been on the ganja. On the way to his house, she fell asleep against the headrest although she kept talking most of the way about a man who attacked his pregnant wife with the claw side of a hammer. She wore the story around her like armour.

Edgar turned off the engine. They were in his garage. I'll be right back.

At first, no, he didn't ask her to come in. He would just go in, why was he here exactly, grab a few things, she didn't even see the stonework, take care of that thing, and then they'd be on their way. He got as far as the inside mat before he turned around, knocked on the passenger window, and beckoned.

+

In the foyer, he sensed she was judging him. She held the house against him like a shirt against his shoulders to see whether it suited him. He looked at her as into a mirror.

The house was divided by a long hallway. At one end was the front door and at the other, the back door, where they'd entered. There were frames along the wall of the hallway. He didn't turn on any lights so she couldn't see more than that. The mat had a rooster on it. The doorknobs were shaped like large crystals. He was embarrassed or vulnerable, emotions to which he was unaccustomed.

She asked him to turn on the lights.

The neighbours, he said.

The neighbours what?

Don't like it when we turn on the lights too late, he said.

Felicia didn't believe that. She went to flick a switch, but he stopped her hand and put his finger to his lips.

How big is it? she asked.

It took Edgar a moment to register what the *it* referred to because her eyes were wandering over the house and him comparatively.

Large, he said. Too large. The yard backs on to woods so I'd say, sizewise, the property is endless.

They probably killing people back there as we speak.

+

He brought her to his house to feed her. Soup. He had canned soup. He offered. She refused. He insisted. When it was ready, he sat on the counter and began eating. She looked at him disapprovingly.

No grace? she said. However humble, we should thank the Lord.

But she hadn't thanked the Lord for the bagel at breakfast. How was it that his food needed to be blessed all of a sudden?

The baby survive and living with the woman family, she said.

You already told me that.

I want to know what they go tell the child about the father.

And her mother, Edgar said.

Well, they can't talk about the father without talking about the mother.

+

She was too tired to stand but she would not sit on the counter like a man. She dug an elbow into his thigh to support herself. At first, it felt like she was massaging a pressure point but after a few minutes he had an attack of leg spasms.

It was altogether possible that he was confusing her with another woman.

+

He calculated the risk of her mouth. But he did not kiss her.

+

As he was driving her home, he asked, Do you mind if I smoke? He was already rolling down the car window.

I do, she said.

9.

After a few hours in her own bed, Felicia took transit back to the hospital. Her mother was worse. There had been a second heart attack, what people in her country would call a massive heart attack, in the night. Her organs were shutting down.

The nurse told Felicia someone had tried to reach her at Christian Lady's house. Felicia said, No. No one had tried to reach her.

Yes, in the log, it says someone tried to reach you.

Nobody tried to reach me. Because if they wanted to reach me they would have reach me. How many hours now? You mean to tell me in six hours, she counted them out with her fingers, twelve, one, two, three, four, five o'clock, nobody could reach me. I is not the Queen of England. I don' have no secretary. You dial the phone and you reach me.

She would not let them throw her mother's body into the Atlantic. Everybody in this hospital would die first.

Felicia followed the nurse out to the station, demanding, threatening, index-finger-pointing, ready to break some nose, shaking her head like a horse clearing flies. The conversation circled and circled. Every time the nurse tried to shake her off, Felicia brought up one of three points: Why had no one called her, turn-for-the-worse, and where's the doctor? She raised her voice. She wanted to know why no one had called her.

The doctor, a different one from yesterday, told Felicia that her mother wouldn't last the day. He was sorry. They did the best they could do. But the outcome was out of their hands. She should prepare herself. He was sorry. Felicia called her sister in the unrecognized island. Her visa came through. Keep her alive until Saturday.

Her mother had darkened and become swollen. Her nail polish was burgundy. Felicia had tried to keep her looking respectable, to keep her hair neat and simple, to lotion her hands and feet. Then in the afternoon, she sat, in what appeared to be resignation but was only fatigue, bent forward, forehead on the bed, arms crossed, hands on opposite shoulders. Around sunset, she opened her eyes to evaluate the precise tint of light in the room. Did the doctor mean end-of-the-day-sunset or end-of-the-day-midnight?

+

Her mother defied both. She lived past sunset, she lived through Edgar's evening visit, she lived past midnight, she lived through breakfast and lunch, she lived and lived and lived. Until she died.

Two nurses tried to pronounce her but Felicia knew only doctors could pronounce (*Mooter, Mutter, Mooter, Mütter*) the dead, so at 4:26 p.m., November 2, one did. Prematurely, Felicia believed. Surely there was a cell that was still on, the last house to turn off its lights along a street. The nurses moved their mouths and Felicia just wanted them to finish saying whatever comforting nonsense they had to, so she could be alone with her mother and continue to lotion her hands until she woke up refreshed.

As with a birthday, Felicia was unable to detect a marked change in herself between one state of being and another. In the hallway, she could hear the nurses ruthlessly going about their business. Outside, she could see the single tree in the courtyard and beyond that a car waiting to make a left turn, very innocently.

Her mother had slipped out the door and would be right back. Hadn't her mother died before? Hadn't her mother died every time she left for work? Wasn't her mother dead when Felicia sat in math factoring polynomials? Wasn't she dead for years while Felicia was ironing her uniform on a small unrecognized island? Wasn't she displaced to heaven and would return with ten thousand times ten thousand angels en retinue? What did she believe about death and the resurrection? Wasn't Edgar dead now? Wasn't the whole cafeteria dead until she activated them? If she left the room and came back, mightn't her mother be sitting up, with a comb in her hair and a jar of pomade open beside her, with wax paper for the curlers? The cloudy feeling inside of her was for the curlers and wax paper, for all of the things her mother did with such earnestness while this terror was surreptitiously conspiring against her. She was counting the number of spoons of oats (seven, the Lord's number) to put into the porridge while her heart was winding to a stop. What could she have done even if she foresaw the moment when she would just be an inconvenient change of sheets to nurses?

XY

9.

Edgar was upstairs in B403 when Felicia's mother died. Felicia did not step into the room. She stood in the doorway holding a plastic bag with both hands to ask if he would take her home.

He asked to see the body, as a point of reference more than as a point of respect, but Felicia said the body was already removed to the morgue. And indeed when they went downstairs, another woman was in the bed. Edgar crossed himself although he was not Catholic.

In the car, Felicia closed her eyes and told him that a group of men caught her uncle one night, put tires around him, and set him on fire. It happened when she was a child, before her mother left for Canada.

He thought she was connecting deaths in her family.

But then she said, Be warned.

And Edgar realized that the story was intended for him, that she was protecting herself.

Nevertheless, he took her to his dark garage.

Felicia refused to get out. I said straight home.

He went into his house and came back with a bag of bagels, cream cheese, a knife, and a tea towel. He spread the cheese on the bagels in the car and they ate, she absently, sniffing snot back into her nose.

He looked at her, reading her profile for a sign. She kept her eyes ahead, glazed. Between her calves was the plastic bag containing her mother's handbag.

She hiccupped a belch when she was done.
He reversed and drove her home.

XX

10.

Waking the following morning at her house, rather, the room she shared with her mother, rather used to share with her mother, in Christian Lady's house, Felicia was struck by how the room itself seemed to have a heart attack. It was stuffed with so many things, greeting cards, ornaments, peacock feathers in vases, creams, boxes of clothes that couldn't fit in drawers, petticoats airing out. By contrast, Edgar's house could be diagnosed with pneumonia. The air was frail and old. It smelled of smoke, rubbing alcohol, cleaning agents, all very thinly, like a chewed flavour on someone's breath.

Felicia tried to arrange her mother's things but her face broke into a cubist painting just picking up her mother's slippers. She tried to make herself a bowl of cream of wheat in the shared kitchen and Dora Maared at the folded napkin her mother placed in the spout of the cereal box to prevent ants from going in as if this were still the small unrecognized island. The attacks of grief were spontaneous: the smell of Dax hair grease on her mother's pillowcase, a belt on a hook in the closet, the blue placemat with the torn edge, the kitchen sponge, her mother's handwriting on a running grocery list. Felicia decided to leave the sorting of her mother's belongings until her older sisters came. Two got visas; her brothers didn't. Her father wanted them to send the body back but it was too expensive and in characteristic fashion he declared he was not going on a plane to bury anybody.

It wasn't yet 9:00 a.m. and the emptiness of the day frightened Felicia. She went to the kitchen to have another try at breakfast. She took hold of a knife. Wasn't there something she had to do? She would go to school and write the date at the top of a page. What was it? She took hold of a tomato. She sliced it. Very thinly. The slices had to be very thin for some reason. Then she stared a moment at her work and swept the slices into a plastic storage container. There was someone she had to call. She started dialling and hung up. Who was it? Right. She dialled again. She would tell the school that she would not be able to write the date today, maybe next week.

Then she went upstairs, lay on her side of the bed and went back to sleep.

It was after noon when she woke up guiltily, uneasily. She chastised herself. At the very least, she could organize her mother's handbag. That stopped at the first thing her hand touched. Her mother's lipstick. Felicia unspooled the tube, reddened her lips slowly, looked at her reflection, and waited a long time for lightning to strike.

+

Although her mother was no longer in the hospital, Felicia could not stay away.

She sat next to Edgar's mother and read *Great Expectations* for Grade 13 English. She sat there and turned pages out of grief or habit or lipstick and none of the nurses objected. She considered Edgar's mother, how she could still be alive when she was so neglected. Then Felicia left before she suspected Edgar would visit.

The next day, she went back, put her watch on Mutter's wrist, and this time read *Great Expectations* aloud. Felicia planned to leave before Edgar arrived (because it was strange wasn't it, wasn't it criminal, for her to be loitering in a hospital room next to a contagious woman) but Edgar arrived early, near the end of a chapter, and surprised her.

Or she surprised him.

I don't have no number for you, she said.

I gave you my card.

House number, I mean.

Edgar unlatched Felicia's watch from his mother's wrist and dangled it back to her. Then he put his gold watch in its place.

He said, She's used to having some—

Weight on her, Felicia finished. I was just— But Felicia had no interest in defending herself. I wanted to tell you about the service.

He showed no interest.

We having a service.

We?

The church.

You called Jerry? His tone was abrasive. It seemed to Felicia that he was somehow jealous of her.

She didn't answer. She beheld Edgar, legs crossed, arms crossed, looking blankly at his mother, looking like he was trying to figure out what to do with her, and his mother, propped up, bobbing to sleep.

I suppose you heard, Edgar said.

She didn't know what he was referring to.

They're discharging her tomorrow.

Felicia smiled but, looking at Edgar's face, she realized that was the wrong reaction. It was her turn to feel envy. How could someone go from Palliative to discharged in a few days?

I'd like to know where they plan to discharge her, Edgar said. Because I, I can't just— This week I have to— Why didn't you call Jerry?

I called him.

Good. Because I told you to call him.

I called him.

All right.

Then they took a few moments to diffuse.

Weakly, he offered to drive her home, at least to the station. It sounded like he didn't want to be alone in a hospital with Mutter on his last Mutterless night. Felicia declined. She slung her handbag over her shoulder.

Wednesday, she said. Remember.

Remember what? he asked.

The service.

XY

10.

According to Edgar, he saw Felicia once between the day her mother died and the funeral. Mutter had been discharged. He came home, ready to apologize to Jazz, the day nurse, for being late, and found Felicia sitting on his couch having tea with Mutter. Her recovering afro was tied up in a black cloth, her nails were painted, her waist was cinched, her tiny breasts pushed up, her heels were kitten, her earrings matched her necklace matched her bracelets. She was wearing lipstick, yes.

Well. Well well. Well well well. What to make of that?

Jazz say to tell you she had to go to her other job, Felicia said. She say you're costing her money. She tell me not to tell you that part.

Edgar had converted the dining room into a makeshift bedroom for Mutter so he wouldn't have to carry her upstairs every night.

What you think about Mutter?

She's drinking tea.

No, I mean her— Felicia circled her face with her palm.

Felicia had brushed his mother's hair into Queen Elizabeth style, put rings on each of her fingers, bracelets on her wrist, clipped on earrings, weighed her down with a pendant necklace. She and Felicia were wearing matching lipstick.

She looks— *garish* is what he wanted to say. He said, A little more subtlety.

Felicia tilted her head and looked again. What do you know about makeup?

She's not twenty-one.

I'm nineteen, Felicia said quietly.

It looks like she's bleeding from the mouth.

Anyway, Felicia said. You should feed her.

She's not a dog. I don't *feed* her. Then he was ashamed for being so prickly. He had to pack and get some sleep, though. He went to the kitchen as if overwhelmed by the choices, when, in fact, he only had a pantry of canned goods.

Felicia followed him to the kitchen, holding his camera to her eye.

Where'd you find that? he asked.

Upstairs. She continued twisting the lens and pushing the shutter. It already have film inside.

Put it away.

Felicia let the camera fall away from her face. She rested the camera on the kitchen counter, opened two cans of soup and poured them into a pot.

Did you call Jerry? Edgar lit a cigarette on the burner.

Not yet, she said. This is another point where their stories diverge.

Call him.

I wanted to ask you a favour first, she said.

So call Jerry. He's reasonable. Edgar didn't tell Felicia that he had already called Jerry, a lanky, pale man with prematurely white hair, born to work in death, to tell him about Felicia. Edgar had told him the story of Felicia's mother in the hospital and at the end told him he'd pay for the plot in Riverside or Sanctuary Park, find her a nice spot. He wanted Jerry to deliver the news that someone had already covered the cost of the funeral.

We don't have big-shot funeral homes where I come from, Felicia said. All you have to do is call Reaper or Horseman when you ready to bury your people. They good. But Horseman does provide better service. From the embalming to the box to the headstone. Reaper does just throw you in a hole, people say.

Edgar searched his wallet and found another of Jerry's cards. He began dialling the rotary phone.

Felicia set her teacup on the table with a click. She took the phone from Edgar's ear and hung it up.

Before we do all that, she said, because I don't have a whole heap of money, I was wondering, she paused, I was wondering if I could use your backyard.

II.

At the funeral, Felicia wore the black dress with the lace décolletage although she didn't really have the curves for it. And a hat with a brim as wide as her shoulders. Her church met in a rented Anglican church that smelled of ammonia. Its members had not yet reached the building fund target despite sending children with baskets through the pews each week.

The organist turned a page and began playing "Abide with Me."

Because the service was on a Wednesday morning, everyone who attended was over forty and female, except for a sprinkling of husbands.

Felicia's mother had requested a closed casket if her hair was grey, open if it was not. Closed it was. Her sisters had seen their mother in private at the funeral home and, for the others on the day of the funeral, Felicia had placed a headshot surrounded by flowers, on a table in front of the pulpit.

Edgar came late. He was the only white man in the church and he didn't stay long.

During Sister Jazz's tribute, he crouched at the end of Felicia's pew, gesturing for her attention. She raised her sunglasses.

I have to get going, he said over the laps of her sisters.

Thanks for coming, she mouthed. She nudged her sister. That's the pneumonia man. But she wanted to introduce them properly. How's your mother?

Alive, he said.

She couldn't go there. She lowered her sunglasses back over her eyes.

Still crouched in the aisle, he glanced at the front of the church to see what he was missing then turned back to Felicia. She kept her eyes ahead. He scribbled on the back of a business card and passed it to Felicia.

That's how the rumour got started that Felicia Shaw would be okay, that she had friends in high places, and, girl, I don't mean heaven.

The earth was frozen beneath the surface, the funeral director announced to the black congregation. A lie. It was early November. The body would not be buried that day. True.

XY

II.

The body was not buried until Felicia's sisters left.

Felicia stood, wrapped to her eyes in one of her mother's scarves and watched Edgar dig a hole at the hairline where his backyard became woods. Jerry and his men brought the body to Edgar's house in a van (the neighbours) at night. Felicia prayed. Jerry and his men filled the grave. Then everyone went into the kitchen and had homemade soup with dumplings.

Edgar stood behind her while she stirred the soup to prevent the dumplings from sticking to the bottom of the pot. He couldn't bring himself to ask her how she was feeling so he just stood behind her and sighed twice.

Felicia did not turn around. I was not nice to you when we first met, she said.

He waved his hand dismissively. There's still time to be nice to me, no?

But by all predictions, they would soon be out of each other's lives. Edgar had rescheduled his trip to Calgary for Monday. He insisted on the date of the burial to get it over with before he left. Felicia would be back in school on Monday as well.

After he was back from his trip, they would meet once more to burn her mother's things in a barrel. Her sisters had taken everything they wanted. What remained was folded in three garbage bags. After Calgary she'd bring the clothes and Edgar would supply the gasoline.

He tried to keep her talking. Your uncle, he began.

Which one?

The one they put tires around and burned, was he into little boys or girls?

Neither.

I assumed he was some kind of sexual deviant.

Felicia shrugged. Does it matter now?

XX

12.

Felicia was supposed to go home the night she didn't. That was the agreement. She couldn't miss more school and still complete the semester.

The night of the burial, after Jerry left, Edgar drank a little on the sofa while she scrubbed Mutter's dentures with baking soda. He told her about Olympic Stadium in Montreal. She told him about defrosting the freezer. He told her about Nadia Comaneci, that tiny body flipping. She told him about Mutter's face when she saw the Buckley's bottle. He told her about the difference between a Montreal bagel and a New York bagel. She was telling him about how Miss Havisham died when, mid-sentence again, he started rubbing circles into her forehead with his thumb.

He kissed where her neck met her shoulder. Mutter was right there, sleeping on a twin bed, yes, breathing heavily, yes, but facing their direction, only a few feet away. Felicia still had her teeth in her hands.

Your mother, Felicia said.

I'll be quiet.

No, she said, twisting her neck away from him like a burning horse.

Her dress just caught on fire? Edgar led her by the elbow. She wasn't smoking? You sure you read that correctly.

Felicia held on to the denture and toothbrush all the way up the stairs.

I think I hear Mutter, she said.

But he had already spun her into his room and closed the door behind them.

+

She was inside that closed door. Outside of wedlock. He had not turned on any lights.

She was not alarmed or surprised. She was unusually alert, thinking of her mother, waiting for her mother to appear to stop her Fleecy from fornicating. It was an experiment against death. You thought you could die. You won't let me do this. At each step of Edgar's advance, she waited for an intervention, a phone call, an aneurysm.

Edgar tried to undress himself, the top half and the bottom half at the same time, which resulted in his pants gathered at his ankles, his shirt unbuttoned and off, but one sleeve attached to him at the wrist where his hand was unable to pass through the buttoned cuff.

His watch—she thought Mutter had it—caught in her hair. He took it off and she heard it thud against the rug near the four-post bed.

He didn't undress her, quite, he tried, he started to. He pushed his hand under her sweater and clawed at her left breast, sliding his whole shirt up there behind him, clawed like the claw of a tractor. Her mother was about to freeze him, to give him sudden kidney pains.

Felicia wanted him to press down on her and crush her face into stone so someone would come in and rescue her. Yet, contradictorily, she kept trying not to get hurt, kicking his zipper away from her ankle, where it was grating, trying to breathe under the weight of his body. He did not remove her underwear, or allow her to, she tried, but he slid it aside. And if not her mother, then the boy with the cow eyelashes from the small unrecognized island would intervene, the same half-muscle half-bone feeling of a turkey neck, in her hand, when she, because he had to be helped if she wanted him to kill her, but in her hand, now inside her, he only felt like a low hum, like a fluorescent light buzzing, despite the earnest thrusting of a snowman's carrot, the smell of his armpit and smoke and alcohol, his face buried in the pillow beside her face, was that his lip on her shoulder, was he dribbling, despite what she felt to be an earnest effort by a man ascending the mysterious and simple heights of male pleasure, already oblivious to her name and face, to whom she had died, despite this man so attentive to the pleasure her body offered him that he wouldn't care if a cat or his mother walked in, despite all that, she could only feel a low hum, the vibration of an automobile in park. Intervene.

Afterward, he took off his shirt and pants completely, finally. She found herself apologizing to him, telling him about human and animal skulls they found behind a church on her small unrecognized island.

Edgar smoked two cigarettes and fell asleep as she was talking. He was tired, after all, from digging a grave. Felicia concentrated on the snail crawling out of her. When his breathing deepened (he slept so quietly, with his lips sealed, his face settled into sternness, very proper, no slackness in his face at all), she got up in the night and went and slept on the couch across from Mutter because she had no way home.

XY

12.

E dgar had no recollection of having transactional sex with Felicia.

Did he have any memory of sex with Felicia?

As far as Edgar was concerned, Felicia was an hungred, and he gave her meat: she was thirsty, and he gave her drink: she was a stranger, and he took her in: [36] naked, and he— Next. She was sick, her mother was, and he visited her, yes, technically he was there: she was in prison, and here ends the comparison.

Did he have any memory of sex with Felicia?

Well, of course, but not as she remembered it.

He had closed the door to the bedroom to access a linen closet on the inside of his room. She briefly stepped inside the master to avoid the door's swing path. He gave her sheets as she was telling him about a wave of girls that went missing on her small unrecognized island. They'd go to school and wouldn't come home. About twenty of them all over the country in a matter of days, she said.

And they turned up dead, Edgar said, because he really was quite tired and wanted to sleep and was used to Felicia's horror stories. I get it, Felicia. The world's a terrible place. You don't need to scare people off.

She held the sheets to her chest. No, not that I was saying. They went missing and the family calling calling the police trying to find their daughters but before they could really declare an emergency, the girls showed up. They had just run off with men, a bunch of old men them.

And, of course, after such innuendo, if he had any desire for Felicia, he quickly pissed it out.

The following morning, sure, he was in his underwear when he came down the stairs, but he was covered in his navy coat. It wasn't like he was immodest. He kissed Mutter on the cheek. He looked for Felicia and she was gone. He went through the first floor, calling for her. Then he went out the back door and found her in her boots and one of Mutter's coats, pouring coffee on the mound under which her mother was buried.

XX

13.

They were almost at her school. Felicia was so worried about whether Edgar would kiss her when he dropped her off and who would see this old man leaning over and kissing her that she didn't really process what he said about his mother. She heard it though.

I have it under control, he said.

He was going to head back home and arrange a day nurse, like the ones he got to watch Mutter while he was at work. There were *rentals*, his word, something like that. That morning he had come down the stairs in his underwear and coat—did he not own a robe—and asked why she slept downstairs and she offered some feeble reason, Mutter wanted water or something. She went to the kitchen to boil eggs and make coffee for Mutter and, well, Edgar and, well, herself as well. He put his thumb on her forehead. She told him no, she had to go to school this morning. He held her face in both hands then tried to pull her head down the front of his shirt, she thought as a weird embrace, and she couldn't understand why until he was upstairs getting dressed and the toaster ejaculated.

He returned and placed his suitcase at the door.

In the car, now, he said, Mutter knows the drill.

I just think someone should be with her.

She'll be okay. I'm heading right back.

He found a lighter in the glove compartment. If he kissed her, he was going to taste charred, like licking the oven rack.

From how he smoked, Felicia could tell that he was nervous as well about being seen with her. And from his tone. All that reassurance transferred on to Mutter.

Old man in his big green Passat. But she didn't want to hurt his feelings. She would turn her head and hug him, convert the kiss to a hug over the car's gearbox. Or maybe he could drop her off at the traffic lights. But, truth be told, part of her did want others to compound the enigma that had become Felicia Shaw. She was already the girl with the dead mother who teachers never called on. She didn't have friends here. The girls she sat next to were careful with her, as if death could be detonated in her by saying the wrong thing. No one from school had called. Or maybe someone had. She hadn't been home much.

Edgar braked in the drop-off zone.

Don't kiss me, she said.

I wasn't going to, he said.

XY

13.

Within an hour, Edgar was back at Felicia's school. The office buzzed her during English and told her to bring her things.

Tell her it's an emergency.

It's an emergency, the secretary said.

He saw Felicia before she saw him. She forgot to bring her things. A student in the office pointed her head to the fire doors, where Edgar had situated himself for privacy, then continued wiping the rouge from her cheeks harshly with a tissue.

Something happen to Mutter?

Sort of. Yes. Edgar turned his back to the office. I called for a day nurse but she can only work for half the day.

So someone's with her now? You couldn't ask me this in the car?

I didn't know in the car.

Or yesterday? Is not now you know you travelling.

I had it worked out but when I went to confirm, the agency told me, you know, what I just said.

How long can she stay?

Until noon. I told you.

Noon!

At the latest. Listen, I can't get into the details. As I was saying, I'll pay you what I was paying her. I have to get to Montreal. People are walking away from the table, Edgar said and imagined a literal table surrounded by duplicates of his father.

Now?

Yes, now. But I can't drive you back either.

Felicia looked between Edgar and the office. I can't miss no more school if I want to get my papers.

What do they need, a note?

She shook her head. It's just for the afternoon?

Today and tomorrow, he said. He knew that she had missed a lot of school already. He knew she was catching up the best she could. He knew she still hadn't finished that brick she was reading.

She chewed both her lips. He didn't want to hear her say no.

Listen, Edgar said pre-emptively, I'll figure something out. Go back to class. And he pushed the heavy school doors and left.

And came back before the door even shut. In the intervening second, their history pulsed through him: the two chairs, back to back, then beside, then facing each other. The flood. The mask. The blood in the Styrofoam cup. Salt gargling by the standpipe. The handkerchief on Grossmutter's face. The front of his wrinkled coat. All that history.

He didn't have to say a thing.

Felicia was nodding. If you get somebody until three, I'll go after school.

Noon, he said.

All you have to do is call the day nurse from the airport and offer her double pay to stay three more hours.

Noon, he said again. The request had turned into a demand somehow. In front of the office glass panels, with the secretary and Rouge watching, Edgar gave Felicia the house key, three bills from his wallet, and somewhat desperately, his watch.

You go need your watch, she said.

He pushed her hand back at her.

That's for a cab and for any expenses, Edgar said. He wasn't thinking of damaging Felicia's reputation. But reading his lips through the office window, he might have seemed to say, That's for a cab after. You're expensive.

And that's how Edgar inadvertently began the rumour that Felicia left school to go awhoring.

14.

When Felicia let herself into Edgar's house at noon, it was obvious that no nurse had been called at all and that Mutter was alone all this time. Her blanket was on the floor as if she had tried to get out of bed. She was still in her nightclothes. She hadn't been changed.

It was clear, as well, that no provisions had been made in case Felicia refused his offer.

The telephone was moved to a table within Mutter's reach along with a glass of water (overturned but no longer dripping on the floor), bread (room temperature although Edgar kept all his bread in the fridge), peanut butter, a knife (both unused).

Felicia dropped her school bag and went on double speed, a bolt of righteous indignation.

You can't just leave her with a knife, Felicia said aloud. She took the knife into the kitchen. She had a good mind to call the number on his business card. (The police didn't occur to her; they were only for violent crimes.) What kind of man? she thought.

Mutter, this is how they treat you? she asked. Monster.

On her unrecognized island, she always heard how white people could be cruel, how they put their old people in special prisons, had nurses, governesses, maids, nannies, and assorted women raising their children. Signs of wealth and signs of detachment in tandem. She should have been prepared.

Let's try to get you up, she said. In your chair. Good girl. She wanted to air out the mattress.

She looked Mutter in the eye. What did she want? Tea. Felicia made her some tea, cooled it, and helped her with some sips. She didn't know what to do about her medication. Had the woman taken all of her pills at the same time? Had Edgar dumped her morning pills or her entire day's dosage on the side table? Was his mother overdosing?

She would have to wash the sheets, bleach them.

You can't just live on bread and soup. Bread, bread, bread every meal, Felicia said.

Felicia put on a pair of yellow gloves. She had a basin, a sponge, some towels ready to clean the woman. Who only has one pair of gloves? Who uses the same gloves to wash dishes and clean the toilet?

Nothing to cook, Felicia said. Nothing to eat in this house. Just sleep and wake up and work. Was she supposed to cook out of the air? She marched into the kitchen and surveyed the fridge. No fruits, no vegetables except a quarter head of cabbage. Black along the cut sides. Some Styrofoam containers, a spoon, chopsticks in one container, scary looking cartons of eggs, milk and juice, three or four loaves of bread in various stages of completion, about as many types of cheese, sticky bottles of condiments, a lighter, packets of sauces, butter, some sandwich shaped things in foil. Only the quarter of cabbage was natural, though not fresh. She had a hard time throwing out food, but that afternoon she filled two shopping bags, tied them up and left them on the inner steps leading from the garage to the house so Edgar could stumble over them when he came in. Then she went back to Mutter.

XY

14.

Edgar returned early the following evening, by surprise because he talked his way onto an earlier flight, stomping snow as he always had on the mat near the garage entrance, but Felicia looked at him disapprovingly, then looked down. She had cleaned.

Welcome back, Edgar, he said to himself.

Welcome, she said with enough reluctance to get his attention.

How was your trip? he continued. Oh, it was delightful.

She was wearing yellow rubber gloves.

He saw that she had slept downstairs in the formal living room on the large couch with blankets she found in the linen closet upstairs. *Great Expectations* was turned down next to the blankets. She did not make herself at home. She did not change her clothes. There was no overnight bag. She was the type to squat over his toilet to avoid touching the seat, then to rip off the first few squares and use the untouched ones.

Mutter was sitting on the couch, dressed in peach, listening to the radio.

Look at you, he said to Mutter, pretty in peach. What did she think in her old age? She always seemed occupied.

Mutter smiled and held out her rock necklace for a compliment.

The house smelled like meat. Did he have meat?

He heard a pot boil over. Felicia hurried to the kitchen. She stirred it. She stirred it. She stirred it. She stirred it. She stirred it. She stirred it. She stirred it. She stirred it. She stirred it. She stirred it. She stirred it. She stirred it. She stirred it. She stirred it. She stirred it.

What time did you get here yesterday? Edgar asked. He made a drink to hide behind.

She looked at him then went back to yellow-gloving.

I'm talking to you, he said.

Noon.

Surely, she couldn't be touchy about— He'd try.

Did you meet Jazz? Edgar asked.

Did I meet Jazz? Felicia said. Did I meet Jazz?

Edgar frowned. He went back to the closet and hung up his coat. She must have left early.

Did I, Felicia, meet—

She didn't show up?

Edgar! Felicia said. Stop it. You didn't call no day nurse.

I did. The agency said—

She threw a sponge at him. It had no effect. Then she went to retrieve it.

You think I left Mutter alone.

Felicia put her gloved finger in his face. If it wasn't for the fear of God in me, I'd leave right this minute. I *know* you leave your mother by sheself with not even something proper to eat so you can go and run down money. There's a God in the sky, Edgar Gross. And I'm telling you that you will have had hell to pay if this woman did die. If you want to kill she, pick up a knife and do it like a man.

No one said anything for a long while.

I'll make you out a cheque, he said, and you can be on your way. The indignity of being spoken to with such hostility after a day of *would you sign here, Mr. Gross* ruptured his pride. The flinging back of his confession. He had nothing to say to her. His face was wrapped up in a leather mask.

+

He came back with a cheque and set it on the table. Felicia kept her back to him, head bent into a canned soup and meat improvisation. Hopefully, she hadn't had to spend her own money on the meat.

You cleared the ashtrays, he said.

You need to buy some food, Felicia said quietly.

There's food.

You can't eat from cans every day, she said.

He opened the fridge. What happened to—

I threw everything out.

Look, he said, for the record, I did call.

Felicia held up her hand, enduring him.

I shouldn't have asked you. So soon.

Felicia braced her hands against the ledge of the sink. One minute you begging me. The next, you acting like a big shot, like you don't want me here.

You should be reading whatever the hell it is you're reading. He smiled and stepped close.

She wiped her nose with the back of a yellow glove. Don't you have a kerchief? she said. Offer me a kerchief. What's the matter with you?

He offered her the broad part of his tie. He had hit the right line. He had recognized her situation, even in the most external and obvious way, but to a girl from a small unrecognized island, that acknowledgement was enough.

We need food, she said. I made a list.

He took the list, left, and came back with his usual afterthought. He said, Food for thought, no pun intended: give up your place. Stay. Take care of Mutter.

I can't do that.

It's just a thought. He left again. They had only known each other two weeks. And he knew she was too Christian to live with a man. She'd need to explain it to everybody, to herself. She could say she was working, caregiving. He didn't want to call her a domestic.

He went back a third time. He said, You'd make someone a good wife.

Then his leaving stuck.

XX

15.

The sex talk that Felicia received had two problems. First, it occurred after she had had sex. Second, it was delivered by the man with whom she had just had sex, had been having sex for six weeks. In its entirety, it went like this:

I don't want to get pregnant.

Then don't.

Felicia looked at the light fixture. Every time she thought of his vasectomy, the absolute certainty of the decision by a man who left a room two or three times before finally leaving, she was perplexed.

I mean not now.

Twin girls. I remember. Edgar reached over her to the side table for his lighter. The heel of his hand pressed her shoulder. His armpit hair was sandy, tan, golden, a lovelier colour than his hair.

But not not ever, she said.

Can't help you, he said.

She didn't have to have twins. Look, he already lopped off the boy from her future. She could be perfectly fine with Edgar, couldn't she, kneading dough and flicking lint from his shoulder and washing his collars. She could spend her life emptying his filthy ashtrays without so much as a tiny lace christening outfit.

So never? she asked.

She settled herself on his chest. She didn't mind this part, minus the smoke. She didn't mind the density of him now with her ear over his ribs. She had seen body hair on men before, of course, but with Edgar she really considered it—how strange that it just grew out of the crook in his elbow and washed over him. All of that hair was hers somehow. She didn't want her body doing it, but she was glad his did.

Come on, Felicia. I have to go. Edgar was trying to sit up.

He didn't have anywhere to go as far as Felicia knew. She wanted to lie and think about his hair a while longer.

He flicked his eyes at her like a reptilian tongue. She felt it on her shoulder.

You know I was married before.

Silence. What do you mean, I *know*?

I don't know. Edgar cleared his throat. It's a saying.

You're divorced?

Sort of.

Felicia pulled down her nightie and stood over him. His face was red, a burn from skiing not from shame.

When you was planning on telling me that?

I told you in the hospital.

You know full well you didn't tell me nothing about no *I'm married* in no hospital. You married this whole time and have me operating under the assumption that you single.

Ancient history.

No. She rapped his kneecap. It is not ancient history. It is present history. It's very present history because, because I'm here thinking about the future

I'm telling you it's irrelevant.

and you come and drop this on me that he's married. He's married. What do you take me for, Edgar Gross?

She dragged the covers off his feet.

He was acting like she was overreacting. He said, I'm not married in any real sense—

Just legally, Felicia said. You're just legally married.

As I was saying, it makes more sense for us to stay married than to get divorced for several reasons.

Name one.

He couldn't find one.

Because you's a good Lutheran boy? Because I here cooking for you like a slave when you have a wife somewhere [he'd said she'd make a good wife] who you don't *want* to divorce.

You're young, Felicia. He found his slippers and started walking to the bathroom. His flat, narrow bottom.

What she name?

Irrelevant.

You turn me into an adulteress in the sight of heaven and have the gall to tell me is irrelevant.

Why do you need to know?

Felicia needed to know everything. She hit him on the back of his shoulder with her fist as he walked past her. She have money?

So what?

Well, go back to having sex with your money.

That's crude.

Go back to your wife and Irrelevant and whatever she name in Calgary.

See, you're a child. You don't understand anything.

I don' understand how you could be married and have me living here for eons—*eons*, Edgar—Edgar tried to close the bathroom door but Felicia kicked it open—and be married from day one.

She was waiting for an explanation, an apology, something. She stood at the door of the bathroom door watching him urinate with a cigarette in his mouth. That's what he meant by go.

XY

15.

Beginning that weekend, the house was frosty.

Before the present blizzard, sure, sometimes Edgar felt like he and Felicia were in an unhappy marriage. She wouldn't talk to him. She moved swiftly around the house, building up charge for the static shock of her anger. He wasn't as malignant as she. He conserved energy, hibernated from the conditions. Occasionally one or the other, him, usually it would be him, would reach out, meet the yipping teeth of an animal he only wanted to pet and retreat to the den to watch the Bulls or the Celtics.

Fair, his timing could have been better. But he wanted to tell her before the end of the year. Fresh start in January. Hence December 29, which made for a chilly New Year's Eve where Felicia told him to take down the Christmas decorations and went to sleep before midnight. He hadn't ever spent New Year's Eve with his paper wife. In fact, the longest they spent together continuously was a drive across the continent and back: Toronto → L.A.→ Toronto. On their way back, they stopped in Vegas to eat and gamble a bit and get married, why not. Within a year of the wedding, she was cast in a soap opera in California. He found out from their weed dealer.

On New Year's Day, Edgar was served a letter on the kitchen table, notifying him that Felicia would be leaving by the fifteenth of the month and that he should take steps now to procure adequate care for his mother. Lovely penmanship, as usual. He read the letter silently in Felicia's presence over his morning coffee and let it drop to the kitchen table. That's where it stayed during the frosty week until Felicia couldn't stand it anymore. She placed it on his dresser under a bottle of Brut.

She wrote, *leaving by*, not *leaving on*. Knowing Felicia, knowing women, she would leave while he was gone to Vancouver in the middle of the month. Catch him off guard. Spite him. When he opened the door on his return, the house would have been converted into a freezer, chips of frost would greet him, he'd have to defrost the hallway to get to Mutter who'd be suspended, mouth open, in an ice cube.

Let her do her worst. If he could take on the vipers at Paperplane, he could take on Felicia Shaw. Move on out. He knew she had nowhere to go. Her former room at Christian Lady's had been rented. Rock, meet hard place.

Edgar beat her to her own surprise.

The morning of his flight, he said, You can leave the key in the mailbox.

XX

16.

Felicia pretended that she didn't hear him. But she was listening carefully through the stages of his departure: his footsteps, the jangling hangers, the crunch of the back door closing, the engine, the grind of the garage opening and closing.

From an upstairs window, she watched the car disappear down the street then she pulled her packed suitcase from under the bed and tucked her toothbrush into her handbag. She had made arrangements with Christian Lady who'd said, My door is always open, my dear, though I don't know where I go put you. The only thing she hadn't done was make arrangements for Mutter. She regretted not specifying an exact time in her resignation letter: *9:00 AM* on the fifteenth of January.

Felicia convinced herself that Mutter was not her problem, poor Mutter. She carried her suitcase to the foyer and stood near the front door for a while, removing Edgar's key from her keychain (she only had one key left, for the lock on her suitcase). When she glanced behind her, she beheld Mutter's eyebrows flickering as if trying to get reception.

Her taxi arrived. She opened the door and waved for more time. No day nurse had arrived. If anything were to happen to his mother, Edgar would say that Felicia was the last person who saw her alive, that Felicia was the one who was responsible for her care, that it was her negligence that caused his mother to fall or choke or starve or however she was to die.

She called the day-nurse agency. There was no booking (monster, an absolute monster) and no one could come on such short notice.

The taxi honked outside.

This is how he was going to fight, was it, using his own mother to manipulate her. Felicia put on her shoes. Mutter wasn't Felicia's problem. Mutter wasn't her mother, her mother-in-law, her great aunt, her friend, her neighbour, her problem. Felicia would leave the key in the mailbox and a certain man fell among thieves and close the door and they left him for dead and walk down the path and a Levite approached and put on her CBC voice to give the cabdriver the address and a priest approached to the room her mother had rented and a good Samaritan approached and see if she could get her Ontario Secondary School Certificate and he bound up his wounds and get her own life and put him on his ass and leave Edgar to take care of his mother's and which of these acted like a neighbour?

16.

E dgar's daybook should have read:

8:00:   Handcuff Felicia. Throw the key in a river on the way to the airport.
8:30:   Check-in
9:00:
9:30:
10:00:
10:30:   Flight to Vancouver
11:00:   Smoke, drink, pursue various in-flight diversions.
11:30:
12:00:   Sleep
12:30:   (PST) Expect Jazz at airport. (Grab girlie mag first from non-Paperplane franchise)
1:00:
1:30:   (EST) Leave a business card on seat for stewardess
2:00:
2:30:   (PST) Presentation from sales
3:00:
3:30:   Merger presentation from finance
4:00:
4:30:   Meeting CFO
5:00:   (EST) Call home.

5:30:

6:00:   (PST) Call home x 2. Mini bar. Girlie mag.

6:30:

7:00:   Hotel Bingo? Find girl??

XX

17.

It bothered Felicia that she could not go an hour without a thought of a certain someone while she was sure he hadn't ever—hadn't *ever*—had a thought of her. Ever. She purposed in her heart not to think about that someone, not to let his name form in her mind, during the morning, then hopefully the afternoon and evening and onward until ever.

She was bathing Mutter in a Christian lady's bathtub. It had been difficult to explain why she'd shown up with Mutter, who could barely walk and hold her head up at the same time. So she lied. The heat broke down in the house while the owner was away in Vancouver. She had no way of reaching him. She phoned repair places in the Yellow Pages and they all said it might take weeks. Weeks? It had been a cursed winter. More work for you, Felicia said. She got one place to send a man, just to look and he said there was a part they needed to order but that too could take weeks. Felicia went deep into the fictional details. Anyhow, she really appreciated this Christian lady's roof over her head. May the Lord richly repay.

The real details weren't sorted yet. A certain deceiver would be back from Vancouver today, stay home for a week, then Montreal. She would not call him when he returned. Let him run frantically to the hospitals, let him call the police, let him worry himself an ulcer.

Close your eyes, she told Mutter.

Mutter squirmed. But Felicia had to wash her hair. She shielded Mutter's eyes and poured some water over her head. The water traced her neck, her shoulders, the long slope of her breasts, and pooled between her stomach and thighs. This is what awaited her, Felicia thought, when the men are gone. This body. She asked Mutter without asking her. Mutter answered without a word.

Felicia began lathering her with a washcloth, systematically, from the neck down. How had her closest friend become a woman four times her age, who did not speak to her, or perhaps English anymore, a woman who asked questions by rolling her great eyes upward, who displayed approval by sucking on mashed sweet potatoes, by turning her head toward the snow? Day after day, she neither lived nor died.

She waited in the armchair for someone who purported to be a certain someone before she found out who the real someone was to go to work and come home.

Elsewhere in the house, the phone rang.

+

A knock on the bathroom door.

+

She stayed on the phone longer than she intended.

When she came back, she was shivering. When she came back, Mutter was. Her hair was wet. It clung to her skull. When she came back, she saw her, herself, she saw him, shivering in the bathtub.

XY

17.

Edgar returned from Vancouver on Thursday morning but he waited until late that night to retrieve Mutter. He was going to be as inconvenient and disruptive as possible.

He didn't know exactly where Felicia was but he began where she would. He went to Christian Lady's house. She told him that there was no room in the inn for Felicia, well for Felicia, but not for Felicia and a woman in his mother's condition. She was staying at another Christian lady's house. It was almost 1:00 a.m. Christian Lady spoke with uneasy fervour, a rush of information, as if she was being visited by a Communist officer.

At Other Christian Lady's house, Felicia opened the door before he rang the bell. She had been warned. It was after one.

Get your things and let's go, Edgar said.

Go where? Felicia was calm in an annoying, rehearsed, pseudo-sophisticated way. She stepped outside and closed the door behind her.

Look, Felicia, I was on a plane all night and worked a full day today. Quit the charade.

And I've been looking after your mother for the last three days because you did not make a phone call

I did not authorize you to take my mother anywhere.

to make arrangements. You should have procured a nurse as I notified you in my letter dated January 1.

He snatched her wrist. She snatched it back. He snatched it back. She snatched it back.

Damn it, Felicia. He gave up.

What kind of man leaves a woman in her state alone?

I left her with you.

That's why she's here, Felicia said. And she's going to stay here until you arrange—and prove that you've arranged—a nurse for her.

Prove to you?

Yes, Felicia said. To me. In writing. Your word is dust.

Edgar looked at the night sky. He needed to guard this part of his past. He feared that Felicia would laugh at him if he told her the facts of his enviable marriage. His wife had run away from her parents. She lived with a roommate in the apartment below his. He was supposed to be in university at the time. She suggested the road trip to California. After they married, they shared an apartment (building) together (she kept her apartment—and roommate). They had more brunches out than breakfasts in. She partied him to exhaustion and brought stoners back to their apartment (building) afterwards. She didn't come home for days at a time. The whole romance happened very quickly. Before Christmas, she had left him and had already been married twice on TV. But in real life, she said she was taken.

Edgar said, Felicia, it's no big deal. She's not based in Toronto anymore. She's moved on.

She's moved on?

Get Mutter, get your things, and let's go.

Your mother's sleeping, Felicia said. Come back in the morning. She opened the door to return inside. The landlady was sitting at the bottom of the staircase waiting to see to it that her front door was locked and all the lights turned off.

I brought you something, Edgar said.

I don't care. Felicia closed the door.

He rang the doorbell immediately.

From inside: Felicia, I have tenants.

I know. He's going.

Edgar rang the doorbell again. Then he knocked. Felicia stepped outside.

Mature people don't slam doors, Edgar said.

I didn't slam it, Felicia said, still holding on to her resolution to be civilized.

I brought you something. Two things.

I don't want anything you have to give me. All I want is for you to find a nurse for your mother and go your way.

As if he hadn't heard, Edgar pulled her hand from her armpit where it was folded, and placed a long narrow box in it. I wanted to give it to you at home, he said.

When Felicia didn't open it, he took the box back, and lifted a gold watch with a small black face out of the case. He held it by the tail in front of her eyes.

Felicia would not give him the satisfaction of a reaction. Edgar took her wrist again and tried to latch the watch to it, but kept fumbling in the dark, so Felicia broke her reserve and clasped it. She wouldn't show pleasure, but he could tell that she was admiring it. The hands were so fine, just a hair thick.

It's for your time, he said. I thought that up on my own.

She snuffed.

And this. He reached into his pocket and held up a ring. She should have recognized it from Mutter's things.

But she asked, What is this?

I resized it, he said.

What is this, Edgar?

Vater used to say that jewellery is to a woman what alcohol is to a man.

Edgar, what—

It's not what you're thinking, he said. He put it on the right finger, wrong hand. You know I can't right now.

What is it?

I want you to get used to having some weight on you.

XX

18.

Upstairs, in a bottom drawer, Felicia had only one pad left. All week while Edgar was in, was where, was away, she kept telling herself, I have to buy pads, I have to buy pads, but she couldn't leave Mutter alone and it was arctic outside [Your hair looks dope, pretty lady]. He'd be back soon. He was probably in the aisle of a plane waiting to disembark. If she could just reach him, she would ask him to— No, she couldn't ask him to pick up pads any more than she could ask him to pick up the still beating heart of a young Aztec virgin.

Let's see. He left for Calgary, yes, on a Sunday. On Tuesday, she convinced herself that she was *only* a week late, not *already* a week late. On Wednesday, she showered vigorously, hoping to hurt herself. On Thursday, she uncovered a complicated biological relationship between grief, motherhood, and childbearing. Why didn't people explain these things to women? By Friday, she had analyzed Edgar's sex talk more than *Great Expectations*. He had a vasectomy. [I heard it.] You heard it? [Loud and clear.] He said he had a vasectomy. [It was disgusting, the two of you talking like that but, yeah, I heard it.] She thought he said he had a vasectomy.

She was inexperienced in these matters but not stupid, despite the rejection of her high school certificate from her small unrecognized island. A man with a vasectomy should release dust or smoke or breadcrumbs or cream cheese or at least a smaller volume of fluid [he's like a Super Soaker] but she always had to wipe herself clean afterward with a rag she kept in the bathroom only for that purpose. She wasn't stupid. She received a patchy, condescending education from girls in Form 5, who said that you couldn't get pregnant when you were menstruating or just after, which left a long middle. The middle-middle, they had said. The closer you get to the middle of your cycle, when you felt most normal, that was the most dangerous time. [You always look dangerous, pretty lady.]

On Saturday, in faith, Felicia lined her panties with one of Mutter's diapers. She could feel the edge along her thigh.

Felicia thought she heard the garage. She thoughted wrong. She thought he said. He had. Hadn't he? He had n't he had n't he said he had n't he said he had n't he?

Something—her concentration, her memory, her reasoning—was off since Edgar left for Calgary. Definitely. She accidentally put the flour in the fridge instead of the pantry. She forgot to put the garbage out last night. She didn't want to do anything but doze in the same patterns as Mutter and think. Mutter. Did she give Mutter her tablets?

The middle-middle. That would be the second week in February. Or maybe there was some aberration. Maybe it was when he just got back from Ottawa and realized he hadn't paid her for the month, for he paid her in advance. He had wiggled out the last of his sawdust into her (soon he would withdraw and flop on his back, soon he would suck a cigarette, soon he would place an arm over his eyes and tell her about the size of Vater's shoes). She had returned from the bathroom, adjusting the back of an earring, and he reached into the drawer of the side table for his chequebook and a pen.

This might be the wrong time, he said when he finished writing. He jabbed the head of the pen on his chest to retract the tip into the barrel.

It was the wrong time. Definitely. But Felicia took the money. At least it was a cheque, not cash.

XY

18.

Edgar's flight, at least, was on time.

Normally, when Edgar returned from a trip, Felicia would be at the door with 360-degree, first-class service. That Sunday, after a week away, he didn't even get economy service. He stood in the doorway of the living room, calling for Felicia, whining the last syllable, waiting, as if he had forgotten how to take off his coat. He had smoked on the flight and in the car, but he wanted a house-cigarette, a drink, a shower, meat. He wanted help taking off his big-boy coat.

Down the hallway, in the dark, he saw Felicia's silhouette sit up and lean its forehead on the inside of its wrist. Then it, she, walked to the kitchen without a word.

It's so good to see you, Edgar, darling, he said. How was your trip?

He met her in the kitchen and pinched her hip.

Don't provoke me, Edgar. Felicia turned on the oven. She took out his plate and laid it face down, a habit from her small unrecognized island where house flies waited on plates for food.

A little conversation, he said.

Don't make none.

Edgar unbuttoned his shirt and eyed her warily. Her hair was growing back. Did he forget something? Was she on—of course.

Ah, he said, knowingly.

Ah, what? Felicia said.

Ah, you're having your—he circled a finger where her uterus would be—your time.

She washed a tomato and began slicing it thinly.

Edgar stepped close behind her. She elbowed him back.

Hard day playing dress-up? he asked.

She turned and pointed the knife toward him.

I want to know how you could go to work or Calgary or wherever the hell you go

Felicia, there's no woman in Calgary or Moscow or the moon.

and come back here like you is Mr. Innocent? How you could look me in the face every day since my mother, bless her soul, and your mother was in hospital and lie

No one's lying.

and *lie* straight to my face. What kind of man— Only a dutty, treacherous, old man have the gall to be so boldface as to take advantage of a girl when she at her most, her most, her most vulnerable condition, to deceive she right to she face, when he know, he *know*, everything that girl suffer in this country,

What on earth are you—

when that girl take she hand and clean up he mother vomit when no nurse was coming, and leave she education to wipe this woman bottom, what kind of man could turn around and lie to this girl—don't look at me—

Edgar looked down.

lie to me to get your way, like all them common, low-class men with no principle? She stopped there.

Click.

Are you—?

You tell me, Edgar. You tell me.

+

Priority number 1: Get the knife out of Felicia's hands without asking for it. Priority 2: Get this baby nonsense out of Felicia's head.

On the plus side, she seemed spacey and unaware that she was holding a knife. On the minus, she seemed spacey and unaware that she was holding a knife.

Edgar began with an assault of facts and ended with the semblance of an argument: you're not a doctor, you're late, your hormones are doing that woman thing, ergo Latin Latin Latin.

I know how I feel.

Edgar opened his hand and beckoned for the knife. Unless you know what it's like to feel pregnant, no, Felicia, I don't think you know how you feel.

I want you to explain to me how I could be—

You can't be, Edgar said.

I can't be?

No, you can't be. You're not.

I'm not, eh? Tell me why I am *not*.

Because I—

If you going to keep on lying, help me God, I go cut your throat right now.

I didn't lie, Edgar said. She was aware of the knife now and Edgar stepped backward to the fridge. He could always swing open the door if she lunged. He never imagined himself as a news story where the neighbours attest that he was quiet, kept to himself, took care of his mother over footage of a bodybag emerging from the house, but Edgar conceived his bloody death now. It was Felicia, after all, who told him the story of the three beheaded girls. Her people killed each other as punctuation.

So, what, I is the Virgin Mary? I have fruit in my womb?

I said I *thought* about having a vasectomy—put down the knife, Felicia—*meaning* I didn't want children, he continued, meaning that precautions should be taken.

By who?

By who do you think?

So this is my fault, Edgar? This is my fault? You gone and defend yourself by throwing this back on me.

How could you not read between the lines?

Because I schupid. She clamped her head. Because I real doltish. Because from day one in this country I was a damn fool.

Edgar saw his opportunity. He darted and grabbed her wrist. They struggled with the knife. He needed to immobilize her entire arm.

That's not what I'm saying.

Then you is a lecherous, treacherous, nasty old man. She wouldn't surrender the knife. Which is it? Tell me, nah.

Edgar had her by the wrist. She crouched, turned her back to him, as if defending a basketball and they travelled from the kitchen down the hallway. When she tried to turn on him, he lifted her up by the waist, her knife-arm flailing, and threw her into the garage and shut the door.

+

Time passed.

Edgar lit another cigarette and turned on the radio.

Felicia banged on the back door. She was howling epithets and threats and comments on Edgar's moral character and manhood and he was shouting back through the door.

Tell me how, was the last thing she said.

Because you're stewpid, Felicia. He drew out the *u*. You're a stewpid minx.

Well, now you talking the truth, she said. You finally talking some sense. I real stewpid.

He paused his pacing at the front door to discipline her with paternal authority. I was perfectly clear with you from day one, Felicia—no children,

You does lie too much.

no children and you knew that marriage was out of the question, which is not to say that I can't commit. I can. I have. I am. Very commitable. But you can't corner a man

I corner you?

into doing what you want. You don't go and manipulate a man because you want a child.

When Felicia began talking again, he strolled to the other end of the hallway, talking to himself, more or less along the same lines. He stopped at the far end of the hallway in front of the parlour bedroom. The weather was bad on Mutter's forehead.

We're going to send her to *die Alpen*, he said. Hysterical. This better not be your child. There's no child. I'm married. Hh. Mutter coughed. You call that a marriage? Mutter said although she couldn't or didn't talk anymore.

+

The garage was having the desired effect. It was supposed to be a padded room until Felicia stopped acting like the girl from *The Exorcist*. But the garage wasn't padded. In fact, it had many breakable things.

After a few minutes of quiet, Felicia slapped the door, an open-palmed sound. Edgar crept down the hall and placed his ear against the door.

Silence.

I hope you listening, she said. Listen real good to me.

Then Edgar heard a crunch, followed by drumming of various depths and resonances.

He didn't even put on his shoes.

He found Felicia standing on the hood of his Passat, which was still dripping from the airport, about to plant a shovel into his windshield. He tackled her by the thighs. She scrambled inside the house and tried to lock him out but he shouldered the door open. She stumbled back. Her heel caught the edge of his suitcase and she fell.

He wanted to pick her up and strike her. He wanted to strike her across the face with all of his strength with the back of his hand, bending it so that the middle knuckle would connect just under her cheek and her head would rotate in slow motion, groan out a deep word in slow sound, flecks of spit in slow motion in the light, until she fell unconscious to the floor.

Instead he knelt and straddled her hips and pinned her shoulders to the runner.

You think I playing with you, she was saying. You think my life is some kind of joke. I bring something to your attention and you not even man enough to act like a man.

If she wanted to be pregnant, he could make her pregnant right now. He tried to undo his belt but he couldn't spare the hand. She was a single muscle, slippery fish. He couldn't get hard either. But he had to do something.

So he opened his mouth and let one string of spit fall slowly from his lips toward her mouth.

+

When Edgar got off of Felicia, when the spit had run down the side of her cheek and settled in a white gob in her hair, he stood with his legs over her face for a moment.

He said, You got yourself into a fine mess with your lipstick and your—he drew a deep neckline along his chest. Then he wiped his wet bangs from his forehead and went to make himself a drink. He said, Nogebligr baby.

What did you say? Felicia lifted her skirt to wipe her jaw and hair. You should have thought about that when you was rubbing up my forehead.

I don't want no baby, he said loudly.

No, say exactly what you said. (For she thought he said *nigger baby* in disgust while shuffling off her.)

Edgar said he didn't say anything. Then he didn't say anything when Felicia continued demanding exact words.

I thought it was the seventies, she mocked. That I had to get with the times. She paused. I'll tell you what you need to do.

He rubbed his eyes and drank. What do I need to do?

You need to do the right thing.

That he would do. He would do the gold-star, best thing.

I'll take care of it, Edgar said.

You better.

But here again was evidence for Edgar of the stupidity of the girl. She heard *take care* wrong.

And soon, she said, putting down her ammunition. She went into the parlour, retrieved her pillow and started up the stairs.

I'll have Polly set an appointment for you, Edgar said.

Felicia stopped. I talking about nuptials. You promise me that. That is the condition on which I come back here.

I didn't promise.

You promise.

I alluded. I did not promise.

You is a real dog, Edgar Gross. You the biggest dog I meet in my time.

I'll have Polly—

Polly is not setting no appointment for me.

What difference does it make?

She don't have no business in this.

Fine, an appointment shall be made for you.

I not having no appointment. You deaf?

No one in his life spoke to him like this. Did she know who he was? Did she know what restraint he was exercising not to open his mouth and consume her like a dragon? Edgar had not slapped her (but she had not stabbed him). He had not destroyed her property (but she had not implanted a foreign being into his body). He had not brought her anything from Calgary (but she did not walk down the hallway to help him remove his coat after a flight across the country).

He spoke slowly in his boardroom voice. Listen to me, Felicia. You will have an appointment and you will go.

(But the chandelier lit her shoulder blade as she walked up the stairs.)

Are we okay? Armistice? Edgar said. I'll drive you there myself.

+

The next morning, he found the knife. In his tire.

19.

During March, appointment after appointment was set for her, in that voice and tense, the details of which were presented on the back of Edgar's business cards. The first three were ignored. On the fourth attempt, she was practically lifted into Edgar's dented Passat to see a doctor, who confirmed that she was indeed pregnant. Eight weeks.

A final appointment followed. Felicia was told by Edgar that he would drive her to the clinic himself, as per their original understanding, but that he would not come in with her this time. This time? He would be waiting for her in the car when she was done. It would take half a day, tops, she was told, but he would be back early.

You're not even going to stay?

He would be there when she was done. Not to worry.

You're not even——?

He would dart to the office and dart back. Not to worry.

If I have to do this by myself, then I go do the whole thing by myself.

She was told not to be impossible.

Impossible? I'll be impossible if I want to be impossible.

+

The morning of *die Endlösung,* money for a cab was left in their money spot under the centrepiece of artificial flowers. Edgar called her from work. She was told to be on her way, not to worry, but Felicia insisted on waiting for the day nurse to arrive. A girl, really, no older than twenty-one, with feathered Farrah Fawcett hair, blown back from her face. Her dress was observed as too short and impractical for nursing care.

Felicia left early enough to be early enough to finish early enough to leave early.

+

When she returned, with her large handbag of unnecessary items, Felicia was met at the door by Feather. Mr. Gross said he would call you at 12:30.

The statement was ignored. An inquiry was made about Mutter's meals.

She wasn't hungry, was said by Feather. Mr. Gross said to tell you that you should—

Of course she not hungry. How you expect her to be hungry in this condition? The air smelled brown.

Mr. Gross told me to tell you that—

Thank you. The door was closed by Felicia.

Felicia's clothes were changed then Mutter was changed. Her stool was dark, deep purple-red, like beetroot, but Felicia hadn't cooked any. Maybe it was Mutter's last egg, decades late, the miraculous one released by God as an affront to Felicia.

The phone rang at 12:30 and was ignored by Felicia. A tomato was being sliced very thinly. It rang again at 12:35 and was ignored by Felicia, who was slicing another tomato very thinly. It rang again at 1:00, 1:10, and 1:15 when Felicia was feeding Mutter mashed sweet potatoes.

It rang from 1:25 to 1:28 continuously while Felicia was upstairs.

Then it rang continually at half-hour periods until the home was come by Edgar.

XY

19.

Edgar cut his work day short and went home.

Why aren't you answering the phone? he called out from the back entrance.

No answer. Felicia's coat was in the closet so she must have been home.

He strode through the house without removing his shoes, calling for her. She was not in the kitchen, not with Mutter in the parlour, not in the powder room, not anywhere on the first floor. The day nurse agency must have screwed up. Had they insinuated something to her? He was hoping only for the barest hint delivered.

Edgar found Felicia in the guest room, her room, lying on the bed with her hands over her stomach looking up at the ceiling. When he entered, she turned on her side, toward the window, away from him.

See, it wasn't so bad. He sat near her head. It's just a quick *whoosh* and everything's better. It's behind you now. He should have said *us*. A woman would expect him to say *us* in a moment like this. It's over.

He placed his hand on her head. She didn't flinch or stir or shrug it off. It was as if she didn't feel his hand, as if he were dead to her. We already have a Ghost.

See, he said again.

He gripped his forearms.

He tried to make casual talk about an upcoming board meeting. No bite. He said Feather always shows up dressed like a vamp. These young girls, he said. Did she upset you? Sometimes you call them in for a job and they get ideas. I bought sandwiches.

He looked down at Felicia. Her eyes were open, unblinking, watering, staring at the window.

Are you happy here, with me, still? He paused. If two people travelling in a straight line meet in a hospital room, is that a vertex or an intersection? I can't tell. I don't know. When you were in hospital I thought that I could maybe be of help. I'm worried that you— You're a good girl. You know what I like best about you?

No response.

You're not the kind of girl, of woman, who faints over spiders or insects. Or blood or vomit. At St. Xavier—you may not remember this but I do—you took *Great Expectations* and crushed some kind of earwig then went back to reading as if—

In the middle of his sentence, Felicia sat up. The bed groaned.

Take off your shoes in the house, she told him and left the room.

XX

20.

Since her appointment weeks ago, Felicia had only gone into Edgar's room to sweep the floor and dust the dresser. She had stopped making Edgar's bed. That Thursday, she gathered the sheet from his bed to wash, else it would stay there forever, when she heard Edgar enter through the front door—unusual— talking to someone—ditto. Female voice. As she was descending the stairs, Felicia could hear them in the dining room. Edgar was introducing Mutter to Feather as if they had never met. She comes highly recommended, he was saying.

Felicia nodded when she entered. Edgar didn't face her. She held on to the spires atop one of the dining chairs, waiting to be acknowledged. Feather was also waiting for them to be formally introduced, but Edgar continued talking to her about Mutter. His voice fizzed.

I'm Feathery, the girl finally said, extending her hand to Felicia. From last time.

Felicia shook it. She thought, What kind of name was Feathery for a grown woman?

Pardon my manners, Edgar said. Felicia here has been taking care of Mutter for— He rolled his eyes.

Six months, Felicia said. She double checked in her head. November, December, January, February, March, April.

Six months, Edgar repeated. Oh, Felicia, this might be a bad time, but while you're here—

Felicia wanted to slap that gassy voice out of his mouth.

He reached into his wallet. Here's your cheque.

Felicia took it, frowning. Why the witness? Why the envelope? Edgar always gave her a cheque directly from his cheque book around the first of the month (or the time he jabbed the head of the pen against his chest). There was an extra zero.

There's some severance in there for you.

She didn't understand. Was she, was he, was she being fired?

Severance? she asked.

Thank you for your service. Feathery comes highly recommended.

Rip it up, Felicia. Throw the snow in his face. [Pretty lady, tuck that cheque into your bra and bounce. Swing your moneymaker out that house.]

Feather looked embarrassed for Felicia. In a second, Felicia thought of her suitcase, the one she had laid on the bed in the small unrecognized island for a night flight, the one she laid on her mother's side of the bed when she decided to move here. She took her hand off the dining chair as if the furniture had become hot. Before she left, she would ransack the house, wreck it until the basement split and hellfire came up. This was very different from the first time, when she found out he was married—married, Felicia, girl, what wrong with you? Or she would white-collar him in her retribution, hurt him where it hurt, at work, call his secretary and tell everything, *seduce, deceive, spit, vasectomy, adulterer.* You're doing this to me again, she thought. I let you do this to me again. Again. She nodded at the thought and not to Edgar or to Feather, as they each might have thought.

Pleased to see you again, Felicia said to Feather.

Likewise.

She started up the stairs, trying to remain composed, and accelerated until she was running up the last few. She brushed at her eyes near the top.

When do you start? Edgar said to Feather, intending surely for Felicia to overhear.

Monday, I thought we agreed on, she replied.

Monday, he said. That's right. As I was saying, I'll be away but I'll leave a key in the mailbox.

XY

20.

After Feather left, Edgar stood in the doorway of Felicia's room. She had emptied the drawers into a pile on the bed and was now shaking out her clothes with a snap and folding them anew into her suitcase, briskly, like it was an Olympic event. Her back was to him. Her shoulders were high, her head bent so low, it seemed to be cut off. All her clothes seemed thin on her. She never wore pants. Always dresses or skirts.

He decided to leave her alone. He walked toward his bedroom. He had to let her go. He had woken up last night when he heard a noise, startled, it was so unlike him, thinking that she would stab him in the thigh. She stabbed his tire. He had to have a cigarette. But he turned back and pushed open her door.

You don't have to leave now, he said.

Tell the jagabat she don't have to wait till Monday.

Felicia. Edgar walked around the bed to face her. Felicia, he said again.

She turned her face from him. But he could see that her sockets were rimmed with water. He held his wrists. He had to restrain himself from reaching to graze her temples with the back of his fingers.

I don't want to do this, he said.

She didn't say anything.

I never should have put this kind of responsibility on you. You're nineteen. You should have been grieving. He didn't want to sound like he was patronizing her but he wasn't used to—did this qualify as an apology?—justifying himself

She tucked a full slip under her chin to fold it.

to subordinates. Subordinate? He was treating her with such respect and care, it was almost embarrassing.

And, think, he said, now you'll be able to go back to school and finish and become a—he had to pause because he could not recall what Felicia's ambitions were apart from being someone's wife and baking cakes on Sundays—become whatever you want.

She huffed handfuls of her toiletries, perfumes, broaches, barrettes, and dropped them into a plastic bag lined with another. She said nothing.

I'm trying to be reasonable, he said. Stay the weekend. Nobody's throwing you out. He reached into the suitcase to unpack for her but she knocked his hand out of the way and his finger got hooked in one of her bras. She snatched it from him.

I know what you're thinking, he said. This has nothing to do with you getting yourself pregnant.

She fixed him with her eyes. Her nostrils flared.

So he left her room. He hesitated at the door because he was going to ask if she had noticed Mutter was leaning to the side lately. But he went into his room and smoked three cigarettes instead.

He heard her voice rolling quietly and seriously to Mutter downstairs, then he heard the door close. From an upstairs bedroom, he saw her put the key in his mailbox and haul her suitcase, her handbag, and a plastic bag of her cosmetics toward the bus stop.

On her dresser, she left the ring he gave her, left the ring and kept the watch.

21.

For four months, Felicia sliced a tomato and waited for her mother to come home. Nobody told her in advance that she was leaving. Nobody told Felicia she was. Once more. Nobody told Felicia in advance that her mother was leaving. The morning of her flight, her mother kissed all the children and held their faces in the gallery then Felicia's father lifted her suitcase down the hill to the village car. Felicia was young, still in infant school, but she knew something significant was happening because her mother was wearing her black dress suit and heels and because Miss Jazz came over to watch them just before her parents drove away. Your mother watching you from where she is, Jazz said to get them to behave. Her father came back in the afternoon, alone, with a stale newspaper. He spoke quietly for a long time with Jazz on the verandah, so familiarly that Felicia wondered if Jazz was going to be her new mother. Then he made the children say goodbye to Miss Jazz and she too went down the hill.

What had changed between then and now? Her mother was still in a distant country. She was as she always was. Elsewhere. Returning any minute. Which meant that Felicia was as she always was. Expecting.

XY

21.

For four months, Edgar smoked a cigarette and eyed the watch on his mother's wrist. Time passes backward too.

When he was a boy, Vater whipped him in the bedroom he had to share with his brother so he, Vater, could have an office, whipped him across the calves with a violin bow exactly ten times while his brother and mother stood witness. He and his brother had been playing a version of hide and seek where Edgar lay on his cot with a black handkerchief over his face and his brother was supposed to find him. Edgar played the part so well—it was as if he were dead, he may have approached sleep on that occasion—that he didn't hear the front or bedroom doors open, only Vater's voice above his veiled face, What do you suppose you're doing? After the whipping, when young Edgar threw himself on his narrow cot (despite their wealth, despite the cloud his parents slept on, which he was not allowed to touch) and Mutter sat next to him and placed her hand on his forehead and he felt the weight of his brother on the other side of him, the voice of his father blasted through them all, Leave him. Then louder, Leave him. And both his mother and brother got up dutifully and went to the voice while his calves stung.

A worm came to the surface of Edgar's mind. Mutter had sacrificed him in that moment to save her own life. He had no ally. And now she was doing the same.

He had told Felicia all of this, though without saying any of it, during their first interminable night together. He told her everything the first night.

XX

22.

You, Felicia said.

Mutter died today. Edgar cleared his throat of four months of dust. Or yesterday maybe, I don't know.

You wasn't there?

It was early, he said.

Felicia hadn't seen him since he doused her with gasoline and lit her on fire while sharing a bag of popcorn with Feather. Where was she now? One flap of Edgar's shirt hung over his pants. Tendrils of veins creeped around his sockets. He had never looked more like Mutter than at that moment.

Edgar gripped his wrists. Can we talk inside?

Felicia hadn't opened the door fully. Only her face was visible. He better think again if he thought she was going to invite him inside and offer him sweetbread so he could triumphansee the room she improvised for herself in Christian Lady's parlour and finger the thin makeshift curtain that apportioned her privacy from the hallway.

Edgar said, I thought you might appreciate knowing.

What you want me do? Raise she from the dead?

Edgar paused a moment. He nodded slightly, as if he expected this treatment, then turned and walked down the concrete path toward his car.

The encounter whooshed by too quickly for Felicia's satisfaction.

You can talk on the bench, she shouted after him.

He turned back. (Are you going to put your head on my shoulder?) She held her position behind the door.

Haltingly, he told her that Mutter's cancer had recurred and progressed. He had mistaken the symptoms. But so had the doctors. She had stopped eating and drinking for two days before he took her to the hospital. Where was Feather? Mutter was dehydrated. Where was Feather? The second time he took her, they discovered that the cancer had *metastasized*, he meant but he said *reproduced*, to her bones. He said nothing about Feather. Three weeks later, she was dead.

You could have told me she was in hospital.

She wasn't. She was at home. Downstairs. There was nothing anybody could do. He pulled out a pack of cigarettes. Do you mind if I smoke?

Yes, she said.

He closed the pack. There's a small private service next Friday. I thought you should know. He stretched to offer her a card with a date written at the back but she did not move so he left it on a corner of the bench. Please come if you're able.

Edgar's movements were too casual, too familiar, for the occasion. Didn't he feel responsible in the slightest for blowing smoke into his mother's face, for feeding her the diet of a prisoner? More than once, she had observed him, sitting on the couch, killing Mutter with neglect the way one kills a plant. (The plants!)

Then, suddenly, Edgar's face crumpled. He crumpled. And Felicia rushed to hold him up. She thought he was fainting with exhaustion. It was the only time his whole life she would see the ugly childlike contortion of his crying mouth. Tense. Pink. Slimy.

All night, in the parlour, he said. I spent all night. Alone. I put on all her jewellery. Last night. This morning.

Felicia pulled him closer to help him up. Mistake.

Edgar looked at her upper arms as if for confirmation.

Felicia? he asked.

She liked to believe that she wasn't quite showing when she wore loose clothes that hung from her breasts, but her upper arms were definitely fatter in this sleeveless top, and Felicia saw in Edgar's face that he recognized a difference in her, as a man who knew her body intimately.

XY

22.

The minister glanced several times at his watch, so Edgar took him aside and asked him to wait for half an hour. But it wasn't any use. Nobody came. That is, except for Edgar's brother, who flew from Germany mostly to settle the estate, Edgar thought, and a bowtied friend of his father's. Mutter had no friends except for the wives of Vater's friends. One of them, when she learned the news, paused, confused, with an expression that suggested that she thought Mutter died years ago. Edgar did not tell Jazz, his legal wife.

Last week when he had sat on a bench outside Christian Lady's house and told Felicia of Mutter's death, she asked him if he was glad.

A branch of lightning blazed through him. Are you? Were you glad when your mother—

Don't bring my mother into this.

I mean, Felicia, what a galling thing to say!

She didn't take it back. She had read his relief clearly despite his best performance of grief.

Felicia's honesty could make her abrasive but not malicious. If she were in the viewing room that day, she would have stood beside him as Mutter's body slid into the furnace and the other men exchanged infuriatingly glib, good-natured memories of the woman, how she used to do this or that for Vater, and asked them to show some respect for the occasion, what kind of animals are you, bowtie or no bowtie. She was not polite but she did display a firm adherence to protocol, occasion, and ceremony so it surprised Edgar that she did not even call. All week.

Jerry entered and explained that the incineration process was complete. The home would remove the residue that could not be consumed—the coffin's screws and hinges, fillings if Mutter had any—pulverize the bones and process the ashes.

Cremains, Edgar's brother said. I was reading about the process.

We prefer to call them ashes, Jerry said. He glanced at Edgar.

Edgar said nothing. On the way home, he sat in the backseat of his own car with the urn while his brother drove and made an international deal with Bowtie.

A week later, a sympathy card from Felicia, addressed to the Gross family, finally arrived. Edgar's brother opened it.

Felicia Shaw, Felicia Shaw, he said. I don't remember a Felicia Shaw. You?

Edgar said nothing.

Whose wife is she?

No response.

Who's Felicia Shaw? His brother dropped the card on him.

There was a Bible verse about trumpets on the inside. One of the girls, Edgar finally said.

On the evening that his brother was to return to Germany, Edgar scooped some of the ashes into a teapot. His brother gripped his forearm to stop him. They wrestled delicately, trying not to disturb the scoop, then his brother, red-faced, word-whipped him for disturbing the ashes, which were to be taken to Germany, before marching up the stairs. It sounded like his brother was ripping paper slowly in half but he was only drawing himself a bath. Edgar scooped the ashes with a teaspoon as if measuring sugar. How cowardly, Vater accused him from the inside, to perform defiance against the dead, you impotent ass. You big man. But Edgar continued scooping Mutter's lungs out.

After returning from the airport, he dug a grave the size of a baby's coffin and buried the teapot. When he looked up, the leaves were rusting at their edges. Early.

+

Two days after his brother returned to Germany and he had buried Mutter, which is to say two weeks after she died, depending on whether it was night or morning, Edgar heard from Felicia, via Christian Lady. He was rummaging through a drawer for a matching sock. He almost didn't answer. Felicia was in hospital. (What you want me to do? Raise she from the dead?) He almost didn't go.

X

1. The drugs were a thick, colourful Ferris wheel.
2. He was there.
3. He left.
4. He turned.
5. He left.
6. He returned.
7. His skirts whirled dervishly around the sun.
8. He could never leave.
9. It was early and he was early. It was early for him and he was early for it.
10. She fed him from her breasts and she fed him from her neck and she fed him from her forehead.
11. She woke up and he was talking in full sentences, though in another language.
12. As I was saying, he was saying.
13. Your father so ugly your own mother run from him, a three-headed girl told her.
14. As I was saying, he was saying. As I was saying, he said.
15. She woke up and she had two mothers, briefly, until they died under a tree in Babylon.
16. She woke up and he was with her and he was with him and they were they.
17. When he squeezed her upper arms, she was supposed to undress and walk obediently into the chambers.
18. She woke up and she was in a movie where he was saying it was all just a dream then she woke from the dream which was just a dream.

19. She was supposed to shovel her grave with a teaspoon and wait to be shot from behind.

20. She woke up and he was crying in an accent that was neither English nor German.

21. Turn over, he said to her once. No. Turn over, he pleaded. What's wrong with my face? For a change.

22. She woke up and he was smoking inside a crematory.

23. She woke up, expecting him to come back as he always did with an afterthought, so she sat holding him and smiling for one minute, two days, three weeks, four years—

Y

Boy oh boy.

THE SEX TALK

Mom, are you my mom?

Of course I'm your mom.

My real mom?

Yes, your real mom.

Then why don't you have a husband?

Who tell you so?

Nobody. But how can you be a mom if you don't have a husband?

I'm your mom. Don't talk like that.

You're not just a lady?

Listen, next time somebody asks about your dad, you tell them that you have a dad. And to mind their business. And to come talk to me.

+

Mom, where's Dad?

Away.

Away where?

All over. He's a pilot. He has to fly airplanes all over the world.

Does he ever fly here?

Sometimes.

And he comes to see me?

Sometimes at night but he says don't wake you.

And he sleeps in your bed?

Yes. In his uniform.

+

Mom, does Dad have a big airplane or a small airplane?

A big one.

How many people can he fit on his airplane?

More than a hundred.

A million?

Not so many.

+

Mom, where's Dad now?

Calgary.

Where's that?

Far.

+

Where's he now?
Still in Calgary.
Is he always in Calgary?
No.
Then how come you always say Calgary?
Because he's always in Calgary when you ask me.
Does he tell you when he's coming home?
No. He just comes.
Does he come through the door or the chimney?
The door. He has a key.
And a key for the airplane too?
Yes, a big key.

+

Mom, where's he now?
The sky.

+

Mom, is that Dad's airplane?
No, I don't think so.
How do you know?
His airplane has a red tail.

+

Look, that one has a red tail.
But it's too small.

+

Is that his plane? It has a red tail and a maple and it's big and everything.
That's him.
Finally.
Wave. Go on. Wave to Daddy.

+

Do you think he saw me?
Yes.

But he was so high.

He tell me he see you with his special binoculars. And he say he wave back.

And what else?

And, well, he tell me you're a big, handsome boy, like a soldier. And he say that you should be a good boy and sit quiet in class from now on and listen to Mommy and do everything she say while he gone.

+

Mom, do you think Dad will take me and you on his plane?

Where you want to go?

New York.

New York?

Or Calgary because he likes Calgary. Or we could just go up in the sky and come back down.

+

Mom, I don't think Dad lives here anymore.

No? Where does he live?

I think he lives in heaven. It's closer for his airplane.

You smart, boy.

I figured it out.

You did. Dad used to be here and then he went up to heaven.

Is he Jesus?

No. But if people behave themselves, they get to go to heaven.

Or if they're old.

+

Mom, does Dad see Jesus when he's up there?

Yes.

Is Dad old?

Kind of.

Older than Jesus.

No.

Older than you?

Yes.

How old?

Old as the hills.
Is he rich?
Very rich.
How rich?
A millionaire.

+

Mom, is Dad dead?
No.
But you said when you die you go to heaven.
Only if you're good.
Was he good?
Sometimes he good and sometimes he not.
That's why he goes up and down.
Exactly.

+

Mom, do you think Dad has another family and that's where he stays
when he's not here or in heaven?
Your dad's either with us or alone. He don't have no other family.
But what if there *is* another one with another boy who's just like me and
a mom who's just like you?
Then they'd be the same as us.
Right, only *they* live in Calgary and sometimes he forgets where he is and
stays with that family instead of us.
There's only one boy like you in the whole world.
Are you sure?
Positive.
Is there anyone like you?

+

Mom, do you think it's good that Dad spends so much time away?
I like being here alone with you.
I don't think it's good.
Why not?
Because if he's not here, he's always doing something with the other boy.
I tell you already there's no other boy.

What if I have a brother who's just like me?

You have plenty friends. There is a friend that sticketh closer than a brother.

Yeah, but I can beat them all up.

Did you beat somebody up? Is somebody's mother going to call and tell me you were causing trouble?

Pretend, pretend. You're such a girl sometimes.

+

Mom, can I have a brother?

How about a fish?

No, a brother. Can you make me one?

It's not so simple.

With Daddy. I know.

What do you know?

And can you make him older?

+

Mom, everybody has to bring a picture of their family to school.

Can't you draw one?

No, Mrs. Henderson says it has to be a photo.

We have pictures.

I want one with Dad in it.

Well, we don't have any.

None?

I don't see what's wrong with a picture of you and me.

Everybody else has pictures with their dads and they have brothers and stuff.

Okay, I'll look.

+

Are these all the pictures of me?

Every last one.

Are these all the pictures of Dad?

Yes.

All of them?

All.

How come you don't have any with me and Dad together?

He didn't like pictures.
Can I keep one?
I'm keeping them for both of us.
But can I keep one for myself?
Which one?
The one with him in the airport with his suitcase.
I'll keep it safe for the both of us.

+

Mom, I think it's time for a new dad.
What's wrong with the old dad?
He's never here.
I'm always here though.
Mom, I'm seven. I can't wait forever. My clock's ticking.
You real old.
And you're not getting any younger, doll. If we get a new dad then that way you won't be alone. Is that what you want? Do you want to be alone forever, Mom?

+

There's a plane.
I'm over him.

+

Mom, how much money do you have?
Enough.
I was thinking that you should marry someone really rich.
Your dad was very rich.
Someone richer.
That go be impossible.
Really? If he was so rich, how come you're not together?
Who said we not together?
Mom, I wasn't born yesterday.
Sometimes grown-ups separate but they still together.
So you're still together?

+

Does Dad send you any money?

No.

I thought you said he was rich.

He is.

If he's rich, then why doesn't he give you any money?

It's easier for a camel to pass through the eye of a needle than for a rich man to enter into the kingdom of heaven.

Did you ask him for money?

No.

Mom, come on. How do you expect to get money if you don't ask?

+

Mom, I need to know where Dad came from.

I thought you tell me you over him.

I am. It's for school. Family tree.

I don't know how far back I can go on his side.

You don't have to do all that. Just his background and I can make up the names.

You will not make up your family.

Why not? It'll sound real. I was going to give him a sister and two brothers. One died in the war—

Which war?

I don't know. The big one. He left behind a pregnant wife.

He has a brother.

It's all the same.

No, you're going to do this right.

+

Okay, so a brother.

He married a European lady—that was his second marriage—and had two children. They must be divorced by now.

I'll need names.

Give me a minute. Let me get the whole picture out.

You're killing me.

I tell you about Mutter. German lady. She died the same year you born. Hurry up.

She was the last one on her side. She had an older sister and a brother who died young. I'll tell you her name just now. And the father died just maybe five years before you born.

That's it?

No. When's this due?

Tomorrow.

And it's only now you're asking me?

I told you I could just make it up.

What about my side?

I did that already.

Let me see.

+

Mom, really, just let me make the rest up.

No, we're going to sit here and do this so you don't bring home another C.

You could be making all this up right now.

+

I would have got an A but she said I didn't use the right format.

What's the right format?

I don't know. Something.

You weren't paying attention.

What?

+

Mom, remember when you used to tell me that Dad was a pilot?

You kept asking.

I used to wave at every airplane. Just in case.

Well, every minute his company was putting him on a plane.

It's not the same as being a pilot. You lied.

Watch your mouth. I never tell no lie.

Because I believed it. It's not a lie to the person who believes it.

+

Mom, what's going to happen to all Dad's money?

He'll leave it for his brother.

I thought they didn't get along. And he's older. He'll be dead too.

His brother's kids then.

And you're just going to let that happen?

He might donate it to some charity.

Charity. Mom, tell me you're joking.

I don't want your father's money.

What about me?

You want his money?

Well, it's kind of mine.

It's not yours. It's his. You will not touch a dime of that man's money. You hear me?

Why are you being so selfish?

+

Mom, do you think I could go and live with Dad for a summer?

Boy, are you trying to kill me?

No disrespect.

You don't know where he is.

I could find out.

Then why haven't you?

It's not the right time. But I was thinking that he might be looking for me. You know, to pass on his legacy.

His money.

His legacy. I'll take over his business.

His business is selling useless goods to stranded people.

Don't you want me to be successful?

Right now, I want you to eat. What are you going to eat?

He cooks.

Now. What are you going to eat now? And, wrong, your father never cooked a day in his life. If you want to eat canned soup and bagels for your life then go ahead.

+

Mom, I need to get my licence.

You're thirteen.

I need to start practicing now so I can get it right when I turn sixteen.

You can wait.

I think Dad's in New York.

So?

So, you've known this?

I don't know anything about your father's whereabouts.

I think he is. Yeah, I have a feeling. Wall Street. He's working for a multi-national.

You think you're driving to New York by yourself when you're sixteen?

You can come along.

+

Mom, I want to get a job. Part-time.

You're already behind in school.

I'm not behind. I'm average.

You're behind half the class.

Only in stupid subjects that don't matter.

You're not getting a job.

Fine, I'll just ask Dad for some money.

You're trying to make me mad.

No, if you don't want me to work, and he's got all this money, then what am I supposed to do?

Finish school, go to university, and get a career, not a part-time job.

Or you'll just have to support me for the rest of your life. If that's what you want.

+

Mom, is Dad dead yet?

When you turn so callous?

It's just a question. Don't act like you love him.

+

Mom, let's say Dad died.

Boy.

Just let's say. Would his estate know how to get in touch with you?

You don't have a dime to get from that man.

Right, but let's say I went to the funeral and introduced myself to that side—

Why on earth would you do that?

Just to pay respects. Honour thy father and mother, you know. And if they didn't believe me, what legal proof would I have that I'm his son?

They know.

Right, but let's say, I don't know, it went to court and I had to prove it.
All they have to do is look at you.

+

Mom, do you think Dad looks like me?
You look like him.
Do you think people will recognize me?
Rich white men in a certain circle, yes.
Those are my peeps.
And what about your black mother who killing sheself for you?
Joke, Mom. Don't go all Rosa Parks.

+

Tell me something I don't know about Dad.
There's not much to know. He worked. He came home.
Come on, Mom.
Okay, okay. He wrote poems here and there.
Wait. Poems?
Like if he was waiting in line, he'd get a sudden burst of inspiration.
Who would've thought?
He used to collect people's business cards too. A card for every occasion.
Contacts. Okay.

+

Tell me something I don't know about Dad.
He worked a lot but leave it to him and he would sail the Mediterranean
in a yacht with a tumbler of scotch in his hand. He was that kind of man.
So he drank?
And he smoked.
I knew that.
From the time he was fourteen.
Hey, that's cool. I need to look into that.
And I don't want you doing either.
Did he have a brand or anything? Du Maurier? Camel? Marlboro?
Ever.
Mom, I'm almost fifteen. I can make this decision on my own.

+

You owe me.
He called his mother—
My grandmother.
his mother, Mutter.
Like moot. I know.
M-u-t-t-e-r.
Mutter. Ima start callin' you that.
And I'll start calling you *Ghostface.*
Oh, can you!

+

Mom, Dad's my dad, right?
Yes. Are you feeling okay?
You're sure?
You don't look so good.
You're absolutely sure?
Here, lie down.
It's not just a story?
Hush. Lie down a minute.

+

Mom?

+

Mom?

+

Mom?

+

Mom?

PART 2

EX

MID-NINETIES

Felicia

●

Exercise

Felicia had a thought the size of a grapefruit in her head that she needed to lie down and peel or slice or squeeze or otherwise process: Edgar was getting divorced. It was in the papers. Edgar was being divorced.

But first she needed to get into the anthill that had become her driveway. She honked. Two teenagers on bicycles looked at her, looked straight into her car, through the windshield and into her eyes, as if they wanted to know what she wanted. She wanted to get into her driveway and squeeze the pulp of this news. That's what.

She honked again.

Army bounded up the driveway right into her headlights, backlit by a spotlight. Where did he get— Was that her good bedroom lamp? He had plugged in every lamp he could find, using extension cords and had turned a few outward, like footlights, so the garage was glowing faintly from street level. The driveway raked downward into the garage so teenagers could sit on the sidewalk and stare down into Army's barbershop like an auditorium, like a show.

Army directed her to park on the street, pointing with one arm and winding a circle from the elbow with the other.

No, Army, get those children out of my house now.

Give me an hour, he said. He leaned on the rubber seal of her window.

Now.

All right, fifteen minutes. Just fifteen minutes until I cut this last guy's hair.

Felicia heard the screen door slam before she saw Oliver, her landlord, approaching her car with his thick chest and tiny legs, like a bison. Here he came with his little bandana, looking like a washed-up rocker.

The teenagers tittered. Oliver ignored them.

Felicia expected him to be angry, like the last time Army had people crawling over his (not hers, Felicia would have to concede; she only rented the basement and part of the main floor) house. That was last month, when they first moved in, and Army had a housewarming of sorts, kids coming out of the backyard, kids going up Oliver's stairs, ringing his bell—so many teenagers, in fact, that they seemed to descend from phantom trees in ninja masks. To avoid future landlord irritation, Army put up a sign near the garage—*Army* with an arrow pointing downstairs—which clearly made little difference in controlling the pest population because Oliver was being teased (Wuh-oh-oh-oh, sweet child of mine) with the entitled condescension of teenagers on his own property at 9:30 at night, though somehow he didn't seem half as angry as the night of the housewarming.

Oliver met Felicia at the driver's door. He seemed calm. He leaned in close as if he had something important to tell her.

The days are long, he said and sighed. She couldn't tell if he was being passive-aggressive or if tonight he was like a dog that wanted its belly rubbed.

They are, she said. Then turned to look ahead, down into the garage. Army blinked *fifteen minutes* with his fingers. Felicia held up one finger. The engine was still on. Her foot was still on the brake.

Oliver sighed again. You see what's going on down there?

He's almost done. I'm sorry.

Oliver was a test to the limits of Felicia's politeness. Holding her smile during his monologues was a feat of muscular endurance, but such was the power of a man who could evict a woman and her child.

It's been like this all day.

Fifteen more minutes, he told me.

He's been saying *fifteen minutes* since this afternoon.

I'll make sure this time, she said. She put the car in park. Oliver reached in and turned off the ignition. She didn't appreciate that.

Your gas, he said.

My money, she should have said.

Nope, she didn't appreciate that one bit.

She tried to open the car door. He sighed. She pushed the door again and only then did Oliver step back and allow her out. She collected two bags of groceries from the backseat, her handbag, her work bag, and her night-course tote bag.

Oliver said, I don't mind a little activity now and again. He's a kid, right? I know I used to be a little hellraiser.

You? she said. She pictured him knuckling his eyes, tugging the skirt of his teacher and pointing at who hit him.

But, Oliver continued, half these kids I've never seen before. I have a daughter to think about.

Interesting that he didn't mention—

And a son.

The son, Hendrix, was under a tree, playing with his ants. He was avoiding a little girl, the sister of one of Army's barbershop clients. She was younger than Hendrix. She had a doll. She had eyed Hendrix before approaching. Hendrix ignored her. She approached with her doll. He didn't look up from his ants.

Were you going for your walk? Felicia said. The bag with the milk was starting to cut into her palm. She jostled. Landlord or not, what kind of man wouldn't offer to take a bag from a lady?

I mean, really, he have a bad back or something? she said to Army later.

I'll leave you now, Oliver said.

Enjoy your walk. Nice evening for—

You know, my ex-wife, Oliver began and Felicia's shoulders fell. My ex-wife, she never used to exercise at all. Just sit around all day, eating chocolate almonds, saying she was tired. Oh, she's tired. Tired from what? Never worked a day in her life after Hendrix. Maybe I told you this. Never lost the baby weight. I mean, come on. How hard could it be? But, oh, she's tired.

Felicia pursed her lips and tilted her head in polite commiseration.

Between you and me, it wasn't baby weight. My cousin has baby weight. I know baby weight when I see baby weight. She just let herself go and couldn't handle the truth. Truth hurts, baby.

It can, Felicia said. Should she tell him the truth right now about himself?

Not that I'm Dolph Lundgren but I'm trying. You know. Being with someone like her, you just get worse and worse until one day you can't even recognize yourself. I used to be fit.

You used to be a contender, Felicia said. She assumed Dolph Lundgren was the one in *Rocky*.

I told you me and my cousin Francis almost got a scholarship to play football in Massachusetts?

How many cousins does this man have? Felicia wondered. But she asked, as Army had taught her, Football or soccer?

Soccer. Oliver looked away. I used to be good.

Some new guys were approaching the garage.

Party's over, Oliver shouted. Keep it moving.

Tomorrow, Army shouted up as a correction. Come through tomorrow.

Army, Felicia called. She heaved the bags to signal for help.

Army sent a couple of boys in his place. She recognized them as Oliver's nephews. They shuffled up the driveway in slide sandals. They took the bags, her purse, and yes they were entering her portion of the house, the basement through the garage door. She was about to follow them inside. Her purse. But Oliver was looking at her over his shoulder, waiting.

I thought you were coming.

Boys, she heard Army call out, Last call for alcohol. I'm going to do Chris and the rest of you come back in the morning.

She had no reason not to (her purse) though truthfully she would prefer to kneel with her arms in the air for an hour than to go for an extended walk with Oliver. But she agreed to go to the bend in the street and turn back.

+

The news of Edgar's divorce had been building up for a couple of weeks.

Felicia first noticed on her break. She was across the street from her office, waiting on her spicy fries to sizzle, glancing through the Entertainment section of the paper, and her eye fell on a photograph of an actress in a teal backless gown, looking over her shoulder. Her partner, an actor in a tuxedo, was looking in the opposite direction. Felicia didn't know much about celebrities. She disapproved of the dress but she paid attention when she saw the woman's name: Sophie Fortin. Reports were saying that Timothy Francis called off the relationship after discovering that Sophie Fortin was married. When asked why she hadn't disclosed her marriage, Sophie Fortin said that she'd forgotten.

A few days later, there was another photo of Sophie Fortin in the Celebrity Briefs section—just a head shot, chin lowered, eyes sultry, eyebrows nicely done. The caption said, *Fortin files for divorce from secret husband.* She was quoted as saying, Some men are forgettable when they get off, hinting at her ex and Timothy Francis, who had broken off the relationship, in one sweep. From then on, Felicia was a fan.

Like a good publicity generator or a desperate, aging actress, Sophie Fortin continued to court controversy.

Entertainment Tonight replayed clips from a semi-dignified sit-down interview where Fortin was asked, How do you forget you're married? Don't you do your taxes?

And Fortin said, Well, I have an accountant like most people. But I've never filed *jointly*. Does anybody? My money is not my husband's.

Asked, Do you want a reconciliation?

With who?

Either man.

Fortin smiled and said, Yes and no.

In the interview, she explained that she thought the marriage was annulled. There must have been some kind of paperwork issue. It was a spur-of-the-moment thing when I turned eighteen. He was older. Loved me more than my father. Who could resist?

Oliver was still talking about his ex. Although Felicia was nodding and para-linguistically responding, she hadn't heard a word he'd said. Rather, she hadn't heard a fact or detail about his ex-wife that she didn't already know. She changed the subject when she perceived a lull.

He returned to his ex.

She tried again. The closet door is giving problems.

Which one?

In Army's room.

He frowned as if he couldn't place it or had trouble imagining anything in his house broken.

There's only one closet in his room, she said.

The mirrored sliders?

She nodded. It came off the bottom track.

Oliver raised his eyebrows. I see the analogy.

Felicia's whole body groaned.

I never—and you can attest to this—I never talk bad about her in front of my kids. But you should hear the things she tells them about me. You won't believe this but Hendrix, little Hendrix, brought a belt for me from Massachusetts in his luggage.

Felicia crossed her arms. The evening was cooling down.

He said it's because I can't keep my pants on. Tell me, where did he get that from? And my daughter's now telling me I have anger issues. She's sixteen. She's telling me I have anger issues. My own daughter? Have you ever known me to get angry, Felicia?

Everybody gets angry.

Without provocation, I mean. You think I couldn't get angry every time Army and his friends run up my utilities? My cousin's tenants shower in cold water.

I talked to Army about the hot water, Felicia said.

Exactly, I spoke to him, very calmly.

Felicia didn't know that Oliver had spoken to Army. She didn't like the idea of Oliver disciplining her son. Ever. For any reason.

I'm going to turn back here, she said. They were at the bend.

Oliver turned with her and began walking back.

The man needs a dog, she said to Army later.

+

The newspapers didn't name Edgar at first. They referred to him as *secret husband* or *wealthy businessman* and once as *heir to a sizable fortune*. Not because they didn't know who he was but because they were stretching the story out.

Soon a source close to the secret husband appeared and spilled salacious details to a tabloid newspaper. Felicia didn't believe the $10,000 plane rides on the Concorde or the lavish parties. But she did believe the rest. The source said that Edgar's was one of the names in the little black book, the leaked clients of an upscale prostitution agency in Toronto. The source revealed that within his company Edgar was well known as a philanderer. He was currently under investigation for several counts of sexual harassment. It was not his first time. He was a man of the slap-and-tickle generation of office interactions. And along with that exposé, Meet the Secret Husband, was a high-contrast photograph of Sophie Fortin with her head on Edgar's shoulder in someone's apartment, it seemed. Fortin is reaching for the cigarette in Edgar's mouth and to prevent her he has turned his head away and upward so the cigarette looks like an erection in the mouth of Alfred Hitchcock.

+

Oliver was already in a sentence by the time Felicia's attention found its way back to him.

—is better. You're lucky you have no contact with your ex.

She never told him that. Army tell you that? she asked.

No. Heather did. You know how these kids like to confide in each other. Oliver wiped his face with his shoulder. He was in finance, was he?

Something like that.

I would have taken that rich bastard for everything he's got.

> Mom, am I a bastard? I can handle it.
> Don't say that word.
> Bastard? I'm using it correctly, no?
> You're not a—
> What? Bastard?
> Army, stop it now. The word is *illegitimate.*

I'm not that sort, Felicia said.

The ex tried to bankrupt me but my sister has a friend who's a big-shot lady-lawyer. Maybe she could help you get—

No need. Thank you.

Whoever gets the kids wins, right? You women end up with the kids, the house, the money, everybody's pity.

Nobody really wins.

I don't know what kind of settlement or alimony he's paying you—

Felicia flared. You see what time I'm coming home tonight? You think Army feeding himself and buying his own—what they called?—Air Jordache?

Jordan, Oliver said. Air Jordans.

Children not cheap.

You're preaching to the—

I'm not preaching.

You're preaching to the choir, Oliver said. I mean, I'm not a Texas billionaire. But I don't work hard (He ain't got no job, Army said later) just to give all my money to a woman who has given me nothing. Nothing, Felicia. Sometimes I'd come home and she'd still be in pajamas with the TV on to some yappety-yap talk show. She wouldn't even brush her hair. And she just gained weight after Hendrix until she looked like a cow. I mean, I might not be a looker, I'm not a teenager—

He complains like a woman, Felicia said later.

Self-dramatizing, Army said.

Yes, that's the word. Dramatizing himself.

An orgy of disclosure, Army said.

Language, Felicia said. But it's sickening. No sense of decorum.

No wonder she divorced him.

Felicia laughed. You bad, eh.

When we met, Oliver was saying, she was— He curved an improbable woman through the air with his hands.

You keep talking about her weight, Felicia said.

All she had to do was to get up and walk around the block. I'm trying at least. I've lost eight pounds, did I tell you?

Yes. You said seven.

It's eight now, he said. How much are you? One fifteen, one twenty?

Felicia was not going to answer that, not because she was sensitive about her weight—she hadn't gained or lost a pound since expelling Army—but because he sounded like he was weighing meat.

Give or take, he answered for her.

They were almost back at the house. Felicia was determined to take charge of the conversation somehow, to change the subject, to set her landlord straight. Walking toward them, but on the other side of the street, was the girl who had been playing with Hendrix. She was crying. Her brother was brushing ants from the dress of her doll.

Listen, Mr. Oliver—

Oliver.

Oliver. You have to let bygones be bygones. I don't know if this woman was fat or what she telling your children, but you have them until September.

He rolled his eyes. Two whole months.

Per the divorce agreement, which Felicia knew by section and article, Oliver's children would spend their summer vacation with Oliver and Christmas with the ex in lieu of constant visitation rights. They arrived promptly on July 1, Canada Day, and had tickets booked for the morning of September 1. There would be no give-or-take of a few days. In the one weekend they had been here, they were already grafted into the neighbourhood scene, thanks to Army. The daughter, Heather, had found a best friend with whom she alternated between chattiness and sulkiness on their daily trips to the mall. The boy had turned Army into a brother, had Army talking all sorts of nonsense as lessons like the king of a poor country with power but no wealth to share.

Listen, Felicia continued, you have them for the whole summer. They find some friends. Just enjoy yourself, nah man. What happened last year is ancient history.

Oliver straightened himself and said, You're right. You're right. I just don't want to see her, talk to her, have anything to do with her.

She's a ten-hour drive away.

Nine.

Whatever.

Then in an attempt to recover from his emotional vulnerability, Oliver went back to talking about the closet. From there the conversation became refreshingly banal: so and so needs to water their lawn, best weed killers, laying out concrete walkways, interlocking bricks, spray guns, paint, interest rates in the eighties, and subjects that caused Felicia to yawn with gratitude.

When they got back to the house, Army was taking coins from a boy at least five years older than him. Felicia stood at the garage entrance and waited because she knew her very presence would kill any remaining energy in the garage.

Oliver, instead of chasing the last of the teenagers away, got the hose and watered the lawn and rinsed his truck, or more accurately, he stood outside holding the hose in the dark for close to an hour.

+

Felicia unpacked the groceries into the fridge.

Did Oliver talk to you about the utilities last week? Felicia asked her son. She couldn't understand why the landlord complained about the utilities when he wasted so much money watering the lawn. She understood how Europeans took pride in gardens but ridiculous.

Did he?

Maybe, yeah.

Army was at the kitchen table counting his money again. He counted it several times that night. He turned the Queen's face on the bills all in one direction. He smelled the bills, arranged them in denominations, then each denomination from crisp to crinkled. It couldn't fit in his wallet, even without the coins.

And what did you say? Felicia closed the fridge door.

Army shrugged. I think I made more money than you today.

For the last time, take that money off the table mat, Felicia said. She knew money to be a dirty thing.

He swept the coins onto the table cloth. You want me to buy you something? Anything you want, you just say it.

Off the table completely, Felicia said.

She had forgotten to buy bread. She was right in the grocery store and bought everything else except what she went in for. Tomorrow she'd have to wake up early to fry bake.

I don't want you getting involved in any adult conversations with him, Felicia said quietly. She could never be sure how much they heard upstairs. And don't let out our business.

You know his ex-wife called the cops on him.

Felicia knew more about this man's divorce than she knew about World War II but she didn't know that.

He told you?

Heather.

Felicia didn't want to ask why, but she wanted to know more. She waited. She made a sound that might be interpreted as curious.

He cut up her clothes. Told her they didn't fit her anyway. There was more but, you know, I was concentratin' on dollar dollar bill y'all.

The man just talking, talking his business, Felicia said. You don't have to ask a thing.

You should see if you can get him to tell you his bank PIN.

Felicia smiled. She was raising a white-collar criminal. She touched his hair. He cut his own as well. She preferred it when it curled as large as bubbles but she was losing the power to tell him how to cut it.

Army twisted his head away. He said, No, really, how much do you think he's worth?

Apart from this house, they knew Oliver had inherited another where he was renting upper and lower portions to different families, either because he was the eldest male child or because he was voted most likely to need a handout. His sisters married well—construction types with massive houses in Vaughan. His brother worked for a developer in Phoenix and had no intention of returning to Canada.

Let your hair grow out a little, Felicia said.

Can't. Gotta be the change you want to see. You still have the old *Ebony*s? I need some more styles.

Far as I see is only two haircut you does give people.

I give them what they want. Business 101. Black style. White style. Done. I cut thirty-one people today.

And how much you charging them?

Half price for your first cut or if you bring somebody.

So if somebody bring somebody for the first time then you working for free.

Mom, Army tapped his temple. Mom. You must think I'm some kind of idiot.

I just posing a hypothetical situation.

I thought of that. I ain' running no amateur operation here. This is a business, Mom. This is profitable. Cash rules everything around me. CREAM. Git da money.

Felicia held up her hands in surrender, though he hadn't actually answered her. She unpacked cans into the cupboard.

He laid a bill on the counter as he walked up to his room. I just busting out everywhere with money. That's for dinner. Buy yourself something nice, pretty lady.

Army

Extension

Army raised the garage door at ten in the morning, expecting a throng of customers, the guys he had to turn back yesterday, but only Hendrix, the kid from upstairs, was outside, poking a straw into an anthill.

You want a haircut? Army asked although he had cut the boy's hair yesterday.

I don't have any money, Hendrix said.

Well, go get some.

Don't have none. I could give you some ants if you want.

Army sighed. He stood at the edge of the garage on the heels of his flattened trainers, his hair-cutting shoes, holding his wrists and staring beyond Hendrix into the street. He hadn't worn a shirt in days. He had downplayed the obvious problem with his business. Sure, he had chosen Monday, July 4, as the grand opening in the spirit of big-business American entrepreneurship, advertised with a flyer on every porch for blocks, incentivized with the half-price offers, even pimpified the garage into lounge cum music shop, but people simply didn't need haircuts every day.

Hendrix placed the straw in the mailbox and clapped his hands clean on his thighs.

What were you doing to that girl yesterday? Army asked.

It was her game, Hendrix said. He explained the rules. It was called Divorce. First they get married. Then the man shouts at the woman. What do I have to say? Hendrix had asked her. Doesn't matter. Just shout. She asks for a divorce. He asked why but she said he wasn't supposed to ask why. His dad asked why,

Hendrix told her. He still asks why. You're not supposed to ask why. So they get divorced. They pretend to sign papers. They divide up the assets. She wanted half the ants. He refused. If I have to give you half my ants then I want half your Barbie. She refused. She said they had to get married again if he wanted to keep the ants. So he has to propose. Then they get re-married. Then they get divorced and fight about dividing the ants. Then they get re-remarried and re-redivorced. And when she wasn't paying attention, Hendrix took her doll by the leg and stood it in the anthill.

Reliving the trauma of playing with a girl caused Hendrix to frown.

She had it coming, Army said.

Hendrix's expression eased. Do you want to play upstairs?

Army shook his head. The house the two families shared was a split-level with a sunken two-car garage. Felicia's half held her car or Army's barbershop, depending on the time of day, while Oliver's half held the remnants of his former life as a married man. To the right of the garage were stairs leading up to Oliver's home. Felicia's entrance was through the garage. Her kitchen and living room were below ground and a bathroom and two bedrooms were above ground, facing the backyard. At the front of the house, there was a balcony off Oliver's living room. Also on that floor was a kitchen and bathroom, and on the upper-most level of the house, three bedrooms: Oliver kept the master for himself, gave Heather the second biggest room, and Hendrix the smallest one. Why does Heather get the big room? Hendrix had asked, emboldened by Army's advice (Your dad must, legally speaking, provide equally for you, was Army's counsel). Because she's a girl, Oliver answered. I want the big room, Hendrix said. Do you want to be a girl? Oliver said. No. Then stop whining. Ordinarily there'd be free flow throughout the house. But because Oliver was renting half (and basically sending half that money to his ex-wife in Massachusetts), he inserted a door between the two households, a black door so in the dark it looked like a portal but felt like a smack.

Hendrix sat on the swivel barstool Army had repurposed. Army, he said, if your dad's a millionaire, how come you're living in our basement?

Army continued gazing into the summer street. That's a bougie question, soldier, he said without intonation whatsoever in his voice, eyes, face.

What's *bougie?*

Bourgeois.

What's *bourgeois?*

Bougie.

Maybe your dad's a truck driver or something. Heather thinks you just make up stuff because you don't know.

Who knows more about my dad, Heather or me?

It's not just Heather.

Is that right? Army turned away from the street. He swatted at a fly and caught sight of his lats or ribs rippling in the repurposed mirror.

Because if he had a million dollars he'd have to give you and your mom half a million, like my dad.

Your dad doesn't have money for a haircut.

That's because he had to give my mom half of everything.

How much?

I dunno. Half.

Army clasped his wrists again.

Did it ever occur to you, soldierbwoy, that I might be making my own million through this humble enterprise? Almost daily he had visions of himself engaged in one of the following: sunglasses, boardrooms, beepers, pagers, airport lounges, complicated drinks but always brown, firing quivering-lipped skinny blond men in tight suits. Yachts, not so much. To be sure, he liked nice things—gold chains, shoes, track suits, hats with sports logos.

You can't make a million dollars cutting hair. You'd have to cut like a million people.

Army blared a gameshow-fail sound. He had attempted to invite nearly a million to the opening—Oliver's siblings, in-laws, nephews, nieces, first and second cousins, unverifiable cousins, pets—but he suspected the word never reached the half of them.

Well, not a million. More like a thousand, Hendrix corrected himself.

What's between a thousand and a million? Army tested him.

Ten thousand, Hendrix said.

All right.

It goes thousand, ten thousand, hundred thousand, million, then billion, then kajillion. My teacher didn't know what came after kajillion. She didn't even know kajillion.

Yeah, so, Army said, I'm gonna make a thousand this summer, then ten thousand next summer, then maybe a couple of years to 100K, and so on. I'll have my first million by the time I'm twenty, twenty-one. Trust me.

Me too. By the time I'm ten.

+

Army was nibbling a slice of cheese from its plastic wrap and watching TV when the bell rang. He thought it would be Hendrix or his dripping-hot sister—aura like beads on a pop can, aura of a close-up burger shot, aura of airplane flying overhead and getting your attention, holding it, until it was gone. An imperious roaring American airline with two huge engines per wing. He couldn't believe his luck when Oliver brought his kids home from the airport. It had only been days but Hendrix was glued to him. The hot sister was a work in progress. He went around shirtless to signal his availability. He was taller than her. She was sixteen, the major hurdle. He was fourteen turning fifteen which was practically sixteen. If you rounded up. He could pass for sixteen himself. On the skinny side—lean, he liked to say—but exotic, muscled, flat, like lines drawn onto his body, no heft to the muscle.

At the door, however, was his first of two customers for the day, a Sikh boy, probably Grade 6 or 7, wearing a patka with a knot tied at the top.

I came at eight but you weren't open, he said. He reached into his pocket and placed a five in Army's hand.

Army hesitated. He was occasionally surprised to find himself in trouble after executing what at the time seemed like a good idea. In this case, however, he could clearly see trouble ahead. Yet he was curious to see under the patka and eager to expand his clientele. He could retire on all the Sikh boys in the neighbourhood.

You're sure? Army asked.

The boy was already seated with the cape around his shoulders. Could you close the garage door?

Army did. There was still enough light through the clear panels at the top. The boy looked around as Army laid out his instruments. The shop was furnished with two adjustable hydraulic barstools, exactly half of Oliver's former family, a narrow full-length mirror, a few divorce chairs in case people wanted to wait around. Army ran a divorce extension cord for his shavers and for his boombox, tuned to 93.7 Buffalo, rabbit ears alert to the best reception. On a divorce bench, he laid out a Mason jar with alcohol to disinfect the scissors and clipper combs after each haircut, a spray bottle with more alcohol for the scalps and brushes. The problem was Felicia's car couldn't be in the garage at the same time that his shop was in swing, meaning he had to set up and take down the business every day around Felicia's work and night-school schedule.

You're sure you're sure, Army checked.

The boy undid his patka. His hair was braided and coiled on the top of his head. It's clean? Army asked.

The boy lowered his head and Army instantly regretted the question. He would be gentler. He would talk him through it. I'm going to have to use scissors.

He uncoiled the braid then held it out like a tail. It was as thick as his four fingers bunched together. The boy sucked in his breath at the sound of the scissors cutting his hair.

Army knew better but he asked, Does it hurt?

The boy shook his head. Shuddered. Should it?

You mean you never cut your hair. Like never?

He shook his head.

Army continued cutting.

I cut a little piece to test it, the boy said. I felt it but it didn't hurt.

Army made one more snip to cut the braid. The boy's hair hung in jagged pieces to the bottom of his ear. He touched it.

How does it feel?

Light.

Honeys be humping your leg, Army said. He told him about one of his first girlfriends, a girl who removed her hijab at school and almost believed him when he said he was Persian but his parents didn't teach him Arabic. He told him about a Sikh boy he knew who used to remove his turban and tuck his hair into his collar and another who wore a doo-rag instead.

The boy smiled but he looked terrified. Can you make it even or is that more money?

I'm not going to leave you looking like you got cut by a lawnmower. Army hadn't intended to charge him extra but since he asked. Chief, it's a big job turning you into a playa. It's not like a regular haircut.

I only have two bucks more.

It's $2.50 but I'll give you a discount. Army dropped the braid in his lap. Bring a friend.

The braid rolled to the floor when the boy dug for money in his pocket. An hour later Hendrix claimed it. Army had recruited him to clean the shop, paid him a dollar a day for unlimited service. His first employee. Introduced a taxation system where Hendrix had to give him back a quarter on every dollar.

Why? Hendrix pouted.

That's how the world works, son.

Hendrix was keeping the hair.

+

Heather came down while Army was cutting the hair of his second and final customer of the day. The kid kept rattling a coughdrop against his teeth and feeling the level of his hair at the back.

Don't make me look like a convict, Coughdrop said for the umpteenth time.

Heather turned the tape in her Walkman. She was wearing eight-hole Docs, cutoffs so short the front pockets were visible, a tank top, and a green plaid shirt tied around her waist. Army wanted to squeeze the juice out of her thighs, just fill his hands with it until it overflowed his fingers.

Heather relayed a message to Hendrix from their father, then started up the driveway. She clipped her Walkman to her itty-bitty waist and unhooked the headphones from her neck. The sponge from one side was missing.

Halt, Army said. He set down the electric shaver. He uncapped the repurposed Milo container, and made a display of licking his thumb and flicking through a wad of bills. Could you get me a root beer and some bubble tape?

Heather descended the driveway and took the money. Before she could leave (him forever, he felt), Army grabbed her wrist.

And get yourself something too. He scooped up some coins and sifted them into her hand.

Yay, she said. I can finally get that pony.

Get yourself a unicorn too. Army picked up the shaver again.

You ever heard about Sophie Fortin? Felicia had asked Army a week ago.

Unicorn, he said. He was designing the barbershop flyer. He'd need Felicia to photocopy it at work for him. She's washed up. She used to be hot.

Don't call women *hot*. I'm not one of your, your homeboys.

You're my everything, pretty lady. He had her.

What was she in?

You mean apart from *Playboy?*

How do you know she was in *Playboy?*

I just heard about it. Army tried to quote Fortin, It's nothing I don't see every day. But I'm every man's unicorn. You don't remember that? Oh and when somebody asked her why she posed nekkid, she was like, I took a picture. It'll last longer.

Are you sure it's not too low? Coughdrop said into his chest. Army was lining the back. My mom got mad last time.

Your mom's always mad, Army said. To Heather: Tell him it's not too low. He'd do anything to detain the chevron her hips made holding up her cutoffs.

Heather grazed her finger against the grain of Coughdrop's hair.

Coughdrop stiffened. He, like Army, was fourteen. What a gulf between them and Heather.

Seeing his reaction, Heather ran her finger over the top of his ear then traced the line around his sideburns, up his temple, around the front of his head.

My mom called last night. She started crying, Heather said.

Why?

She's just like that. Heather straddled Coughdrop's legs to see the other side of his head. Aren't your parents divorced?

Separated, Army answered for him. Coughdrop's parents were the most recently infected by an epidemic of divorce that had swept through the neighbourhood. Locusts might be another way of explaining the suddenness and mysterious biblical scale of it.

Heather readjusted the spotlight. My mom and dad separated a bunch of times and they got back together a bunch of times.

She backed away and leaned against Army's repurposed suitcase (now a counter) with her elbows behind her and her chest out.

Army made a note to himself to wear thicker shorts. To camouflage his excitement, he spun Coughdrop so his belly button was now in Coughdrop's face.

Don't cut the top, Coughdrop said.

I'm not cutting the top, Army said.

Because if I go home looking like a convict again—

You say the word *convict* one more time and I'll cut your ear off.

Convict, Hendrix said, entering the garage, sucking a freezie and holding one out to Army.

I'm not kidding, Coughdrop said.

Cut off his ear, Hendrix said.

I'm just fixing the part. Relax. Army held up his hands. Is that all right? Can I fix the part or do you need to ask your mom? He kept his back to Heather while speaking. Did Mr. O and your mom fight all the time?

That's so cliché, Heather said.

Army thought it was a perfectly legitimate question but she had said on a previous occasion that he didn't know how families worked and that hit a sensitive spot. He tried again: Did Mr. O beat up your mom? Does he just go around beating up women?

Heather didn't answer. She studied her reflection a moment before fixing her hair with the fine handle of a comb.

He got fired for beating up a kid, Hendrix said. His lips and tongue were purple. The police came by our house to talk to him.

We're not talking about that, Heather said.

Mom used to beat him up, Hendrix said. Mom got tired of Dad going out all the time and coming back late. He used to get drunk lots. But it wasn't just that. Like it was a bunch of things.

But it wasn't because they were arguing, Heather said.

She used to hit him, Hendrix said.

She didn't hit him.

I saw. He hit her.

He *did not*, Hendrix. You're always seeing things that never happened, Heather said. He threw things but never to hit her, like, just to— I don't know.

Heather applied lipgloss then wiped her teeth with her tongue. Army thought he would burst.

Coughdrop tried to claim the spotlight. I think my dad felt emasculated, without the job and with mom telling him what to do.

What's *emasculated*? Hendrix asked.

When they cut your nuts off, Army said. Then to Heather: To what?

To, like, warn her. So, yeah, sometimes they argued, but most of the time, they just didn't talk to each other. They were living together in the same house, but me and Hendrix would have to talk to them for them.

Hendrix said, That's not why.

Why then?

He hesitated. And just when no one thought an answer was forthcoming, he said: Because she was fat.

Heather went red. Mom's not fat.

Dad said she's fat.

She's not fat-fat.

She has a boyfriend, Hendrix went on divulging. That's why she sent us here, so she could kiss him.

Filter, Hendrix! Shut up!

No, because you and her fight all the time over you and—

Shut up. She struck him hard on a shoulderblade. He punched her thigh and was about to hit her again when Army stayed his hand.

You and who? Army asked. Any name would drive a stake through his heart right now.

An ex, Heather said.

Army couldn't bear the thought of Heather with anyone else. He removed the cape from Coughdrop and changed the subject: Maybe Mr. O could hook up with your [Coughdrop's] mom.

So gross, Heather said.

Get his rocks off, Army went on. Better her than strippers.

Are you done? Heather squeezed her lipgloss into her pocket and pointed two fingers at Coughdrop. Mall?

I'll walk you partway soon as he's done.

I'm done soon as you pay me my money.

Coughdrop slapped five dollars into Army's hand. He briefly admired himself in the mirror before leaving with Heather.

Bring me some business, Army called after them. He sank into the chair when they rounded the corner.

+

She has a boyfriend, you know. Hendrix swept the hair around Army's feet.

The *you know* struck Army as bizarre, as jealous and malevolent. But he didn't show it.

Oh yeah? Army said.

Yeah.

Army shrugged. So what?

Heather and him used to do stuff.

What kind of stuff?

I'm not telling you. Hendrix swept the hair into a scoop. But I know.

You don't know nothing.

I heard them.

Come better than that, G.

They were talking and then I heard them kissing.

How does kissing sound?

Quiet, but I knew. Because I heard her kissing before. Hendrix emptied the scoop into a Zellers bag, tied a knot in the bag of hair and tucked it into the divorce rubble.

What are you keeping all this hair for?

Nothing.

It places the lotion in the basket, Army said.

What?

It places the lotion— Forget it.

Army noted the resemblance between Hendrix and Oliver, the same need to divulge.

Hendrix continued, I was going to drill a hole in my bedroom wall so I could spy on them.

Soldier, you can't do stuff like that.

I didn't though. Because she'd see the hole when she was putting on her lip gloss—that was from before she was allowed to wear makeup—and she'd know I was spying so what's the point so instead I just hid in her closet.

G, what's wrong with you?

I was just practicing. I was going to jump out and surprise her. Anyway, I saw Heather and Bruno.

Kissing?

More than kissing.

I need you to promise not to do that again.

I need you to promise, Hendrix echoed, not to do that again.

Serious, little man.

Serious, little man.

Hendrix is a punk, Army said. This had worked in the past.

Hendrix looked back undaunted. Hendrix is a punk, he said, nearly spitting out his purple ice.

+

In the kitchen later that day, when Army came back from balling and was ready to eat a shelf of the fridge, Felicia asked, What did you do today? From her tone he could tell she was after a confession of some sort.

I don't know, Army said. What did you do today?

She told him what Oliver told her. Two women in saris and a boy rang his bell this evening. They started berating him in a language he didn't know. The boy said they wanted to know if he had seen their recycling bin, maybe accidentally taken it. But Oliver knew that translation was false. The women kept turning the boy's head from side to side, brushing upwards to suggest what was missing. Oliver told them that the person they wanted was not his son. He pointed downstairs.

I'm going to ask you again, Felicia said. What did you do today?

I just provide services. Army thought outrage was the right strategy in this case. I mean, it's on him to clear it with his moms. I'm just an instrument of the Lord. I can give him back his hair if that's what he wants.

Felicia seemed tired.

Army changed his tactic. He asked, You know where Mr. O goes in the day?

I don't care, Army.

It ain't by Tia Maria, I tell you hwat.

Oliver doesn't want you cutting hair in the garage anymore.

Army was aghast. His shop had officially been open two days, although he had been cutting hair—and cutting it well—for a year. You're paying rent here.

I know. Just shut it down a few days. Can you do that?

Heather

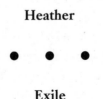

Exile

Heather and her best friend of less than a week, Diane, were taking their daily constitutional to the neighbourhood mall, a twelve-minute walk from their street by catwalk through mid-century houses. Cars were parked on both sides of the street, which left a narrow passageway, like a clogged colon, for cars to negotiate. One side of the street, she thought, the police should only let people park on one side of the street. She and Diane slipped into a catwalk, crossed the street, and walked diagonally across the mall parking lot. Beyond the mall was Army's school, the one she'd be attending if she lived here.

The mall itself was anchored on one end by Zellers and on the other by an Asian grocery store with a poorly ventilated room of fish tanks. When Heather had to take Hendrix with her, she usually left him there and he'd converse with the Chinese fish-cleaners, who spoke little English apart from numbers, while they hacked off fish heads. She and Diane, meanwhile, might get a patty from the Jamaican stand in the atrium or peek at the girlie mags at Becker's (gum for Army, she almost forgot) or shoplift makeup from the Dollar Store before finally heading to Zellers.

He stocked shelves at Zellers. He was a skinny boy who flicked hair out of his eyes. He didn't wear a name tag. A rebel. His red shirt was always untucked from his black pants at the back. Without a cause.

Despite her best efforts at stalking, Heather couldn't predict his shifts so she had to go to the mall two or three times a day if she wanted to see him and be seen. That day, as Heather and Diane entered the air-conditioned store at ladies' wear, the skinny stocker was pulling his trolley of abandoned and rejected items toward them. He didn't smile. He didn't nod. But for the first time Heather felt his eyes flood her in the aisle. Heather touched her undercut. Sweaty. Sophie B. Hawkins was singing, Damn, I wish I was your lover.

And then, when the skinny boy was close enough to smell her, Heather dropped the single most brilliant line of her life. She turned her pink breath toward his passing head, looked at his belt and said, Need a hand? It seemed like it happened in slow motion, with close-ups of her lips and his belt, but it happened very quickly: she was passing, she said, Need a hand? *Need a hand* was at once so banal as to be forgettable and so full of insinuation that it could not be. Did she throw cotton panties or lingerie at him?

He paused. He was trying to figure out which. His neck tinted.

She pulled a sleeve from the cart. Menswear, she said.

His jaw mottled red.

She tugged the tip of the hose with her thumb. Garden centre.

His cheeks. His temple. Vines of blood climbed his face.

Diane affected boredom. She said, I'll meet you at the nails place. She had been considering her nails like a posh wing-girl the whole while, with the palm facing outward instead of like a man with the fingers curled inward. She knew when to scat. The power of two hot girls in all their skimpy, tanned, moist-necked, bubblegummy glory had already overloaded Skinnyboy's senses.

You were here yesterday, Skinnyboy said.

In the mind of a lesser girl than Heather, rotating alarm beacons would go off. *Danger! Danger! Evacuate immediately!* But Heather simply frowned. Was I? I guess. Right, looking at CDs.

You're here pretty much every day.

She screwed her face up into concern. You're not some kind of creep?

Good song, he said.

Radiohead.

I think I listened to it for like two months straight.

What the hell am I doing here? Heather quoted.

I don't belong here, he finished.

For a few moments, everyone in the world vaporized, and left the two of them standing in the wide aisle among endless plains of consumer goods.

Where're you heading? Heather asked.

He pointed his head without releasing her eye.

She pointed her head in the same direction, but as a question.

He answered by inclining his head more deeply.

So you look for me every day? Heather asked when they had straightened up.

Yeah, no, I can just tell the people who come here because they don't have AC at home.

Then the two of them walked toward the garden centre, Skinnyboy trailing the cart behind them. From the garden centre, they walked to health and beauty to men's wear to electronics back to the garden centre. He greeted other employees with the barest facial tic, perhaps a slight pout of the lip, and impressed Heather by saying cool things like, Hi Paula, and, That was my old supervisor. Real adult things.

She offered him bubble tape among the CD racks and lilies.

But his real passion, his words, was music. Of course. He played guitar. Acoustic and a little bass. He was in a band. Their sound was like Nirvana meets Joni Mitchell with a little bit of Bob Marley, he was explaining while up on a red ladder, restocking items from the cart.

What's it called?

What's what called?

The band.

Mmrm.

What?

Murmur.

You always do that?

He snorted. First time, he said. But I should. Watch your head. He lifted a large flowerpot from the top shelf.

My dad had a band, she said. He quit it because he has tinnitus.

Coo'.

They used to play covers.

We only do original stuff, Skinnyboy said. I mean, some covers. If you're playing a three-hour set in a bar to a bunch of old dudes you better bring the Eagles. But like 90 percent original.

They started off making their own music. Heather wanted his respect. Like one of their songs got pretty big.

What song?

Pine Cone.

The skinny boy shook his head, or cleared his hair from his eyes. He was wearing the flowerpot on his arm like a large thimble.

It wasn't huge-huge. But it was on the radio and stuff. Not his version. A cover version from a French band. Péter covered it, sort of.

French or French-Canadian.

French-Canadian. Montreal. Anyway, some band—she made finger quotes around the word—covered it. They kept the chords but changed the lyrics so it was different enough to be their song. Whenever my dad sings it, it sounds like he's Weird Al. It's a complicated story.

The skinny boy twirled the flowerpot from the inside for her to continue.

So Heather complicated the story further. Their band had a record deal. My dad and mom got married. They broke up. The band, I mean. And my parents too, I guess. I doubt it was all my mom's fault, although my dad calls her their Yoko. They had the usual band problems. Creative differences. There's only so much guitar my dad wanted to play in the background. Anyway, the label dropped 'em before they broke up. And Pine Cone was big in Quebec for some reason.

Coo'. The conversation had strayed too far from him. Hey, I should—

Heather wanted to be the one to end it. I should find Diane. She stuffed her hands in her pockets but kept her elbows locked so her body stretched itself out lean and her shirt rode up and her shoulders rose high and sexy to create a valley for her face. She took a few steps back while he took her in. From his vantage, he'd be able to drop coins down her tank.

I'm Heather.

Heather, he repeated but he didn't give his name.

They revived the routine.

I live a couple of blocks that way. She pointed her head.

That way. He pointed his head.

At 55 Newcourt. By the catwalk.

He climbed down the ladder and walked her to the edge of the store. Between the electromagnetic shoplifting gate, he finally asked, You have a number?

Just come by, Heather said. Maybe change first. 55 Newcourt. With your guitar.

He very gentlemanly opened a door for her. It was automatic. But still. He reached out a hand.

+

Heather found Diane outside the manicure salon, reading the covers of tabloid magazines and sucking on an eighteen-inch freezie. They passed the ice between them on the walk to Diane's house while Heather went on and on about Skinnyboy. They talked about him through a makeshift dinner of instant noodles on Diane's bed (her parents were divorced). Now that Heather had seen him up close, she tried to convey what a rare creature he was, how he had reached in between the upper buttons of his shirt to scratch his chest, how he didn't laugh once—possibly couldn't—with his tiny Edward-Scissorhands mouth, how he was a man who would have had a horse centuries ago, a man whose coastal village people must have worn white, silk puffy shirts and stood on cliffs, looking into the moody sea.

It was almost dark when Heather walked back to the garage, strutting in among Army's boys, with a can't-put-your-finger-on-it confidence and glamour, like she was in front of an industrial wind machine.

Where's my bubble tape? Army wanted to know.

She had finished it all. She took the gum from her mouth and stuck it on his improvised counter. Then she slapped his butt and went upstairs.

+

Two days Skinnyboy didn't come by. Were she in Grade 8 she'd stuff a note with her feelings, with the kind of flattery that no guy in a band could resist, fold it into a fortress, and send it off with Diane for secure delivery, analysis, and reportage.

On the third day, she returned to Zellers without Diane. On the way, she unbuttoned her shirt to expose her midriff under her tank top. She'd find him and ask him whether she should pierce her belly button or not.

I came looking for you yesterday, he said.

Yesterday? She was home most of the day except for dinner. Oliver had finally cracked under their complaining and taken them out.

There was a guy in the garage who kept trying to give me a haircut. I thought it was your brother.

That's the guy in the basement. Army.

Army, right. He didn't know you.

He knows me.

He said he didn't know you.

You went to 55 Newcourt?

Yeah, 55 Newcourt. Army was the kid's name. How many Armies do you have on your street?

Heather still couldn't believe it. He was a half-black kid, right?

Yeah.

About this tall? She held her hand five inches over her head.

Low hair, talks kinda fast, no shirt, thinks he's a stud, Skinnyboy finished.

It was Army. Was my brother with him?

He was alone. Anyway, the kid said I had the wrong address and then he tried to sell me stuff, actual stuff, not like weed or anything.

When Heather had climbed out of Oliver's truck after dinner, Army was still in the garage.

Did you bring me back some fries? Army had asked.

Hendrix gave him a box.

Heather specifically but casually but clearly asked, What's up? Meaning, Did anyone come by for her?

Army filled his mouth with fries and shook his head and she went upstairs and called Diane.

Skinnyboy looked over his shoulder. He couldn't spend his shift talking to her and Heather wanted to get home and deal with Judas. Which was the one who denied Christ? Her biblical knowledge was fuzzy. Peter. With a kiss? Someone's ear got cut off. Van Gogh.

You have a pen? she asked.

This time Skinnyboy was ready. Heather wrote her number on the inside of his arm. In the time it took to write seven digits, they exchanged information. She told him she was almost eighteen. He was twenty-two. She looked young, yeah, she knew. She was a dual citizen. No she wasn't in university. She might study journalism in a year or—because he didn't seem impressed—pursue acting. And she issued a warning. If you call, just say you're looking for a haircut or something. My dad can be a dick on the phone. She capped the pen.

Coo', he said.

Sorry, she said. Just a general, blanket sorry for the inconvenience of her presence and absence and attention and residue.

I got a guitar out of it so, I mean, whatever.

Skinnyboy walked away from Heather with the back of his shirt untucked into an Employees Only area before she could ask him whether she should pierce her belly button or not.

Oliver

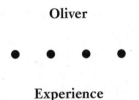

Experience

When Felicia showed up to inspect the basement with her swivelheaded son, Oliver liked them immediately. They'd be quiet, appreciative people. There was secrecy in her face but not the scheming kind—past secrets, not future ones. Army had spoken like Felicia's lawyer. Did Oliver require first and last? Were utilities included? What was the average utility cost? Would he consider including them? Shovelling of snow and grounds maintenance? Oliver found himself trying to please them, courting them. There was a nearby stripmall. The house was a catwalk away from the bus route. Army wouldn't have to change schools. But Oliver was firm on the occupancy date. Felicia wanted to wait until the end of the school year for Army and herself—a July 1 move in—but Oliver insisted on June 1, emboldened by the advice of two brothers-in-law. The basement had been empty for a month already. Others were willing to rent it. His other choices were a family of five which would put pressure on his utilities plus the wife looked telenova dramatic; a Portuguese couple with a baby but the man looked like a drunk and together they made him feel Portuguese Lite; another couple where the wife didn't work and looked depressed while the man looked oppressed as if he wanted to but could not divorce his wife; a single man who had too many factory jobs in the last few years and was trying to get a place so the courts would grant him visitation rights; a large Indian family with grandparents. Felicia was neat, in heels, skirt, professional, attractive, direct, had a checklist. He spied in her car; it was clean.

Oliver had taken his divorce out of storage between the time she rented the place and moved in, after the year's contract was up, and squeezed everything into a hill on his side of the garage. The divorce rubble sloped from ceiling to floor, back wall to garage door. It took up so much space that Felicia could barely open her car door. Oliver had seen her squeezing out, eyeing a bicycle wheel or gas can or printer box.

She told him, curtly and professionally as if she planned how to tell him, to clean it up.

Army offered to help for a fee. Then he cannibalized it for free.

When Army was setting up for the grand official opening, he found a leather footstool (which he carried upstairs and rang the doorbell and asked Mr. O if he could use), a box of Mason jars (which he carried upstairs and rang the doorbell and), a standing scoop (which he carried upstairs) and an alarm clock (which he) until Oliver just said he could use anything he wanted, just don't wreck anything.

All of the furniture in Army's barbershop was salvaged from Oliver's divorce rubble. Until recently, he used to cut hair in the bathroom, in the bathtub, and wash the hair down the drain. As landlord, Oliver had to clean the drain with a coat hanger and Drano.

Today Oliver was going to sort through the garage. Monday seemed an appropriate day for that kind of work. He backed up his truck so he could toss whatever he or the kids didn't want into the bed. Heather was still sleeping, at 9:00 a.m., so it would just be Oliver and Hendrix. They'd just put her stuff in a pile.

Maybe we can get the barbecue going, he said to Hendrix.

When he opened the garage door, Army peeked out from the basement entrance, sleepy-faced, half-naked. He put on some sneakers and strolled out. He asked for Heather, which Oliver did not appreciate first thing in the morning, the boy still thick in the shorts, asking for his daughter. She was sleeping and to remain sleeping.

Holla if anyone comes by for a cut, Army said, then went back inside, yawning.

After half an hour, Hendrix said, I'm getting Army.

For what?

It's kind of his garage too.

It's my stuff. Oliver caught himself thumbing his chest. The boy was such a provocation sometimes. So very different from Heather. Before either of them, he had hoped for a son, but Heather had taken to him or after him so easily, preferred him even as a child, as though she knew his ex was unworthy of attention. And Hendrix, no, not the same.

Oliver said, I might have some of Grandpa's old hunting stuff in here.

Guns? Hendrix asked.

It was time to get down to business. Oliver opened a Zellers bag and met instant opposition.

Don't throw that out, Hendrix said.

It's hair.

I'm going to feed it to my ants.

Ants don't eat hair.

They do too. At least mine do. Hendrix took the bag from him.

Oliver sighed. Maybe the hair of teenage boys was the poison that could finally rid his front yard of ants.

After another thirty minutes, Oliver was overwhelmed. No, irritable. No, thirsty. He was thirsty. He sent Hendrix up for some juice. Hendrix returned, weird satisfaction on his face.

Where's the juice?

Oh yeah, Hendrix said and went back.

Oliver had spread piles around the garage and he was becoming convinced that there wasn't too much of use in any of them. There were sentimental things. Everything he touched had a memory and place in his old house. Yellow sprinklers. Boxes of records. Boxes of clothes he used to wear in high school. Boxes of shoes. That area was a high school zone. Toys and furniture. Helmets. Duplicate tools. Old drills. Box, box, box, box, ab-roller, rope, tools, tools, bumper, plates, box, box, books, candles, a fan, lamp, wooden bowl, Vovó's hair pins in small tin boxes, velvet dining chair, a bust a friend made of him, car rims, fringe curtains, wooden rods, lampshades, a portable AC unit, some wood, fireplace irons, (gentleman's mags missing,) two ornamental gold cats, (also some VHS tapes missing,) wooden hangers, wire hangers, a wicker hamper, books from university, teaching textbooks, posters, sheet music, table legs, bookshelves, sneakers, clothes, rackets, hockey gear, hockey sticks, what was he looking for? Really, what was he looking for?

A hundred years went by. He shouted for Hendrix.

Hendrix came out.

Moments later, Heather came.

And finally, Army came. He was ready to set up his business but Oliver's divorce rubble had spread into his shop space.

But, Mr. O. This is my livelihood. You and I reached an agreement, if you recall, Shaw versus Soares, last Thursday. Right to practice? We shook. We had witnesses.

I was the witness, Hendrix said.

I mean, that's like legally binding.

Take it inside, Oliver said. Or use the driveway. I'm looking for something.

Guns, Hendrix said.

When Army said there were no guns, Hendrix promptly lost interest in the divorce rubble and turned to look for his ants next to the recycling bin.

Army pulled out one of the barstools and sat, looking out at the street, and explaining to Oliver the principles of running a good business. Business 101. You had to be open.

A pile teetered near Oliver when he tried to dislodge a case from the middle.

Grab that music stand, Oliver said.

Mr. O, Army said, you know I don't work for free and I'm losing money as we speak since—

Hurry up. Oliver was straining under the weight.

Army grabbed the stand and together they prevented an avalanche.

Damn it. Oliver wagged his finger. He had cut himself.

I reorganized that corner, Army said.

Just leave my stuff alone, all right? I know where everything is.

Army took his seat on the barstool, looking out into the street with his back hunched.

Oliver cooled down. He'd been snapping at people or storing up hurts then confronting people. This moodiness was an effect of the divorce that worsened when his children were around. Their presence activated surges of elation, frustration, rage and despair, sometimes within an hour, like New England weather.

I see your tan line. Hendrix pointed to Army's thigh.

He doesn't tan, Heather said.

I bronze up, Army said. Whut?

Not like us.

You're white. Hendrix poked Army's leg.

He's not white. His mom's black.

So, he can still be white.

Focus, Oliver said. But he was privately amused by hearing his children talk, working out their own lives so earnestly. Their busy conversations. Their little debates. He wanted to apologize to them. To embrace them when they talked like that, especially after he had been a big bad wolf.

Heather wiped the back of her neck and Oliver glimpsed bare skin underneath. Under her hair, the back and sides were shaved.

Looks dope, right?

Heather reddened. Oliver lifted her hair to the top of her head to better examine the damage.

It's getting stubbly, Army said. I could touch that up today if you want.

Army tried to finger Heather's scalp. Oliver slapped his hand away.

You better find the rest of your hair and put it back or I'm going to shave you bald.

I can find it, Hendrix said.

No phone privileges tonight, Oliver said.

It's just hair, Dad. It'll grow back.

Or tomorrow. You want to keep going?

They worked in silence after that.

Now it occurred to Oliver what he had been looking for. The guitar he played when he was a teenager. He found two other guitars, strings broken, scratched. But his first one, the one he had saved up for, worked weekends with his father, and had made the case himself out of wood, put on the hinges and lined the inside with crushed velvet. The outside had stickers from all the places he and a friend and his friend's girlfriend had been to when they drove the girlfriend home from Vancouver to Toronto during university. His ex was supposed to come but her parents wouldn't let her. He was a third wheel.

Near the other two guitars, he found the songs he had written, tucked in a half-ripped envelope. Maybe six—he hadn't remembered that detail about himself in at least two years—songs. His longhaired self had written songs for his high school girlfriend, but they became songs for every girl he dated up to the dragon he married.

Oliver felt like he had recovered something of his life, from the time before his ex-wife. He was going to live in poverty and play music in shops, smoke cigarettes and wake up late next to topless blondes in squalor. He was going to have fans write him letters, a small, dedicated base of fans, and failing that he was going to teach music. What did he end up teaching until the debacle? Math. $Y = mx + b$ year after year, parabolas, plotting. That was a failure too, as his father predicted while he was in university. He had wasted three earning years, singing fado and drawing on paper (his father was illiterate in English and barely literate in Portuguese), when he should have been sweating, married and with a two-year-old.

Oliver thought the guitar would be close to the others. I could have sworn, Oliver began.

I sold it, Army said. On the weekend. The guy wanted the Kramer originally but he didn't have enough cash, so I sold him the old one.

You sold my guitar? Oliver said.

Wait, which guitar are we talking about?

The Conn, the Japanese one in the case with the stickers.

Yeah, the crappy one, Army said. It needed new strings. I thought you said—

I didn't say anything about selling my guitar.

Some kids dribbling a basketball were approaching down the driveway.

Closed! Oliver shouted at them.

Hold up, Army shouted in correction. Then to Oliver: You can't be turning away my business like that, Mr. O.

Army went inside and came back with an envelope. I sold a bunch of stuff yesterday. Here's half.

He pressed the money into Oliver's hand and went chasing after the boys.

You better be going for my guitar, Oliver shouted after Army. I want my guitar back in this house before your mother comes home tonight or you— Oliver couldn't think of a threat quickly enough. You hear me?

+

Oliver and Heather were waiting for Felicia when her car pulled up. The divorce rubble was still spread over the entire garage so she would have to park in the driveway overnight.

Oliver presented Heather. I want an explanation as to why your son feels he has the right to shave my daughter's head?

What?

She's bald.

No reaction from Felicia.

Show her, he ordered Heather.

Heather tilted her head and flipped her hair over her face. The back was shaved. Oliver lifted up the sides as well.

This, Oliver said. This is what I'm talking about. He squished Heather's cheeks in one hand and turned her head.

Army do that to you? Felicia asked Heather directly.

She looks like a punk.

You don't even notice it if I wear my hair down, Heather said.

I noticed, Oliver said.

Well, you didn't. It's been, like, a week.

I see a lot of girls with the sides like this, Felicia said. And boys too. Is the style.

Heather combed her hair with her fingers.

I don't like it but it look good on her, Felicia continued. She young.

Heather smiled. And because Felicia made Heather smile by her simultaneous disapproval and admiration, Oliver couldn't protest. He couldn't bring up the guitar heist. Heather said she was going to the mall.

I started cleaning up, he said to Felicia, wanting one of Felicia's mixed blessings for himself.

I see that, she said and went inside.

Felicia

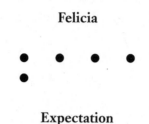

Expectation

Tuesday after work, instead of attending her first night class of the summer, Accounting Procedures, Felicia found herself for the first time on a vertiginous floor of a building at King and Bay in Toronto. It was after six but employees milled about, holding mugs of coffee and manila folders.

Felicia licked a finger and turned a page of *The Economist*. She'd prefer to read the book in her bag, *The Silence of the Lambs*, but felt she might appear lowbrow.

He'll be right with you, Polly said. Her title was Administrative Assistant. It's so good to finally put a face to the name.

Felicia nodded. She crossed and slanted her legs so tightly she had to raise one hip off the seat. With one hand, she felt around her bag for a mint.

She quickly popped the mint into her mouth when she heard Edgar approaching. But she did not stand up. After fifteen years, she wanted him to find her poised in the centre of his reception couch, looking dangerous, as Army liked to say, in her black French heels, polka dot skirt, chiffon blouse, her arms braceletted in gold, her face powdered, her hair pulled back like Sade.

Edgar rolled down his sleeves when he saw her. Someone had bought him a new shirt. She knew better but his shirt seemed like a detail deliberately offered to anger her, an explosion of questions. She accepted his hand to stand up but when he tried to kiss her cheek—the gall of that man—she twisted away and dropped *The Economist* on the couch behind her.

He opened one arm toward his office. The other, she felt hovering just behind her back, daring to touch her. In an office. She recalled the exposé. Was he groping women in the office? She couldn't quite see it.

He had gained weight in the face so now he looked like three rectangles stacked on each other: head, neck, the rest. His hair was between the colour of pennies and loonies, but streaked throughout with dimes.

Thanks for coming. He closed the door but it hardly mattered: one side of his office was a window wall to the city and the opposite, interior wall was entirely transparent, looking out into a hallway with the company's name and logo on the wall in silver metal. Can I offer you something to drink?

Felicia held up a hand in refusal. Yes, let him roll out the pleasantries now that he needed whatever he needed.

Tea? Coffee? Anything?

No, thank you.

Water? Edgar refilled his coffee then added a splash of rum. He took a gulp and frowned. Have you been well, Felicia? You look well.

I'm doing fine, thank you.

Yes, yes, I'm sure. Someone walked along the hallway outside the glass wall. Edgar nodded at him and smiled a grimace. Poor design. He was condemned to acknowledge everyone who walked along that wall while they looked into his zoo cage. We renovated, he said. Now everyone shares my view.

There was a silence. She was not going to rush him. She could luxuriate until he got to his purpose. His desk had nothing on it except a name plate, a phone, and his business cards. Not a file, not a pen, not a sheet of copy paper.

It looks like you never moved out of Brampton.

That's correct, she said.

It must be really developed now, he said. I haven't moved either. Same house in good ol' Toronto the good. Sometimes I kick around out back and have a cigarette, pay my respects to Mutter. He paused here, Felicia thought, to remind her of a debt. And your mother. Geraldine.

Her mother's name in his mouth was obscene. She turned back to small talk. Still travelling?

You remember. Edgar sparkled. Still, yes. I just came back from—

Calgary, she said.

New York, he said. We acquired Zoomin in America, so now we have stores and concessions throughout all the airline hubs, JFK, Atlanta, O'Hare, and some of the second-tier airports. I wasn't travelling as much for a while, but these days, it's probably best if I—

This time she didn't finish his sentence.

If I, well, he said with finality. Did Polly offer you something to drink?

I'm fine, thank you.

Edgar swigged from his mug. Are you sure? Because we have this machine, it hasn't even hit market yet.

He was shaking a little bit. Maybe even sweating. He needed to dye his temples. He got up and went to the bookshelf and poured himself another splash. Bit weak, he said. Was it a problem that I called you at work? You're at Brownstone College?

Yes, she said to both questions.

Is De Rosa still there? He used to be dean of Business?

He's provost now.

Provost? We used to play tennis together at High Park.

You don't play tennis.

I took it up for a while. Public courts. Nothing schmancy. This was years ago, years ago. Edgar leaned back in his chair. How determined he seemed to waste her time. And your sisters, he continued, how are they?

You remember. It was her turn now.

Of course, he said. You used to write them every week.

Darlene took early retirement. And last year Glenda's first boy got married. Lavish thing.

You went back. Alone?

No, Felicia said. She allowed her back to touch the back of the chair. Let him say it.

He didn't. He said: I think about your mother from time to time.

Sixteen years this fall, Felicia said. Sixteen for you as well.

You remember when—

Edgar, Felicia said. Did you call me here to reminisce?

He exhaled. He never showed signs of inebriation, no matter how much he drank. Finally he asked, Have you been paying attention to the news?

She knew exactly what he meant, but she said, I was listening in the car. The man who beat his stepchild to death then threw her off the balcony to make it seem like the child fall down on her own—

Edgar tried to interrupt.

but the autopsy say that the child had all kind of internal bleeding from before the fall.

Felicia, he said. He dipped his head, lowered his brow to look at her.

People real wicked, she concluded.

Another man walked by the window and Edgar grimaced out a smile. You know what I'm referring to.

Oh, you mean—

Yes, I mean that.

The scandal, she said unable to hide her delight.

Cut the charade, he said.

Multiple scandals.

There are no scandals. Sip. Sip. It's all blown out of proportion.

Then they were back fifteen years and the conversation went underground into a lair where they knew each other, always would. She had seen him on the toilet. She knew every last one of his shirts.

You make your bed, Felicia said.

Don't pick sides

I am a side.

until you have the facts. You don't know everything there is to know. And I'd like to let you know that none of these women were from the time when we were together.

Felicia perceived that this shred of moral conscience was meant to endear him to her, to separate their relationship from the others.

All of these allegations stem from before you—

Felicia was shaking her head. What a dog he was.

Or after you. Never at the same time.

Except your wife.

That's a slightly different matter. I'm talking about the allegations.

But now Felicia wanted to talk about Sophie Fortin. She asked plainly, If she didn't file for divorce, Edgar, would you have filed?

I don't know. Let sleeping dogs lie. But the allegations. I'm concerned that—

This is what I don't understand, she said. On the one hand, you are the most passive, laissez-faire man. Married for what, twenty to twenty-five years without making any effort to line up your real life with your on-paper commitments until all this public pressure. But on the other hand, you're aggressively preying after young girls. Girls young enough to be your daughter. What did that one say?—all sorts of sick things, you used to rough she up.

Now, wait a minute, wait a minute, he raised his voice. He was walking back to the bookcase. When he returned, his voice was controlled again. I am not a violent man. Was I ever, ever, Felicia, violent with you?

More than one girl saying that.

Because it's a conspiracy. That's how these things work. Women make all sorts of egregious accusations because they're angry.

About what? Tell me what we so angry about.

Not you. Other women are angry about— He stumbled. About not winning.

Felicia had to laugh. You mad. But even as she was ridiculing his arrogance, she hated herself for finding it plausible. His rejection had made her nearly crazy. No, Edgar was not violent with her. He was insistent. She did things she didn't want to do. She remembered him pushing her head down in the kitchen. But it was no crime. She heard girls did that in empty classrooms at Brownstone. Felicia said, They all can't be lying.

They're exaggerating, making a caricature of me. Edgar was sweating.

Felicia took a handkerchief from her purse and tossed it on the table. He wiped his face. His eyes.

I am not, he said slowly, by any stretch of the imagination, what you would call a good man. But I am not the kind of man that these women are making me out to be. Or maybe that you think I am. I admit that maybe there are things I would have done differently in hindsight.

Felicia wanted to know what things. Edgar held up a hand and ducked his head to prevent her from interrupting.

As I was saying, I am concerned that the media or prosecution may try to contact you. It's not a legal case so much as it is a public case. I am asking that you watch out for folks trying to lure a story from you and if there's anything I can do to convince you to cooperate with me and my team then I would oblige.

By cooperate, you mean keep quiet?

The media will come out to seduce you and to spin a story. You understand, they're not interested in the truth. They're interested in selling papers. And it's not just damage to my reputation I'm concerned about, but yours as well. A scandal is a scandal for everybody.

I thought you say there was no scandal. Felicia was delighted.

There is no scandal. I am preventing a scandal.

He never named Army, Felicia noticed. Your lawyers making you say all this?

I am asking you, Felicia,

[to be my lawfully wedded wife, in his tone]

not to approach the media with your story.

Don't call my house, Felicia said. She took up her bag and walked out, smiling politely at Polly on the way out. Polly's eyes followed her right to the elevator. She knew everything.

+

Oliver wasn't home when she returned. Yet his presence hovered. Even when he wasn't visible, she sensed that he could burst into physical form at any point with a sound like a confetti party popper. She liked him best when he was washing his truck (as opposed to flagging down her car, watering the lawn, or interminably pacing the streets) because it was the only time he seemed uninterested in talking to her. And this evening she couldn't bear a conversation where the word *ex* was said. She did not want to be compelled into taking the other side, that is, the side of a man, as he smushed the face of his ex into topsoil with his foot.

He wasn't home. His truck was gone. Army was surely out playing basketball behind the rec centre. She didn't even want to see her guysmiley son.

And so why did she feel as if she were carrying a boulder in her uterus, so much so that she had to cup both of her hands over the area, after she unlocked the door and deposited her bags near the couch?

+

Edgar didn't call her house.

At work on Thursday, while she was trying to sneak in some reading/scanning for her night course on Payroll Fundamentals, she answered the phone: Brownstone College, English Department. How may I help you?

I need to see you promptly, Edgar said.

For what?

About a matter.

I'm not available. Felicia was in no rush to see Edgar again.

I'm going to Halifax in the morning.

Maybe when you get back then, she said.

This evening works for me, Edgar said.

I have class.

A student entered, holding a pink add-drop form for the summer session.

I have to go. I'm not driving back to Toronto, Felicia said.

Is your class at Brownstone?

Don't come here. She enunciated. I am not available.

I get back at two on Sunday. It's either going to be your house or my house. I'll be at one of those two places.

She hung up and snatched the form from the student.

Army

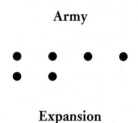

Expansion

Two weeks of the summer had gone by. Army's business underwent a series of expansions that began with a short-lived lucrative franchise in the backyard, thanks to Oliver's unearthed barbecue.

People don't need haircuts every day, he had said to Felicia. But you know what they need?

What?

Food. He parted his hands over his face as if unveiling a marquee.

Army's BBQ was cheaper than the patty shop in the mall and offered a greater selection. He barbecued hotdogs and burgers and topped them with crushed ketchup chips. He also sold house specialties such as barbecued patty and the extremely popular grilled grilled-cheese sandwich also known as g^2 or broke man's beef. At first, Oliver didn't want anyone touching his barbecue and insisted on doing the barbecuing himself. But within a few days, Army wore him down with ill-timed demands—once waking him from a nap in the backyard—until Oliver handed over rights to the spatula.

Someone had a bright idea to barbecue chocolate bars. It wasn't that Army didn't understand the basics of thermodynamics. The intent was to merge all chocolate bars into one mega chocolate bar with a signature smoked flavour. After a mall run, they emptied every brand unto the hot grill and waited. Some guys were tossing a football around in the backyard as well. It got tossed too far, a guy jumped to catch it. As he was in the air another guy tackled him into Oliver's wooden fence. The fence got busted. Oliver came out when he heard the commotion. The boys scattered, leaving Army and Hendrix to explain the fence, a trampled tomato plant, and the melted chocolate in his barbecue.

I offered to pay for the fence, Army said to Felicia later.

What kind of man takes money from a child?

It's all right. I offered. But he refused anyway. I think he just likes to suffer and complain.

That was more or the less the end of barbecuing on Oliver's grill for the summer. But not the end of quote dollar dollar bill y'all unquote.

+

Army was usually outside when the mail arrived mid-morning. He and the post-woman were tight.

He did his customary check for a letter from Publishers Clearing House. The envelopes were usually big and brown. Felicia had told him not to get his hopes up. He told her he was getting closer. His friends laughed at him. He thought their disdain would make for a good story when he received the final *Congratulations! You've won!* He thought the final *Congratulations! You've won!* letter might be disguised in a plain white envelope with more time-sensitive information to trick the winner into not opening and thereby forfeiting the prize.

No *Congratulations! You've won!* letter today, but there was a letter for Felicia from a place called Paperplane, which word was emerging from the fold of a paper airplane in profile. She had received a similar letter last Friday, exactly a week ago. A ruse. Another ploy from Publishers Clearing House. He was on to them. They had discovered he was under eighteen and addressed the letter to his guardian from one of their subsidiary addresses.

He put the letter on the coffee table for Felicia but, oh, he'd be home when she opened it.

+

It was the deadzone in the middle of the day. Most of the parents were at work. Most of his friends were indoors. Heather was off somewhere, passed out in a cocktail of moody sixteen-year-old hormones probably. No, that's unkind. She could be as cruel as she wanted to him, but he would always love her with the high, delirious pitch of Whitney Houston.

Army could only find Hendrix for company. They had spent almost an hour trying to break their own speed record. They were determined to ride the length of Newcourt without toppling. They tried it with Hendrix on the handlebars for

a while, then with Hendrix on the seat while Army pedalled standing up, sprint-
ing. They were about to try again.

You ready? Army asked Hendrix.

Hendrix stopped sucking the knuckle of his thumb, climbed on the saddle,
and held on to Army's waist.

Army pushed off. The first few metres were wobbly. They corrected quickly.
The faster they went, the easier it was to balance.

About a week ago, early July, Heather had come back from the mall and caused
a scene in his shop, reminding him that he lived in the basement and needed to have
a little respect for everyone else, that maybe he should stop selling his piss and get
a real job like most people. And Army had to save face in front of his one customer
and Hendrix so he pointed out that she didn't have a job herself and wouldn't know
anybody on this street if it wasn't for him. Then she rolled her eyes and said, Mr.
Social. You're so cool. I just want to hang with you all summer. And he asked her
why she was being such a cunt all of a sudden. And she started for the stairs. Don't
go around acting like you own the place, she said. He opened his palms to Hendrix
and asked, What was that about? PMS, Hendrix said. She's like that with Mom. He
didn't know what the letters stood for or the biological reasons for it. Hendrix
sometimes applied it to himself, as in I feel PMSey today.

Army and Hendrix accelerated down the slight incline toward the corner. It
felt faster than last time.

Slow down, Hendrix called out.

Hold on.

Army felt Hendrix's little hands squeeze his waist.

At the speed they were travelling, Army couldn't stop easily. He couldn't
keep going straight either, else he would crash into a green electrical box. He had
to turn and follow the curve of the sidewalk. Yet they had never made it this far
before and Army was unprepared for the weight calculations of rounding the
corner.

The bike kicked up at the back. Hendrix spilled off. Army toppled sideways
and the bike skidded out from under him. He lay on someone's lawn a moment
and closed his eyes. Heather.

He had tried to be the adult with her. He knocked on the upstairs front door
the morning following her tiff. She answered with her hair up, wearing an oversized T-shirt that slipped off her shoulder. She was still smoking. He apologized,
specifically for calling her a cunt. She said nothing. Then Oliver came to the door
with his eyebrows up and when he realized there was no tenant-landlord issue,

shooed Army back down the stairs. And since then there had been a lot of sunglasses and gum chewing between them—mostly from her; he felt himself looking longingly after her while trying not to look. Maybe Heather found her crowd,
Army didn't know.

Army opened his eyes. Hendrix was holding his digital watch above Army.

I broke the band. The silver thing's gone, he said. A rivulet of blood was running from Hendrix's knee down his shins.

Army sat up and took the watch from him. It still worked. He could fix it.
They walked to retrieve the bicycle. When Army looked up from the watch, he
beheld the future of his business on the other side of the street. He left the
bicycle on the ground and stood, holding his wrists. His bottom lip slackened.

Hendrix followed his eyes. You're gonna take them?

Hell yeah.

They left the bike behind and crossed the street.

Grab one, Army said.

+

Their find consisted of a set of weights: two fifty-pound flat metal weights, four
plastic-shelled twenty-fives, four tens, two fives. The weights and bench weren't
in great condition. The bar was rusted, the vinyl on the bench was ripped and
stuffing was coming out but Army could duct tape that new.

Someone in that house had given up on fitness. Hendrix and Army also
scored a belt for around the waist that had electrodes in it. Army figured patrons
could just use it as a weight belt.

With that lucky garbage find, Army's business expanded yet again from barbershop to BBQ stand to gym. By the end of the summer, most of the boys would have
V-shaped torsos and tiny legs, like martini glasses.

He spent the afternoon cleaning the weights, and singing under his breath
for Heather. Bleach didn't work but CLR and a scrubbing brush did. The rust
came off, ran down the driveway. Within a few hours, he'd set up the bench at the
front of the barbershop, almost directly under the garage door. He lined up the
free weights along the wall with the recycling bin. He found a ThighMaster from
Oliver's ex in the divorce rubble. That would be good for the girls. He imagined
Heather squeezing her thighs together with a little arch of her back, a push of
her tush, then opening them, her nipples straining in a leotard, and had to think
about basketball immediately to avoid the erection. The thought of basketball
wasn't strong enough. He had to play.

+

Army missed Felicia's arrival home because he was out playing ball and drumming up clients for the soon to be launched Army's Gym. When he got back, the letter was no longer on the coffee table.

Did you open your mail? Army asked.

Nothing came for you.

The corporate letter, what was that?

A notification. They received my change of address.

Twice?

Yes, twice. Processing error.

What's the business?

Some magazine subscription promotion thing from work.

Can I see it?

I ripped it up. What's the matter with you?

Army wondered. Would his own mother—? Naw. Would she? Nah. But would she though? No.

Mom, I'm going to be straight with you here.

Yes, be straight with me.

I'm expecting a cheque. From my sweepstakes.

You have to give up that foolishness.

Hear me out. It should come any day now and I'd like to be sure that you, my own mother, wouldn't— He stopped short with enough suggestion in his voice.

You accusing me now?

If you accidentally destroyed the first one, I won't be angry. We'll just contact them.

The letter was not for you, Army.

+

The gym was immediately popular. Testosterone was at an all-time high. You could smell it—exactly like elk anus.

It was a chest, bicep and abs day. There were only two days: the other was shoulder, triceps, lats, abs. They made a half-hearted attempt at calf raises and squats but it didn't feel like much work on the equipment. They worked their legs with basketball anyway. The muscle magazines with men with veins as big as their fingers advised them not to work the same body part every day, to take a rest. That advice was for old people. They were all going to get Van-Damme jacked before the end of the summer and get girls next school year. That was the plan in complete detail.

The pricing structure of the gym was a failure, though.

Patrons paid a one-time five-dollar membership fee. Army would come to realize that he should have monetized it differently—on a subscription basis, five bucks a month, or five bucks for twenty-inch biceps, whatever would guarantee steady cash inflow. For now, one-time fee. He'd take some of the money and buy more free weights at Zellers. The message was, Look, the money comes right back to you.

Money slowed down. He couldn't go back to his customers with a new pricing model for the gym when he had promised a flat fee. At that point in the summer, he decided it was time to use his secret weapon. Before Oliver had cleaned out the garage, Army had found a few girlie magazines buried in an unlabelled box. *Juggs.* He did not store them between his mattress and box spring because Felicia rotated mattresses by the season. Instead, he slipped the magazines into some folded T-shirts and stored them in an inside pocket of the suitcase he used for a counter.

He couldn't run the girlie mag business openly from the garage and he couldn't advertise it either. One-on-one, in private, and only to select trusted, undoubtedly horny friends, he said, I've got something to show you. He took the magazines up to his room and together they read the articles.

That business provided daily income.

Heather

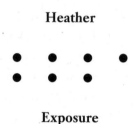

Exposure

Oliver's truck was gone when Heather returned from a mall run. She was a bit miffed with Skinnyboy. Everything was about him, the music, constantly topping her in conversation, and she wanted things to be about, well, her. No one was in the garage, except for Army, adjusting the Velcro of his—everybody's—weight gloves, though not actually lifting weights. She acknowledged him today.

So you think my dad's a truck driver? he said.

Okay, she said, unsure of what she had stepped into.

Not that I have to prove anything to you or to anybody.

She shrugged and was going to go her way, but the way he was flexing his hands, so earnestly, so simply, made her pity him. She said, You have to admit this lovechild business—

I don't have to admit nothing.

She tried again, Where's Dad?

Hm. Army put his finger to his chin. His truck's gone. Maybe he's driving it.

Hendrix must have blabbed. But come to think of it, she wasn't even sure she said the truck driver bit. It might have been Oliver. No, it was her. Hendrix said Army's father was a millionaire and Heather said the truck driver bit and then Oliver started talking about his former life as a bus driver. In any event, she'd said that a long time ago, when she just arrived.

Yeah, whatever, Heather said and started to leave.

Are you still mad at me? Army asked to stop her.

He looked at her, baby-don't-hurt-me in his eyes. Oh, she could tell, he had it bad. She remembered something she heard about him recently.

She looked both ways before she said, I have something to show you.

He took off the gloves and held his wrists.

Go inside and open the door when I tell you to.

There was a deadbolt on each side of the black door so mutual consent was necessary for a member of one household to enter the other. No one ever consented. All transactions were made at the respective front doors: the door inside the garage for the Shaw residence or the upstairs door for the Soares residence.

She undid the bolt on her side.

You ready?

She heard him undo the bolt on his side.

Okay, open the door, she said.

When he did, she was standing with her plaid shirt unbuttoned, her bra unhooked and lowered beneath her breasts. She leaned forward, crossed her elbows so her breasts spilled between her arms. Then she closed the door on Army's opening eyes. It was about twenty years ahead of Snapchat.

+

The first time Heather laid her lips on Skinnyboy, she was on the trunk of his car, after he drove them to Port Credit on the lake and played her songs until she was bored with the music and with giving him compliments, so to end it all she beckoned to him and kissed him while he was still singing, the guitar pressed between their bodies, his hand still attempting to strum but getting stuck under her breasts.

+

Immediately, Army tried to duplicate the event. Oliver and Hendrix were not back yet.

He knocked on the black door. I have something to show you.

I don't want to see, Heather said.

A few moments later, he knocked again. Do you have something else to show me?

Heather remembered his type in Grade 9. Dressed in Fubu with the fade and the gold chain, awash in cologne, frenching girls at basement parties, fingering them in the pool, grinding against them on their little beds, twitching out their orgasm.

She went to the black door again and turned the knob. Army was sitting on the floor in a position of desolation, one foot resting flat on the inside of the other, elbow on the raised knee, forehead on elbow. When she stepped over the threshold, he stood up with his back against the hallwall.

You ever kissed a girl? She took another step.

A bunch of times. He nodded. I I I think you mean how many honeys, you know, you know?

How many honeys?

How many honeys? How many?

Yeah, how many? Heather took one more step and let her hair fall into her face. Ballpark, how many?

Too many. Lost track. You're asking me to count the stars. After graduation we made out in the parking lot. Army's body stiffened, all of it. I have to—

Go on. I'm listening.

Heather's breasts grazed his chest then she set them firmly against him like the paddles of a defibrillator. The very tips of Army's body stiffened. She perceived the contrary forces of his hope and suspicion, that she might kiss him or tease him, that he already saw himself in the aftermath, made ridiculous, played.

Army swallowed. So many I have to— Army started and swallowed again. Have to, like, beat them off. With a stick.

Heather didn't have to tell him to close his eyes. His eyes lowered themselves to her lips and closed automatically. His head was craned forward. She pushed his hips against the wall with the heels of her palms. She could feel the heat from his hands hovering around her cheeks but afraid to make contact. She opened his mouth with her mouth. His tongue had all the exploratory zeal of a hamster sniffing out a new cage. He was trying to impress her now. To settle him, she pinned his neck against the wall in the web between her thumb and index finger. He went limp, as if she were an alien sucking the life force out of him, rendered with the graphics of blue mint breath in a gum commercial. But in a lower country, she sensed an insurrection so she withdrew through the black door before the riot.

+

The first time Skinnyboy laid his body on Heather was in his basement room one afternoon after his shift. They entered through the side entrance. The house was air-conditioned. Heather already imagined herself living there. She looked through his things with her fingertips, as if in a store, politely, not too much probing, while he poured a Coke elsewhere. A ukelele came out—in that respect,

Skinnyboy was ahead of his time—and again with the singing. Heather liked his lyrics, Heather liked his voice, but somehow that didn't make for good music. She drank the Coke and while he was singing, fell asleep on his futon and woke up hours later. He was still playing and making notes on a music stand with a pencil from behind his ear, as if he was trying to get as much work done as he could while the baby was napping. He seemed both unaware that she had fallen asleep and consciously drawing inspiration from her as resting muse.

There were many commercials for *Phantom of the Opera* in those days.

+

Every time they were alone, Heather kept showing Army things. She was a veritable how-to manual of a softcore Kama Sutra. Of everything but.

Heather opened the screen door, saw him, closed it, and wordlessly, they met at the black door.

Hendrix? Army asked.

They're gone to Canadian Tire, she said, meaning that they'd probably drop by one of her tias' or tios' houses on the way back. Power to them. There was only so much fado a girl could listen to, even in the background.

She and Army went to his room. They knelt on his bed. They approached each other on their knees.

Army broke away suddenly. But seriously, Heather, I need you to believe that my dad's not a truck driver.

This again. She said, I thought we settled that. Your dad's not a truck driver.

Don't just say it. I need you to believe it.

I believe it.

You don't.

You want to talk about your dad or you want to make out?

Army nodded desperately, which Heather noted was not a choice, but a hormonal pupil dilation, the ascendancy of his limbic system.

The kissing, the groping, the push-ups, the orifices, the hair, the sweat were all innocent to Heather. Fizz in water. A little bubbly. An alternative to TV or talking on the phone or going to the mall. She knew it was more to Army. He kept pushing for some kind of status. Official. He asked her if she wanted to go out with him, like officially, and her answer was simply, I'm sixteen.

At the number, Army said, I'm super horny right now.

I've got two years on you, she said. And, kisssmack, why, smack, buy the cow, kisssmack, if you can get the milk for free.

He turned businessy. If there was a way to bottle—

Army! Heather was exasperated. Shut. Up.

He did for a while. He held her by the back of the head and rolled on her then she rolled on him and they rolled on the blanket rolled through their limbs rolled.

Moments later, Army's mouth was making speech sounds. I'm sorry, he said with his hands deep between her legs.

No, no, don't be sorry.

But I don't get why Mr. O's so mad at me?

It's not just you, she said, while her fingertips were just stretching the elastic of his underwear.

About the guitar. He had months to handle his business. He told me I could take anything I wanted.

Use, Heather said. Not *take*.

Take anything I wanted to use, Army compromised.

Just let it go, she said, while tightening her grip around the long neck in his pants.

His breath caught.

No one wants to think about a parent while getting busy but Army had opened her memory. Damage had been done. While she was pulling down his pants and he was trying to lift his hips to help her, she was thinking that her father had wanted to be a rockstar, that he had made tapes, that he used to do shows but he fell out with the band, then tried solo. There's a family video of Heather and Hendrix swiping their hands down the guitar as Oliver was playing then scurrying away. She didn't miss that time. Her father might. She rarely considered her father from within his head, say, as he must see himself when he remembered that video, his skinny self in a long Jimi Hendrix headband.

Army was fluttering his hand mechanically between her legs. You're right, he finally said. It's not just me he's mad at. He's got some toxic anger issues. Against your moms and stuff. Like every day he's ragging on her.

What was with these distracted Canadian guys, multi-tasking when she was trying to get off?

Is Conn even a Japanese name? Army said. If he had said, Don't sell the Conn—

You're killing my boner, Heather said.

Army smiled. Shortlived. You think I should get braces?

Heather slid his hand along the side of her hip, into the band of her panties.

Go out with me, Army said. Come on.

I'm—

Sixteen. I know, I know. You probably already have a man? Army asked. I mean, don't you?

Heather was below him at that point. She reached up to kiss his face but he backed away.

An American?

I don't have a boyfriend. She held her expression neutral.

Do you call him?

Heather pushed him off and sat up. No, she didn't call him. She wrote him one letter when she first arrived for the summer and he never wrote back. After months walking around with his dick in her mouth, he couldn't write her a damn letter.

She began, I— then changed course and began, You—

Then they heard the truck doors thud and Hendrix's high voice outside and left each other conversatio interruptus.

Oliver

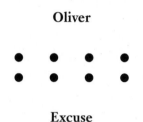

Excuse

Oliver felt worried, no, afraid, no, annoyed, no, he felt mild apprehension about the legal cast to Felicia's tone lately. He had had tenants before. He knew that tone. So over the past week, he pre-emptively upgraded a number of items in her unit. She wanted a peephole. He gave her a peephole. He installed new mirrored sliding doors in Army's room and Army promptly claimed the old ones for his garage/barbershop/BBQ stand/gym. When she saw the sparkle in Army's room, she wondered if she could have mirrored sliders in hers so she wouldn't have to go into Army's room all the time to see herself. Oliver obliged. He promised to sort through the divorce rubble by the end of the summer at the latest. It would not encroach on her forever. Felicia made suggestions. He made suggestions. They made suggestions jointly.

Yesterday, he began fixing the wobbly doorknob to Felicia's bedroom, something he was aware of before she moved in. She had gone with him to Canadian Tire to choose a crystal doorknob. In his truck with Hendrix leaning his head between the two seats. He might have talked a bit too much about himself, he realized now, yet he was falling into the same current while Felicia sat on her bed, doing a poor job of supervising because of the tabloid newspaper spread on her lap. Oliver was telling her about the time his ex-wife suggested that he was responsible for the deaths of his parents because he was living off their fat, even as a grown man, that he had worked his parents to death. Felicia always seemed so interested in his past, even though he was trying to move forward.

Back then, I was working two jobs, Oliver said. *Two.* During the day, I was supplying at a Catholic school if they had work for me, and then I'd drive the evening or night shift for Brampton Transit so those guys could be at home with their families. Plus, if I didn't have a route on the weekends or couldn't get shifts in the summer, I'd work as a mover or do landscaping with my uncle. That's *four* jobs. Sweating to put food on the table and she was at home.

Mm, Felicia said.

I mean, Heather and Hendrix were already in school. She wasn't working. I'm talking three years ago. She hasn't worked a day since we got married. And now she already has tentacles around her next victim, Hendrix was saying.

He said *tentacles?*

Hooks, I think, is what he said, Oliver lied.

You married people—

I'm divorced.

Same thing. You're always condemning your spouse. If she was so terrible, why'd you marry her?

I ask myself that every day, Oliver said. But it was just the next step, the next line in a math problem. You know, like when you have to show your work step-by-step.

Can't you find one good thing about the woman?

Oliver made a display of considering the question. Honestly, I can't.

Make something up.

He pursed his lips, resisting for a while, then finally said, She was punctual.

Punctual? That's the best you can do?

And she used to be good at planning family stuff with my sister. They used to talk long on the phone. Maybe still. We all went to Disney together one year.

Disney.

Don't get me wrong, Felicia. Everybody liked her at first, even though she wasn't Portuguese.

Portuguese, Felicia said to her paper. She had opened a gate in him to a kind of hell.

She could talk to anybody, Oliver went on. Came from a blue-collar family. Her father worked in a paper mill in one of those New England towns. When we were dating she took a bus from Boston to see me. I don't know if she told her parents or if she ran off.

Did she now? Felicia said.

She used to sing harmony to the Carpenters with me. Carole King. Oliver sang, *It's too late, baby. Now it's too late.*

Though we really did try to make it, Felicia finished. She licked a finger and turned a page.

You know it?

Of course.

Oliver inhaled and his chest swelled. I'm not a bad man, Felicia. If I'm providing and you're—she's—complaining about the spark, the magic, then someone has their priorities wrong. The spark. What's the spark? You need to rub something, get some friction going, if you want a spark. How romantic do you expect me to be when the children have chicken pox or my mother's in the hospital? I was working twelve, fourteen hours, those days. And she's saying she doesn't feel loved? I don't feel loved but am I complaining?

Maybe she was depressed.

About what? She had nothing to worry about.

Mm, Felicia said.

Oliver snorted a small laugh. She and my sister planned a birthday party for Heather when she was six or seven.

That so?

He snorted again at the memory of Heather in a princess costume, leaning over a cake. His smile faded slowly.

Felicia was fingering her clavicle. The ex used to stroke hers unconsciously when she was feeling amorous. Was Felicia aroused? When was the last time she had a capable man like him in her bedroom? But he couldn't—right now? In so long. He hadn't been with— He should at least lose a few more pounds first. She was probably used to a. Different sort. Of size. And energy. Stamina. Attack in the initiation.

He blurted out, I'm not looking for anyone right now.

She looked up from her paper. Good, she said, after a slight pause.

Maybe I'll get married again, Oliver explained. Down the road. You know she had the nerve to tell me, to tell *me*, that I had—I can't even repeat some of the things she said to me in front of the children—that their father had the musical talent of bad brakes, and then Oliver found himself babbling about the ex-wife while thinking of Felicia's pubic hair and the grey in his.

He was suddenly thirsty, needing a drink the way smokers needed a cigarette. Felicia was not saying anything. He felt the need to speak louder and faster—the voices of the children outside, Hendrix watching *Beetlejuice* upstairs. And the lock stile could be planed down. Maybe he should plane down the entire side of the door. He dropped his awl abruptly and said he'd have to finish tomorrow.

Why can't you finish now? Felicia asked.

Her face was hard to read but he took a deep breath and accepted what he believed was an invitation to stay (she didn't want to be alone) and tell her about how Heather, when she was little, came home three times in a month without pants. Where are your pants? I asked her. And Heather, she said, How am I supposed to know? The ex thought that was cute. Then he followed up with the time the ex dragged him to the taping of a talk show on women who complain about how men look at them, where he was one of the only men in the audience, and he said, Don't wear short skirts if you don't want to get looked at or raped and the audience booed him. Followed by the time the ex told Hendrix that he was more of a man than his father would ever be, etc. etc.

+

That was yesterday. Today he knocked on Felicia's door, ready to finish installing the crystal doorknob.

Army answered. Look, Mr. O. I'll get it tomorrow. I tried. The kid was talking about a trade. How you feel about that?

Who is it? Felicia said in the background.

I feel no, Oliver said. He held up his all-purpose screwdriver. Doorknob.

Oliver's cologne rose to his nose. His eyes skidded ever so slightly from Army's. He had sprayed a little to mask the scent of his unwashed T-shirt. That was all.

Army smiled. You'll have to come back in a bit. Mom's getting ready.

So?

Mr. O, seriously? I need to teach you about women.

Who is it, Army? Felicia called out.

Mr. O. He wants to finish the doorknob.

Tell him tomorrow.

Felicia, Oliver called out, but Army took him outside. He was as tall as Oliver already.

Listen, man, he said quietly with his hand on the doorknob still. I know you're trying to get with my mom and everything, but you got to run better game than Mr. Fixit.

Oliver opened and closed his mouth like a fish.

And I know Hendrix wants a big brother. Trust me, I was like that too. Army put his hand on Oliver's shoulder and walked him to the front exterior stairs. But, mano a mano, I think you're overexposed. Absence makes the heart, right?

Oliver shook his head out, shook the words into sense.

Think about that trade, Army finished.

Army slipped inside and closed the garage door.

+

A few moments later, while Felicia was reversing from the garage, dressed nicely (a date? a late church service? a date?) Oliver motioned for her to stop and wind down her window. He wasn't going to stop her. He felt compelled to. Then he felt compelled to tell her something.

There's something you need to know, Oliver said sententiously. (With a man? Who?)

Felicia kept her foot on the brake.

Some time ago, your son took some property of mine without my consent.

I'm running late, Felicia said.

She had a way of making him feel ridiculous, a grown man tattling on a child.

Oliver pressed. I could go to the police with this, Felicia. My brother-in-law's brother's a cop. I could have Army charged. For theft.

I'll get Army to give you back your—

Guitar.

Guitar? Army doesn't have any guitar.

Oliver reached into the car and blew the horn to summon Army. They would get this straightened out there and then.

It's not just a guitar. This was my first guitar. 1978. I got it in a shop in east Vancouver. How are you going to return that experience to me?

Army poked his head out of the house door.

Give him back his guitar, Felicia shouted.

I've spoken to Army already.

Then why you involving me in your affairs? Felicia looked what people call *visibly upset.*

Army started walking toward the car.

The word *affairs* unsettled Oliver.

He sold my guitar. Are you getting the picture now?

You want me to ground him?

Oliver wanted the boy punished in a meaningful way. With conviction. She had grounded Army before, for the barbecue incident, for example, but Oliver had seen him dribbling a basketball from the mouth of the garage while Felicia was at work.

Army ducked his head through the passenger window. Oliver was on the driver's side. Felicia between.

You're grounded for the evening, Felicia said to Army.

You can't ground me for something I've fixed. Mr. O and I— Army reached into the car and twirled a coil near Felicia's hairline. You're sweating.

I can't, uh? But Felicia was distracted. She lowered the sun visor and inspected her makeup in the mirror.

Oliver folded his arms on the roof, as if he were trying to press the car in place. Army spoke to Oliver above the car roof.

Mr. O, I was trying to spare you the details. I've spoken with the kid and explained the situation, that you had a sentimental attachment to the guitar, and the kid—I shouldn't call him a kid, he's like done high school—the kid *proposed* an exchange of that guitar for another guitar.

Absolutely not.

Exactly, I told him that all guitars were off the table and I couldn't interest him in anything else and he said that he already put strings on his guitar.

My guitar.

Right. Your guitar. So I said I'd refund him. Fair, right? Full refund. And he said to me, get this, he wanted me to pay him *double* because he was now selling it back to me.

Do it.

Wait, Mr. O, you gotta understand that this kid's trying to outhustle me. I ain't paying double. I can't just be turning over money to people.

Get my guitar back.

I offered him a full refund and a free haircut in exchange, final offer. And he said he'd think about it.

Inside the car, the visor snapped up. Listen, Felicia said. Work it out. Both of you, work it out.

Army stepped back and looked inside the car. I'll get it back, he said as Felicia took her foot off the brake.

The car moved backward under Oliver's forearms.

Today, Oliver said.

I can't leave the house, Army said. You heard the woman.

I said, work it out, Felicia called.

Oliver was confused. She was supposed to unite in a front with him against the wildness of youth. His ex would have set herself behind his shoulder and folded her arms mercilessly. She liked him to handle Big Discipline.

Oliver stepped back from the vehicle. Enjoy your—

Felicia put up her window.

How you gon' play me like that? Not cool, Mr. Fixit, Army said, shaking his head. Not cool.

+

Oliver got in his truck and drove, not following Felicia, but driving in the direction he thought her car had gone. He ended up at The Mansion. That's where he found himself whenever he had a fit of akathisia.

The club was lit by wall sconces and very dim stage lights. The bar also emitted a dull blue light. Apart from that, darkness. The stage was half an octagon with a low gold restraint around the bottom both to prevent the girls from falling and to keep the men from reaching. The girls would come close and crouch for their dollars. The men respected that. They drank and looked. Hooted and clapped, almost more for the music than the girl. They were middle-aged, beaten down somewhat, bleary-eyed, wore baseball caps, shuffled, trucker mesh hats, went outside to smoke, coughed, spat, came back and hunched forward from their barstools looking from their beers to the girls and back again, shyly. They had wives, most likely, and kids, and spent more nights watching TV than having sex.

Girl in uniform, girl in nurse's outfit, bad librarian, the stock characters. The Mansion's steady patrons knew the canon of routines and spoke passionately about the girls' artistic development and their bodily virtues. The real old-timers spoke of the girls as fondly as daughters: she did that throwback number last year, bone in her hair and everything. Took the bone out at the end. Shook her head. Haha. And she gave Dale a kiss every night he cried out Wilmaaaaa! Wonder what she's doing now? Because, truth of the matter, is that the girls went on, had last dances the same night their replacements were introduced. Oliver thought he might see them in the mall one day, just catch up with them, as if he knew something about their lives. At the checkout. But every girl to whom he said, You remind me of— Did you ever— (for he couldn't finish) looked at him strangely, without the sympathy of these girls. These girls who would drag on your cigarette outside wrapped in a parka with their little knees showing, their shoulders slipping out before shuddering and running in. He wanted to help these girls. True. Superman fantasy be damned. It was true.

The private rooms didn't have doors, for the girls' safety, but beaded curtains, and the back of the couch was turned to the doorway, so if you ignored the red card in the pocket on the door frame, you'd only see a guy's head lolled backward, arms spread across the back of the seat. There was a no-touch policy as well. The private rooms each had strong coffee tables that could be improvised stages, depending on a guy's taste. Most of the girls didn't use them.

The woman on stage now was black and new. This might be the first time they had a black dancer. How could that be? Not the first, but definitely the best—prime. The others were a bit dumpy, a curiosity more than a pleasure, they were good fun though, athletic or matronly, he wouldn't mind lying on their breasts, being clutched into comfort. Or giving them a little slap to test the reverb of their flesh.

This one had long thin braids. Flag theme. A military outfit with patches that peeled off. Different parts of her body had different flags. Oliver could identify most of them. The epaulets were union jacks with fringes. Clever. Entertaining *and* educational. This girl went to school.

Onyxxx untied the knot from her waist and unbuttoned her shirt. Revealed a Jamaican bikini. Stars and stripes on the bottoms.

One of Oliver's Mansion friends (whom he never saw outside of this place, never discussed children, or work but only sports scores and girls) shouted, Show me the Beaver, and Onyxxx slipped down the waist of her pants and flashed a maple leaf thong.

Oliver held up a two-dollar bill, which she took with her teeth, some jungle reference. He allowed himself ten dollars whenever he came here. That would be five girls or maybe a dance every couple of weeks.

He should go to the police about his guitar. Felicia had told him that some young boys on her island skinned a pig and hiked the skin up the flagpole of the central police station to protest the acquittal of two Indian officers who murdered a deaf black teenager after a fête. Oliver wanted to know the logistics of getting pig skin up a flagpole under twenty-four-hour police surveillance. She shrugged. When she told stories like this, she never seemed particularly interested in the *how*.

The music ended with a few bars of O Canada, where her salute dropped from her forehead down her shoulders, her breasts, her waist, to her hip and circled around the groove of her pelvis into her crotch.

The DJ said, Give it up for Onyxxx. Happy belated Canada Day, boys. (It was, in fact, two weeks after Canada Day.) She set off some fireworks for me. Make some noise, fellas.

The Mansion provided theatre for Oliver, so stimulating, often surprisingly tasteful. No lower nudity. In Montreal the girls bared all, and in the States. Where else could one get a show with lights and sound, plotless plots, good girls and bad girls, histories, post-routine analysis, mounted sports TV in the background and two pounds of chicken wings for the price of one on Wednesdays? Come on. What red-blooded man could ask for more? (More of a man than you'd ever be, the ex had said.)

Onyxxx approached the steps. There was no backstage adjoining the stage so the women had to walk through the crowd to get to their dressing rooms while someone else scooped up their clothes. The men weren't allowed to touch the girls but they might accept your hand to come down the stairs in those towering heels. They were sweet.

Thank you. Onyxxx took his hand.

They'd accept a few more dollars one-on-one. Maybe he'd get a lap dance later.

Where you from? he asked her.

Windsor, she said.

He meant, *Really*, where are you from?

Long way from home, aren't you? he said.

She laughed.

Oliver hadn't made anyone laugh in so long. Flirting. He still had it. Only here.

I wouldn't say no to a ride, she said. All wink without winking. Then she left.

What day was it? Tuesday. Oliver hoped they kept her on.

He walked to his truck. He usually parked at a far end of the lot, under some trees, near the dumpster, because, he was prepared to say, he didn't want anybody dinging his truck, because that spot kept his truck cool, he was prepared to say. He laid an old Entertainment section on his lap. He closed his eyes. For the first fifteen seconds, he was lying on the left side of the bed and his wife was stroking her clavicle. For the remaining forty, he was sitting on the floor of Felicia's bedroom, looking up at her legs. When he opened his eyes Sophie Fortin's backless back was wet.

Felicia

Exchange

The Sunday she told Army she was going to a church function and felt Oliver's eyes all over her, she sped to Toronto, hoping she hadn't crossed Edgar on the way, forestalling him from—how did he find out where she lived when she had only been there since June? Weeks. Who did they know in common?

Edgar didn't invite Felicia inside. Instead he kicked his feet into some flattened loafers and walked her around the outside of the house toward the woods.

I wasn't sure where we left off last time, Edgar said. I didn't feel we could speak frankly in my office.

Her heels perforated the moist earth as they walked so she took them off and wore his shoes while he walked barefoot and held hers. There was something honeymoon-on-a-beach-in-silhouette about their stroll.

Also, he added, I hadn't heard from you so I was wondering if that was a sign of, he hesitated, a sign of something.

Felicia frowned and looked at his shoes.

Have you had dinner? Edgar asked.

It really didn't suit him, the small talk, the solicitousness. Felicia said, You don't have to be nice.

I'm not being nice, he said. I mean, I'm not trying to be nice.

What's the matter now?

Nothing's the matter.

The matter you wanted to discuss.

Edgar caught on. Let's walk some more.

The matter, as far as Felicia could discern, was a kind of mid-life crisis. He wanted to sell the house. He wanted to resign. He wanted to move to the mountains or maybe buy a cottage. He wanted to join a men's basketball league. He wanted find a pair of soft, comfortable jeans. His first.

He showed her the two trees he had planted at the head of their mothers' graves.

I got the Japanese maple for Geraldine and I got this one, he said, pointing to his right, the cotinus coggygria, for Mutter. It's also known as a smoke tree. That's the only reason I got it. But out of death, life, he said. That's in the Bible somewhere. Or the Bard. I don't remember.

It wasn't until an hour had passed and they were sitting on a stone bench near the graves that Edgar approached the heart of the matter. The evening had cooled down. Felicia folded her arms when she caught Edgar looking at her breasts.

I don't think people take me seriously anymore, he said.

Why?

Isn't it obvious?

To me, yes, but to everybody?

He sighed a sigh that made her think of Oliver. I'm a man in the prime of his life—

Past.

In, he insisted.

Felicia was unprepared for the sudden touchiness.

And what do I have? A house. That's all I have. A house.

A job, Felicia continued the list. Money in the bank. You've travelled up and down.

Garbage. Edgar waved dismissively. I suppose next you'll say I have my health.

Count your blessings. Felicia saw her opportunity. What you saying now is something I telling you donkey years ago. What does it profit a man to gain the whole world?

When you're in my world, Edgar said, and you're in your forties—

Fifties.

He froze her with a look. And all the other men around you keep talking about their wives and their kids' soccer matches and they bring around those fundraising pledge forms and you don't have any of those things, two things happen. One, you want to take an axe to their faces. Two, they start to think you're kind of funny.

She had never had that doubt about Edgar. Everybody knows you don't like men.

I don't mean like that. He eyed her covered breasts. I'll get you a sweater when we go back. I mean—

They don't take you seriously.

They used to envy me and now—*pity* is a strong word but I feel, he hesitated, condescended to. I lack gravitas.

Felicia felt anger rise in her. Oh now he wants a family.

I am ungrounded by commitment. I always wanted to be married. That's probably why I married Sophie so young. And you too. In the hospital, you told me you wanted the husband, the kids, the white picket fence. Remember? I'm talking too much. How about you? Are you seeing anyone?

Off limits.

I don't see why that should be off limits. We used to be able to say anything to each other, he said with a false, pleading tone that irked Felicia. Devious through and through.

I think you're forgetting vast swaths of things you neglected to tell me, she said.

How's work? he said, bypassing the prompt.

Edgar, she said. Stop asking me the same nonsense.

Okay, he said. Yes, I was wondering if, well, two things. One: Has anyone contacted you?

Does anyone know I'm out there?

Not as far as I can tell.

She wouldn't say it but Felicia really thought that Edgar was worried over nothing. No one was going to contact her. She was not the main story. The main story was the bad actress who forgot she was married to a man with a shady reputation for harassment in his father's company. But he was so self-centred and self-important and, what was Army's word, *self-dramatizing,* yes, that he thought even the Russians were spying on him.

There's your answer, she said.

That's good.

And you would like to keep it that way.

Yes, that was what the second thing was going to be. How could I help you maintain your privacy through all of this?

What if I don't want privacy, she said, but she was just being contrarian. She mentioned nothing about the two Paperplane envelopes that had arrived in the mail.

If they haven't contacted you, I don't see why you would go after them. There's nothing to gain.

Are these women charging you or is it just an HR thing? She wanted Edgar to come clean, stop trying to play her for a fool.

Edgar ignored the question. Initially, we—

Who's *we?*

My team and I. He paused. Right, yes, as I was saying, we thought that the best strategy was to lay low and to solicit a settlement under whatever terms worked for both parties, but in the last week or so we've been toying with the idea of another strategy.

I don't want to be part of any strategy, Edgar, if that's where you're going.

No, he said. Well, not exactly. I thought of this before the divorce and the allegations.

Why should I be part of any strategy?

We can come to the why later, he said. Just hear me out.

She straightened her shoes between Edgar and herself.

And for the record, Felicia. I don't care what happens with these women. I just want the true story out there for the record. Your story.

That's not going to help you.

Or our story, which is that we met while I was married, yes, but while both our mothers were in the hospital, dying. And that you and I entered a relationship, the seed of which was grief. He pointed her shoes at the trees. You cared for my mother. I cared for you and for our son. I've never denied him, Felicia. You know that.

Felicia bit her lips. This was rich. Meet my black wife and son. Maybe they could get a profile story in a women's magazine with her and Army seated on a settee, Edgar standing behind them with his arms spread over the engraved frame. Maybe he had political aspirations.

Edgar was still talking: We remained committed to each other although you chose—

I chose? *I* chose?

to live a separate and private life.

I have to stop you right there. Felicia looked up. Lord, grant me the serenity.

But regardless, he said, of how it came about, this is our—

It is not our story a*tall*, Felicia said.

I don't know what your story is but this has been my story. You know, not a day goes by that I don't think

Stop it, Edgar, she said. He was embarrassing himself.

about you and little Armistice and how we could have done things differently, maybe got a station wagon, with some planning.

He's fourteen, going on fifteen.

But you left in such a hurry.

You put me out, Edgar. Felicia withdrew her feet from his shoes and took hers from him. She ground her heels into the tongue flap. You brought me down the stairs and beheaded me in front of some prostitute you had masquerading as a nurse—for Felicia had discovered that the agencies he used to watch Mutter were in fact escort agencies—and told me, she slapped his arm with each word, to leave the key in the mailbox.

I was ending our work relationship. It wasn't fair for you at nineteen, twenty, to care for Mutter. You were in school, finishing up your— You finished?

Of course I finished.

It just wasn't right to put that responsibility on you. I don't remember saying anything about the key.

You said it. You told me to leave the key in the mailbox by Monday morning. I remember clearly.

I don't have any recollection of that.

He was talking like he was in court already.

If your version is true, then why did I come see you in the hospital? You can't have a selective memory, Felicia. I was right there when you named him *Armistice*. He was in the premature ward. Your *Canada and the World* history textbook was on the side table. There's nothing wrong with my memory.

And yes, she remembered, Edgar had held Army, with his shoulders up to his ears, held him carefully, and Felicia thought, I did this. I brought this child here so you could look at yourself while looking at me, look into a mirror reflecting a mirror. She remembered the blue gown. She remembered how large Edgar was in contrast to how small the baby was, and how the baby, Army, white as a piglet, yawned his toothless mouth and how his upper lip was larger than his lower, and didn't care who was holding him, just wanted to sleep while being held. She had hoped that the baby's presence would create some change in Edgar. How could it not? The baby was an offering, a peace offering, something she was offering him at great personal cost to her reputation, but she was willing to let that be. She had trembled with hope. She had, in motherhood, ascended to another state of being where she had to forgive, where she couldn't be angry, where she was willing to sacrifice even more for this one thing, one thing. Just make us a family. It's the only thing she would ever ask for.

And after that, Edgar? Felicia asked.

I—

He, indeed. He came to Christian Lady's house a few months later and sat in the formal living room drinking some juice, probably cursing that Christian Lady's house was a dry house. Felicia was bouncing Army with a cloth on her shoulder. She was constantly in profile. She asked him if he wanted to hold the baby. He said no. She extended the baby to Edgar and he shook his head. Felicia thought that if he had just held the baby that day, things might have been different. But they fought instead about why he didn't want to hold the baby, and he dug in, and looked incapable, distanced, and uncomfortable on the formal Italian settee. He left and came back, as he used to do. Not to see the baby again though. All Edgar wanted was to tell her that she should have been honest with him if she wanted to have a baby. They fought in the foyer. She said she didn't want to have a baby, and his last words to her for fourteen going on fifteen years: If you didn't want to have a baby, then why did you have one?

You have a penchant for the macabre, Edgar said.

Felicia protested. I just remember everything.

How come you don't remember good things, Christmas, eggnog and cake?

Because that never happened. I wanted to make eggnog and you said it gave you gas and when I made ginger beer you filled yours up with rum. And I asked you to measure the currants and raisins and you made me make a mess of the cake and—

Okay, okay.

What I don't appreciate, Felicia returned to the matter, is how you think you're outsmarting me somehow. If you had come to me at the beginning of your troubles and said, Felicia, girl, I know I don't deserve anything from you

I don't.

but I in some real hot water now

I am.

and I was hoping you could help me out

Yes, yes.

by pretending we stayed in touch over the years and that I was providing for you and your son.

Edgar opened his eyes wide as if that was exactly what he intended to say and was now waiting for her response.

She opened hers wider. The answer is—

That you'll think about it, Edgar interrupted. Think about it and tell me soon. I'm not doing this to position myself favourably before a magistrate, Felicia. You don't think I couldn't just write cheques to these women.

I could answer you now. And she wound up to say a big, fat—

No, think about it, he said. There's one more part.

She stood up and stepped off his shoes. She'd walk back to her car in her impractical heels or barefoot but not in anything belonging to Edgar Gross.

I don't expect that you, he began then began again. I said last time, if there's anything I could do or offer to secure your cooperation then I'd be willing to, to, to oblige.

She mentioned nothing about the two Paperplane envelopes that had arrived in the mail.

+

(Felicia knew the nurses/caregivers were hookers only years after the fact.

She recalled a conversation where she wanted to call the agency herself and Edgar refused to give her the number. She couldn't understand why. She thought the problem was her accent.

No, I should call. As a man.

That puzzled her more.

As son. Just tell me when you're going and how long you'll be and I'll make arrangements.

It was a clue.)

+

On the drive home, the Barenaked Ladies taunted her from the radio.

She would not go back fifteen years for a million dollars. *Well, I'd buy you a house.* There was no way in hell, in heaven or hell, short of the Lord himself revealing an alternate will to her in a dream. *A nice Reliant automobile.* She felt a swarm of Latinate locusts crawling over her: transaction, cooperation, manipulation—business people loved to invent new words by adding *tion*—strategization. *Like little pre-wrapped sausages and things.* Notfortheworldtion. *Yep, like a llama or an emu.* And the calculation of his presentation was offensive, sitting at the graveside. *Well, I'd buy you John Merrick's remains. All them crazy elephant bones.* Some bigger news would drop, Felicia was sure. He was bribing her or playing with her or recruiting her in advance. *We wouldn't have to eat Kraft Dinner.*

A million dollars now could not make up for the time she didn't have enough for food, before she got this secretary job, and had to send Army to school with a mayonnaise sandwich, how she took a cash advance on a credit card that she repaid at 29 percent interest when he came home and said, You forgot to put meat in my sandwich but Jason gave me some of his salami. *Well, I'd buy you a green dress. But not a real green dress, that's cruel.* Oh no, no, no, Edgar Gross. She would find a way to afford fixing Army's slight overbite and ragged bottom teeth if he'd consent to wearing orthodontics. Just lower braces, the orthodontist said. *Dijon ketchups.* And now that she was above water, Edgar Gross wanted to swoop down and skim along the surface of her life so men would take him seriously. *Haven't you always wanted a monkey!* Seriously.

Felicia came home to a full-out barbecue in the garage. Army was jangling over a black round charcoal grill (whose? whose charcoal? whose permission?) with a spatula in one hand and a can of coconut water in the other among a bunch of guys. Condiments (hers), cartons of juice (hers), the emergency bread (hers) she started keeping in the freezer were laid out on a lounge chair she hadn't seen before. She realized that to ground Army well—in a way that was intended to teach him a lesson— would require more vigilance than she could afford. Or possibly an ankle monitor.

I can't help if they come here, Army said. They're not grounded.

Well, I can help it.

The garage is still part of the house, he said.

She clarified: You are not to step foot beyond this doorway. You grounded another day for disobedience. Who all this belong to?

Not Mr. O.

Who?

Not Mr. O.

Felicia shut down the affair, put a sign on the door: *Army is grounded. Do not ring for him.*

Army contested that grounding him at fourteen was unfair and embarrassing but by the next evening he didn't seem particularly bothered by the punishment. He was a child of forgiving disposition, like an empty plastic container one could not hold underwater for long. Felicia suspected that he had taken down the sign when she went to work and put it back up when she was to return. He was smiley but he was playing dirty. Instead of finding evidence for her suspicion and upsetting his keel, she let it go. And it occurred to her that in marriage she would be as silently prudent and longsuffering but unfooled a wife as she was a mother.

But that night when she heard Army talking to someone out his window, she ordered him back to bed from her own bed.

I'm in the house, he said. Are you trying to kill me?

She placed a hand over her eyes, considering Barenaked Ladies, though not in the way Army had been from the abutting bedroom.

Army

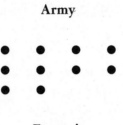

Exegesis

Army was talking to Heather on the phone, trying to figure out how to make more money. He walked into the kitchen with the cordless.

Let me ask. Mom, would you have a problem if I sold drugs?

We are going to church this week, Felicia said.

I wouldn't be using drugs. I'd just be selling them.

I need to place you before the altar.

Put aside your moral objection for—

That's all I have.

She's going righteous, he said to Heather.

I can hear, Heather said.

Felicia said, If you stop breaking fences, you might have some money save up.

Heather yawned on her end. You could just bank everybody's money, no? My business teacher said banks don't actually keep your money. They know that most people won't come in and ask for all their money.

That's not true.

At least, not at the same time. Something like that. They invest it.

I should be a bank? He sat at the kitchen table and spun a banana.

You'd have to promise them interest in return.

Felicia: You are not taking any money from any child on this street so their mothers could come to me complaining. Remember Nick Greco.

Nick Greco's a punk, Army said. You want me to invest your money?

Who're you asking? Heather asked.

Both of you. Mom?

No, Felicia said.

He covered the receiver. How about Dad? You think he might—

Stop threatening me with your father, Felicia said. We are going to church this week.

Army uncovered the mouthpiece. You want to come to church with me?

+

At church, Army was to find the answer to his questions / of money. He encountered two things that would lead to the end of his world.

The first was the scripture reading, Revelation 18:9–14.

> 9 And the kings of the earth, who have committed fornication and lived deliciously with her, shall bewail her, and lament for her, when they shall see the smoke of her burning,
>
> 10 Standing afar off for the fear of her torment, saying, Alas, alas, that great city Babylon, that mighty city! for in one hour is thy judgment come.
>
> 11 And the merchants of the earth shall weep and mourn over her; for no man buyeth their merchandise any more:
>
> 12 The merchandise of gold, and silver, and precious stones, and of pearls, and fine linen, and purple, and silk, and scarlet, and all thyine wood, and all manner vessels of ivory, and all manner vessels of most precious wood, and of brass, and iron, and marble,
>
> 13 And cinnamon, and odours, and ointments, and frankincense, and wine, and oil, and fine flour, and wheat, and beasts, and sheep, and horses, and chariots, and slaves, and souls of men.
>
> 14 And the fruits that thy soul lusted after are departed from thee, and all things which were dainty and goodly are departed from thee, and thou shalt find them no more at all.

The second was the Praise Team, two guys on guitar, one on drums, another playing keyboard, another piano, and a kid with a trumpet. They all seemed epicene, long hair falling into their eyes. Maybe a family? The tallest one was the one he sold Oliver's guitar to. His brothers were slightly more attractive and closer to Army's age. Jackpot.

+

Army found it titillating to write the word *sex* on an offering envelope. He shaded it with his hands so Felicia and Hendrix couldn't see and showed it to Heather.

Sex, it said.

She glanced askance at him. Grow up.

It was her first time in church in a very long time and she was extremely attentive to the service, so attentive she made Army want to pay closer attention. She sang. She said *Amen*. She crossed herself and Army had to tell her, We don't do that here. Yet Army wondered if he was missing something. Hendrix was fighting sleep on Felicia's shoulder.

During the prayer, Army came to a more nuanced question. He whispered to Heather, Who the sexiest brutha in here?

Heather exaggerated her offence when she looked at him.

She looked good praying. There was a little bit of fat in her cheek that he liked. It seemed amplified in prayer. Did Heather love him? He wanted to know whether Heather loved him, not liked him, but loved-him loved him, I-ee-I-will-always-love-you-loved him. If when she moved back to America she'd lie on her bed with her hand clutching her heart. Was it possible, he wondered, for her to know how physical his longing was for her, curled up on his bed, his hand fondling his pubic hair? He loved her. He loved her, loved-her loved her, he loved Ha-h-hh-hh haa-ha. I know this much is true.

When they were seated again, Army nudged her and directed his eyebrows to various middle-aged men and Heather twisted her face into various forms of horror. Then he became more reasonable.

How about him? he whispered during an offertory appeal, right into her ear. Which one?

Guitar. With the hair.

She paused a long time, Army would think in retrospect, before answering. She pushed out her bottom lip. Why? she asked.

Army shrugged.

The younger one's better looking, Heather said. She was red.

Felicia shot him a look and pointed to the other side of her, intending to separate them. So Army laid off for a while.

While they were singing the offertory response, he started up again into Heather's ear: He sexy? Meaning the guy with the bangs playing guitar.

I don't know. Why?

Do you find him sexy?

Kinda. Stop saying *sexy*. Why?

Army desisted for a time.

You know who be the sexiest girl in here though, he said.

She snorted her appreciation.

Then he went to the bathroom. For a very long time. More than fifteen minutes.

I need you to do something, he said when he returned.

What?

Just promise.

Promise, she said, too hastily, just to get the mystery over. She couldn't know she was selling her birthright for pottage of lentils.

After church, he said. Then *Amen* after *Amen* to the preacher.

+

After church, Army led Heather to the back wall of the building, a narrow strip of asphalt where the cars couldn't park or pass and that was not visible from the street. Just a footpath, really, a shortcut for teenagers. Three guys, one with a guitar case, were exiting the rear, brown metal door of the church. They were still out of earshot.

I dare you to flash those guys, Army said.

I'm not flashing them, Heather said.

Just real quick. Up and down. Real quick.

No.

Heather, come on.

I said no, Army.

You promised.

I didn't promise to do that. She folded her arms as the guys entered earshot.

Boys, Army said. This is my friend, Heather. We've run into a little problem.

He stepped back with Heather, turned his back to the boys, and begged. He tugged at her shirt. They skirmished. But her eyes glinted.

Finefinefine. Stop it, she said finally and slapped his hands away.

She looked at him while quickly unbuttoning the top half of her shirt. Before she could lower the straps of her bra, a side door opened and Skinnyboy emerged, holding his guitar case and talking to someone behind him. It was just enough time for them. Heather spun toward the rear fence. Army shielded her. The boys walked away as if nothing had happened.

Skinnyboy approached too familiarly, Army would observe in retrospect, although they had history, the guitar, the refused haircut, the failed negotiations.

Skinnyboy greeted them both with a nod but his eyes spent more time on Heather than Army.

Army thought he could capitalize on the boy's obvious interest. Hey, you want to see something?

Heather walked away with her arms folded and her shoulders high. When Army ran after her, she kept shrugging him away although he was not touching her.

+

In the backseat, Hendrix was twirling a cardboard lollipop of King David. Felicia asked Heather what she thought of the service. She said she was still thinking about it and looked out the window in what could be interpreted as deep religious contemplation. Heather didn't say a word to Army.

Felicia was irritated because she couldn't find Army after church. She had wanted to leave right away to avoid some prying, disingenuous Jazz.

I thought you wanted to talk to them, Army said.

You don't know some of those women, she told him. They just digging and digging from before the time you was born. Then you should have hear them when you was born. My mother warn me. Once you see I take out my keys you know is time for we to go.

I was about my father's business.

Army had effectively silenced her. It was the first time he had gone to church in about six weeks *and* he had brought visitors *and* he stayed awake *and* he was more pious than when he left home.

Who you was talking to so long? Felicia asked.

I saw, Hendrix said.

Thou dost not know the work for which I have to do. Army slid his hands along his forearms and clasped his wrists.

Don't make a mockery of scripture, Felicia said.

+

That evening, he located his red, illustrated children's Bible in a drawer under some essays from last year.

He underlined *and fine flour, and wheat, and beasts, and sheep, and horses, and chariots, and slaves, and souls of men.*

He double-underlined *and horses, and chariots, and slaves, and souls of men.*

He placed the frayed tongue in the Bible to mark the spot.

Heather

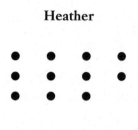

Expression

The Monday after she went to church, Heather met Skinnyboy after his shift at Zellers and confessed the truth because she figured he might have heard it already from the boys at church. Her truth went, Her neighbour was trying to force her to flash some guys. She said no. Thank God you came out when you did.

Yeah? he said. He was still in his uniform. So hot.

She tried to look contrite. She wanted his forgiveness to be grudging and slow, though she knew she didn't need it from him. He wasn't going to bestow, to make the sign of the cross over her. Her point in the gesture was contrition.

She tried to work herself up into tears outside his car in the Zellers parking lot.

He said nothing. Perhaps he already knew. He was not surprised. He tossed his knapsack into the trunk where his guitar and a notebook lay.

You never play me anything, she said, although he had.

I don't play for just anybody, he said. But, hey, we're doing a show in a couple of weeks. You should come. I don't really make music for people though. If they like it— Here he shrugged. Even as he was protesting, he was lifting the guitar out of its case to play her a concert.

He began. The guitar was slipping from his grip. He looped the strap around his neck. He restarted. He messed up on a chord. He restarted. He forgot the words. He got out the notebook. He restarted. The wind was lifting the pages. Heather held the pages down. He restarted.

This song was so about her, Heather thought.

Same

The chords disappear quickly as if he only knew three.

Once Heather got a book out of the library about analyzing handwriting. Skinnyboy's handwriting—well, first of all, he prints, no cursive—is arthritic, tiny, inscrutable sometimes—crossed out. The only thing she remembers from the library book is that the size of handwriting matches the size of a person's ego. Skinnyboy's self-esteem is a procession of ants.

A-   C- C#- D-

I sing the same thing over again

A reference to her father's cover band. She had told Skinnyboy that the band would rehearse the same 70s songs in the garage until her ears bled.

A-

I sing the same thing over again

= Heather. But was he like saying that his ex had Heather beat in the body category but Heather had her beat in the face?

I taped your face on my ex girlfriend (I said)

She asked him if he had a type. He shrugged. She said she always ended up with pretty much the same kind of guy if you swapped out their heads.

Clearly there was a dumpation of some sort.

Why did he sound like he was from California?

I put your head on my ex boyfriend (she said)

She played it for Army over the phone without context. He said, Cool, and went back to talking about the gym.

When she played it again and asked him to listen carefully and offer an informed response, Army confessed that he couldn't quite make out the lyrics and that he stopped listening at the part about a guy giving some guy head.

A reference to her early pursuit of him in Zellers.

You want to find me I'm already dead

The other thing she remembered from the handwriting book was that the slope of one's writing reveals one's inclination toward optimism or pessimism. The ants were on a worrying decline.

You go looking but you're in my head

Even Heather recognized this as cringeworthy, youthful, poetic melodrama. There was a goth girl in her English class with a stud choker who threatened suicide by the week.

I already found you in my head

She turned off the stereo but not before Army gave a final comment: Just head, head, head everywhere. Like seriously, bro, go find yourself a chickenhead.

She was being foolish. Did she want to get caught? It was her first time juggling two guys. But who was she cheating on with whom?

Yesss!

I already loved you before I said

Not punctuated. Fruitful ambiguity to ponder before sleeping.

Chorus

E-   A-

Be me, be with me

So they were official. He was asking.

(Playing the song for Army was like holding a 3D puzzle to Army's face then berating him for not discerning the pattern.)

D-   G-

Be me. Can't you see

This part of the song was her favourite. The melody sloped downward as she and Skinnyboy sat on a riverbank and inspected their reflections.

C-   F   B-

Be me, be with me

E-   G-   G#-

If you don't want to be yourself

This is the soul pour-out moment.

A-

Be me

Oh, she does remember a third thing. One's ambition can be determined by how high one crosses one's t's. Skinnyboy's crossbar floats above the stem of the letter (a good sign), which is odd considering the downward slope of his lines. Ambitious but doomed? Delusional?

3.

When I'm done I'm gonna do it again

Skinnyboy squeals *again* on the tape but he didn't when he sang to her live in the parking lot.

Said when it's over gonna say it again

Heather would suggest *Live in the Parking Lot* as a title for his band's album.

Your best friend is never your friend

She opened up to him and he competed against her, as he always did, so they ended up pitting their childhoods against each other.

Heather: I was in constant fear that my dad would be my supply teacher and humiliate me in front my friends.

The girl in her English class also had an eating disorder and said that her choker was not merely decorative.

Ugh, Heather hated her.

Your best friend is more than dead

Skinnyboy: That's nothing. I think my ex-girlfriend's mom tried to Mrs.-Robinson me.

Chor

Be me, be with me

Be me. Can't you see

Be me, be with me

If you don't want to be yourself

Be me

Yeah, she was tuned-out for most of Grade 10 English but she remembers Narcissus and the pool (she knew that before the class though) and something about being chased by deer and Echo being cursed to repeat after people for talking too much. Her teacher was like fifty but used to flirt with the jocks, touch their shoulders while reading, and behind her back they would mock her.

Just the chords from the chorus.

Guitar solo

Chorus x 2

This was neither on the tape nor in the live performance.

Guitar thing

It's new, he said as an apology when he was finished.

It's good, she said.

It's a bit darker than the stuff I normally write. It's not really done yet.

Sounds done to me.

Skinnyboy tried not to smile. Various throat clearings, hair swinging, clothes adjusting motions. Heather knew from a PBS documentary that primping activity was the mating call of primates.

Here, you want it? Skinnyboy ripped the page from the spiral.

Don't you need it? she asked.

It's up here. He tapped his head. He tapped his heart. And here.

In retrospect, she would label him a cornball. But at that moment, in the parking lot, she couldn't resist his wuthering heights. She tiptoed up to his six-foot-two bendiness and kissed him. The guitar was still between them. He went red when she pulled away and to cover he ducked into his car.

I've got a copy, he said, as he was rummaging. I record raw versions. You never know. He emerged holding a tape, which he gave her.

She kissed him again. Redly.

It's just a working demo, he said, as if nothing happened, and wiped his nose in a circle with a paw.

Are you going to keep giving me stuff if I keep kissing you?

Heather wasn't thinking about Oliver's guitar in the backseat. Her gaze was in the general vicinity, never quite rising to his eyes, but she was making sure Skinnyboy saw her see him twist the lower half of his body away from her. Soon he would put his hands in his pockets to disguise the bulge.

She wagged her jaw, took two steps back then turned and walked toward the catwalk. She wanted him to see, she wanted him to see her, she wanted him to see her walk away on the catwalk yeah I shake my little tush on the catwalk.

Oliver

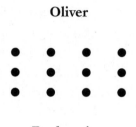

Explanation

What was going on? Oliver started to see black women everywhere. He saw dozens of them, pushing carts at the Asian supermarket, ahead of him in the bank line, holding tissue to their kids' noses, taking Legos out of their hands, managing strollers, looking into newspaper boxes, framed by the bus window as he waited on the traffic light to change, cashing out his food, paying cable bills on Rutherford Road, modelling bras in the weekend catalogues, on Dolph Lundgren in an old *Playboy*, just everywhere, like an unearthed Chinese army, only black and female and often quite animated or exhausted. Even a cousin was dating a black woman from Cape Verde. Where did they come from all of a sudden with their shake-shake, racks, skirt-and-sneaker combinations, morning skin, lips, lips, lips, short hair, long hair, braids—he didn't understand how the hair was so lustrous or crackly, who could he ask about weaves? Army? He'd think Oliver was interested in Felicia and that was not the case. Heather? The women held their shape better than—just better, though he didn't much like their faces—the clownish look of makeup on some of them—but their bodies, well.

Felicia, of course, he saw her in some form every day. She smelled like cocoa butter and something else. He tested some on his hand in Zellers. Strange smell. Not unpleasant. Smelled like it should be associated with a memory of a grandmother or a house or a summer.

And, of course, he saw black women at The Mansion.

+

When he came back from The Mansion, one night, Hendrix walked into the house bloody.

Naturally, Oliver required a series of explanations.

Oliver and Hendrix were waiting for Felicia in the driveway. If she thought she could brush him off, she would— she better— Oliver was a little drunk.

First the record-breaking bike nonsense, now this.

Soon as Felicia shut her car door, Oliver said, I want an explanation as to why whenever I leave my son in your son's charge, he comes back covered in blood from head to toe.

Felicia looked at both of them in turn.

Show her, Oliver said.

Hendrix twisted his forearm toward Felicia's face. There was a large raspberry on his elbow and grated skin along the inside of his wrists but no blood.

I'm going to have to take him to the hospital, Oliver said.

Felicia inspected Hendrix's elbow. Army did this?

We were doing double cartwheels, Hendrix began, but I fell when it was his turn to go up. He's so heavy.

This was after you grounded him, Oliver pointed out.

What more do you want, Oliver? I just don't get it. He *was* grounded, Felicia said. He's not anymore.

That was for something else. And frankly, Felicia, what you do with your child is your business. When it comes to my children, I deserve an explanation.

From me? Felicia asked.

From you.

I wasn't there.

I can tell you what that boy needs.

What?

Oliver relented.

No, Oliver, go ahead, tell me what my son needs.

He hesitated but in front of Hendrix the ex-wife had said that he'd never be a man. He said, A whoopin'.

What he really wanted to say was *a good whoopin' from a real man*. But he didn't want Felicia to think that he was accusing her of being a single mother or that he was interested in parenting the boy. But, for the record, if he were that boy's father, he'd give him a whoopin'. Not true. He wouldn't hit a fourteen-year-old boy. If he were that boy's father, that boy would never have gotten to this point. He would not need a whoopin'.

Felicia privately addressed Hendrix. Let me see it again. She touched around the wound. You just need a little ointment, she said. Come.

Felicia took his son away and closed the door on Oliver.

Oliver went upstairs. Heather was on the phone. He took the remote from her and switched the channel. What more do you want? He wanted— He wanted to call someone, a brother-in-law. No, he didn't. What he wanted was— He wanted explanations. The black door was locked when Oliver checked it last night and in the morning it was unlocked. He wanted someone to explain to him how Felicia could leave her son home unsupervised all day. Explain to him why he was sending money to his ex-wife in the summer when she had no kids to care for. She should be paying him. Explain why Felicia thought she was superior to him when he was the one renting his place to her. Why women everywhere thought they could get away with clawing out the eyes of men who spent their whole lives doing nothing but good for them and the children.

Who are you talking to? Oliver asked Heather.

Nobody.

Give me the phone.

Heather got up and went to her room. He wanted an explanation as to what happened to his clarinet-practicing Heather.

Nobody better have long hair and wear a dress, Oliver called after her. He started thumbing through the channels.

+

By the time Hendrix returned, Oliver was listlessly channel-surfing and recalling the ex's gift for disaster preparedness. She made him keep a medical kit in his truck. Hendrix's arm was wrapped in a bandage from his upper bicep to his mid forearm.

I sat on their toilet, Hendrix said.

Oliver didn't stop his clicking. It's my toilet, he said to himself. Technically.

There are a whole bunch of Band-Aids under the bandage. She told me I can't shower for three days.

You can shower, Oliver said. Now his son was lying to him. Just don't get it wet.

No, she said I was allowed not to shower. Army's towel is green. Do we have green towels?

Enough, Oliver said. Why his son idolized a thug instead of his father, he didn't know. Go eat something. Heather! he called. Make your brother something to eat.

She let me have a granola bar, Hendrix said. He sat on the coffee table keeping up with the flickering channels.

Heather trudged back downstairs, still on the phone. Put it on thirty-six, she said.

It's time to eat something. It was the *something* that made him feel sorry for himself, trying to keep his children alive, these organisms he had brought into the world.

Heather took the remote from him. To the phone, she said: No, my dad was watching. Then to Oliver, Army says hi.

Oliver sighed.

Nothing. He didn't say anything. I don't know why he didn't say hi back. He's watching TV. To Oliver, Army says he's sorry about Hendrix. He'll make it up to you. He has a special membership deal for people over forty.

Great, Oliver said.

Senior's hour. Private gym time around your schedule.

Not a chance in hell, Oliver said.

He said not a chance in hell. I don't know. Talk to him tomorrow. To Oliver, He wants to know what would make gym membership attractive to you or Tio Ricky?

I'm not paying to use my own garage. Get off the phone, Heather.

You heard that? Army says, A service, not a location. Yeah, I get it. Totally. He's just being curmudgeonly. Look it up. Crabby. What time?

Heather, Oliver said.

If she thought she was going somewhere with Army, she better think again. She was spending too much time with that boy when she already had a brother. (The voice of reason: They live in the same house, Oliver. What do you expect?) When they weren't in the garage together or wandering the mall among droves of teenagers, they were on the phone with each other. Too much. Too much. And Oliver knew the boy was behind all this symbiosis. He was always calling.

Hi, Mr. O. Is Heather there?

You just talked to her.

I forgot to tell her something.

Hi, Mr. O. Is Heather home?

You saw her open the door and come inside.

I know. I'm just being polite.

Hi Mr. O. Is Heather? Is Heather? Is Heather?

Oliver used to answer the phone. He would try to listen on after Heather took the extension but she screamed at him. Once he picked up while she and

Army were talking to hear what they were talking about and Heather, sensitive to every abnormal click, screamed at him about privacy and her rights and compared him to the ex, which hurt. And now he didn't answer his own phone anymore. Didn't or couldn't. She banned him.

Right. Heather banned him after the time she was ignoring his demands and he banged on the door between the two households and shouted at Army to get off the phone. He assumed that Heather was speaking to Army. But it so happened that Felicia was on the phone.

He heard her talking to Army, probably covering the mouthpiece. He crazy or what? she said. Who he think he talking to? He don't know I paying rent?

Army's voice: He wasn't talking to you.

Who he talking to then?

Heather.

But soon enough his phone would go back to being his. His sisters would make each other call him when they thought he was having a daily pang of loneliness.

I already told you that I only brought one pair of heels and I'm not wearing them, Heather was saying. I'm not wearing a dress either.

Off the phone now, Heather, Oliver said. I need to call your tia.

For what?

I don't answer to you.

I gotta go, Heather said. That's a Nirvana song. Being an ogre.

You're not going anywhere with that boy, Oliver said after she hung up. But he knew where she was going and could not morally object.

You don't want me going to church?

To pre-empt an unwinnable argument with his teenage daughter

(We have Vovó's memorial at Tia Maria's house.

That's in the evening.

You're not going anywhere with that boy.

Dad, he's fourteen.

If you want to go to church, I'll take you to Vovó's old church.

But I don't want to go there.

Since when are you religious?

Since when do you care?)

Oliver turned up the volume.

Felicia

Extortion

Three Fridays ago, a cheque arrived in a Paperplane envelope for $1,500. The sticky note read, *A hundred dollars for each birthday. EG.*

The cheque was easy. She would not deposit it. The note, however, occupied Felicia while she was idling in traffic or soaping her legs or disposing of breadends. There was no verb in the sentence. There was no sentence, technically. It was a crumb of a sentence, the tiniest pubic-hairy soapcake of his wealth (whatever activity she was engaged in at the moment determined the appropriate metaphor), an indication of his late glacial benevolence. Not even a full sheet of paper. He couldn't take two seconds to write her name? Or Army's. *Dear Felicia.* She deserved that much. *I am enclosing a hundred dollars for each of Armistice's birthdays that I missed.* Yes, man, bear responsibility for missing them. *I recognize that this humble token can never be adequate compensation* Yes, offer a scrap of humility *for the years of your life that you devoted to raising our child, the countless unnoticed sacrifices you have made, while I was gallivanting from bazaar to bazaar and chit-chatting all over the planet without a thought as to where his next meal was coming from or money for his field trip to the Royal Winter Fair was coming from because I'm a slimy, selfish, good-for-nothing abomination who will have to answer to the Creator come Judgment Day.* Ahem. *With regrets, EG.* The *G* on his initial was poorly constructed. Revealing. It was more like an overgrown child's *g.* She could have crafted a better cursive *G* when she was in Standard 2, despite the rejection of her certificate from a small unrecognized island. *EG.* What was he an example of? Was the money supposed to be an example of a pulsing conscience? And furthermore, Army's birthday was not until

September 14. Did he even know when his child was born? Not *his*. Her child. *Her* or *their* but certainly not *his* alone.

Two Fridays ago, that is, a week after the first insult, as if Edgar's canine ears had pricked forward and picked up her thoughts, another cheque arrived. This time for $15,000. And in a one-word bark on another yellow sticky note Edgar managed to respond to all of Felicia's ultrasonic whistling: *Better? EG.*

Uh no. Nonono. He could add zeros until his pen ran out but it—what was it? *It* was it, damn it—would never be *better*.

And days ago, yet another cheque arrived. The handwriting suggested that he must have been drinking. Tremulous, furry, like a mint coated in fuzz. The cheque was for $150,000. The note said, *Words are not enough. EG.*

+

The day after the Civic Holiday, Felicia skipped her Tuesday class yet again to drive to Edgar's house. Her class had become an automatic alibi in case Army got suspicious about her whereabouts. She was going to leave the three cheques in Edgar's mailbox. She walked up the path, dropped the envelope in, walked down the path. What if he didn't see it? She walked up the path, pulled a corner of the envelope out, lowered the flap of the mailbox on it, walked down the path, started her car. What if he thought it was junk mail? She walked up the path, took out the envelope, slid it partly under the door, walked down the path. But what if he didn't enter through the front door for weeks? She walked up the path and rapped the edge of the envelope against her palm, deciding, deciding. She would have to do what she wanted to avoid. She knocked. During the daytime, there was never any evidence of occupation from the front of the house. No newspapers. The garage was at the back. Felicia waited. She repositioned the envelope in the mailbox. She walked down the path.

She heard the door open behind her.

No way, Edgar said. I was just thinking about you.

She was determined not to fall into his pick-up-where-we-left-off-a-decade-and-a-half-ago familiarities. Felicia retrieved the envelope and served him. But the transaction happened too quickly to make an impact. Edgar held the envelope without any emotion while gazing into her eyes without any emotion. She should have thrust the envelope at his face while making her point (which was? which was? which was leave me alone), then ripped up the cheques one by one, sprinkled the flakes in his face, and wagged her hips down the path.

She peered into the house. Nothing had changed. Not even the floor mat. Fifteen years and he hadn't bought a new mat. The house smelled more thickly of itself.

Step in, Edgar said.

Violins whispered near the bridge. Don't go into the house.

Felicia found herself on his couch in the parlour, same couch, sitting with an arrow up her back, her knees together, her handbag on her lap.

I have someone come in to clean twice a week. Edgar moved an ashtray from the spot beside her. What hospitality. Then he wandered around looking for his cigarettes which were in plain view on the dining table. How is work? How is Armistice? You know, not a day goes by that I—

Why you sending me money all of a sudden?

He shook a few cigarettes out of the pack and extended it to her.

You mad? She had never smoked in all her days with him.

Might relax you.

Edgar sat next to her. It wasn't a controlled sit. It was like he released himself and fell beside her, so close their hips touched.

I've never seen anyone refuse free money.

Well, you seeing it now.

As I was saying, he blew smoke away from her, this girl comes in and cleans. Nothing like how you used to have the place, mind you.

Felicia was tempted to have him go on. But resist the devil and he will flee from you. I not here to talk about your domestic.

The cheques, he said. And she's not a domestic.

Edgar, stop provoking me.

I'm getting our process started.

We don't have any agreement.

Our understanding, then. He took the cheques out of the envelope, read the amounts, and dropped them into the slot between Felicia's handbag and her stomach. Think of them as expressions of my sincerity.

Metaphors from the last three weeks came to mind and with them came the various little unaccounted moments of Felicia's life where she felt herself to be most ontologically herself, outside of relation to anyone, just her lone single continuous self.

Am I the only one? Felicia asked.

You're the only one I would approach, Felicia.

But she meant more than that. How many children you have?

You mean apart from—

I talking German? She spoke slowly. How many other children you have?

None.

Not a single one? She didn't believe him.

I mean, I don't know. None that I know about. He positioned the ashtray on his lap. That's the truth.

Could a man really not know how many children he had the same way he didn't know how many quarters he had in his pocket?

I am trying to be honest with you, he said. I know you like that.

Sentences like these caused Felicia to flip out. As if she were some simple-minded anomaly. As if honesty was a preference like green or black olives.

Felicia retained her composure a second longer. No more cheques. Do you understand me?

Felicia, cut the high-and-mighty business.

I'll cut the high-and-mighty when you cut the—the charade. She raised her voice. You not interested in me or your own flesh and blood.

There's where you're wrong. I *am* interested.

Oh, he was infuriating. You wasn't interested for fifteen years

People change.

and all of a sudden when women say you rape them left, right and centre, you interested in we?

Edgar leaned over her to place the ashtray on a side table. Then he stood. For a moment, Felicia thought that she had crossed a line.

Have you eaten? he asked, unruffled.

Felicia tracked him as he walked toward the kitchen, past the spot where Mutter's bed used to be. There was nothing there now. Felicia could almost see the woman, eyeing her wrists, tilting her head to feel weight in her earlobes. She, Felicia, used to keep a package of diapers on a dining room chair, tucked in, where no one could see it and so she wouldn't have to go up and down the stairs when she needed to change her.

Edgar returned with bread, a knife and a tub of margarine. Few things activated the nurturer gene or socially conditioned response in Felicia like seeing a man unable to perform basic and daily tasks that she regarded as basic and daily. How could he not, after all this time, prepare a decent meal for himself? How was he going to offer a guest in his house bread and margarine? Why did he need to hire a woman to clean the house that he himself dirtied? Uncleaned. Defiled. Too far. Still. Get it together. *It* what? Everything. His life. Get it together already.

No more cheques, she said.

Edgar spread margarine on a slice. Have you given thought to ending our separation?

Before she could reply, he got up and walked back to the kitchen. He returned with plates.

More civilized, he said. And for the record, Felicia, I did not rape anyone left, right and centre. She was making copies. I was standing behind her. There was small talk. I tucked in the tag of her blouse. That's all I'm going to say on the subject from here on. You understand?

There was only one?

That is all I am going to say on the subject.

The china cabinet faced them, the arrangements untouched in fifteen years: gravy boat on gravy tray, flanked by sets of standing blue and gold plates, which were propped behind teacups on saucers. She had never bought herself a set. China always seemed to her a wedding gift. To buy oneself china was like a woman buying her engagement ring. One of her sisters had inherited her mother's china. Edgar's eyes followed Felicia's to the hutch.

He took another bite of his bread and margarine. His grey eyes, like Army's. He said, Help yourself.

Felicia said, No more cheques.

+

The following Tuesday (yet another class on Payroll Fundamentals missed), Felicia was back on Edgar's ancient couch with a blank, signed cheque.

What did I say, Edgar? Stop trying to buy me.

Let me be blunt because I don't think you're getting me. I am trying to make amends.

Don't make none. I not keeping up any malice regarding you.

There are good schools here.

Nobody's moving.

You don't have to move right now.

You and me, we done. To this day you never so much as say you sorry for what you do to me.

Regardless. Edgar waved a hand as if to suggest bygones, which incidentally Felicia always thought was a yam-like root vegetable because her grandmother used to utter the phrase while cooking. Edgar clasped her hands between both of his. Felicia had to look down to double check the sensation of his hands on hers. Just take the money, he said. Just take it, Felicia.

When Felicia looked back up into his eyes, she was squinting. He had communicated something of the truth by touching her. She suddenly understood what was happening. Edgar was transferring his assets.

Are the women suing you?

He let go of her hand. We're not talking about that.

For how much?

Later, much later, Army said, Question for you, pretty lady. How much does a lawyer cost?

The word is *retain*, she said.

Noted, he said.

She waited for him to ask it correctly.

How much does a lawyer retain?

How much does it cost to retain a lawyer? she modelled.

Yeah, that.

You better not be in trouble. Across her mothermind, various likely offences presented themselves, mostly forms of theft, fraud, and racketeering. What kind of trouble you in?

Mom, you need to seriously, like, chill with the juvey fear.

He had called her *pretty lady* and she had already convicted him of being a disappointment. She felt a pop of shame followed by an intuitive moment similar to this one with Edgar where she knew that Army was planning to set himself up as an arbiter of petty teenage dramas. You will not be a lawyer, she said with finality. And regretted it.

Edgar sighed. I have decided to take a leave of absence.

I thought you was going to resign.

I have changed my mind.

The way he was talking, so formally—I have this or that—made Felicia suspicious. She asked, You decided or they making you?

Ultimately the decision is mine.

Felicia recognized that as Edgarspeak.

I have decided to take an indefinite leave. He glanced at her to see how the announcement was being received before going on. And the damage is already done to my reputation.

Since when you care about your reputation?

Felicia, stop rubbing salt. Whatever the outcome, the damage was done by the accusation. There'll always be a footnote next to Edgar Gross. How am I supposed to recover?

You know by running away, everybody go think you guilty.

He shrugged.

You won't regain your status by trying to protect yourself.

Then?

To err is human; to forgive, divine. But our Lord and Saviour stood in the breach.

English. Talk to me straight.

Penitence. Tell the truth. Confess.

I told the truth.

The real truth.

Which one is that? He seemed genuinely confused, as if he had told her multiple versions of his situation.

Humble yourself, Felicia said. That was as much tenderness as she was willing to grant him.

He walked to the kitchen through a bead curtain she had put up when she lived there. Wooden beads interspersed with blue crystal discs. Her heart fractured open, as thin as a crack on a teacup.

Edgar couldn't say the next bit to her face. He called from the kitchen, I'm not joking about reconciliation, Felicia. In fact, I'm just going to come out and say it. I want a child.

You have a child, Felicia said. But she knew he meant something like a child from scratch.

Another.

So you could have something to coo at during your leave of absence?

I'll help.

You'll *help*? If, *if* I took you seriously, and I'm not— She forgot what she was going to say. She was positioning Army in the mix. She said, You go turn your back again.

I won't. He was becoming exercised. Trust me.

She laughed. It was the *trust me* that made her laugh at first but her laughter converted itself into something less caustic, into something genuine and diaphragmic. There was joy in her laugh but she was not entirely laughing for joy.

Edgar tried to laugh along.

If somebody better come along, Felicia said, trying to settle herself, you go tell me to pack up my things and go.

Better? Edgar opened his arms. Come on.

Felicia would need to use his bathroom before she left.

Anyway, I'm not playing hypotheticals, Edgar said.

Who you go leave me for this time, Edgar?

That's a stupid question.

No one? Felicia pushed. She was a little giddy.

You? That's what you want me to say.

You'd leave me for me?

Yes, I would leave you for you fifteen years ago.

Felicia took mild offence. You're saying I'm old.

Don't ask stupid questions if you can't take the answer.

And that was the sentence that quelled any further sound that might resemble laughter.

Don't call me stupid, she said.

I didn't call you stupid.

There's a way, Edgar. There's a way to be in a conversation.

He laid his head on her shoulder and heaved. I don't know anymore.

She had to console him. Her Christian duty. So she took her thumb and pressed his forehead.

Not a day goes by, Edgar said.

Army

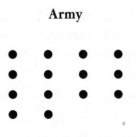

Extravagance

A few days earlier, there was a letter from Paperplane. Not addressed to Felicia. Addressed to him. Full legal name: Armistice Gross.

Boys, Army said. He wiped haircrumbs from his hands. He had stopped talking about the sweepstakes with them, but he felt something special emanating from the envelope. He held the letter in both palms like a Samurai sword.

Troops, Army said. Gather round.

Weights clinked. Hendrix put away his bag of hair.

I thought you were going to feed it to your ants.

I'm saving it so they'll have something to eat in the winter.

Army felt the occasion called for a speech. Once in every man's life, he began, there comes a moment that divides the men from the boys, the haves from the have-nots. You, boys, are witnessing such a moment. Now, I'll never forget you. He turned to each person gallantly, letter still in his hands. Coughdrop, I'll make good on replacing your bike (it was stolen in June while in Army's possession, official story). Hendrix, little Hendrix, ants, bees, wasps, anything you want.

Guy, shut up and open the letter.

This envelope, this envelope that I am holding, he slapped it with his knuckles for emphasis, from Paperplane Canada, contains our futures. Dramatic pause. He wished Heather wasn't at the mall. The people we are now will cease to exist. These clothes. This house. This is the last time you will see me like this.

Boy thinks he's Jesus.

Swimming pools and Lamborghinis, Army raised his voice, are just the start of what will be a future full of fullness.

Someone went to grab the letter out of his hand.

All right. Army stopped speechifying, tucked the letter in his armpit, and wiped his hands. Then he slipped his finger under the flap and pulled out the letter.

It wasn't a letter because there was no writing. It was a blank piece of paper that enclosed a cheque with a sticky note on the front. His heart accelerated.

The Post-It read, *Dear Armistice, For your birthdays. Yours,*. Army turned over the Post-It. That was it, *Yours,*.

The name was on the cheque, where it belonged. Edgar Gross. And the cheque was for $1,000.

Army fanned it in the air and whooped. The boys held their fists to their mouths. Everybody wanted to see it.

+

Army didn't tell Felicia about the cheque.

I want to start keeping my own bank card and bank book.

When you're sixteen, Felicia said. I not stealing your money.

Mom, mom, I'd never accuse you of that.

You was accusing me just recently.

I'm trying to save you time. I'm trying to save money. He unleashed a smile. Do you want me to be responsible or do you want me to be dependent on you forever? It's time I start managing my affairs. I'm practically fifteen, which is practically sixteen.

Give me the cash and I'll deposit it for you, Felicia said.

I can do it myself tomorrow.

Felicia eyed him as she dug into her handbag. She gave him his card and his book. Deposit only, she said.

Of course, of course.

And both the card and the book come back to me tomorrow evening.

To exit the room, Army made an offensive drive to the hoop, whirling around imaginary defenders and laying up and slamming the lintel over the door.

+

But Army held on to his property and Felicia seemed to forget. That is, until one evening she came out of the house into the garage, holding his bank book, which she must have retrieved on her own.

Above her recent deposit was a deposit for $1,000.

Everybody go home right now, she said.

She pointed Army into the house and closed the garage door.

Where did you get $1,000?

He sang, *I work hard for the money. So hard for it, honey.*

I not playing. Since when people paying you by cheque? she said, for she had read the deposit line carefully.

Oh, you're talking about that thousand. That's from a separate enterprise. Paperplane, he said.

When?

He shrugged. Last week.

And you didn't tell me.

I didn't? When I asked you for my card.

You did not.

There wasn't much to tell. He retrieved the note from his room and showed it to her. She confiscated it.

You not keeping that money, she said.

+

The money disappeared from Army's account and a package appeared in the mail.

Boys, Army said. Gather round.

It was the size of a gold bar, but not heavy. Very light in fact.

I want to know who you doin'.

Who yo' daddy is?

Sometimes fortune smiles on the brave, Army's speech began, and rewardeth the humble of heart. Sometimes a little box containeth great reward. Whatever could it be? you ask. He began unwrapping the package. Could it be thousands of dollars rolled into a ball? Or could it be South African diamonds? Perhaps, a Fabergé egg.

It was a cassette.

The shop laughed. Army reddened.

It probably has instructions on it, Hendrix said. He was the only one undeterred.

Army put it in the double-cassette stereo and they listened for the first few moments. Nothing. Army held his wrists. He turned up the volume until he could hear crackling. No message. Not even breathing.

It was clear that there would be nothing on either side of the tape, but Army let it run, just in case. When the play button clicked off automatically, he had already forgotten that the background soundtrack to their chest and abs workout was his father's bungled attempt at music.

+

Not counting the cheque or the blank tape, Edgar sent Army fifteen birthday gifts that got progressively more eccentric. (When Felicia asked Army, he said that Edgar had sent him "nothing.")

The blank tape finally had given the boys some advantage over Army, whom they regarded as most likely to become an aristocrat.

Hey, Army, I have a message for you, one might say, then freeze, eyes open, mid-step.

Hey Army, message coming through, another would say, then press play on his sternum and release a massive belch.

Yet receiving the cheque and the blank tape had energized Army's business in a way that no amount of strategic expansions could. Everybody on the street hung around, expecting something to happen: romantic drama, a weight record, a spat, blood, a package.

Almost every day for two weeks, a package arrived for Armistice Gross.

Whack, a boy critiqued when Army held up the first gift.

Army felt something he never had before, but that Heather seemed to experience often: embarrassment over his father's effort. But when he thought more about it, he realized that the boy was jealous. Each time he opened a package and the guys dropped their weights and huddled their sweaty selves around him, they were all spending Christmas with their fathers.

+

On the first day of Christmas my true love sent to me:

1. A family tree, sans partridge. Edgar constructed his side with tiny black script that Army appreciated more than the information. Now he could practice more than Edgar's signature from the cheque. The note said, If you still need one for school.

2. A Chicago Bulls hat. Note: I play in a men's league, which confirmed to Army that he'd grow tall. Dark and handsome were givens.

3. Leather wallet. No note inside, just Canadian Tire money, which was fine because Army could use it to trick out his bike.

4. A case of Jolly Ranchers. Not a roll. A case. Note: Addictive. Army sold these.

5. A wooden carving of his name, the kind you get at Canada's Wonderland and place on your dresser. He would have preferred five golden rings.

6. German candy. Gross.

7. A wool sweater. Note: Not sure your size. The sweater was the colour of dust and out of season yet Army put it on immediately. Felicia asked where he got it. Zellers, he replied.

8. A brass ring with *Gross* carved into it. Apparently Boss spent a lot of time at Canada's Wonderland.

9. A twig. Okay. All right. Dead insect in the box as well. Note: Makes a good switch.

10. Tabs from a pop can. Note: Apparently people collect these?

11. A metal lighter. Note: I'm quitting.

12. A silk pouch with colourful stones inside. Note: Got these years ago from a charlatan in Arizona. Supposed to make dreams come true.

13. Red shoelaces. These were dope because surely Jordans would be next.

14. A Bulls jersey. Note: I'm thinking of joining a league. Surely, surely, number fifteen would be Jordans.

    There was a three-day pause between gifts 14 and 15.

15. A crystal keychain of a fish. Army held it over his head to see if there were Jordans underneath. Instructions maybe? Nope, just a keychain of a fish. Was he supposed to sell this to finance his sneakers? Then he read the note: Still working on one more thing.

    Make it good, old man.

+

The final gift was not a pair of Jordans. It was like the first. A cassette. But this time there was music on it and Edgar's tiny black script outlining the songs on the J-card. The music was classic at best and out of touch at worst, contradictory: Bob Dylan, Leonard Cohen, some guy named Nick Drake, Spandau Ballet's True, Billie Jean, A Whiter Shade of Pale, Ebony and Ivory, The First Time Ever I Saw Your Face.

+

Felicia would not find out for months about the gifts. Army lied about the tape he played in the car. Define *lie*. I made it for Heather, he said, and truthfully he did copy Edgar's tape onto a 90-minute tape as a parting gift for Heather, complete with more contradictions: Creep, Right Here (the SWV remix of Human Nature), The World Is Yours, Gypsy Woman, Juicy. If you don't know, now you know. When Jordans finally arrived in the fall, Army was careful to wear them outside of Felicia's presence. He changed before he entered the house and stored the sneakers in his backpack. The only mistake he made was discarding the shoebox in the recycling bin. He hobbled into the house from the arcade on garbage night and found a curious assembly of objects, notes, and envelopes with familiar writing from under his bed categorized on his comforter like the evidence of a police raid. Army was furious. Felicia was furious. She accused him of playing his part in a grand deception. He accused her of the same. She stormed into the kitchen. He heard the cutlery drawer rattle. She returned with a knife. He bosomed his Jordans and defected upstairs to the *Republikflucht* of Oliver.

Heather

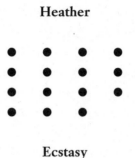

Ecstasy

The third Friday in August, Skinnyboy drove Heather to a bar on Queen West, between Bathurst and Spadina. Heather was underage, she had no ID, so she tried to be as inconspicuous as possible by carrying parts of a drum set into the bar. With makeup she was a passable twenty-one. Security said of course they believed her but they could lose their licence if they gave her a wristband without ID, they didn't care if she was two hundred. She sipped from Skinnyboy's glass. He told her not to worry and put a pill in her mouth.

Skinnyboy's band, Murmur, comprised a boy skinnier than Skinnyboy with a big nose, the drummer who wore eyeliner, and Skinnyboy, who that evening wore a black undershirt torn at the armpit, black jeans and black trainers. All the band members had the same haircut as Skinnyboy. They all initiated sentences by flicking their hair out of their eyes. None of them used their hands. None of them had girlfriends.

They got there at nine but Murmur didn't go on until eleven. Heather sat through three bands trying to be Nirvana, gazing at their shoes, mumbling and dragging their lip over mics, then stepping back and headbanging at least once per song. It felt like a talent show more than a show-show. Murmur, though, did an Unplugged version. Brushes on the drums. Skinnyboy sat on a stool, let his hair cover his eyes, and lifted his voice into the Alps. Phrase after phrase he never took a breath. The crowd was silent, split between boredom and rapture.

Afterward, Skinnyboy's friends kept asking her what she thought. She went through all of her adjectives: *cool, mellow, sick, dope, fly, tight* (more Army's words than hers by the end) and the one they seemed to like best was *real*. You guys were really real. Skinnyboy cupped her skull and put another pill in her mouth. She just wanted to be alone with him.

So you thought we did all right? Eyeliner said.

I'm telling you, she said.

You heard how I changed up the ending of "Same"? Skinnierboy said.

We should keep that, Skinnyboy said.

Totally, Heather said.

They went up Spadina and had Chinese food in an orange-lit takeout place. They ate on the curb, then Eyeliner drove them down to the lake in Skinnyboy's car. He kept looking at her and Skinnyboy in the rearview mirror. She was tired, deeply, in her muscles. She wanted to lie down. She put her head on Skinnyboy's shoulder, he kissed her head, she kissed his neck, he fondled her shoulder, she ran her thumb along his zipper and closed her eyes. She initiated, he could say. She opened her eyes when he kissed her on the lips. Her eyes met Eyeliner's in the rearview mirror.

At her new school in Massachusetts, they joked about orgasm face. Mindy Lauren did the best imitations. For one girl she bucked her teeth and twitched her upper lip, for herself she sloshed her hands through her hair and coughed in slow motion, for Heather she lowered her lids disdainfully, put her elbow on her wrist and pretended to smoke a cigarette. While brushing her teeth, Heather would sometimes practice an orgasm face and end up laughing into the foam. Sometimes she'd practice how far back she could push her toothbrush into her mouth.

The car had stopped. She wanted to lie down. She was lying down. She heard car doors close. She wanted to lie down deeper. She heard gravel. She heard smoke voices. She thought about all of the orgasm faces as the shadow of Skinnyboy's hand crawled under her shirt. Maybe, as he looked at her face through his hair, he was seeing orgasm face, not dying face.

+

The second time, if there was a second time and not a third or fourth, it was like Skinnyboy was angry with her. Only it wasn't Skinnyboy, it was Skinnierboy, was it, then it was Skinnyboy again, then laughter, and smoke and the muttering, all like the beginning of a headache between her legs. She didn't feel anyone dragging her jeans down to her knees. She woke up on a Ferris wheel. But even that she couldn't be sure of, how their faces kept changing, every time they swished hair out of their eyes, and she was awake, but not. How many pills—what pills—had she had? It was just Ecstasy, no? She wanted to be awake when he opened her centrefold. She wanted to set her face a certain way. Why was he so skinny? The top of her head was counting against the door handle. How many sips was this? She felt like she was upside down. She decided that she was asleep. It was dark. There was no way.

And when she awoke, definitively awakened by someone shaking her shoulder, she was curled up in the backseat with her head on Skinnyboy's lap. Skinnierboy and Eyeliner were gone.

The sunrise, he said. Watch a little bit.

She sat up. She had to twist the waist of her pants to sit right and set the seam of her shirt along her shoulders. The sunrise. Right. She couldn't muster enthusiasm for it. Saturday morning. She felt her hair. It was frizzing. Her stomach boiled. She opened the door and threw up in the pocket of the interior panel.

Skinnyboy reprimanded her for being a drag, a joykill, sorry that he woke her in the first place, and she said that it was early, that she hadn't seen the sunrise in years, and he said all the more reason to feel something now, you know? I'm not dead, she said. Of course I feel something but like you always want me to express, like give it a rest, it's like five in the morning.

He didn't say anything for a moment, looked at her eyes, then her lips, then smoothed her hair, and said he was sorry. Sometimes all this beauty, you know, makes my soul, like, quiver. Like, my music's dark and everything, but inside, I'm like more sunrise than sunset.

Heather wanted to roll her eyes but didn't have the energy.

He took her to McDonald's for breakfast (she vomited a second time in the parking lot, the motion of the car, she couldn't hold until the bathroom), counted out his remaining change to buy them each coffees. He offered her a bite of his Egg McMuffin. She couldn't. He ordered her to eat something. His authority, she liked. He was so concerned about her. She picked at his fries across the acrylic table and gathered extra napkins to clean the vomit from his car.

I have the whole day off, he said.

Heather already knew that.

We can do anything you want.

She wanted to go home and have a shower. She didn't want to go back in the car and hear Soundgarden, whose songs had warped like hot vinyl, whose music she would never be able to listen to again when it came on overhead in a clothing store, say, without thinking of Skinnyboy, the standard car, the interminable night and the interminable sunrise.

+

Later, she omitted the part of the story between Skininierboy and McDonald's to Army. But he asked her directly, Did you have sex?

Heather considered whether she could tell Army the truth and she must have paused too long. Any answer apart from an immediate and definitive *no* would be problematic and she was too late to respond immediately now.

So you did, Army said.

I didn't want to, Heather said.

And then Army said the most devastating thing that anyone had ever said to her.

+

Heather put three fries in her mouth and went to the McDonald's restroom. Her period might be coming soon, she thought. That explained a lot.

+

The whole day off. Joy.

We could make it to Montreal, Skinnyboy said.

Why don't we just head back? Heather said.

He accused her of not carpedieming and she conceded that they could hang out in Toronto for a while.

Skinnyboy took Oliver's guitar out of the trunk and put it in the backseat. Respect the art, he said. Heather wished she was with anybody else so she could say, It looks like a coffin for his music career, but she was stuck with SkinnyboyWhoFlickedHisHairOutOfHisEyes in a car that smelled like Egg McMuffin for some reason, bleach, and boy. Did she even like boys? she wondered. Would she even like them if they weren't always tickling her with their attention?

Skinnyboy knew where every Zellers was around the area.

He stopped for allergy medication.

He read the free entertainment papers with his ankle on his knee like a grown-up.

Heather could tell from how often Skinnyboy was looking over, checking the side of her face, that he wanted to make sure they were cool. It wasn't that he didn't want to get in trouble, because she didn't think that he thought he did anything wrong. And she didn't want to make him feel like he did anything wrong because, she realized, she didn't know him very well and he seemed pretty normal, like with his own room and posters of Soundgarden on his wall, and because she wanted to go home. She knew Skinnyboy would not take her home until she was herself again.

He tried to make amends. He offered her Oliver's guitar. Piece of garbage, he called it. He wrapped his plastic bracelet around her wrist then gave her a gimp bracelet he was wearing. She didn't say much. Her hair needed attention.

Skinnyboy was waiting for her to stop being such a, what, joykill. He said, Why're you acting like you're in Grade 8? which intimated that maybe it was normal for sex to be pressed out of you in a lemon squeezer after high school. She thought about her mother, not the plump always-on-a-diet version of her, but the girl she must have been when her father used to write her songs. (Skinnyboy never wrote her songs.) Her mother's top getting ripped by her father, no, a boy like her father. His fist, gripping the fabric beyond reasonable force, like a hammer pummelling a grape into skin.

Skinnyboy was saying something. Heather had to squint in order to listen. He had been talking for a while now, she realized. What's the deal with her energy? Something about what happened in the car and something if you're just going to suck and something—for she really could not process any of it—and she came onto him and what did she think they were going to the lake for—exercise?

I'm tired, Heather said. I'm tired, okay?

He went on.

She pretended to be asleep most of the way through afternoon traffic. When they were nearing home, she said just take her to the mall and she'd walk home.

He said, Whatever. And nothing else until he pulled into a parking space, turned off the ignition. They both sat there staring ahead.

+

And she would say to Army later, He made me feel as if it was all my fault. Like I was the one who made the whole trip miserable and whatnot. Like I don't get why guys do this. Like you turn it back on me somehow.

Army shrugged.

Like, you're doing it right now, Army, she said. I'm telling you something and you're—she folded her arms and pushed out her lower jaw.

I'm listening.

Well, don't listen like that.

What do you want me to say? You shouldn't have gone off with him.

+

Heather tried to smile. What was she doing smiling? She wanted to run from the car, have a shower and eat some cereal with her feet up on the coffee table.

What was she doing making a feeble joke? Now you can write a song about me.

He snorted.

She undid her seat belt.

Bye, she said.

Bye, he didn't so much reply as repeat.

+

Heather walked up the street with her hair up in a loose, shaggy ponytail that made her head look twice as big. The sun was setting huge behind her. Not really. But it seemed to. She seemed a silhouette against the suburban backdrop, a shadow walking on a person.

Army spotted her from the garage then dominoed to Hendrix who was training his ants then dominoed upstairs to Oliver who came pounding out then to Felicia who heard his footsteps and Hendrix's shrill announcement from downstairs. They all lined up at the edge of the garage. Army was holding his wrists.

I'm back, Heather said, glittering jazz hands.

You think this is funny? Oliver said.

She knew she would be in trouble while she was planning her escapade with Skinnyboy but with less than two weeks left in Canada she didn't care. She said, Just do whatever you're going to do.

You don't tell me what to do. I tell you what to do.

I'm sorry, all right. I was going to tell you, Heather said.

It's over, Oliver said. Over. Over. For you.

It just went late. I was supposed to come back, but—

You could have been dead, Heather! What kind of—

I'm not dead, all right.

The least you could— And now you come back with attitude.

I don't have attitude.

With lip. I have a good mind to send you back to your mother. Now.

I said I was sorry.

Oliver pointed Heather up the stairs. She looked at Army but he looked away quickly. When Oliver saw this pass between them, he grabbed Heather's arm to lead her away.

Don't touch me. She pulled her arm away with such force that her elbow was pointing at Oliver's face.

But when Felicia took Heather's shoulders and lowered her elbow it was somehow okay. Without saying a word, Felicia told her everything that was blacked out. Some man had bought her a bagel and talked and talked and she thought she was the first girl, and then he rubbed circles into her forehead, and opened his chest as he would open a shirt and showed her his bleeding sacred heart, and she took a white washcloth and dabbed at it and stitched him up and made him soup and tuna sandwiches, all the while he was promising that he would buy her a unicorn.

Then Heather ran up the stairs and Oliver chased her.

+

The skinny boy who flicked hair out of his eyes had a name. It was Carter Hardwick.

Oliver

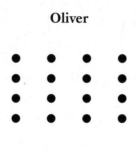

Explosion

The time had come. Thursday, September 1. The Thursday before Labour Day. Per the divorce understanding, Oliver drove his children to the airport. Check in two hours early at 10:20. He tried to be light, to make their last memories of him those of a father who was going back to an incredible life, full of vague happiness.

Hendrix was sniffly in the car. Oliver had been stern with him when he was loading the luggage and found that Hendrix had scattered all the hair he had gathered over the summer across the lawn. A slight breeze lifted the curls up from the grass. In the rearview mirror, his lawn looked like the crown of a gigantic baby emerging from the dirt.

Hendrix was also sniffly because he wanted Army to come to the airport with them and Oliver, enraged by the hair he'd have to rake, said no. The night before, Hendrix had wanted Army to shave *Army* into the side of his head. But the boy had just enough decency to make Hendrix ask permission (Oliver said, Absolutely not, of course) and Army shaved a series of *X*'s instead. His seven-year-old son was going to school with *XXX* shaved into his hair and he thought it was the coolest thing. The ex-wife would, no doubt, be on the phone. And now, Hendrix was rubbing his eyes under the camouflage hat that Army had given him. It was a lot of stress for a little boy. Why was their mother doing this to them?

Baby, Heather said from the passenger seat. She was fingering a gimp bracelet and another that looked like a hospital bracelet.

Hendrix slapped her hand away when she leaned from the passenger seat to

flick the brim of his hat. Oliver didn't intervene. Tough love. It was good for
Hendrix to develop some fortitude. The boy was sniffling far less than he would
have at the beginning of the summer.

Oliver looked out the window. Out the right side along Airport Road, planes
were queued for takeoff. Heather turned to Hendrix again and screwed her
knuckles under her eyes and Oliver finally said, Leave him alone.

Heather said to Oliver, He's going to miss his boyfriend.

Oliver was about to make a little joke himself.

But with all the disaster his little voice could contain, Hendrix said, Yeah,
well, you're the one who was kissing him.

Oliver turned his eyes from the road to look at Heather, who was going red.
A plane seemed to land on the roof.

I wasn't kissing him.

I saw you.

Shut up!

I saw you guys.

What's he talking about? Oliver said.

On his bed, Hendrix said, kissing and rubbing on each other. Then he
wrapped his arms around himself and wiggled and wormed and kissed the air.

What's he saying, Heather? Oliver shouted.

He's making stuff up.

But Oliver knew. He knew. He *knew*.

And your hands were in his pants.

Heather! Oliver said.

Dad, he's just causing trouble.

Heather Elizabeth Soares. Oliver slapped her bare thigh. Even her shorts
were too short. You tell me the truth.

I am telling you the truth.

You tell me the truth right now. Oliver slammed her shoulder into the side
of the car. You've been messing with that boy right under my nose all summer.
All summer, Heather! From one thing to the next.

Heather's face crumpled.

Baby, Hendrix said. Baby. Baby. Baby.

Shut up! Oliver said, then turned to Heather. When did this start?

I didn't do anything, Heather said.

They used to go through the black door when you weren't home.

You're dead! Heather's face was puffy and red.

Oliver turned his attention back to the road. Barely. He was driving manically, winding around the terminal toward departure parking.

I'm going to kill him, Oliver said. With the Mr. O and the Mr. O. And you, Heather, when I [he thumbed his chest] went to bat for you against your mother and you come and do this to me. What is wrong with you?

I didn't do anything, Heather said. With her forearm, she swept her hair back over her head.

How many guys, Heather? Oliver said. How many? What is wrong with you?

I'm telling you the truth.

If you turn up pregnant, I swear—

I'm not pregnant. We didn't do anything.

Whenever Heather tried to explain, Oliver turned up the radio incrementally until they settled into a parking spot and classic rock was blasting through the dark underground. Oliver slapped the steering wheel and shook his head. He took Hendrix's suitcase and walked quickly in front of the children; Hendrix kept pace with him, running a little. Heather struggled behind with her luggage.

At the departure gate, Oliver was cool to both of them. He was going to leave without hugging Heather, but she opened her arms weakly, like a question, so he answered with a hug and passed his lips across the top of her head, then turned away.

+

Oliver intended to open the garage and drive his truck straight through into the barbershop, into Army, and pin him against the wall.

His only daughter. Right under his nose. By this boy who just wanted to take, take, take. He still didn't have his guitar. Where was his guitar?

The hair Hendrix had scattered was blowing down the street like mini tumbleweed from a Western.

No one was in the garage.

Oliver banged on the house door. He had a key, not on him, but it didn't cross his mind to retrieve it. He had a different idea. He ran upstairs. He strode to the black door and undid the deadbolt. The other side was locked.

Army! Oliver called. He punched the door four times. Army!

He threw his shoulder into the door.

Open this door! Oliver rammed the door a second time and it exploded with the sick sound of wood cracking.

He snapped his head around, searching the hallway for Army. Then he went straight for Army's room, the nasty, sweaty, bleachy smell of teenage boys. Bed unmade as well, mattress indented with groin weight, underwear on the floor.

I need you to identify yourself immediately, you hear me, Oliver said. His voice sounded like a monitored alarm system.

I heard you, I heard you, man, Army's voice came from the bathroom.

Where else would the horny little bastard be?

The toilet flushed.

I just in here taking a dump and minding my business and you're waking the dead. The faucet opened. Damn, Mr. O. The faucet closed. Can a brother have a second to himself?

When Army emerged from the bathroom shirtless, drying his hands on his boxers, Oliver was occupying the entire doorway, standing on his hind legs like a bear.

Put on some clothes, Oliver said. He couldn't look at the boy's skin.

I'm all right.

Oliver went into Army's room, picked up a white T-shirt from the floor and threw it at Army in the hallway. Put on some clothes. I don't know if people dance around naked where you're from but—

I was born here, Mr. O. That's some offensive KKK—

I said, *Put on some clothes!*

Fine. Chill. Army stretched the shirt over his head. You don't have to go busting down doors and stuff before a brother can get a little Froot Loops in his system. Don't you have a key to your own house?

I want an explanation.

About?

About? Oliver opened his eyes wide. About? You're going to ask me *about?*

Army started walking down the stairs toward the kitchen.

I'm talking to you, Oliver said.

Yeah.

Don't *yeah* me. Oliver barrelled down the stairs into Army and the boy lost his footing and slipped down two steps before rebalancing.

What's your problem? Army asked.

Boy, who do you think you're talking to?

Listen, Mr. O. I ain't given you nothing but respect all the—

I want an explanation, Oliver raised his voice and enunciated. What were you doing with my daughter all summer?

Army paused in the living room.

Heather told you I was doing something with her?

Yeah, she told me, you bastard, you son of a bitch.

And you sure she was talking about me cause I, I, I, no sir, not me. He made his way to the front door. I don't know what you're, what she's, what you're talking about.

Oliver charged again and Army flew out the door into the garage.

You see all this here? Oliver said, motioning to the barbershop, the barbecue, the weights. Finito. I want you and your mother out of my house.

Look, Mr. O. We didn't do nothing. I swear.

Oliver picked up a glass bottle of blue alcohol and aimed at Army.

Hey, hey, hey, hey, hey, Army said. He held up his wrists over his face.

Oliver threw the bottle. Army deflected it with his forearm and it shattered against the weights.

Oliver crouched and rotated his body so he was blocking Army from exiting the garage. Army was pinned between the weight bench and the back wall of divorce rubble.

You haven't given me my explanation yet, Oliver said. You must think that I'm a woman you can charm. You must think I'm playing with you. You must think you can take whatever you want from whoever you want whenever you want and not have it come back to bite you. Well, son, I'm older than you and I'm smarter than you and your mother put together. God help me if I don't kill you now.

Mr. O, it's absolutely not what you think.

Where's my guitar?

I'm working toward finding you a suitable replacement and believe you me—

I want an explanation.

And that's what I'm providing.

I said I want an explanation. Oliver approached. Army was losing ground.

Heather was real sad after that guy in Boston and we just got to talking.

And you thought it was okay to stick your dick in my daughter. Oliver lunged. There was only the barbell between them now.

It wasn't like that, Mr. O. We talked. I didn't even touch her. I mean—

How many times?

How many times what?

How many times didn't you touch my daughter?

Like one one once maybe twice maybe I don't know like not more than a couple of times she came on to me—

Oliver lunged. You're blaming *Heather* now?

No, of course not, Army said. I mean I had, like, what do you call it, like feelings for her.

Oh, you love her now?

Not love-her love-her. Like brother-and-sister love-her.

Oliver wrong-sided Army and grabbed the tail of his T-shirt. You're disgusting. You hear me?

Army surrendered. If that's disgusting, then I guess I'm disgusting.

That's your explanation then—you're disgusting?

At the time, it wasn't brother-and-sister. I thought she was— I mean, before she ran off with that guy, I thought. Maybe. But I don't expect you to understand.

I understand that you wanted to get off. He took Army's shoulders and slammed him against an unstable wall of divorce rubble for punctuation. And that you saw an opportunity. Slam. And you took it.

A box toppled.

Look, Mr. O, you're going after the wrong fish in all of this. I didn't run off to Queen West with her. Heather's no Mother Teresa.

That infuriated Oliver more. He hooked his forearm under Army's chin and pressed into his throat.

I want an explanation.

Army tried to shake his head, which was turning the colour of an engorged penis. The ex had told Hendrix that he, Hendrix, was more of a man than his father. How could a woman say such a thing?

Something fell behind Army and gave him room to escape. He spun around so he was facing Oliver's back. Oliver turned and lunged. Army took a running step backward, stepped on part of the smashed bottle, and his hip collided with the side of the barbell—and in a long, slow-motion second, he fell to the floor, the barbell tipped over and the unsecured fifty-pound weight plate slid down the sleeve of the bar unto his foot. The edge of the weight struck the inside hump of his ankle.

Army closed his eyes and grit his teeth. He leaned back and lay in the pool of broken glass and alcohol. His shorts were soaked. Oliver saw the boy's flaccid penis through the leg holes of his boxers.

Oliver scanned outside to see who might have seen.

I want you and your mother out of my house, he said.

Army didn't say anything. It was unlike him. He was sucking in sharp breaths. Frowning and breathing. Frowning but breathing.

Oliver stepped over Army's body and entered the code to close the garage on the boy.

+

But Oliver couldn't stay upstairs.

There was an unusual quiet in his house. The whiff of his children taunted him. He froze, trying to identify or preserve it. Not a sound downstairs. Hendrix had left a belt on the stairs. Heather left her cereal bowl on the coffee table, spoon still inside. She used to put her feet against the table's edge, and watch TV while talking to Army or "Diane"—how many guys, Heather?—on the phone.

Oliver decided to get in his truck and go to The Mansion. He didn't want to be home when Felicia got home, not because he was afraid of her, he convinced himself, but because he was afraid / of what he might do if he saw that boy again. That was why.

In fifteen minutes he was at The Mansion.

Yes, The Mansion to see *les danseuses*. Yes, in the middle of the day. It was night inside.

Two other fellas sat on stools right against the stage. The girl was already topless, doing a classic routine, school girl or librarian, and not one of the more topical routines, sexy military, sexy Québécoise, sexy Olympian. She was crawling on beat to Cotton Eyed Joe. Oliver made eye contact with the bartender who used to be a *danseuse* earlier in her career. She was moving up. Good on her.

He deserved it. He had it coming to him. Whatever it was. He wasn't dead. Felicia could call the police on him if she wanted. Oliver knew how to talk to the police. All they wanted was an explanation. And he'd give them an explanation, oh he'd give them an explanation that would make them chain their daughters to their desks.

Disgusting was the ex-wife's word. Disgusting. With the strip clubs. If that's disgusting, then I guess I'm disgusting. I'm just in here taking a dump and minding my business. But I don't expect you to understand. She became a fat nun after Hendrix. No Mother Teresa, Army had said about his daughter. Not love-her love-her.

Me and my big house, Oliver thought. I have a big house to shuffle my big fat self around.

+

Oliver was planning to kill the rest of the day at The Mansion, but around three o'clock, he realized that Felicia might be returning late (orientation weekend was coming up at Brownstone) and the boy was on the garage floor—he wasn't bleeding—injured.

He wasn't tanked yet. He was actually in the best shape to drive, he believed. Relaxed. So he headed home as inconspicuously as possible through the early rush-hour traffic.

As he expected, Felicia's car wasn't in the driveway when he arrived at home.

Oliver didn't open the garage door to see if Army was still lying near the weight bench. Instead he walked downstairs through the broken door (could he fix it before Felicia got home?) and into Army's room. The window was open. Army was lying shirtless, listening to his Walkman. His foot was already swollen. The skin was blotchy.

Oliver slid Army's closet door open. Army jerked awake.

Put this on, Oliver said. He tossed a T-shirt and a pair of shorts on the bed. He would take the boy to Emergency.

+

Army and Oliver waited a long time in the ER waiting room. There had been no service since they returned a questionnaire (a questionnaire!) to the intake nurse and she arranged a wheelchair for Army.

He fell, Oliver had said.

I'd like to speak to your son privately, the nurse said.

His son? That confused Oliver's feelings. But he didn't correct her, which confused his feelings even more.

He's a minor, Oliver said.

Have a seat, sir. The nurse was black. Oliver was sure Army would go in there and rat on him. And he'd be charged for child abuse. Plus he had the incident that cost him his teaching job.

Presently, Oliver and Army watched a muted TV in the corner. They were on mute themselves. Oliver periodically went to the triage desk to speed up the service. What was wrong with the health care system?

We're doing the best we can with the staff we have, the nurse said.

Oliver returned and sat next to Army's wheelchair. Army froze him out. It was hot in the waiting room. Wasn't it hot in here?

What did you tell her? Oliver asked.

That I fell.

I mean, that's the truth, isn't it? Oliver asked.

Army shook his head. Nope, it ain't.

They returned to watching *Wheel of Fortune*. Army seemed more interested in it than Oliver. It was after seven and no one had called Felicia. Oliver bounced his knee. He read an old entertainment magazine. Enough with the Sophie Fortin nonsense.

Moments later, Oliver was striding toward the vending machine. He came back with two Pepsis and a bag of Skittles. He opened one Pepsi for Army and waited for him to sip before opening his own.

Army wasn't going to talk to him, although Oliver felt that he should be the one not talking to Army, all things considered. Oliver would not be brought down to the level of a fourteen-year-old. He was the adult here. He'd have to model good behaviour. He took a long drink of his Pepsi in preparation. It could use a good shot of rum. All right. Now.

Are you going to tell Mom or am I? Army said first.

Oh, that's the game he was going to play?

I don't know that we need to call her right now, Oliver said. We're not even sure if it's broken.

It's broken, Army said. Mom was going to take a bunch of us to Wonderland. She can barely afford it but it's my birthday, y'know?

Oliver took the fiduciary hint. We can still go.

Well, I can't anymore.

Let's wait on the X-ray. Oliver was at a loss. But either way, they'll patch you up and we'll get ourselves going, won't we?

Army said nothing for a long time. He folded his arms with the Pepsi in one hand, dangling at an elbow.

Oliver wrinkled his forehead.

When do you want us out by? Army asked.

Let's not think about that right now, Oliver said and immediately imagined himself in the house alone again, inspecting the rooms, opening and closing the windows, walking up and down the stairs as if searching for something he full well knew the location of.

The nurse gave them an eye from her station.

Let's get you healed up first, soldier, Oliver said and slapped Army's good leg with gusto. He made sure the nurse saw.

Army was no fool though.

I think you need to stop charging us rent, he said.

Oliver wagged his jaw.

Yeah, Mr. O. I think you need to stop charging us or drop the rent or something. Army adjusted his leg with his hands. Else this situation could get very expensive for you.

I'm not dropping the rent.

Have it your way, Army said.

Oliver leaned on the armrest of Army's wheelchair and whispered, I'll drop it fifty bucks.

I was thinking more like two hundred, Army said.

Fifty and I'll take you to Wonderland.

Two hundred and I won't tell Mom you broke my leg.

A hundred and I won't tell her how you spent your summer.

Oliver reclined. Army reclined. They both took sips of their Pepsis at the same time and that's how the deal went down.

+

Five and a half weeks later, the Sunday before Canadian Thanksgiving, when Oliver had returned from dinner at his sister's house, the ex-wife called.

Who is this? Oliver said, trying to kill her.

Heather has something she needs to discuss with you, the ex said. Hold.

Three times in one month the ex let his kindergarten-aged daughter come home without—

Hey, Dad.

Call me directly, Heather, if you need to talk to me.

I wasn't going to call you. Mom's making me.

And then a plank in reason broke and he was sinking to the kitchen chair, flickering, because he already knew what she was about to say now then now then now then

THE SEX TALK

I think I have the wrong number.
Peace.

+

Hi, I just called. May I speak to Felicia Shaw?
She's at work.
At work. Of course. At work. I'll call back later.
Peace.

+

Hi, it's me, I just called. Who's this?
That depends. Who dis?

+

Hi, I called a week ago for Felicia Shaw. Is there another number where
I can reach her?
At work.
I tried her work number.
Yeah, well. She'll be home at six, six thirty. Is there a message?
No message.
Do you want to leave a number or anything?
She has it.

+

Hi, sorry. I hate to call back so soon. Am I speaking to her son?
Yeah.
Armistice?
Army.
Army. How are you, Army?
Been better. Broke my foot. You want a cut?
Of?
A haircut. Best in Brampton. It's 55 Newcourt. Come through.
I'll come true. You think your mother—
It's through. Come through.
Cool. I don't know what you kids are saying half the time.
Listen, call back later, okay? Peace.
Peace.

Hey, no offence, Boss. I can say peace but you can't say peace.

+

Hi, sorry, last time. Is your mother avoiding certain calls?
I don't know.
Do you know who this is?
Yeah.
Who?
The guy who just called.
I mean—
I know who you are.
And you think she would appreciate my call?
Probably not.
I see. Well, do me a favour then, Army. Don't mention this call.
Silence is golden.
Thank you.
You're not hearing me, Boss. That was for you to say, What's the price
of gold?

+

I know I said last time last time, but your foot. You said you broke it?
It was broken.
Oh, I assumed it was presently broken.
Passive voice, Boss.
You were in a fight?
You could say that.
Over a girl.
What else is there to fight about?
Money.

+

It's not too late.
Black people don't press charges.
You shouldn't identify as black. You're biracial.
I'm okay with black. Like I don't feel German or whatever it is you are.
German. It's German.
I know.

You sounded vague.

I had to do a family tree.

You got it?

Trust me, I know. Nazis and all that stuff. I got it.

+

That's the version your mother gave you? Nazis and Heil Hitler and skinheads?

I mean, I had to fill in the blanks because why else wouldn't she talk about you. I figured you guys must have been— She talks about Mutter.

+

Do I sound old when I say peace?

Yeah. You can't pull it off.

I'll stick to bye then.

You could pull off later.

+

I hope you don't mind that I call from time to time.

Free country, Boss.

Please don't call me Boss. I'm nobody's boss right now.

Don't you run a company?

Did. I'm taking a leave. It was a whole deal that we don't need to get into.

What do you want me to call you?

How about— I guess Boss is fine.

+

How could you not hear about this?

Boss, I've got my own problems.

Nothing at all? The allegations? Felicia didn't say anything? I don't believe that.

You're probably thinking it was a bigger story than it was.

It was huge. Is. Still.

Boss, people get divorced every day. I could name you ten kids on this block who're in the middle of a divorce.

It was more than the divorce.

Girls get raped.

I didn't rape them.
Assaulted. Whatever you call it.

+

I tried a little bit when you were young, but Felicia, your mother,
I know who she is.
made it very difficult.
She said you were a pilot.
She should have told you the truth.
Which is?
Which is, which is long and a bit complicated for now.
Give me the quick version.
She was a flight attendant.
True?
Of course not. I'm kidding. Kiddo.
You guys just keeping lying and lying to me.

+

Excuse me.
You need to get that cough checked out, Boss.
It's nothing. Smoking. Don't ever smoke.

+

Haircuts? That's the business?
It started as a barbershop then we found these weights so we had a gym
plus I sold freezies and Popsicles for half what the Hasty Market charges and
there was the barbecue franchise until a guy busted the fence.
Hold on. Actually, I'll have to take this.
Is it true that guys always run off with their secretaries?
What? Later.
Peace.

+

We got cut off last time.
Right, your ex-wife.
You're fishing.
Your mistress?

No, I'm completely single. No wife, no mistress, no kids. I mean—
It's all right. Hey, Boss, look, I gotta go.
Army.
Peace.

+

I should pass through. If Felicia—
Boss, it's come through. And there's nothing to see. Since I broke my
foot, business tanked. But I have a better business now and I don't need
Mr. O's garage.
Who's Mr. O?
The landlord. Not really anymore but. He's the guy upstairs. He's prob-
ably a lot like you, no? Do you have a problem with the honeys?
I wouldn't call it a problem.
Yeah, he wouldn't either.

+

Blackmail is not a business model.
I was just buying lunch at the West Indian place, minding my business,
and he was coming out of the strip club. Middle of the day.
Good thing he doesn't work for the Secret Service.
I don't get it.
Discretion.
Long story short, he dropped the rent.

+

You have to be careful who you're doing business with.
Do you, like, hate Jews and stuff?
Of course not.
How about black people?
Obviously not. You can't believe everything your mother says.
She didn't tell me that.

+

Again?
Yup, he dropped the rent again.
Is he molesting you?

I thought of that. He's pretty straight though.

Don't joke about that.

No, no, every time he does something to me—

Something like what?

Stupid stuff. It doesn't even have to be to me. I told you I saw him in his truck with a woman.

So?

Like it was the mall parking lot near The Mansion.

That's the strip club?

Right. He was probably getting a blowjob.

+

But that's no reason to pay you.

Like I don't care if he's humping shorties near the dumpster.

And it's not Felicia's business if your landlord's cavorting with women.

She doesn't care if he's doing it. But she doesn't want me knowing about him doing it. He's a corrupting influence. You gotta know the psychology of women, Boss.

+

How much now?

Fiddy bucks. But it would be suspicious if every month he went up to Mom and told her he dropped the rent. So she keeps on paying the rent and Mr. O refunds it back to me.

You're basically making money off your mother.

Nants ingonyama bagithi, Baba. Circle of life, baby.

+

He finally just told Mom to pay whatever she could. And she told him she could afford the current rent.

Stupid.

That's what I thought. But it's about dignity.

It's stupid. That's what it is.

Anyhow, I'll work him down until we're living here practically free.

+

That wasn't my fault. I asked the lady in the store what the kids were listening to these days and she said you guys were just taping music off the radio. Mix-and-match tapes, she said.

It's mixtape. I opened up the package in the middle of the barbershop. You don't just give somebody a blank tape.

I fixed it. I made you a mix and match.

Come on. It's mixtape. It's not some German kleinleiderkampfchatzenwunderword.

+

No, I can teach you. We'll start with die Lebenskraft und Lebensfreude.

Is that all one word?

Two. Die Lebenskraft und die Lebensfreude.

They sound similar. I got the und.

The only difference between them is joy.

+

Later.

Don't hang up. I have something to ask you.

Sure.

Okay, promise you won't get mad.

No, I knew you'd ask someday. You have a right to know what happened between—

Just promise.

It was the seventies. Both of our mothers were dying—

You know I've got all these businesses, right?

Right.

I was wondering if you could spot me a dime.

How much is a dime?

Well, not a dime-dime.

+

She came by and made a big show. So you're saying she took that cheque from you too?

She keeps my bank book. Plus Hendrix told her that I got the cheque.

But I made it out to you. She had no right.

Exactly. So can you?

I'm not in a position to give you money right now.

Boss, if you don't want to, just man up.
No, that's not it. My records are being monitored.
Whatever.
I'm telling you the truth.

+

You sound surprised.
I haven't heard from you in a while.
I was away.
You're still away.
Are you all right? Is this about the money?
No, this phone call may be monitored.

+

Do you always answer the phone?
No. I only answer if no one's home.

+

Next year's too far away for me to know.
They're making us choose courses already. I'm gonna take Business as my elective. Try and figure out how to keep my money working for me, you know.
Easy. Don't get sued.

+

Nothing's going on.
You're in the papers.
I already told you that I was in the papers.
Yeah, but you're in there again.
I am aware.
Are you going to lose everything?

+

If you had to choose between me and a trust fund.
Trick question.
Honest answer.
How much is the trust fund?

I suppose that's the answer.
Ballpark.

+

Shoot.
And if you had to choose between your money and, like, me?
I don't.
If.
There's no if. There's no choice.

+

How's the girlfriend you can't tell me about?
Summer girl? She's back in America. We had to keep it on the down-low.
You might know her. Boston?
I'm not chummy with too many prepubescent girls.
She wasn't prepubescent. She was real pubescent.
Either way.
But I have a new girlfriend I can tell you about. You want to talk to her?
Well—
But don't call her my girlfriend.
I don't really—
Hang on.

+

She sounds very pretty.
He said you sound hot.
Not hot, Army.
She said, Ew.
I didn't say hot. Please tell her that I—
She's gone. Ew, she said.
I'm glad you find that amusing.

+

When's your ex coming back?
December. Oh, I didn't tell you. She's preggers.
With?
We don't know. She thinks it's a girl. I think it's a boy.

I mean, is it your baby?

No, but I can still have an opinion.

+

It's not your baby. Why do you care?

I mean there's like a 0.1 percent chance. Maybe a 1 percent chance. Like broken-condom, vasectomy-odds.

And she was your girlfriend when she got pregnant?

Sort of yes, sort of no.

Either way. If it's not your kid and she wasn't your girlfriend then there must have been another guy.

I don't know. Maybe. But she wasn't into him.

+

Listen to me, Army, and listen good. It's not your kid. Run.

She's not suddenly some kind of ghost because she got pregnant. You don't know her.

Run. It's not your business.

It's not yours either, Boss, but you're all up in it.

+

I don't usually go around advising people on their personal matters.

And what if it was my kid?

Then that's a different matter.

But same advice.

What?

What? Nothing.

+

Get yourself a new girlfriend.

You don't have to worry about me.

Don't get anybody pregnant.

I know that, man. I wrap my junk up tight. Like say something original.

It's the worst thing you could do with your life.

+

I just thought. It's been a while.

I know I got a sexy voice and everything but why do you keep calling?

Just to see how you're doing.

I'm doing fine.

What's happening?

Nothing. I mean, you call and you talk and that's great, but I've got money to make and you've got money to make to pay off all those honeys you were assaulting—

I was not—

Allegedly. Anyway, talk don't pay the bills.

If you're suggesting I stop—

I think you've got some stuff to work out, like you and Mom.

You told her?

This morning. She asked.

Just out of the blue?

She keeps the newspaper articles about you. I was doing a little browsing and I didn't put stuff back exactly like I found it. Anyway, she's going to change the number.

+

Hello. Are you there?

I'm here.

Why are you so quiet?

Mom doesn't want me talking to you.

You're taking it very literally, don't you think?

+

I saw the Jordans you were talking about.

You don't have to get me stuff anymore. Buy me stock.

I could put you together a portfolio.

I already know what I want.

What company?

Two, actually. And I don't know the names. I just want this ticker symbol. ARMI is the first one and ARM is the backup.

Which index?

Index?

The TSX, the DOW, the FTSE, the NIKKEI?

Boss, I'm paying you the big bucks to find out stuff like that.

+

Well, I can't wear them.

She's making me return them. Mom says you've got to stop with the gifts.

She actually said that?

I'm paraphrasing. She says you're trying to buy me. A guilty conscience needs no accuser. Exact words.

She thinks I'm guilty? You can't take these women— I don't mean to sound like der Frauenfeind. A misanth— missyg— like a mis—

Don't hurt yourself on the English.

You listen to rap. You know exactly.

Unfair. That's the divorce talking.

Take my word. They just want your balls in a nutcracker.

Personally, I think Mom could do better.

Than?

In general.

But you were implying that she could do better than me?

Do better? It's not like you're together.

We're not.

She's done okay without you.

+

I don't want to talk about the divorce.

Question for you, Boss.

Does it concern the divorce?

I asked Mom but you know how she is.

I hope I'm clear when I say that I'm done talking about the divorce.

Let's say there was a high-profile divorce case where it was discovered that the man had a child—let's say he had a son, but not with his wife. That would be, like, evidence of infidelity or, like, a history of poor conduct with respect to women.

There's no question in there.

I guess.

Little Blackmailer.

Moi? I guess my question is, Would a lawyer find that interesting? If this dude was negotiating a bunch of rape settlement cases against him and stuff. Just a question. I wouldn't do that to you. Although I could, I guess, right?

Is your mother seeing a lawyer?

Silence is golden.

+

You know when we started talking, you never used to say Mom, Mom, Mom all the time.

Sounds cold, but she pays the rent, Boss.

Which you steal back.

See, now that's cold.

What's happening to you? Now all you say is, Mom, Mom.

I'm just saying what she says. I am forbidden.

When I was a kid, we'd call people like you mama's boys.

What's the alternative?

+

I didn't mean that you were a mama's boy. I'm just tired of hearing what Felicia says.

Why don't you ever call after six when she's home?

I didn't think I needed to.

She's got feelings, you know.

Of course, she has feelings. I have feelings. You have feelings. Let's work on one set of feelings at a time.

Yours?

No, yours.

+

Don't you enjoy talking to me? You, not Felicia. You.

Lately, it's been hit or miss. You're very abstract.

I don't think you're abstract.

Because I'm not.

+

So you're just going to stop talking to me?

Boss, don't act like you love me.

+

How's business? How's your girlfriend?

That's really what you want to talk about?

+

You think it was easy to find you? And now you want to give me hell because your mother's fed you some Nazi story about me all your life.

Boss, easy on the yo-mamma business. You stumbled on me. You were looking for her.

+

If you close this door, it's final. I'm not going to come looking for you again. You hear me? It's your call.

Stage four. Bargaining. It's okay. I'm here to get you through this.

+

You think I don't replay my life every night now that I know you're out there? You think I don't wish for a time machine?

Invisibility. That's the real superpower.

How can you take this so lightly?

I have fifteen years on you, Boss.

+

You'll understand when you're grown up. At first, you think it's okay being single and then all of a sudden it's not. Then one day you wake up rolling down a hill. The momentum is enough to make you tumble along. Although you're alone. I can't go back to pretending you're not real, Army.

Who's pretending? I'm just a voice on the phone. Think of me that way.

+

What do you want me to do?

Yeah, Boss, I don't know. But my mojo's all messed up with this energy. I'm not well, you know.

Don't go there. You're doing well.

I sometimes look at kids on the street and think they might be you.

They might be.

When you turn eighteen, maybe you'll come to your own decision?

Maybe.

So. Later then.

Peace.

PART 3

X^2

I.   PERCENTAGES   *Army*

At first, Army was 99 percent sure, then 98 percent sure, and now he was down to 96 percent sure that he couldn't be the father. It was biologically impossible from what he understood about reproduction. He would have had to had had, have had to had had, sex.

He may have told Coughdrop and the others that he had had sex with a girl from his old neighbourhood—

Who? they asked.

You don't know her, he said.

Who?

I gots to protect shorty's rep. I ain't like you hounds.

—and he may have had had lots of sex in his head with lots of women, both local and famous, unknown to them, but Heather never let him put it in.

2.   A CLARIFICATION   *Army*

—and he may have had had lots of realish sex with his pillow and lots of simulated sex with his palm and lots of concocted sex with a girl on his former street, and lots of mindblowing, albeit entirely imaginary, sex with lots of real women, but Heather never let him put it in.

3.   HEALTH CLASS   *Army*

Army's 4 percent of uncertainty nagged him well into November.

During the two-week Health block, his class had to sit in a portable that stank of wet-boy (umbrellas were for chumps) and learn about bodies instead of playing indoor kickball.

Army was being disruptive that day because he excelled at kickball. And he was bored of etching penises into his tablet-arm desk.

The uterus sheds its lining every twenty-eight days, Mr. Collins said while colouring a uterus red on the overhead. The correct term, and the one I expect you to use, is—

Army interrupted: I have a friend who said he got a girl pregnant through her belly button.

The other boys turned their attention from their penises.

True story, Mr. Collins. He was pumping on her and his juice—

I've told you twice—

Sorry, sorry, his sperm, got all over her stomach, in her belly button, everywhere, I mean it totally covered her, soaked her to the bone, and like a month later she was pregnant.

You finished? Mr. Collins asked. He uncapped a fresh red marker. Can we get back to menstruation now?

I thought you was supposed to be answering our questions and stuff.

Mr. Collins stretched his back. A male cannot impregnate a female through her belly button anywhere in nature.

I know that. That's what I told him. But he swears that his sperm ran down, because she was like drenched, ran down into her 'gina, *va*gina, sorry, and then swam up into her uterus.

That's some Olympic sperm, someone called out.

Ben Johnson sperm right there, someone else said.

You done now? Mr. Collins said.

Army danced the worm with his arm. You know, jet propulsion tails and stuff.

Mr. Collins continued colouring the uterus red. Army made the penis erupt on his desk.

4. . REVISED CURRICULUM   *Army*

Army lay in bed, strumming his pubic hair.

What if, in fact, he had had sex with Heather and didn't know it? What if his Olympic sperm had been absorbed through her skin directly into her uterus and was like, *How you doin'*, to the egg and the ovum was like, *Not interested*, and the spermatozoon was like, *Can a brother say hello?* and the ovum was like, *Hello*, but really stush, and the spermatozoon went, *You gon' offer me a glass of water?* and the ovum was like, *I ain't got none*, and the spermatozoon was like, *I thought y'all was supposed to be hospitable*, and the ovum was like, *I don't know you*, and the spermatozoon was like, *Stop playing, girl, you know me*, and the ovum was like, *Army?* and the spermatozoon was like, *Who you expecting? Bill Clinton?* and the ovum was like, *I didn't make you out*, and the spermatozoon was like, *Turn on a light up in here. Let me see what I'm working with*, and the ovum was fine and the spermatozoon waggled its neck toward her face and, boom, baby.

5. CAESAREAN   *Army*

If you could cut a baby out of a woman's stomach, then surely you could put one in through her stomach. Surely maybe couldn't you?

6.   TEST TUBE   *Army*

Or what if one of Heather's Tic Tacs fell out into her panties then slipped down her pant leg and he stepped on it in the barbershop and then while cutting his toenails he got it on his hands then while he was sleeping it brushed against dried ejaculate on his sheets and the next morning he touched a doorknob then Heather touched the same doorknob then went to the bathroom and the zygote crawled back into her vajayjay while she was wiping herself?

7.   ALTERNATE ROUTE   *Army*

and the next morning he touched a doorknob then Heather touched the same doorknob then pulled some hair from her mouth and the zygote jumped in and got tangled up in her digestive system and ended up in her hooha and, boom, baby.

8.   A ROSE AIN'T A ROSE AIN'T A ROSE   *Felicia*

Armistice's birth certificate identified Edgar Gross as the father because he is the father, because Felicia thought he might change his mind about participation, because the child should not bear the indignity of fatherlessness nor should she bear the iniquity of whoredom, because, because, because. Consequently, Armistice's surname was Gross not Shaw.

And in all situations where she and Army must appear together and did not require proof of identity, Felicia went by Gross. In parent-teacher interviews, for instance. To his friends, for another. Yet on her bills she was Shaw. At work, she was Shaw. Before the Lord, depending on which church she went to and whom she was speaking to, she was either Shaw or Gross. As far as possible, she took the example of Madonna and Cher and encouraged Army to emulate Bozo.

Bono, Mom.

9.   FATHER   *Heather*

Heather said the father was not the father.

10.   IDENTIFICATION   *Heather*

She looked between her legs at the floral pattern on the loveseat and agreed with her mother.

Yes, she said with the *s* and everything.

Same boy you brought into this house in June?

I just told you.

Her mother counted months on her fingers. July, August, September, October, and it's only now you're telling me. Four months, Heather. What do you expect me to do after four months?

It's not four months. Heather's thigh obscured a pink carnation. I saw him after that.

Heather, I told you I did not want you seeing him anymore.

Yeah, well.

From this minute, you understand me, I don't want you seeing Bruno or talking to Bruno. You're not going to tell him about this baby.

I knowwuh.

Repeat after me.

Mom, I'm sixteen. Save that for Hendrix.

Repeat: I will not see—

I'm not repeating after you.

I will not see Bruno—

I will not see Bruno again and I will not tell him that I'm pregnant and I'll just sit in the house all day playing clarinet and repeating after you until I die. Happy?

II.   W5: HARD-HITTING INVESTIGATIVE JOURNALISM   *Heather*

What she did know was that she didn't know *who* the father was for sure, but she couldn't tell her mother that. She also knew that she didn't know *what* happened to her in the backseat. Or *why*. She was pretty sure about the *when* and *where*.

She could have pronounced—you husband and wife, you may kiss the bride—Army the father but that wouldn't be true.

Not that her lie was any truer.

12.   *THE MAURY POVICH SHOW* HAD NOT YET DESCENDED INTO
      CASE AFTER CASE OF PATERNITY TESTING.   *Heather*

                              HEATHER
     I is 100 percent, no, more than that, I is 256 percent sure that Skinnyboy is the father of my baby.

                               MAURY
You sure sound sure.

HEATHER

That's 'cause I is sure, Maury. Just look at them.
(A projection of the baby, split screen with SKINNYBOY, appears. The audience vocalizes agreement.)

SKINNYBOY

That baby don' look nothing like me.
(Audience boos.)

I don' know 'bout Tom, but she been sleeping around with Dick and Harry.
(Audience laughs.)

MAURY

Well, we don't need to speculate anymore. I've got the results right here in this envelope. Is Carter Hardwick the father of Heather's baby? (Beat.) We'll find out, *after* the break.
(Applause. Music.)

13.   AFTER THE BREAK   *Heather*

MAURY

I have the test results in this envelope right here. Are you ready?

SKINNYBOY

Ready as I ever gon' be.

HEATHER

We don't even need to open that envelope and go through all that, Maury. I done told you what's up.

MAURY

With respect to the unnamed child of Heather Soares, Carter (pause) you *are* the father.

HEATHER

In your face! In your face!
(She stands up and slaps the bill of his cap.)

14. AFTER THE BREAK, ALT.   *Heather*

MAURY

I have the test results in this envelope right here. Are you ready?

SKINNYBOY

Ready as I ever gon' be.

HEATHER

We don't even need to open that envelope and go through all that, Maury. I done told you what's up.
(To herself)
Waste people's time. (Bleep.)

MAURY

With respect to the unnamed child of Heather Soares, Carter (pause) you (pause) are *not* the father.

SKINNYBOY

I toldjou! I toldjou!

(HEATHER runs off stage with her face in her hands. An eruption of bleeps.)

15. CLARINET   *Ex*

Because once upon a time Heather had played a lovely clarinet, a mean clarinet, the kind of clarinet only a middle-school girl could play behind her closed bedroom door. Joyful, Joyful, We Adore Thee? That was her jam.

She kept her music in plastic sleeves in a black binder. The worst thing that could happen on the face of the earth was to break her last reed. Then she woke up from a glass coffin in dark lipstick, plaid, and Doc Martens and decided she didn't want to live anymore, or at least not happily. She started listening to amplifier feedback. She was no longer the kind of girl who played clarinet.

Her exact words were, You play it.

And now what was she putting in her mouth?

16. SCALE   *Oliver*

He thought eventually it might even out, his feelings for Heather and Hendrix. Yes, he loved both his children equally, but he preferred Heather. She was his image. If she and the ex were contemporaries, Heather would walk past her in the high school hallway and snarl. If he and Heather were colleagues, she would never demand his resignation from the school board or lay him off from the transit company or take steel wool to his masculinity in general. Hendrix might.

Maybe if Hendrix had come first, the dynamics would be different. But Oliver and Heather had some good years before Hendrix. Hendrix was always his mother's. His mother had determined to make him her own after Heather had taken to Oliver so easily from day one.

They could have divided the children evenly in the divorce agreement.

17. RECORD   *Oliver*

But, for the record, he loved both his children equally.

18. LIFE BEGINS AT   *Hendrix*

Hendrix was under orders not to say a word about his sister's pregnancy to anyone.

Do you understand me? his mother asked. Not a soul.

He put on his hat and his Beetlejuice backpack and went out the front door. He got as far as the end of the street, then he turned and plodded back to the house and rang the doorbell.

Except? he asked.

What does *not a soul* mean? his mother asked.

Does that mean I can't talk to Heather about the baby?

Heather knows she's pregnant.

She's a soul. Or Dad? Or you? Can I talk to the baby about the baby? Is the baby a soul? Can I talk to the baby without talking to Heather? Does the baby share a soul with Heather? Can I—

Hendrix! His mother clamped his shoulders. Do, not, tell, any, body, you, see, today, about, the, baby. Got it?

Then she spun him around and sent him down the street in an enormous soap bubble of silence.

19.   THE PARTS OF A LETTER, A CLASS ASSIGNMENT   *Hendrix*

Dear Army,

How are you? I am fine. Are you still cuting hair? I made it to level 5 of double dragon. You have to click back fast when the guy throws ~~die~~ dynamite. How's Dad? Something hapened to Heather but I cant tell you what.

Sincerely,

Hendrix

20.   SHE SAID   *Heather*

Heather said, I can't talk long, but she was saying she was pregnant. She said, Are you alone? but she was saying she was pregnant. She said, Even if your cast is off, your ankle's gonna hurt every time it rains, but she was saying she was pregnant. How much clearer could she be? When she finally said, I'm pretty sure I'm pregnant, she was saying, Do you think I'm a slut?

21.   HE SAID   *Army*

With incredible longsuffering, Army endured the eons it took Felicia to remove her shoes when she came home. Before she could place them on the shoe rack, he burst.

Heather's pregnant, he said, but really he was saying, Heather's pregnant.

22.   WORD TO YOUR MOTHER   *Skinnyboy*

Skinnyboy had heard from Diane who heard from Army that Heather was pregnant. Skinnierboy had too.

Among themselves, they didn't entertain the possibility that it could be one of them.

She used to follow me around work, Skinnyboy said.

Yeah, she used to flash her tits for money, Skinnierboy said.

She was a ssslut, they said.

Nevertheless, Skinnyboy very hastily joined the Reserves.

23.   GUITAR   *Skinnyboy*

After Skinnyboy enrolled in Royal Military College and moved to Kingston, the church needed a new guitarist.

Old dude subs in from time to time, Skinnierboy said. Heather's dad. I'm gonna quit Praise Team.

24. SHOULDN'T BE   *Oliver*

The current topic under discussion between Oliver and the ex-wife was where Heather should have the baby. Where not whether. Ideally, she should be sent to a girls' school in upstate New York and come back thin in a poodle skirt and a tiny chiffon scarf around her neck with her arms empty.

She shouldn't be having a baby, Oliver said.

And that made the ex-wife disagree immediately. Heather would have the baby.

Oliver meant *shouldn't be* differently.

25. IT'S ABOUT TIME   *Oliver*

If Heather had the baby in Brampton she'd become a proverb to all the kids on the street, causing Oliver's stock to descend into white trash, and Oliver didn't want that.

If she had the baby in Leominster, her whole school, all the neighbours, her mother's conservative friends, would know, and the ex-wife didn't want that.

It's about time people knew the kind of father you are, the ex-wife said.

Don't start on me. The high-pitched whine of Oliver's tinnitus broke into his consciousness. This is not something you want to start.

Time people knew the level of utter ineptitude I was putting up with. I sent Heather to you for one summer and you send her back knocked up like a Jersey cow.

She was pregnant when she got here.

It never ceases to amaze me how unfit you are for fatherhood, she said.

This happened on your watch, not mine.

For fatherhood, yes, *and* also for marriage and manhood generally.

26. ADOPTION OPTION   *Oliver*

Oliver and the (not *his* but *the*, because she was nothing to him) ex-wife were undecided about whether Heather should give up the baby for adoption.

You don't throw your children away, the ex-wife said, intending, no doubt, to land an uppercut.

I didn't throw my children away, he said.

No one said you did, the ex-wife said. You're always so defensive.

You took them from me, Oliver said.

Let's not get off topic, she said. But Oliver could hear in her voice that she was satisfied.

27. DISCLOSURE   *Oliver*

The ex-wife said she was not going to tell the father (as Heather identified him) about the baby.

Oliver said some of what he was thinking: Because you don't want to be the one to ring their doorbell and sit on their couch and look them in their married faces and tell them that their son knocked up your daughter like some black street thug.

I never called him a thug, she said.

I never said you did.

That's your language.

Oliver recalled her habit of clearing herself of blame. In the fifteen years they were married, she had never been wrong once.

It's unnecessary to blab any of this to anyone, the ex said, until Heather knows what she's going to do.

It's not Heather's decision.

I mean, as parents—you're still a parent, aren't you?—we have to decide.

And you don't think the boy has some say? You might be comfortable with deception but I certainly am not. *Jab.* How are you going to keep a man's child from him? *Jab. Jab.*

We're talking about a boy, not a man. Some men, though, never—

We are talking about doing the right thing, Oliver said. Believe it or not, some of us have principles.

28. UNTIL HEATHER KNOWS WHAT SHE'S GOING TO DO   *Oliver*

They decided that Heather would return to Canada, where it was free to have the baby, after Christmas.

Why *after* Christmas? Oliver asked.

The divorce agreement clearly states—

I know what *the divorce agreement clearly states.* I just don't see why the two of them can't come for the holidays if she has to come anyway.

No one said anything about Hendrix.

Oh, come on!

The divorce agreement clearly states that both children will spend Christmas—

But we're talking about exceptional circumstances.

What happened to Heather does not change my right to spend Christmas with my children, so Heather will not be travelling until Sunday, January 8, and Hendrix will be back in school on the ninth. End of story.

You don't decide end of story.

The courts decided.

Through similarly arduous point-by-point fighting, they decided that Oliver would home-school Heather for the winter semester, aka the final trimester, that she would be kept indoors when she started showing, that she would return to Leominster in the fall to finish her last year of high school, and that she would apply to a state college for Nursing.

29. WHAT ABOUT HENDRIX?   *Ex*

Oliver tried again. Then you have to send Hendrix for March Break.

Says who?

You can't separate them for so long, Oliver said. A boy needs his father.

End of story, the ex-wife said. You're not taking Hendrix to your strip clubs.

I never. How did that—

And you will never.

30. OPTIONS   *Hendrix*

While his mother and father were debating whether Heather should keep the baby or not, Hendrix, who was on the *not* side, suggested feeding the baby to ants. The ants could eat the baby and leave no trace at all, but he'd need African army ants for that.

31. PROVERBS 6:6–8   *Hendrix*

Let us read responsively.

⁶ Go to the ant, thou sluggard; consider her ways, and be wise:

⁷ Which having no guide, overseer, or ruler,

⁸ Provideth her meat in the summer, and gathereth her food in the harvest.

It said right there, right?

32. DOUBLE DRAGON   *Hendrix*

Hendrix was not allowed to play his handheld video game for two days because of his modest proposal. He was on the brink of beating Level 6 when his privileges were taken away.

That's no way to talk about your sister, his mother said.

You called her a Jersey cow and no one took away your—he scanned her—your fingernails.

Three days, the ex-wife said. You want to keep going?

But I didn't call her anything. And here Hendrix began crying. I was talking about the baby.

33. FALL   *Edgar*

Edgar spent his fall in a boardroom facing male lawyers, public relations consultants and boardmembers, then in Berlin facing his brother, who was putatively male, and now on a train facing an unbelievably blond teenager.

I sometimes look at kids on the street and think they might be you.

They might be.

So blond that it took Edgar a morning of furtive inspections to figure out the gender. Right now, he was going with male.

34. HIS/HER   *Edgar*

No, female.

In the aftermath of the harassment allegations, but before the enforced leave of absence, the board mandated that Edgar complete a course in sexual sensitivity (their words), a course that Edgar blamed for messing up his most basic perceptive and intuitive skills.

For example, he caught himself saying to a friend, an escort friend whom he no longer slept with, not really, I like a beautiful woman, same as everybody else, but the important thing is that he or she gets me, you know.

There was a microexpression of concern across the friend's face.

A woman, Edgar clarified. I'm not froufrou.

I understand, the woman said.

A female woman, he said to make sure.

I got it, Edgar.

But he wanted to be absolutely certain. Feminine.

35. ø   *Edgar*

The blond teenager was already seated when Edgar boarded so there was no opportunity to evaluate his or her voice or movements for confirmation of his or her gender. S/he was reading a book where one of the letters on the cover had an o with a slash through it. So s/he was either a ghostbuster or Danish.

And therefore male or female.

Edgar felt he should err on the side of female.

36.   ALTHOUGH ARMY WAS FORBIDDEN TO SPEAK TO HIM   *Edgar*

Edgar often heard Army's voice in his head. How did you end up here?

Well, I'm nowhere yet. I'm in transit.

No, I mean, how did you end up being such a sorry wreck of a man?

Thank you, Army. Thank you very much.

Plain talk, bad manners.

But, yeah, I've never been up north. Change of scenery. Fresh air.

Don't you smoke?

Used to. I've quit. More or less. I'm considering it. The plain gendered teenager began eating from a plastic bag of granola. Maybe s/he was a horse. And to answer the real question, I'm here because I wanted to be alone for a while.

Don't you live alone?

37.   BETWEEN SOLITUDES   *Edgar*

I mean, you're not a total train wreck, Boss.

I'm doing all right.

More like a car wreck.

It's just a little rough patch.

Yeah? Things went downhill after you got the boot.

I'm on a leave of absence.

Getting away for a month in Berlin was supposed to be good for Edgar's psychic realignment. Change of scenery. Fresh air. Five years ago, his brother had divorced his second wife and married a woman much like the first two, with a trickle of royalty in her veins. Good thing Edgar didn't invest in getting to know the first couple of wives or the two children from the second marriage. When he arrived at his brother's house, he offered his new nephews chocolate eggs he had bought at the airport.

Gender neutral, Edgar pointed out. *Kinder Überraschung.*

His new sister-in-law made the children thank him. Edgar told her it was sexist to have only male children. His brother told Edgar he smelled worse than a fruitcake. Edgar told him he was getting fatter than Vater. By evening, his nephews were sneaking up on him, tagging him, then running away, shrieking, Drunkle, Drunkle. (Edgar had had a sip or two on the flight.) And by night, Edgar was tired of the children.

Seems to be a pattern.

I'm not tired of you.

I'm waiting for it.

Yet.

There we go.

After a week of *Drunkle-Drunkle!* and *Fatter-Vater!* and the blunt life-planning of his brother, Edgar and his brother got into a nasty fight. It began unremarkably. At dinner, his brother criticized rosé as a *Mischling* drink. Pick one, red or white, he said, but don't suck the teat of a halfbreed. Edgar bit down. The riff to the Final Countdown began. The brother told him he would create a position for him to manage a couple of regional airport stores in Eastern Europe now that the wall was down or, better, he could give him a portfolio of airports through Greece and Turkey, a portfolio that Edgar knew his brother planned to axe in a few years, so Edgar could run the division into the ground if he liked and retire at that point or go back to Canada once the Canadian branch had rehabilitated its image but Edgar declined both offers and his brother kept insisting until they were shouting at each other and Edgar was digging up all sorts of family bones and inventing Emersonian quotes under the auspices of translating them into German, and alas the next day Edgar packed his travelbag from the seventies to much headshaking from his brother and politeness from his sister-in-law who dressed the children and instructed them to bid Uncle farewell while she took photographs for the album. His brother dropped him off at Lehrter Station. Edgar called him a Bolshevik, which sounded to him like an appropriate insult to part with, and his brother called him a Gypsy, which Edgar didn't mind.

Inside, Edgar promoted the ticket vendor to a travel agent. Throw something together for me.

Just anywhere?

Amsterdam maybe. He'd grow his hair out and wear a gold glam suit. Or no—north. He said, As far north of Germany as you can. Three weeks. A big circle that gets me back to Tegel. And he gave the agent the date of his return flight to Toronto.

So the travel agent booked him a ticket north to Hamburg then farther north through Denmark. From there, Edgar intended to take a boat across the North Sea, another train up to Oslo then east to Stockholm then south again to Copenhagen and back to Germany, drinking moderately all the way.

Well, that was better than what I was doing.

Which was?

Worrying.

Sweet, but—

Not about you, Boss.

38. NEVER AGAIN *Edgar*

When the blond gathered up his or her grey belongings to leave, Edgar felt a gust of disappointment pass through his lungs. The train was nearly empty. The tone of the car converted itself from German to Danish and as he travelled through his itinerary he became, if it were possible, more silent.

The trains were better than the cities. He didn't want to do anything touristy.

The highlight of his misadventures through Scandinavia occurred in Stockholm. He was rummaging through a display bin outside of a gift shop in Gamla Stan, the old town, when he saw two black men, first their heads over the incline then their bodies approached, then their shadows. They were very conspicuous. Together they appeared formidable, walking toward the sun. Taller than Edgar. Thin too. He'd describe them as giraffey but the sexual-sensitivity-trained Edgar would not. Edgar poked around the bin until the men came close. He was sure that they'd recognize him, not with the electricity that he beheld between black strangers but as a fellow foreigner, perhaps with a nod. He scattered his mind for a pretext to stop them. The time. Directions. He could trip them. Nothing seemed appropriate. So they passed him. He trailed them for a while and still could not find a reason to stand between the pair. Were they brothers? How did they end up here? Did they speak English? They seemed more African than American. Could he say that? He didn't know what was reasonable anymore. The sexual-sensitivity course said he should ask a woman if she wanted to be addressed as Miss, Mrs. or Ms. Then they entered a dollhouse, the Negroid men of African ancestry, and Edgar continued through his itinerary without seeing another primarily Congoid person of colourful, African, or mixed ancestry until he reached the airport in Toronto.

39. HO HO HO *Edgar*

He spent Christmas in a hotel room on Lake Louise.

His brother's wife had encouraged him to return to Germany for Christmas but Edgar found himself saying into the phone that he already had plans to spend the holiday skiing in Banff with a woman. The lie got more and more elaborate to the point where he bought new Völkl skis and flew to Alberta.

He went skiing one day. That was enough. On Christmas Day itself, he slipped out of the hotel around noon as if he were heading to visit family for dinner then he hiked one of the closed trails, smoking and calculating how high up he was from the lake. When he got to the top, he cleared a log of snow, sat, smoked a cigar and ate the pack of M&Ms he had brought for lunch. The rest of Christmas, he watched TV on low volume in his room, mixed experimental ratios of red and white wine, and ate from among the assorted snacks he had prepared, for he didn't want room service or the hotel staff to think he was spending Christmas alone in a hotel room.

40. ARE YOU THE LEAF, THE BLOSSOM OR THE BOLE?   *Edgar*

What are you getting me?

What I wanted to get you didn't quite work out.

Nothing seems to work out for you.

You are a life-vest to a drowning man, Armistice.

And why should he get Army anything for Christmas after the way Felicia had forced the boy to deracinate their blossoming chestnut tree?

They made their choice. During the summer, Edgar had acquired a list of traditional anniversary gifts, and painstakingly selected gifts for Army because he assumed that Felicia was grooming the boy into a chippy British butler. Year 1 was paper, year 2: cotton, 3: leather, 4: fruit, 5: wood (he considered a Frost poem for this one), 6: candy, 7: wool, 8: bronze, 9: willow (a hassle), 10: tin (at a loss), 11: steel, 12: silk (maybe for a little Liberace), 13: lace, 14: animals (he came within seconds of buying a dog), 15: crystal. Plus the mixtape.

For Christmas, if everything had gone according to plan, Edgar intended to give Army the ultimate gift. He would present himself. Make a present of himself. Be present. But their relationship was prematurely razed and sold to a developer. Yet if the thought counted, on Christmas he and Army hiked up a snowy mountain trail side by side.

41. MIXTAPE   *Army*

Army planned (and would forget) to bring his Walkman to the hospital so Heather could listen to the Quiet Storm while having the baby. *You give me, you're giving me the sweetest taboo.* Or he could grab the mixtape from the car. He had made her a mixtape of his father's mixtape by dubbing Edgar's 60-minute mix on a 90-minute cassette and adding some songs of his own. Crystal Waters, Gypsy Woman, *la da di, la di da.* Deee-lite, Groove Is in the Heart. Nirvana, The Man Who Sold the World.

Later, in a letter to him, Heather wrote that it was hard to know where his father's songs ended and his began. Edgar had attempted to put some nineties music on there, at the end of side B. It was the most meaningful thing Heather had said to him to that point; it was exactly what Army wanted to achieve with his curatorial efforts.

It was hard to know where his father ended and he began.

42. CHRISTMAS 1978   *Edgar*

For better or for worse for Edgar every Christmas echoed Christmas 1978 for Edgar for better or for worse.

He remembered seven things about that Christmas.

1. He had willed himself to tell Felicia by December 31 that he was married so that they could go forward into the new year with their mouths open to snow.

2. He hadn't celebrated Christmas in years but Felicia discovered an artificial tree in the basement and pulled her what-kind-of-man-(in-this-case)-doesn't-celebrate-Christmas-especially-when-every-year-could-be-his-mother's-last trip. Together, they connected the three sections of the tree, fluffed the limbs to hide the space where the tree was joined, strung the lights and the fat, blue tinsel boas, hung candy canes and angels, threw out the broken balls, sprinkled tinsel into a gaudy mess, and crowned the tree with a gold star.

3. She placed two gifts below the tree. But then she removed the gift that was for him.

4. He bought her several gifts over a period of days. The first one, she wouldn't open. He opened it for her. The *Jackson 5 Christmas Album*. He shook it in front of her face. Nothing. He put it on the record player and within a minutes she was humming ruh-puh-pom-pom, ruh-puh-pom-pom, ruh-puh-pom-pom. A victory. Within a matter of days she should have been back to herself.

5. One evening, when he came home after dark, he found her sitting on the rug between Mutter and the flashing tree, painting her toenails. Her skirt was modestly arranged, her chin was on her knee. In that moment, he thought his eyes could hardly take more pleasure.

6. On Christmas Eve, she sat Mutter in the kitchen with a recipe book on her lap to supervise the cake making. She dressed Mutter in a red sweater and bejewelled her, combed out her white hair.

7. Most importantly and unfortunately, Felicia had served him a letter and she had herself in a fine tangle where she wanted to enjoy Christmas but was committed to her resolution to coldshoulder him.

43. TRAVEL   *Edgar*

The trick with travel was to have people believe that you were dashing off to clink glasses and have your photo snapped while they were eating leftover sludge from their trough. One should give the impression that one would be busy in a distant city, too busy to think about or call the leftbehinder.

In the seventies and eighties, when he was jetting across the continent, Edgar never spoke about the monotony: the gate numbers, the reserved strangers, the buttons on the hotel TV remote, the white sheets, towels, tiles, cards, smiles, handshakes, the numbing expenditures, revenue, projections, questions, explanations, on what basis.

Often he stayed at a hotel near the airport and because airports tend to be on the outskirts of cities, he had never, for instance, actually seen Winnipeg in close to twenty years, apart from the airport and his hotel.

44. PACKING HEAT   *Heather*

The nippy morning of her flight to Canada, Heather decided to pack some extra clothes. Minding her own business, she folded a couple of her old padded bras and stuffed them into the side of her suitcase. Her mother, not minding her own business, entered her room as she was struggling with the zipper.

Maybe we need to get you another bag, she said.

Because Heather was sixteen and the sort of highschooler who excelled in insinuation, passive aggression, cut-eye, grudge archaeology, and colourless odourless poisons, she understood her mother's *Maybe we need to get you another bag* as a comment on the size of her clothes.

45. THE KIND OF EXHAUSTING TEENAGE FIGHT THAT WAS
TURNING HER GREY   *Ex*

Everything I say is not an attack against you, Heather. You don't have to take everything so damn personally.

So how should I take it when you're talking right at me?

I'm talking to you, Heather, not about you.

You were too talking about me. You said, We need to get *her*. Who's *her*? Did Nefertiti join us?

You're your father's problem now, the greying ex said. She turned to leave Heather's room. I can't talk to you anymore.

Yeah, don't talk to me. You never talk to me anyway.

And so another grey hair was born.

46. XXL   *Hendrix*

Hendrix was in the doorway as his mother was leaving. Heather's room was plastered with posters of boys—Joey Lawrence, Kurt Cobain, Mario Lopez, Kirk Cameron, Luke Perry, Andrew Shue, Johnny Depp, David Duchovny, Ethan Hawke. The Soundgarden poster was covered over by Will Smith.

What? Heather shouted.

Do you have space for one more thing? he asked.

I'm not taking your hair back with me. You're so gross.

He sat on Heather's bed, lifted his shirt and pulled his Double Dragon game from the elastic of his trackpants.

It's for Army but you can play it too, he said. While you're waiting for the baby.

Heather took the game and squeezed it into her luggage. He wanted her to put it in her hand luggage but Hendrix hesitated to make suggestions. He always got punished. He pushed down on the top of her suitcase while she tried to inch the zipper closed.

As he was applying weight he had another suggestion but he knew better than to offer it: Wouldn't it make more sense for the fattest person in the house to sit on the suitcase and the person with skinniest fingers to work the zipper? Honest, he didn't say it but Heather scrunched up her face like she heard it somehow and was on the edge of tears.

47. EDGE   *Heather*

She realized Hendrix would no longer be the youngest Soares. He would get lanky and wear his pants sliding off his butt with a stud belt. He'd hole up in his room with a guitar, flicking his bangs out of his eyes and eating the hearts of girls from a cereal bowl.

48. HAIR   *Hendrix*

Heather hugged him in the airport. Did I feel fat just now?

Not everywhere. Hendrix tiptoed to get a better look. At least your hair's thin.

49. SOLO   *Army*

At the appointed time, Sunday, January 8, 1995, Heather arrived in Brampton. Army wanted to go to the airport with Oliver but he wasn't allowed. She's not family, Felicia said.

As an excuse to be the first person she saw when she arrived, Army shovelled the driveway, the stairs, and the sidewalk. When Oliver's truck pulled in, Army took off his toque and stuffed it in his pocket. Heather grinned from the front seat. Oliver tried not to smile at the reunion.

Army put away the shovel and swiped up his gift from the abandoned weight bench in the garage.

Mom said you need extra folate, he said. He handed Heather the multivitamins.

Felicia heard them arrive and came out wiping her hands on a dish towel.

Help her, Felicia said, and Army ran to get her suitcase.

50. HORMONES   *Oliver*

You don't look fat, Oliver told her.

I'm not fat?

That's what he said. He thought. It was a very confusing moment.

You expected me to be fat.

He expected her to look pregnant.

Pregnant is not the same as fat. Then as suddenly as they came, Heather's hormones turned like a flock of swallows or tiny fish that swim in glittering packs. You thought I'd come back here looking like Mom. That's what you wanted. So you could go around divorcing all the fat women.

51. DAMAGE CONTROL   *Felicia*

You not fat, girl, Felicia said and sat Heather down at the kitchen table. Don't listen to him.

I never said— Oliver began.

What you want to eat?

So I could get even fatter?

Heather's cheeks were moist and mottled red. Her bottom lip looked fuller than Felicia remembered. She had gained weight. On the small unrecognized island, it would be a compliment to tell Heather that she looked nice and fat now.

Without seeming to realize it, Heather took an avocado from the fruit bowl on the table and began peeling it with her thumbs. (Before Heather arrived, Felicia was reading yet another article about Jeffrey Dahmer, who was in the army, deployed to West Germany, discharged, worked in a delicatessen, then as a phlebotomist, then in a chocolate factory, before the cannibalism and all that.)

Army and Oliver exchanged looks and Felicia jumped in to save Heather's dignity. She sliced the avocado for Heather and sat down and ate half.

52. YOU'RE YOUR FATHER'S PROBLEM NOW.   *Hendrix*

Hendrix was allowed to make the phone call to find out if Heather had arrived. Felicia answered. Do you want to talk to her?

No. Is Army there?

Army told Hendrix that Heather already had a fight with Oliver about whether she was fat or not. Hendrix told Army that Heather had that fight all the time. Last night when she was packing, she said that none of her clothes fit anymore, that they should just buy her tents to wear, that they should roll her around the house naked like a pot-bellied pig, that they should tie her to a tree outside then shoot her in the neck and eat her carcass since they all hated her so much. Did you get my gift? Hendrix concluded.

53. GIFT   *Army*

You have a gift for me? Army asked. He passed the phone to Oliver.

Multivitamins, Heather said.

In the nanosecond before he realized she was joking, his heart dipped, then he had an *aha*.

Touché, he said.

Pregnant Heather was scary.

54. TOUR   *Heather*

Army gave Heather a tour of her house. She would still sleep in her room, yes. He had his room downstairs, but also had an office upstairs in Hendrix's room. There were undelivered newspapers and envelopes requiring stuffing in there. His mother kept her room downstairs. Mr. O kept his upstairs. Felicia used the downstairs bathroom because she didn't want to clean up after Army anymore, so he and Mr. O shared the upstairs bathroom. The baby would be in Heather's room or the office.

I'm not keeping it, Army.

Pshh. Whatevs.

The kitchen upstairs was now the main kitchen and extra food was stored in the kitchen downstairs.

Really, Army, I'm— She didn't care one way or the other what happened to the piglet. On the floral couch, her mother had asked her what she thought and Heather had shrugged.

Give it thirty days, Army said. Moneyback guarantee. Including shipping and handling.

55. CHRISTMAS   *Heather*

Merry belated Christmas, Army said when he insisted they both take a multi-vitamin immediately.

She clinked her pill against Army's. Merry Christmas to you.

And Happy New Year! His spirits were indomitable but not contagious.

It's gonna blow, Heather said.

56. BILL   *Army*

The boundaries of the house had collapsed when Oliver destroyed the black door.

Army had suggested that Felicia and Oliver collapse the phone to a single line.

Nobody don't call you, Mr. O.

My sisters—

Apart from pity calls. Anyway, we upstairs most of the time anyway. You can't have me running down the stairs with a broken foot to answer the phone.

Felicia was against the idea. She kept the line downstairs while Army told his friends to call the upstairs number first then the downstairs number until he got permission to get a pager.

57. THE DOOR   *Edgar*

She almost always met him at the door like a dog.

He didn't care if he wasn't being sexually sensitive, but he liked knowing that while he was enduring the drudgery of work, Felicia was at home smelling perfume bottles on Mutter's dressing table and offering her tail to him.

He almost got one for his son, a dog, a little schnauzer mix.

58. OLD TIMES   *Army*

He and Heather talked in Heather's room the Sunday she arrived until Felicia had to physically remove him and apologize to Oliver.

Same thing the next night. And the next.

Felicia would order Army to his room, apologies would be made, then Army would call Heather and they would talk until Felicia had to pry the phone from his cold, dead hand.

59. SHE WAS BEST KNOWN   △

Sophie Fortin was found dead in her Beverly Hills home over the weekend. Early reports from the Coroner's Office indicate the cause of death as an overdose of prescription pain medication. A full toxicology report has been ordered.

60. THEY WERE BETTER KNOWN AS   *Heather*

The skinnier boy's name was Mason Reed. The boy who wore eyeliner was Dylan Kennedy.

Her whole life, Heather would never meet a Mason, Dylan, or Carter who wasn't a complete dick.

61. GRIEF   *Army*

It never came up during their internal phone conversations but for weeks after the fiasco between Skinnyboy and Heather, Army kept the garage door down. He ignored the bell. He shut down all his businesses and did his homework in front of the TV until Felicia came home.

The real betrayal wasn't so much that she had run off with Skinnyboy, whom Army considered blindfolding and executing with a single gunshot to the back of the head, but that all summer Heather was playing him for an inferior specimen. The duration of her duplicity was far more egregious than the climax of it.

62. THEY KEPT WORDS BETWEEN THEM   *Oliver*

Army never told Felicia that Oliver broke his foot.
Oliver never told Felicia that Army broke Heather.
But the two men kept their fingers on the red button.

63. FAMILY AND CLOSE FRIENDS ONLY   *Edgar*

When Sophie died, Edgar smoked a cigar, drank indiscriminately, and listened to records. In the morning, he awoke outside of his body, near the ceiling, with an aerial view of himself lying on the couch, records strewn all over the floor, the coffee table, two bottles on their side. Then the room spun back into his body.

When he learned about the memorial service for her in Toronto, Edgar got himself cleaned up, put on a black suit, and tried to enter the service. But the funeral director, more bouncer than funeral director, stopped him.

May I help you?

Private funerals Edgar had heard of but not private memorials.

May I help you?

Yes, excuse me, Edgar said.

It's private.

Private?

The bouncer said he would pass on his condolences to the family.

Pass on?

Tell me your name.

Arthur, Edgar said.

He heard the organ music as he was leaving. How strange that the organist would play Here Comes the Bride, he thought, before realizing that it was actually the same rhythm as Chopin's Funeral March.

64. FOUND DEAD IN HER   *Felicia*

She slipped in church the week after Sophie was discovered and instead of *grace*, sang, 'Twas grief that taught my heart to fear.

65. EVANGELISM   *Army*

I got baptized, Army told Heather.

Oh you've become [one of those people].

Saved, sister. I'm trying to get Mr. O to give his life to the Lord but he likes them strippers too much.

Ew. Don't tell me stuff like that.

66. INCENTIVE   *Army*

I told the outreach department that their missionary strategy was played out. Like these days you got to incentivize. If they gave me a hundred bucks for each person I brought into that church, I'd have it full every week. A thousand if I make the conversion. But they thought I was joking, like.

67. THE HOUR   *Army*

What bought Army an hour on the phone some nights was that he shouted back at Felicia that he was telling Heather about Jesus.

Well, tell her fast. You have school in the morning.

Every time he heard Felicia's footsteps nearing his door, he'd abruptly switch mid-sentence to a point from church, beatitudes, how he occasionally does the Scripture reading, most recently Hosea 8:7—For they have sown the wind, and they shall reap the whirlwind—but they don't ask him to pray anymore after he denounced the poor-in-spirit for their poverty. He kept his Bible open next to him so it would appear to Felicia that he was referencing it.

The money he collected for a view of Heather was still inside. Purifying.

68. HOMESCHOOL   *Felicia*

Couldn't I just get homeschooled like Heather? Army asked at breakfast in February.

Army had always liked school, though. All those people around. Felicia remembered her own attempt at homeschooling, *Great Expectations* on a sofa. She couldn't imagine getting Army to read a book that long without a cocked gun at his head.

I gots companies to run during business hours.

69. MERCIES   *Felicia*

Felicia thanked the Lord that the baby was not Army's. Or hers.

70. THOSE WHO CAN'T HEAR WILL FEEL   *Christian Lady*

 If I was you, I not going back by any man who treat he mother so. Job or no job, Christian Lady had said to Felicia. I was young too, girl. You going to mess up your life if you set foot in that man house again.

71. WARNINGS   *Felicia*

I don't want you fathering this baby, Felicia told Army.

I'd kinda need a time machine, Army said.

Don't take this for joke. When the baby born, I don't want you acting like the child father. Heather make she bed and she certainly done lie in it.

72. DO NOT DISTURB   *Edgar*

While the others were approaching March Break, Edgar was downing rosé fortified with a touch of crème de cassis in the same hotel where he spent Christmas.

Edgar glugged wine from the same bathroom glass that he used to rinse his mouth.

73. MARCH BREAK   *Oliver*

The week before March Break, Hendrix called. Did Heather have the baby yet?

No, Oliver said. What's your mother saying about March Break?

Nothing.

Don't you want to see Heather and the baby?

I thought you said she didn't have the baby.

Well, inside of her.

I can't see inside her. Anyway, Mom said it was too late to buy a ticket.

I drive.

I know.

Put your mother on the line.

Can I talk to Army first?

After. Call your mother.

Tell Army I was thinking that Heather should have twins so that when the baby goes to the orphanage it would have a brother already.

74. CARRIAGE   *Oliver*

Oliver was thinking of a way to get Hendrix to Canada for a week. He was not worried about Heather, except in the low-frequency hum that he was always worried about Heather, because the only thing that could happen eight weeks before the due date would be a miscarriage.

75. TRADITION   *Edgar*

It was the same hotel where he spent Christmas for the last several years actually, sometimes alone, sometimes with a friend of the female persuasion.

76. FUN FACT   *Edgar*

If you drink before bed, you don't need to brush your teeth as alcohol serves as a mouthwash. A health benefit, see.

77. BEANS   *Heather*

She kept telling Oliver to shut up because he talked nervously every time she had a contraction. He didn't think it was happening. He thought it was the red beans, why did Felicia like cooking them so much if they just gave everybody gas. It's early, isn't it? I mean it's getting late, it's almost what time is it, it's not time yet, try to sleep. So clueless. She got up and was chewing ice in front the open freezer door. She went downstairs to knock on Army's door, Oliver tailing her, spouting theories, and Felicia

78. GOOD OL' FELICIA   *Felicia*

took one look at Heather, sweating, sucking an ice cube, hair sticking to her forehead, the vibration in her eyes, top of her nightshirt wet, and told Army to call an ambulance.

Now, Army. Call an ambulance.

Oliver was jibberjabbering nonsense:

79. JIBBER JABBER   *Oliver*

Are you sure because we still have a couple of months before anything happens I mean something should happen first no there's a sequence to these things you can't just decide (the boy came out with his hands in the pockets of his sweatpants to hide his boner) and if this was it then you wouldn't be able to walk your mother she was a mess she still is but you're just take an aspirin and go to sleep and if the pain comes back in the morning we'll go to the doctor to see what's going on

80. WHAT'S GOING ON   *Felicia*

Felicia pulled Heather's hair up and fastened it in a high ponytail atop her head. Then she took Heather by the upper arm and walked her up and down the hallway.

I want to sit down.

No, walk, walk.

Heather squeezed her eyes shut and grimaced. Her legs went slack and Felicia held her up.

Army, call an ambulance.

Mind your business, dammit, Oliver said and pried Felicia's hands off Heather and looped his neck under Heather's armpit for support.

Then Oliver looked around for his keys and Felicia knew where they were but did not bring them for him.

81. CURLERS   *Army*

If he think he can handle it, let him handle it, Felicia said. Is his child, not mine.

Army opened his eyes wider.

If we go, we not staying long. You have school in the morning.

It's March Break.

Still. You finish reading *Macbeth*? I don't see you reading anything.

Hurry up. Army held Felicia's keys while putting on his boots. She was taking out her curlers.

He want act like a big man, Felicia said, let him take care of his daughter if that is how he want to get on.

Army started taking out her curlers but she pulled her head away. Then he dropped a scarf on her head and pushed her by the shoulders to the front door, like a snowplough.

The minute they were in the Brampton hospital parking lot, he opened the car door and ran to the entrance. Felicia called after him.

82. TRACK   *Felicia*

She had a good mind to sit in the car and remove the rest of her curlers but the boy bolted, so she followed him with her hair covered, half in curlers, half out, praying she didn't see anybody from work or church.

She could see Army in the light beyond the automatic doors, looking both ways before running left.

83. SQUATS   *Oliver*

Heather banged on the dashboard, on the seat, on the handles. She gripped the handbrake and pulled it up. At a red light she ordered him to go. She elbowed the door. She took off her seat belt and leaned forward.

There was a sound like a wet fart and then Heather looked down at her thighs.

Then she raked her hands in her hair in aggravation.

Oliver pulled over to the shoulder.

Just drive, Dad, what are you doing?

But his truck, the seat, maybe she could do some of that outside, not that his truck was important right now but maybe she could just—

I'm not having the baby in the woods.

Of course not. I— Don't you want to, like, squat it out? Make sure you get it all out. I don't know. I'm trying to help you, Heather.

Heather screamed and whipped her head from side to side until Oliver pulled off the shoulder and sped the rest of the way to the hospital.

84. WRONG   *Army*

Army couldn't find Heather or Oliver in Emergency and he couldn't just walk to the back.

The receptionist checked her computer. No Heather Soares had been admitted.

What about Oliver Soares? Army asked. He's the dad. Not the dad-dad, but her dad.

The triage nurse shook her head. Sorry. Are you sure you're at the right hospital?

85. A PLAGUE OF DIVORCE   *Felicia*

Of course. Oliver had refused the Brampton hospital after Felicia told him about a series of deaths from a meningococcal outbreak. Four children in all who were there for other longterm but treatable illnesses until beds opened up at Sick Kids ended up dying because of their parents' postal code.

86. HEADING BACK HOME   *Felicia*

She had taken Army back home once when he was nine. It was for her father's
funeral. It was the only time Army had been on an airplane. He kept watching
the gate to see the pilot then he turned to her when they crossed with their black
wheelbags, holding coffee, laughing with the stewardesses, he turned to her but
did not say anything.

87. THE SMALL UNRECOGNIZED ISLAND   *Felicia*

was largely unrecognizable in the capital and around the coast. In the eleven
years she had been gone, Germans had come over and bought up the beachfront
property, built hotels and casinos and docked their cruise ships nearby like goats
tied to a tree.

In her village people cursed the Germans for taking over and Felicia joined
in. They knew everything about Germans, down to the way they held cups for
their mothers to spit blood into. The islandfolk cursed their government for selling them into slavery, although some were happy their children could get jobs at
the hotels. They talked a lot about the sagging triceps of German women.

88. WHITES ONLY   *Felicia*

Felicia tried to take Army to the beach although her sisters told her the beach
was now private. She went. Sure enough, one of her own people, a boy she went
to school with came out and said she couldn't use the beach but he was friendly,
how you doing, you looking nice, and so on. When Army asked if he could use
the swimming pool, he said, Go ahead. Felicia went after him but her schoolmate
clarified, Because he's a child.

A white child? Felicia said.

Unashamed, the mate said, He go fit in.

Felicia called for Army and went back up the hill to the village.

89. REROUTED TO ST. XAVIER, FELICIA SENT EDGAR
     TELEPATHIC MESSAGES   *Felicia*

Not once did you tame a baby's wild foot with a sock.

90. BY MYSELF   *Felicia*

I lined my eyes and lips carefully that day.

I dressed my irresistible in a snowsuit and hat. It was -24 degrees Celsius with
the windchill.

I curled an *S* in the front of his hair with baby oil.

I bought everything with my own money.

I lifted the stroller on and off the bus in the winter as you looped your Passat to and from the airport.

91. BY OURSELVES *Felicia*

We waited on your porch for a door to open.

I bounced Army on your unshovelled porch and stared at the door.

92. BY YOURSELF *Felicia*

You were in Calgary. You were in Geneva. You were in New York. You were in heaven because it was closer for your airplane.

93. BY MYSELF AGAIN *Felicia*

When it was clear that you were not home or would not answer the door, I looked up and down the street to see who saw us. Then I lowered Army back into the stroller and pushed it, with its one trick wheel, through dough.

I did all of this while you ambled around the world, shaking hands, men's hands.

94. THE USE OF DICTIONARIES IS PERMITTED DURING THE EXAM *Felicia*

When I lay the child down on the bed and unzipped his snowsuit, he looked up at me the *exact same way* as when I had zipped up his snowsuit, although you or I had failed him since then.

A baby teaches you the meaning of the word *regardless.*

95. CRY *Felicia*

Three months in, the child was supposed to drink two ounces of breast milk every three hours, but he drank four. He would not refuse her. He cried when he was gassy, or alone. He cried when he was sleepy and she'd pace the hallway with him, his ear feeling for her heart. He might cry when he needed to be changed or he might lie in his own feces smiling. She saw how other babies clenched their fists during bowel movements but Army always had soft hands that reminded her of a pigeon.

He smiled when he was smiled at. It was remarkable. Without any words, he kept talking to her. He said, Hey pretty lady, you're back. I thought you were gone forever. Don't go again. He said, Can we do that thing where I look at your face and you open your eyes really wide or that thing where you make all those sounds with your mouth? That's amazing. Or the one where you hold me against your chest—you so warm, lady—and breathe oceans until I fall asleep. How are your breaths so big? Haha, he said, you thought I said something else.

She studied Army as he slept. He slumped to his right if he fell asleep in his swing. He curled to the right in his crib. It was a good sign, her mother would have said. When he was about to wake up, he covered his eyes with his pigeon hands and kicked out his legs. Then she'd pick him up and he'd blink slowly and stick out his bum in her arms. Yeah, yeah, pretty lady. I'll be right with you.

96. BY OURSELVES AGAIN   *Felicia*

Felicia realized that after having Army, she'd never be alone again. Always a question about the baby. Who would watch him? Was he sleeping? Even a few years ago, when she worked at a post office inside a convenience store and had no one to watch him, she left him in the arcade next door, bleeding quarters from her. It was the cost of childcare.

97. HIGHWAY   *Army*

Do you want me to drive, Mom? Because you're only going, like, a hundred, Army said.

He wasn't sixteen yet, but he had already studied the Ministry of Transportation's driving handbook and cozied up to Oliver for shared use of the truck.

I'm going the speed limit, Felicia said.

It's the middle of the night. The road's clear.

Are you gonna pay the ticket?

And the speed limit doesn't apply if you're in an emergency situation.

Felicia didn't accelerate. Army rewound the mixtape to a seventies song and turned up the volume a touch and then Felicia sped up gradually so he wouldn't think it was because of him.

98. EVIDENCE   *Felicia*

Army did not resemble Felicia or Edgar in the watery way resemblances usually work. Instead, in the right light his face leapt forward exactly as Edgar's or as hers or in less light as her mother's or in darkness as Mutter's.

And one day when she picked him up from preschool, she found him gripping his wrists, like an ouroboros, his face set like Edgar's when he needed a cigarette.

Why are you standing like that?

Like what?

Like that.

He released his wrists and shrugged. You're late.

She wondered if she might have transmitted the gesture to Army unwittingly but she had never known herself to hold her wrists that way. From which gene is the adjusted figleaf position expressed?

99. EVIDENCE OF A SORT   *Felicia*

Fifteen gifts Edgar sent the boy last summer and not so much as a mint for Felicia.

In the car, she couldn't bear to see how carefully Army handled the tape, like an heirloom, how gently he turned the volume knob.

What about her daily work, meal after meal, day after day for fifteen years? What about the constant enforcement of nutrition, the presentation of growing portions as he pulled in his chair year after year?

Army still ate absentmindedly, like a child, without a thought of where his food came from. But he was starting to sit and eat absentmindedly, like a man, with his mind elsewhere, on money.

100. MONEYMONEYMONEYMONEY! MONEY!   *Felicia*

What was it with these modern men and money? Felicia's father provided for eight of them without curbside trash or customized stationery. He set out in the morning and came home in the evening with fresh blessings by the day. So-and-so sent you some breadfruit, so-and-so say she lime tree bearing real nice, and her mother, before she migrated to become a domestic, would accept the Lord's provisions and lay them on the counter.

101. RESPONSIBLE   *Felicia*

In those days, Army may have been her sole responsibility but she was not solely responsible for him.

102. RESPONSIBLE MEN   *Felicia*

At the end of last summer, Felicia came home and found her son in a cast upstairs on Oliver's couch, the black door busted open.

I heard a crash in the garage, Oliver said, but the garage door was jammed and so I had to break down the black door to get to him.

He carried me up the stairs, Army said. Like one of them brides over the threshold.

103. EXIT   *Army*

Are you worried the baby's gonna die? Army asked. Felicia was driving as if she was falling asleep.

When are you going to Casa Loma? was Felicia's response. Did I sign that permission form?

I signed it for you. He could have lied but he could tell Felicia was in no mood to ride a high horse. I took the initiative, you know.

What about the money?

Well, you still have to pay twenty dollars. She looked over at him. Life and death are in the hands of God, she said.

So you think the baby's going to— Army hanged himself with an imaginary rope.

I don't know.

I'll bet you twenty the baby's gonna live. Twenty bucks on life. Come on, come on.

104. PROPOSITION   *Felicia*

Felicia did not accept Edgar's proposition to have another child. Nor did she not not accept it. She laid down two conditions to test his seriousness. He negotiated hard.

Why didn't he come with that nonsense eight, nine years ago when the boy was asking for a brother? And even then, she— Who knows what she would have done at the time for a roof of her own?

If he backed out of his sacred paternal duty once, he was capable of backing out again. Simple. But this time, Felicia would place her arms around the shoulders of her children, and she and her two boys (boys surely, though everybody needed sisters) would watch him drift away from their desert island. The three of them would look dangerous, as Army would say, their limbs agloss with Vaseline, a terrible serenity on their faces as his raft floated down a river of fire toward a cave. It was a vivid image in her mind. Edgar would be wearing cutoffs and his shirt would be in tatters. All beige.

105. THE SECOND   *Edgar*

She told him the first condition, which he reasoned was preposterous, and she got huffy and wouldn't tell him the second.

106. THIS IS NOT DENIAL   *Edgar*

One of Felicia's conditions was that he give up smoking.

His objection to that demand, as he explained it to her, had nothing to do with smoking itself but with the penance she expected him to pay. He pointed out that he did not even smoke a pack a day. He did not go broke buying cigarettes. Was smoking a problem if one could afford it? Did one have a cocaine problem if one could snort one's way through the Alps? The real problem behind drug addiction was poverty. Ergo Latin, Latin, Latin.

Since she was so interested in the subject, he told her that nicotine was a naturally occurring compound that had a number of health benefits unmentioned by the anti-tobacco propagandists. He could name ten right now if he wanted to. But that was beside the point.

Until she could understand his principled convictions against *not* smoking, he would not be yielding to that condition, no. Smoking was no different from making a phone call several times a day to someone you loved. *Cogito veni vidi vino e pluribus de facto rasa in vitro veritas et cetera.*

Remember I used to call you from work? he said.

Then Felicia got a soft look in her eyes, exactly what he wanted, yet he regretted the reminder and began talking about the candy cigarettes he and his brother pretended to smoke in their childhood.

107. NEITHER IS THIS   *Edgar*

He could stop any time.

He knew that sounded like the talk of a chronic smoker. But a non-smoker would say the same. So *ho-ho.*

In total control. And, purely hypothetically, even if he wasn't in control, so what? Was he in control of his breathing or his swallowing?

His relationship to cigarettes was just an autonomic bodily function she'd have to get used to again.

108. NOR THIS   *Edgar*

In the last few months before he went on leave from Paperplane, he had begun to break longer flights into multiple segments so that he could stretch his legs outside the terminal in the fresh air.

In advanced societies like Germany you could still buy cigarettes from vending machines.

109. DRUNKARD   *Edgar*

That was Felicia's word.

The drinking didn't seem to bother her as much, though. If he asked her to pick one—I either give up drinking or smoking—she'd pick smoking, which would be the greater sacrifice as he was not what people call a big drinker. He was a social drinker. Who drank only on special occasions. Which he usually celebrated alone.

The exception was when Sophie died and he drank hard for weeks. He drank until he recovered a memory of Sophie at a gas station in the Midwest, deveining a leaf on the trunk of his car. And another at the altar in Vegas, because it was a joke to her, kissing his forehead in holy matrimony.

110. RUM SHOPS VS. WINE SHOPS   *Edgar*

Felicia told him the most marvellous stories of rum shops. In a tropical, far-away land, men sat in sheds under the intermittent breeze from an electric fan, watching a little mounted TV in the corner, reading newspapers, practicing politics, and drinking away their family money.

He would drink crystal, drink ruby, drink amethyst, drink amber, drink onyx. Drink all Mutter's jewellery.

There was a privately owned liquor store that he enjoyed visiting in Toronto and a better one in Calgary. The one in Calgary had wines laid out in nooks like future closets for rich women's shoes. Dark bottles. Standing, lying in geometrical mosaic patterns from a Turkish mosque.

The store was owned by either a Spanish man or a blonde woman who employed either a blonde woman or a Spanish man. They sorted the store by region. One could walk from North America to Chile to Argentina to Portugal to Spain to France to Italy to Australia to New Zealand within a few feet.

111. PROVERBS 20:1   *Felicia*

Wine is a mocker, strong drink is raging: and whosoever is deceived
thereby is not wise.

112. SOMETIMES THE ONLY   *Edgar*

He was on a first-name basis with the Spanish man and the blonde woman. They shipped him wine and cards of thick toothy paper at Christmas.

The quality of the postcard paper impressed him as did the quality of the pen used as did the class and gossamer of their humour.

But the bass note of their friendship, if he could call it that, was the money, thousands, he had spent travelling the globe in their store.

113. PAIRINGS   *Edgar*

While the blonde woman had excellent recommendations about wine pairings, she missed its more adventitious combinations with Mars, Reese's, Caramilk, Crunchie, Bounty, Crispy Crunch, and of course M&Ms.

The Spanish man and blonde woman would make a good couple. He teased them gently together but had spoken seriously to each of them separately. When he spoke to the blonde woman, she thought that he might be asking after her status because he himself had interest in changing it. He noted her disappointment as she frowned when he said the Spanish man's name.

Edgar could see himself swirling and smelling his way through Europe with this blonde woman. She'd wear a broad-brimmed hat and he'd monitor the tan on her shoulders. But there was something vulgar (ah, Sophie, why'd you act out your life to the end?) about her. For example, the day he cast the Spanish man as her love interest, she tested one of Edgar's large bills for counterfeit then lifted up the drawer of the cash register to hide it. Did she suddenly think he was some kind of criminal? This was not a cheap American liquor store, darling.

114. INTEREST   *Edgar*

Felicia never held his bills up to the light or questioned his cheques, until recently. Edgar recalled her confidence in his finances while leaning against the hotel headboard. He could leave his bank book lying around and she would treat it no differently from a misplaced sock. If he had shown it to her, she would not have understood where all his money was. She might have expected more money in his chequing account.

And, bless her little heart, Felicia was so proud to have her first savings and chequing accounts. Solemnly, she told Edgar how the woman in the bank explained to her that one made more interest than the other. *She* tried to teach *him* something about money.

115. GREEN   *Army*

Seriously, Mom, if you don't drive this car like a winged demon is chasing us, I'm going to take the wheel.

They were off the highway. The light was about to turn green, Army calculated. Felicia glanced at him. Did you change that undershirt all week?

Army looked down at his chest, exasperated. I guarantee you that whatever you're worried about right now is wholly unimportant given the fact that Heather's baby is busting up through her guts. Green.

I don't see what so hard about putting on a clean undershirt every two days? It's green. Focus!

116. RELENTLESS   *Felicia*

Felicia had not gone a day since meeting him without at least one, and if one then at least a dozen, thoughts of Edgar.

Sometimes the thought was, I have not thought of Edgar today, and that thought would itself count as a thought of him.

117. TULIPS, CERTAINLY   *Felicia*

She could have been the wife of a good man if it wasn't for Edgar. And now, Felicia thought, Heather's chances of a respectable marital bed, high thread counts, floral curtains, floral gardens, were dashed. Or maybe not. She was white.

Felicia signalled her turn into the hospital parking lot.

Wouldn't it be good to plant a tree, plant flowers on her own soil? The simplicity of wanting to drop a seed, a bulb, a sapling into the ground and wait for it year after year to open its arms up in praise of our Lord. Year after year, to grow taller and outward, but not away. Even Army would leave her at some point, no? The kind of boy he was, he'd leave her at eighteen, go panning for gold dust in a creek.

Army's eyes were red.

You should have slept while I was driving, she said.

Both of us couldn't be sleeping.

Felicia steupsed.

Jokes, jokes. I'd never do that to you.

118. LASHES   *Felicia*

It is one of the arbitrary cruelties of the universe that women never had eyelashes as lovely as little boys.

Little Army was a lamb in church. He would slide close, lift her arm and place it around him. Nobody had to teach him that. He centred himself in her attention so innocently as if he didn't know who she was and under what circumstances he arrived on God's green earth.

119. JOYFUL, JOYFUL, WE ADORE THEE   *Ex*

Such a lovely tone she had, something out of a forest. And that attentive look with the clarinet's mouthpiece tucked behind her upper teeth and her lips curled—what happened to that Heather?

120. FAIR QUESTION   *Felicia*

Would Felicia trade Army, return him to as-if-he-never-were, if she could marry Coweyelash from the island and sleep on half of a respectable marital bed? Would she trade Army for other DNA, well behaved, attentive, neat DNA?

121. CORRECT ANSWER   *Felicia*

No, Felicia could not leave Army floating in space, in the purgatory of not being. He would be conscious out there in the cold, a giant baby among the stars, looking at her on earth and setting his face like Edgar when she was laying down the first condition.

This must be what it meant to have no regrets. Yet she had some. She didn't regret the child. She regretted the father. Minus the hair.

122. OB-LA-DI, OB-LA-DA   *Felicia*

She had to get her hair done.

Colour this time. Felicia liked to lighten the shade—not that she wanted to look white, but she did need to look like she could be Army's mother.

123. THERE WERE NO SIGNS TO THE DELIVERY ROOM   *Army*

They won't be in Emergency, Army.

Of course they will.

Emergency is not for that. We have to go up to maternity.

Walk, walk, walk. He dragged her until she was half running. Her guts are probably everywhere by now.

They found Oliver sitting alone in a waiting room, bouncing his leg. The room was unusually calm and dim for a hospital. Army looked around. He expected fathers biting their nails.

Slow night, Oliver said when he saw them.

Did she have the baby? Army asked.

You're not in there with her? Felicia asked.

Oliver shook his head.

But she's in labour? Army checked.

So-so, Oliver said.

Did they say you can't go in or something?

No, that's not it.

It was either slap Oliver across the face or bolt.

Army, no— was the last thing he heard but he was through the doors already.

124. MISCARRIAGE   *Oliver*

He was no obstetrician but he was a father and he suspected that Heather was early because she had tried to abort the baby.

There was no baby behind the doors. Oliver was sure he should feel some larger metaphysical grief, but he felt only personal loss.

If there was to be no baby, only a red pool of floating doll parts, did that mean that Heather would return to school in Leominster after March?

125. RELATIVE   *Oliver*

The nurse escorted Army outside. She spoke to Felicia as if she were Heather's mother. Oliver didn't correct her. Heather was entering active labour, according to the nurse. Dilated five centimetres. Oliver had no reference point, despite having two children.

Army presented himself as the brother but the nurse said that given the patient's circumstances, the premature baby, the sensitivity of the situation, they would allow only one person into the room—the father of the child if he was available.

Felicia gave Army a look that stopped him. Oliver waited for him to change his story.

An adult, the nurse punctuated.

In Heather's case, given her age, the mother's mother would be welcome. The child's child was in a precarious situation so the doctor wouldn't want a thoroughfare. The nurse addressed that point to Army. It's hard to know what the baby's chances are at the moment.

The nurse handed Felicia a gown and a mask. To Army and Oliver she said, Make yourselves comfortable.

Felicia was swallowed up by the doors and Oliver and Army paced outside and watched TV and awaited her updates.

126. COMPLEXION   *Oliver*

Although he had a niggling suspicion, he'd wait and see how dark the baby came out before jumping to conclusions.

127. LEAVE IT TO BEAVER   *Oliver*

And then, depending, he would castrate the boy with a cleaver and feed him his own balls.

128. VIABLE FETUS   *Heather*

There's a 50-50 survival rate for fetuses at this point, the Explainer explained to Heather and Felicia. Slightly better than 50 percent. You're still early in the third trimester. Even if the baby survives delivery, it's not out of the woods. Birth defects are common. We're looking at potential heart problems, low blood pressure, anemia, infection. We'll put it on a respirator. I'm not saying this to scare you, Heather, but I like my patients to know all possible outcomes.

Are those all the outcomes? Felicia asked.

Well, there are others. Cerebral palsy, autoimmune disorders, vision and hearing iss—

What about a normal baby? Heather asked between contractions.

Well, yes, there's that possibility too.

129. DISINFECTANT   *Felicia*

Serves him right, Felicia thought when she learned that Heather's water broke in Oliver's truck. He'd have to clean it, though she knew he would not clean it properly. He'd need rubber gloves and Dettol and a basin. He owned none of those things.

The story she heard: Oliver pulled over on the shoulder. Did you get all of it?

130. NAME   *Heather*

What should I name her? Heather had asked Army in their seconds together.

Or him, Army said. Pick a name that could go either way.

I think it's going to be a her though. Heather couldn't imagine having a boy inside her.

131. ARMIES   *Edgar*

I'm a mutt. But mostly German shepherd. The family's German, Polish. Some of them migrated and married so now we have British and Irish in the family. Cousins. We don't really speak to each other.

You're your own world war, Boss.

We get along. We just don't speak to each other.

Any Jews?

No.

So I guess I'm a mutt too.

More of a mutt than me.

Mutter than you.

132. CRYSTAL   *Felicia*

Felicia remembered Edgar's crystal doorknobs. She thought they were a nice touch. When she first moved there, she thought if she should ever own a house of her own, she'd like crystal doorknobs. She thought of sending a package home to the small unrecognized island.

She wanted to take the doorknobs the first time she left.

If Heather's baby was a healthy girl, Felicia would suggest the name Crystal.

133. CASH OR CHEQUE   *Edgar*

She used to send cash to her father on the small unrecognized island but Psychoanalyst Edgar thought that she was really sending that money to her dead mother.

He told her that she should send her father a cheque. It was safer. But she said that her father wouldn't be able to cash a cheque on that small unrecognized island. She mailed him cash in her letters.

Her mother used to send cash in an envelope, Felicia told him.

Her sister said her father didn't exchange the Canadian currency for unrecognized currency. He liked the look of the Canadian bills. He showed it to the family when they visited as proof that she was doing well.

134. UPDATE   *Army*

Forty-five minutes later, Felicia emerged with an update: They'd given Heather some injections to help the baby. Steroids. And they put her on antibiotics as a precaution in case she was fighting off an infection.

Tell them to check if the baby's upside down, Army said. Health class was paying off.

I think we should leave the health advice to the professionals, Oliver said.

You have any money? It felt like millennia since Army had eaten.

135. NAMASTE   *Army*

Outside the canteen (open, surprisingly), Army said they needed to name the baby if the baby was to have any hope of living. It couldn't just lie around like no-name brand toilet paper.

136. NO NAME   *Felicia*

However, Felicia was adamant about not naming the baby. It would be too hard on Heather if she lost Crystal. She shouldn't look at the baby much, Felicia told Oliver. Life and death were in the hands of God, she said. She was praying for the baby, she said, for God's will to be done, she said.

She told Oliver all this while selecting refrigerated bagels. Army was going through her purse for change for the vending machine. She limited him to a dollar. He worked her over for $1.50.

137. FEMINISM   *Felicia*

Felicia didn't believe in all this women's rights business, but then again, she didn't know much about it as a theory.

All she knew was that every time she lifted a bag of soil or a case of printer paper she wondered why should she, a woman, be lifting this while men went around shaking each other's hands?

138. FEMINISM, IN PRACTICE   *Felicia*

She found her son a place to live, no? All these years on her own, the Lord prepared a gourd, and made it to come up over them, that it might be a shadow over their heads, to deliver them from their grief, while Army remained innocent of what it was to stand in front of a landlord, listening to him and thinking of the rent this paycheque and car insurance the next one, the phone bill this cheque and the cable bill the next. No, we cannot get Pay-per-view.

139. POVERTY   *Felicia*

Felicia may not know much about feminism but she knew a thing or two about the unconscious.

The barbershop, the barbecue, the gym, the other rackets she didn't know about, Army was making sure he would never tumble into what he feared most, what he smelled in her hair—poverty.

140. SO, YOU WERE IN THIS SITUATION BEFORE?   *Oliver*

Oliver knew he couldn't ask Felicia about Army's father unless he wanted to receive her thirty-day notice. Everything he knew, he knew from Heather, who knew from the boy, who knew nothing.

141. ACETABULA ET CALCULI MAGIC TRICK *Oliver*

Though, more or less, he already knew the story: Felicia was an unwed teen pregnancy. That happened a lot with her kind. There was a black girl in Heather's old school, same thing. The girl was fifteen.

Felicia was that girl in Heather's school. And now Heather was Felicia when she was that black girl.

142. MORE OR LESS *Oliver*

Felicia Shaw is a woman of secretarial age with a fifteen-year-old son. She is a woman who is also a black woman. Calculate her age when she got pregnant?

Let x represent Felicia Shaw's age when she had her son.
$x = a - b$ where a represents Felicia's current age and b represents Army's age
$x = a - 15$

143. SOLVE FOR X *Felicia*

A few moments after Felicia caught Oliver looking at her, he sidled up next to her with specious casualness as she was reading the expiration date on milk cartons.

If you don't mind my asking, he asked, how long you been at Brownstone?

Felicia shrugged. He was questioning her job security all of a sudden? He was going to increase the rent back to the original amount?

I mean, did you start right after high school or was there a training course or—

I did a program, yes.

That's what I thought. He coughed. And you must have stayed home with Army for a couple of years before that.

Until he went to school, yes. She figured out his game. Pathetic.

That's good. That's good. One more thing, if you don't mind my asking.

I'm going back up to Heather, she said and walked away.

144. SUBSTITUTION *Oliver*

$x = a - 15$
$x + 15 = a$
$x = (x + 15) - 15$
$x = x + 15 - 15$
$x = x$

∴ Felicia Shaw was x years old when she had Army.

Ding, ding, ding. Correct.

145. HE KNEW THE TYPE WELL   *Oliver*

Felicia had had sex with a boy in her high school. The boy was one of those scrawny, visibly virginal types in Grade II who grew two inches in height over the summer and became the plain girl's kryptonite. As a recent virgin, he was a fervent and mechanical lover. Like a busy signal. Felicia was his flat-chested lab partner who felt pretty and useful when he fondled her on his twin bed in the attic.

146. TOUCHED FOR THE VERY FIRST TIME   *Oliver*

When she told him she was pregnant, he kneed her in the stomach.

She doubled over, for although the boy was no longer a virgin he still had virgin dust in his hair and she did not expect such unvirginlike violence from him.

She was away from school the next day. And the next. He went to see if she was okay. She would not speak to him.

She did not return to school until he graduated. By then Army was weaned and she could leave him with her dead mother. That is, until her dead mother died and she left him with Christian Lady Army told Heather about. She took a typing course. Then she got a few temp jobs until Brownstone opened up, which meant $x = 31ish$.

147. THE RICH FATHER   *Oliver*

Right. There was that story from Army via Heather. His father was a count, a Rothschild, gold incarnate. Oliver snorted. That's why they were renting his basement. He had tried to talk to Felicia about it once when they were out for a walk but she put on her legal voice and he retreated. She was so secretive.

148. KNIGHT   *Oliver*

In a sense he had saved her from all the men who kneed her and her son. He set them up in relative luxury.

Last summer, after they moved in and he heard the gentle clatter of their lives downstairs he would find himself walking heavily in the clouds above them—he didn't know why he was doing this—or calling for his children and expressing irritation when inwardly he was bursting with happiness.

It was the happiest he had been in a long time, having his children without his wife. Even now, he'd prefer to have Heather close to him and pregnant than far away and menstruating.

149. UPDATE   *Felicia*

The next time Felicia came out to update Oliver and Army, Army was chattering in a sleep-deprived way and making a series of worrying connections.

I was a preemie too.

You were.

Tell him, Mom.

Thirty-two weeks.

Is that so? Oliver said.

Like Heather, Army said. I came out and they were like 50-50, blah-blah, and I was like, Watch me. And I was in the hospital, for, what eight weeks.

Until term.

Until term. And Mom slept in the hospital for eight weeks, pretty much, until I was like, We need to bust up outta this joint, pretty lady. You didn't even have baby stuff. You probably thought I was going to die.

I didn't.

Then Dad came and bought you everything.

That's enough, Army.

She took me home in her mother's handbag, I was so small.

Felicia stood up. She should get back to Heather.

She's all right, though? Oliver asked.

Heather's fine, for now. It's the baby they don't know about.

Tell Heather to hold it in until tomorrow.

She can't just hold it in, Oliver said.

Felicia left as they were bickering.

Just until midnight. We're almost there.

The baby's not a fart.

150. TOMORROW, TOMORROW   *Army*

Because tomorrow would be March 14, exactly six months away from Army's birthday, and Army believed that the fourteenth was the Valentine's Day, the sweet centre, of every month.

151. BLAME   *Army*

When Felicia left, Army slouched and closed his eyes. The waiting was tiring. He was not a waiter, he was a doer. He should be in there asking for surgical instruments and saying *stat*.

Heather's body was the first image that appeared when he closed his eyes. This occasionally happened. In a decade, he'd recognize this chain of events—close eyes, hot girl—as a kind of personal screensaver. A decade ago, he'd have ripped her month out of a calendar and pinned it to the wall in front of his bed. Note to alert self: Make a calendar of hot high-school girls from the neighbourhood. Sell. Omit Heather.

Last summer, he had taken money from other boys but he had never taken any from Skinnyboy. Okay, he took money for the guitar but not for Heather. Therefore he was not to blame for what happened to her.

But he intended to, didn't he? For as a man thinketh in his heart, so is he. For the love of money is the root of all evil. For where your heart is, there will your treasure be also. That one's backward. For where your treasure is, there will your heart be also.

What if there was no heart in the baby? Literally. Army opened his eyes. He looked at the side of Oliver's face. The sides of his goatee looked like marionette lines.

Anybody ever tell you that you look like Chucky from the side? Army said. Aren't you scared the baby's gonna come out looking like Chucky?

Hendrix put you up to that? Oliver crossed his thick arms over his thick body. I act alone, Mr. O.

152. MARKET VALUE   *Army*

How much would Heather cost? the boys in church wanted to know. A few of them happened to be congregating at the bathroom sink when he went down to relieve himself. It was just supposed to be bathroom talk.

Depends on what you want her to do, Army had said. She'll flash you but no touching.

How much for touching?

The guy just said no touching.

No touching right now. Maybe later. A handful's going to cost.

How much for a pinch?

You're so desperate.

Army had collected a downpayment, their offering money, but the following week they complained that they only received a partial view of Heather's breasts so Army issued them a partial refund.

153. WHICH WHILE SOME COVETED AFTER, THEY HAVE ERRED FROM THE

FAITH, AND PIERCED THEMSELVES THROUGH WITH MANY SORROWS.   *Army*

Army closed his eyes again.

He was over her (except for the screensaver issue) but couldn't Heather see that he was the beginning of a good story? Basement to penthouse. BMX to BMW. In five years, after he made his first million, they would walk around Manhattan wearing enormous sunglasses, coffee in one hand, schnauzer leashes in the other.

Did you have sex with him? Army had asked her when she returned that day.

She paused a very long time.

So you did, Army said.

I didn't want to, Heather said.

Then she told him a story about rape. He believed her. But she didn't cry or get choked up, which made him wonder—God forgive him for sounding like Oliver—if there was another explanation.

Maybe, *no*, Heather wanted to go, maybe she voluntarily, *no way*, hooked up voluntarily with those guys, *no*, voluntarily, despite knowing how much he Romeoed her.

He understood where his loins were because of her.

154. SHABBA!   *Army*

Army wouldn't have said no to some Pringles at the moment. Something crunchy. He should have brought his Walkman.

When Heather came back in January, he wasn't supposed to offer grins and folate pills and long talks into the night. He had moved on. He was supposed to be like, Heather who? See him sitting with a cigar, surrounded by a traila load of video girls, gyrating around him like hummingbirds.

The word *twerking* had not yet been invented.

155. SLAVE MARKET   *Army*

In the barbershop, he had negotiated another trade deal for Heather that fell through.

That ain't right. You'd be the African that sells his own tribe.

First I'm only half African. I'm, like, Rican, know what I'm sayin'. Second, she ain't from my tribe; this is karma for what her people did to my brethren them. Fourth, third—I'm not selling anybody. The fee is for my services, not hers.

How much?

Well, what is she worth to you? She's leaving in a week, man. You're not leaving me a lot of time to make something happen.

I know, I know.

Then very quickly: Cash preferred, trades accepted. I guarantee results or your money slash trade back. Fine print: I can't guarantee how far you'll get.

Man, it's not even about that.

Because I can't control if you screw things up.

So what am I paying you for exactly?

For Heather's attention.

I can get her attention.

Army cocked his head.

Sometimes.

And for me to talk you up to her so she might *see* you. Right now, you're invisible to her.

So she'll go out with me.

Is that a question?

It's like a confirmation I need.

He had to return that punk's money too.

156. BUSINESS EXPANSION   *Army*

But what does it mean? Does she, like, like me?

I don't traffic in meaning. I traffic in results. You want meaning, talk to— Here Army pointed upward.

157. SILVER   *Army*

  4 Saying, I have sinned in that I have betrayed the innocent blood.
     And they said, What is that to us? see thou to that.
  5 And he cast down the pieces of silver in the temple, and departed,
     and went and hanged himself.
  6 And the chief priests took the silver pieces, and said, It is not lawful
     for to put them into the treasury, because it is the price of blood.

158. WORD CHOICE: PIMP   *Army*

The word *pimp* was never used. In the mid-2000s, when *Pimp My Ride* blew up, Army would always hear the verb inflected by the memory of the summer of Heather.

159. WORD CHOICE: PROSTITUTE   *Army*

The word *prostitute* was not used either. Neither was *hooker, whore,* or *whore of Babylon,* even to himself in the days after—could he say it?—she cheated on him and he wanted to set her on fire. That wasn't his thought. Where did that come from?

160. BULK   *Army*

A traila load a, a traila load a, a traila load a traila load a traila load a girls, girls, every day. From London, Canada, and USA.

161. THE UNHOLY SPIRIT   *Army*

Yes, but how much was Heather's body worth? That wasn't Army's thought. But it entered his head.

He slapped himself across the face. Too hard.

What's the matter with you? Oliver said.

Demons, Army said. He opened his eyes.

Right, it was an unholy spirit trying to make him think that he actually thought that thought. But he would never reduce Heather to flesh. That wasn't him.

He closed his eyes. Heather again.

162. SURFACE TENSION   *Army*

The first time she opened the black door, she lifted her breasts over her bra and he could see the puddle of jiggly giggly flesh spilling over the top. Sometimes when he filled a glass to the very brim, the memory returned to him, and he would bend to the counter and sip. She runneth over.

163. HOW AM I SUPPOSED TO LIVE WITHOUT YOU?   *Army*

Unpardonable. His every imagination was evil, like the people in Noah's time.

Army resolved to stay awake. He debated asking Oliver the magnum question: Mr. O, how'd the missus leave you? But that would turn into a bedtime story, complete with a witch, a casa and a prince. Plus he already knew multiple versions from Heather, Hendrix and Oliver himself.

Think good thoughts.

Army would get Oliver a Michael Bolton CD for Christmas. Good one. See, that was the Holy Spirit just now. He hadn't grieved it yet.

164. NOW THAT I'VE BEEN LOVING YOU SO LONG   *Army*

Would God bless his business? He should pray more. He should wear a crucifix. He should hang one in the garage. He could ask his mother to buy him one. No, then God would think that he didn't want to spend his own money on Godstuff.

165. TELL ME, HOW AM I SUPPOSED TO LIVE WITHOUT YOU?   *Army*

He got baptized in the fall after his cast came off. It was so easy. He didn't have to memorize anything. He didn't have to carry kindling up Mount Moriah.

166. HOW AM I SUPPOSED TO CARRY ON   *Army*

Abraham was willing to cut his son's neck. Isaac was obedient unto death. Pink tongue sucking a lollipop that had gone purple with the colour. Army bet his father, Paperplane, would do likewise, would cut his throat.

Army would let him. He would lie on the twigs and joke all the way until his father cut his voice.

167. WHEN ALL THAT I'VE BEEN LIVING FOR IS GONE   *Army*

After all, his father was cutthroat in business. Shooting lasers out of his finger in the boardroom, dumping his lukewarm coffee over an intern's head.

168. MAKING A KILLING   *Army*

Before the final end, his father stopped calling so much and got busy (with women? Black women? Asian? German? Puerto Rican?) but he probably loved him. His father. Probably he loved him too. Probably he loved him as much as he loved him. Probably one of them loved the other.

169. A NICOTINELY CHALLENGED MAN   *Edgar*

To make his son—his son?—his son a mixtape he bought a new double-cassette stereo and a portable tape recorder. To record from records he held the portable recorder close to the record player and kept really, really quiet.

But he was smoking really, really quietly in the background.

He also made a mixtape for his secretary's daughter, who never mentioned it. His secretary said she said thank you, but Edgar knew she, the secretary, was just being polite. The look she gave him suggested that he'd be better advised to spend his evenings handling sundry legal matters than making mixtapes for teenagers.

How difficult it was to get the attention of women. That is, until they love you. Then they never lift their attention from you. Even after you try to pull off their antennae, flip them on their backs and pluck out their legs.

Was there more wine?

If he had raised Armistice, the child would know his way around a good wine by now. He would have been tasting some at dinner.

He would never encourage a child to take up smoking though. Filthy, filthy habit. For a child.

170. SMOKING   *Army*

He tried smoking, after playing ball by the Catholic school, and when he came home Felicia was like a canine on him. She smelled it in his hair, on his clothes, although he couldn't smell anything, and she banned him from playing ball for a month and talked herself to sleep, scolding him about his lungs and this and that, and what kind of cancer, and what next, snorting cocaine in her house, and if he thought she was the kind of mother who, even when she stopped talking he heard it.

171. JUST A PUFF   *Army*

But he and Heather smoked sometimes nevertheless. They passed a cigarette between them but he had more of it because she was pregnant and he was a gentleman like that.

WHEN WERE THEY GOING TO PULL THE BABY OUT OF HER COOCH?

172. DRIVING MISS DAISY   *Army*

Maybe his father had a driver. He imagined his father rolling up Newcourt in a black Cadillac, rolling down the rear window just enough to let out a white-gloved hand. Then he'd roll up the window again and be gone. He'd continue to be, but gone.

173. FOR EXAMPLE, MOSES   *Army*

Moses asked to see the face of God and only saw his back.

174. RIDDLE   *Edgar*

Last summer, the last story that Felicia tangentially inserted into conversation, with the chilling calm of someone both unmoved and fascinated by horror, was of a man being sued for child support.

They're suing him, she said.

They who?

The woman. She saying he's the father. He saying he is only a sperm donor. And when they investigate further into this woman's past, she had a number of hospitalizations for hysterical pregnancies. She claim she get pregnant by this and by that—by a man on TV, by milk, by a dog bite.

Where's this happening, Felicia?

Back home. And she was a virgin the whole time. Very devout. So when she actually get pregnant, everybody was surprised because she was still claiming to be a virgin. And she was. Anyway, she had the child and like her senses kick in and now she suing the man.

As usual, Felicia's story ended prematurely with unspoken, parable-like accusation.

Is he the father? Edgar asked.

She say yes but her own testimony say she never had sex with the man. He say he's a sperm—

You already said that.

We go find out in the courts up above.

175. OF DARKNESS   *Edgar*

Of course he could but could he really end up with a black woman? Like, *really*. Could he take her anywhere? When his present sister-in-law cooed about the piazza outside the Uffizi Gallery, what would Felicia have to say? He would always have to rescue her.

She couldn't even conjugate an English verb properly when he found her. Error after error out of her mouth. Yet she wrote perfect grammatical cathedrals. How could she both know and not know the same language?

176. HEART   *Edgar*

And yet she presented all sorts of opportunities that appealed to him. He would get to sit all day in the rumshops when she took him to wherever she was from. He could talk the code to the dread who made sandwiches in the lobby. If his brother came up with some withering witticism and called him, say, a *negrophiliac*, Edgar would get to call him a mayo-faced, Saltine, Kartoffel, Kraut Bosche, blue-eyed devil. He'd have to work on the syntax.

He had lived with her longer than any other woman in his life. Those months felt like amber was thickening orange around them, like the ash from Vesuvius was settling over them while they lay face to face in bed. She had stayed with him in the hospital. She came back even when she didn't have to. She might be the only woman who ever bought him jockey shorts. Somehow she knew what size. What a fool he must have looked like with his old self in black socks and bare legs trying to seduce a young girl like her, who was shiny and didn't know it.

177. ORDER   *Felicia*

She had a gift for order. Army pointed it out. He told her that when she put a mug down, the handle would be parallel to the wall so it looked, somehow, aligned. Without thinking, she turned all the hangers the same way in the closet. She did these things effortlessly.

Observe, he said as he removed a tray of hashbrowns from the oven.

And indeed, she had arranged the six hashbrowns in a grid.

Things should be neat, Felicia said, feeling accused rather than complimented.

You might have OCD, he said.

178. TAG   *Edgar*

She was family of a sort, because of the child. But then Army made it sound like he and Felicia lived in a sort of family and Edgar didn't want to ask whom he would choose, this Mr. O or himself. Instead he asked about movies.

Have you seen *Sophie's Choice*?

Boring.

You thought so?

I haven't seen it.

Well, how do you know it's—

I know she does an accent in it. She's German.

Polish.

Tomaito, tomahto. My homeroom teacher had a nervous breakdown last year. Did I tell you? All we did was watch movies anyway. But one day, we were talking, whatever, and he snapped the metre stick, Hulk-Hogan style, across his thigh. Buh-bwap. Then he didn't come back.

And that's why you don't know any history or geography.

I think he was sexually frustrated.

Anyhow, as I was saying, you need to watch—

We had this scrub for a supply teacher for all of June, which was why my report card didn't accurately reflect my performance.

Felicia bought that?

179. LACES   *Oliver*

Army was trying to remove his size ten shoes by peeling the heel of one with the toe of the other while keeping both feet on Oliver's lap. He did that from time to time after the cast came off. A remembrance of things past.

You think she's dead? Army asked.

Dead? Oliver frowned deeply. Dead? Why would she—

Yeah, I don't know. Mom's been gone so long. Give a brother a hand, will you?

Without undoing the laces, Oliver tugged off one sneaker then folded his arms again. If she was dead there'd be some kind of alarm system. Code something or other.

Army held up the other foot. There was a standoff of looks.

My hamstrings. Army massaged the back of his thighs.

Oliver removed the other shoe. He did have a streak of Felicia in him, Army did. To raise death at a moment like this and just leave it on the table with such detachment was a classic Felicia move. Dead? Ridiculous. He would never hear the end of it from his ex-wife. He hadn't called her yet. Imagine calling her and saying, Heather's dead. The doctor said it was a genetic abnormality passed down on the mother's side. Oliver shook his head. What was he thinking?

Army wiggled his toes. You want to hook me up with some Pringles?

180. TAG   *Edgar*

The last time they met, she wanted him to show her exactly what he did to deserve a "leave of absence."

I tucked in her tag, Edgar said.

Felicia reached across the back of his couch and pulled Edgar's neck forward, toward her face. Like this?

She was mocking him. He imagined that for years she had been mocking him, wherever she was, in her house getting railed by Mr. O while tomatoes grew on a trellis in the backyard. He twisted his head away.

She laughed a broad, acrid laugh. In that moment on his couch, what Edgar felt was a German feeling with no Canadian equivalent. *Weltschmerz* crossed by *verschlimmbessern* and a guillotine-like *Torschlusspanik*, a feeling that rose up sometimes when he was looking into the fridge or loading the washing machine and remembered Felicia. He had the hot sensation that she was watching him with satisfaction from an omnipresent tree, her clawed feet wrapped around a branch.

And how about all the other women? Felicia asked.

I made it clear last time that I wasn't talking about this anymore.

What you do to them?

Nothing, Felicia. Words. Just words.

181. SEDUCTION   *Edgar*

He had one move.

182. SPECIFICALLY   *Felicia*

What were the words specifically?

I don't remember.

Were you drinking?

It was just a bunch of compliments.

Specifically.

I don't know.

Because there's a difference between, You look nice today, and, You looking fine when you squat down in that tight skirt.

That's not what I said.

Well, tell me. I waiting to hear your compliment.

183. TO BE COMPLETELY HONEST   *Edgar*

His mistake had not been in offending the women but the men.

Thinking the all-male board would understand, he'd said, This is my company.

Some of the men looked at each other. Others looked down at their expensive pens.

Edgar felt emboldened. Order was being re-established. You can't fire me, if that's what you're thinking. You're all here because of me.

And the chair of the board, an ancient man who still wore bowties and spoke his consonants with German crispness, the only one who had not looked away from Edgar, said, You're mistaken, my dear boy. This is your father's business. He crossed himself. And Heinrich's. You both flatter and forget yourself.

184. TO SUGGEST MOTIVE OR ASPERSION   *Edgar*

The chair of the board had two daughters and four granddaughters, one of whom interned at Paperplane a few summers earlier when she was on break from reading economics at Cambridge, all of which facts, when taken into careful consideration, disclosed the chair's leaning toward believing the chicks, the weakness of his sperm, his fetish for bowties, his unctuous devotion to Vater, his father's disappearance during the Third Reich, and possibly also his prim attention to careful pronunciation.

185. PROVERBS 23:29–30   *Felicia*

²⁹ Who hath woe? who hath sorrow? who hath contentions? who hath
    babbling? who hath wounds without cause? who hath redness of eyes?
³⁰ They that tarry long at the wine; they that go to seek mixed wine.

186. ZUGZWANG   *Edgar*

The white was finished but the red wasn't. He was saving a bottle of rosé to take back. With the lights off in his hotel, Edgar could see Lake Louise cupped between the mountains.

Such a pretty girl Felicia was. Lean body like an Olympic marathoner, the fibres of her thighs twitching. When she lifted her back off the bed, he could wrap both his arms around her waist or grip her shoulders from behind and she would turn into a slippery fish. And the little anterior tilt of her pelvis when she stood in the kitchen in a low-slung skirt. Not bad at all. But of course she was dishonest. She went and got herself pregnant and thought he would comply with her Jesus. Edgar disliked being compelled.

If she had just waited, she could have gone on cooking for him all the days of her life.

Man, do you hear yourself?

I'm not sexist. It's what she wanted.

Apparently not.

It's what she wanted. Maybe not now. Because her pride's eating her. She would have been happier doing things my way.

And you?

187. PROVERBS 23:33–35   *Felicia*

³³ Thine eyes shall behold strange women, and thine heart shall utter perverse things.

³⁴ Yea, thou shalt be as he that lieth down in the midst of the sea, or as he that lieth upon the top of a mast.

³⁵ They have stricken me, shalt thou say, and I was not sick; they have beaten me, and I felt it not: when shall I awake? I will seek it yet again.

188. REVERSE SEXISM   *Oliver*

Whoever said that women love their kids more than men do had never been inside the chest of Oliver Soares, had never seen him stand outside Heather's bedroom door knowing she was in there, breathing and filling up the house with her mystery. When she was a little girl, she used to erupt in terror and laughter as he dropped her from above his head and caught her at his belly.

Again, she'd say when he set her on the ground. Again, and reach up her arms.

189. PERIOD   *Edgar*

Sometimes he used to walk into the bathroom and smell her blood.

190. INTERVAL   *Edgar*

Not all the time. It was something he noticed but not something he missed.

191. LUXURY   *Oliver*

Army's feet did not smell like pine trees or little tree air fresheners. But you'd expect a boy who spent so much time in the shower to at least smell human.

What could he possibly be reading in *Chatelaine?* Where was Felicia with a report? How was his little Heather and her little Heather? Oliver had been stalling with the adoption process. The ex wanted a closed adoption—no contact whatsoever between future Heather and the family. He had resisted such a severe separation on various grounds—personal and moral mostly but also spiteful and punitive.

Heather was under two years old when the ex left him the first time.

He had settled his little family into 55 Newcourt, one of his father's rental properties. His ex said, sarcastically, Look at me in the lap of luxury, which hurt Oliver because his father had been slaving ever since he was taken out of school at seven years old to work on a farm in Portugal. He had moved to Canada with holes in his shoes, sent for Oliver's mother, and landscaped his way to a family home and multiple rental properties. Within a few months in the new house, Oliver discovered that his American wife had been writing letters to an American ex-boyfriend. When he confronted her about it, that he was working hard all day so she could write her ex-boyfriend, she took off with the child and went to stay with her parents in Massachusetts. He was ready to end the marriage, but his mother, from her hospital bed, made him go and retrieve his wife, his ex-wife.

What are you going to do at your age? she asked. Oliver was younger than Edgar was when he met Felicia.

What's she going to do at her age? Oliver responded. His wife was twenty-two.

It's disgraceful, his mother said in Portuguese.

You should have married Teresa in Portugal, his father said. She no leave you. Teresa was his cousin.

192. A SOLUTION HENDRIX MIGHT SUGGEST   *Oliver*

Oh, he wished the ex-wife, that woman, would die. Just spontaneously combust, but comically, like combust into smoke and feathers, so he could have his children back.

193. FITNESS   *Oliver*

Army had taken a strong interest in the *Chatelaine*. The cover promised diet tips, fashion tips, home tips, and—for shame—50 Ways to Leave Your Lover.

Read something with nutritional value, Oliver said.

Army looked over the top of the magazine. You sure you don't have any change?

Oliver could feel his eyes heat-scanning him for the location of his wallet.

We can share those Pringles, Army said. They're healthy. I'll even let you choose the flavour as long as it's not Nature.

If you come up with half, I'll come up with half, Oliver countered. Somebody needed to teach this kid responsibility.

The ex-wife did not contribute a dime to the household GDP, as Army would say, *and* she let herself grow to that size. He was not a shallow man, no siree, but have some pride, have some self-respect. Surely when she looked in the mirror, she had to feel some stirring of nostalgia.

How about I pay you back when we get home?

194. NOT TO HARP ON HER WEIGHT *Oliver*

He could have stuck with her even when she posed for Rubens. Her weight was the one thing he could attack reliably because she was so sensitive about it. It bothered her far more than it bothered him. She was never thin-thin. Heather had a way of saying *fat-fat*. She always had hips. Nothing wrong with hips. They were the body part he initially wanted to grab most on her.

How many times and ways did she leave him before leaving for good, packing up all her stuff and going back to America with their kids? No real reason for the divorce, like all the others on the street. The woman was unhappy. Everything the man did was wrong. Every single thing.

Did Hendrix say she was dating a guy with hair like Bill Clinton? May the force be with that poor shmuck.

195. NEW YEAR'S RESOLUTION *Oliver*

The ex-wife tried to lose weight every January but she had no resolution.

By Valentine's Day, she got conveniently tired.

Whenever they went walking, she always wanted to rest after a few steps. He could keep going and going. But she wanted to rest. What was the point of dragging him out there if all she wanted to do was rest?

196. THE REST *Oliver*

Frankly, she embarrassed him. There he would be in some public park, technically a division 3 athlete, with someone he wouldn't look at if he had accepted the offer from the division 3 school and not stayed in Canada. She sat on a curb, ready to argue or cry while all the other men were passing them, jogging and biking. He marched on spot, picking up his knees, barely sweating, waiting on the ex to catch her breath.

197. TRAP *Oliver*

Go ahead, she said. It was a bright, in-focus winter day. Go ahead without me if that's what you want to do.

198. DON'T FALL FOR IT *Oliver*

I'll catch up, she said, but he knew she wouldn't.

199. SHE'S TESTING YOU *Oliver*

He knew he couldn't go on without her. She was on the verge of tears. She was saying go ahead but she meant, *Don't leave me.*

200. VOW   *Oliver*

She meant, Don't leave me.

201. OW   *Oliver*

She meant, Don't leave me behind on this trail

202. HOW   *Oliver*

to find my way back to the car alone. She meant, Don't leave me, Oliver. For God's sake, you can't leave me in this condition. You're the only man I know here. Don't leave me.

203. BUS   *Oliver*

Listen to this, Mr. O. Army began reading aloud from 50 Ways to Leave Your Lover. Number 36. Buy a pair of sunglasses and a one-way ticket out of town.

Nonsense, Oliver said.

On his wife's encouragement, Oliver became a bus driver for Brampton Transit before he got laid off. (He used to teach high school mathematics but was dismissed for upholding school policy.) He got bad shifts. He drove around suburbia late at night. Sometimes he was the only one on the bus. He thought, Why am I driving myself around Brampton?

Army said, Just think about how many women you helped leave their husbands by public transit.

204. ROUTE   *Oliver*

There were sections in Bramalea where all of the streets began with the same letter. He screwed up the turns: G-section, H-section, M-section, N-section. Later, when word arose of the G-spot, he thought how similar an ordeal it was to navigate the G-section of the city.

205. ROAD CLOSURE   *Oliver*

His wife wouldn't let him sleep with her in any case. Before the divorce they hadn't had sex in months, which was like dog years.

206. SIGNAL   *Oliver*

She used to touch his thigh late in the night when they were younger, before Heather.

207. USED OR UNKNOWN CAUSES *Oliver*

Number 47. Burn the bridge, Army continued reading from *Chatelaine*. You can't leave your lover if you keep going back to him. Destroy all traces. Army looked up. But what if you have children with him?

Would you stop reading that garbage, Oliver said.

Part of him believed that the ex only wanted a child and nothing else from him. A second child was a bonus.

He had wanted more than children from her. He'd wanted her before the thought of children. Oliver tried to remember why, what was the attraction, and could only come up with, She used to be nice and thin. Mostly nice. And she could be relied on for potato, pasta, vegetable, or bean salad at family picnics, even before the kids. And she used to sing with him spontaneously in the car. Oliver didn't want to go down this road.

Number 50, Army read. Love the one you're with. He fluttered his eyelashes at Oliver and said, Aw.

(It was a Portuguese kid, Army's age, who got him fired. Could have been his own. D'Souza. Oliver had asked him to remove his gum and when he refused to comply Oliver led him to the garbage can by the back of the neck.)

208. POEM *Felicia*

A student came into the office one day, holding a poem from her class. She said her professor, an Asian woman, was forcing them to read offensive and racist literature. Felicia could remember two lines of the poem: Oh fat white woman who nobody loves / Why do you walk through the fields in gloves.

209. THE BARD *Felicia*

Edgar used to write her poems. One. He wrote her a poem. One poem once.

Clouds. For Felicia Shaw. He coughed then conducted his cigarette like a baton.

I wandered lonely as a cloud, that's not me. That's the Bard.

There's only one Bard.

Right, listen. I wandered lonely as a cloud / and to the deepest sea / to find to find to find someone / who was finding finding me. Good, huh? That was all I had for a while but then I got a second wind when the stewardess came round with nuts. Her mother departed up above / in a paroxysm of pain. Paroxysm, Edgar raised his eyebrows, just came to me. Up into the clouds she went / Saying

Felicia's name. Poetic licence, Edgar commented. He raised his cigarette high for the finale: But down, down, down came the rain / And washed the spider out / And now the little girl / lives with me in the clouds.

You wrote that all by yourself? Felicia asked. She set a glass of grapefruit juice in front of him.

Believe it. He gave the napkin to her.

She sat on his knee. She reread the poem. It was terrible and he seemed to know it yet also seemed to be hoping that she didn't know it.

She said, *Out* and *clouds?*

Out, cloud, out, cloud, he said.

He blew his smoke the other way, then he asked, Are you going to put your head on my shoulder? and began rubbing her forehead and he kissed her until the ice melted and made the top of the grapefruit juice watery.

210. CRY   *Heather*

Heather clutched Felicia's hand and cried, Don't leave me, don't leave me. God, don't leave me.

She had told a lie that she needed to confess. She felt like the waves wouldn't subside until she confessed and they threw her overboard to be swallowed by a whale. The lie she told her mother was that Bruno had driven to Brampton to see her and that when she took off that night it was to be with him. Of course, he would deny it. Of course his parents would say he was accounted for. Alibis. Of course they'd do anything not to financially support a kid for eighteen years. She had ended her speech to her mother with a whimper meant to invoke pity for the suffering of their gender. The unspoken words were, I'm telling the truth, Mom. Don't you believe me?

211. RECTANGLE   *Felicia*

Heather's cries crossed from sobs into dry retches. Her mouth prolapsed into a rectangle, so the inside of her lips was visible to the gums. Felicia patted Heather's forehead dry, wiped her nose, her cheeks. She did not leave again, stopped updating the men, whom she imagined in the waiting room, pacing around a cage, flicking their tails, then falling asleep on top of each other.

212. EPIDURAL   *Felicia*

You have to hold still, Felicia said. You don't want the needle to break in your spine.

Horror on Heather's face. Was it *needle, spine,* or *break?* A very sensitive generation, this one.

It's not too late to change your mind, Felicia said. Heather had rejected her earlier advice but Felicia gave it one more shot. Pain was ordained since Eden. I wouldn't take no epidural if I was you.

She knew of someone from her village in the small unrecognized island who went abroad and took an epidural and the odds were one in ten thousand that she would be paralyzed and she was the one.

213. HOO-HOO-HAA-HAA   *Heather*

They didn't think she was worth teaching how to breathe, was that it? It was stupid anyway, this breathing business. It's not like there was a right way to breathe anyway. She didn't want to breathe anyway. She didn't want to go to those classes anyway. Not with her dad. Gross.

Not with Army either because she didn't want to appear among the older women in track pants as a teen pregnancy. They would regard her not as a woman who happened to be pregnant, but as a teen pregnancy.

She made the point in college, years and years later: Person who is incarcerated. Person with a disability. Not pregnant woman but woman who is pregnant. Person first.

214. BACKSEAT   *Heather*

Heather didn't tell anyone, except Army, that she had been raped—sexually assaulted—because in her heart of hearts she believed that she had invited multiple penises into her body, that if she hadn't decided to take off with Skinnyboy none of this would have happened. In theory, she knew she shouldn't blame herself (years later, enrolled in a State College, she understood the psychology of victimhood, Patty Hearst with gun and beret) but still when she boiled facts down, the conversation went like:

Were you raped?

Yes.

Where were you raped?

In a car near Lake Ontario.

Would you have been raped if you didn't go to Toronto?

I don't know.

Would you have been raped if you didn't go to Toronto?

Maybe. Anything could happen.

Would you have been raped if you didn't go to Murmur's show?

He could have raped me behind the church or dragged me into the mall bathroom.

Would you have been raped if you didn't go to Toronto? Yes or no, Heather.

No.

Speak up.

No.

215. HOO-HOO-HAA   *Heather*

She was an unwed mother too. Don't forget that. She was a teen pregnancy and an unwed mother and the pain here it comes again are you serious?

216. BYE, BYE, MISS AMERICAN PIE   *Felicia*

If she could bear some of the pain for the girl, Felicia would. She would slice its syrupy filling onto a white plate and serve some to Oliver and to the ex, because no good mother would let her daughter run wild, yes I'm judging you, and a sliver for Army so that he would never touch a girl until he was married at twenty-seven, such a good age for a man to marry, and then pieces for Heather and herself, and grasp Edgar by the back of the head and slam his face into the remainder.

217. MIRROR, MIRROR   *Heather*

The boys had rested and were back for more. Inside her the skinniest one of all was spasming his little death for dear life as if the rape had gone into remission until this most aggressive recurrence of poisoned fruit. Something like that. A colourful Ferris wheel.

218. RELIGION   *Heather*

You believe in that stuff? she asked Skinnyboy.

Yeah, I guess. He shrugged. I believe. But not like a redneck.

They were on his bed or in a store or a parking lot or in his car. The anticipation of pain was clearing her memory.

He asked, Don't you think there's a God?

Ask me that now, she said from her hospital bed. She believed the emptying of her body into car pockets and parking lots and her father's truck and now a hospital bed had a divine origin.

219. THE LIGHT   *Felicia*

Ask you what now? Felicia dried Heather's neck.

Am I close to done?

But Felicia misheard. You're not dying.

How close do I have to get to death without dying before this thing gets out of me? I'm not Nefertiti.

220. LAST WORDS   *Edgar*

In the hospital room, that endless first night, he had told her that apart from *Schatz*, the rest of Mutter's vocabulary consisted of varieties of pain, *der Schmerz, das Leid, der Kummer, die Qual.*

So starke Schmerzen.

And then she let those go, dropping down to the article: *der, das, die.*

It had been the same with his oma.

221. FIRST WORDS   *Edgar*

Unknown.

222. HOW WAS SHE TO KNOW?   *Felicia*

While Edgar was out smoking, Felicia turned the chairs to face each other and placed her feet on the chair that was formerly his.

When he came back, he asked, Are you going home?

She shook her head.

Then, he said, implying that he wasn't either. He looked at her feet in his chair before settling on the floor with far too much effort and drama for a man between thirty-five and forty-five. And once he was down there, he shuffled and groaned lightly, raising one butt cheek then the other.

Sit in your chair, she said but did not remove her feet.

He protested.

We past politeness.

Edgar rose with much effort. Felicia moved her feet to one side of his chair and crossed her ankles. She patted the side of her chair for him to do the same.

She took off his shoes and instantly regretted it. Perhaps they weren't past politeness after all. But soon he had fatigued her receptors and she could smell nothing and hear nothing and see nothing.

223. MED SCHOOL GENDER QUOTAS   *Heather*

No man should be a doctor. Not just an obstetrician but a doctor. No man understands nuclear fission in a uterus.

224. REVISITING THE OPTIONS   *Heather*

She would be willing to die for this child because she almost died having this child.

No way she was giving this baby up. Have your own damn baby if you want one.

225. SKIPPING CLASS   *Heather*

How were all the other girls her age spending their week? Not lying on blue sheets with their legs open.

Okay, maybe a few of them were.

You have no idea, Heather thought at them, you have no idea what happens elsewhere, by which she meant inside of you.

226. PINK DISPOSABLE RAZORS   *Heather*

She hadn't shaved her legs, because it was difficult bending around the baby-belly and also because it was winter. She was conscious of the hair on her legs as she prepared to be inspected by a man who could be her father.

227. PAIN HAS AN ELEMENT OF BLANK.   *Heather*

228. IT HAS NO FUTURE BUT ITSELF/ITS INFINITE REALMS CONTAIN/
ITS PAST.   *Heather*

229. JUST CUT ME OPEN   *Heather*

Why isn't it working? Cut me up. Feed me to the dogs.

Nobody going to cut you open, girl.

Don't let go.

Nobody letting you go. Once you pushing, it almost over.

230. EVIL LAUGHTER   *Heather*

Her father was out there thinking she got what she deserved. Her mother said she was going to come and didn't. Felicia stabbed her in the back with a poison needle. They all tricked her into dying. In the background, they all plotted her death as part of the German expressionist film with weird shadows that they had been shooting for the last seventeen years.

231. WWED   *Oliver*

She said she'd come to help after the birth, Oliver said, referring to his ex-wife.

The baby's early, Army said.

They were still in the small hospital waiting room outside the birthing rooms. Army was using Oliver as a pillow. He lay the back of his head on Oliver's shoulder and extended his legs outward on the vacant bank of seats.

Yeah, but if I told her to get on a plane and—

You know how much one of those get-me-on-the-next-flight flights costs?

Let me put it this way, Oliver began again. When he was uncertain, he could quickly come to a decision by asking himself, What Would Ex-wife Do? And naturally he found merit in the opposite course. If *she* called *me* and told me Heather was in the hospital, I'd be in my car driving to Massachusetts right now. Oliver clapped and slid one hand forward. Fast.

Me too, me too. But let's face it. There's nowhere for her to stay.

That's not why, Oliver said.

And what she gon' do once she gets here? I mean, what's she really going to contribute to the little GDP we have going?

Oliver imagined the ex as she surveyed his new situation. She would find Oliver living with a slender woman who—imagine—cooked, cleaned *and* had a job and a boy who called him *mister* and was already begging to drive his truck.

She don't want to stay with you, Mr. O, Army continued. No offence. Once was enough.

232. AKIN   *Heather*

Did her mother really lie on her back while a cackle of hyenas tore open a zebra inside of her? Did Felicia when she was her age? Why didn't someone say something? How could this ring of sabre-toothed fire not have come up before?

233. BECAUSE   *Heather*

Would she have believed a woman who told her not to have children?

234. TRUE   *Heather*

Everything comes out, Heather told Army later. Not just the baby. Everything down there. You can't help it.

Ach, Army said, as German a sound as he had ever made.

However Heather was beyond being disgusted.

235. AIR   *Heather*

The baby made no cry. It didn't move for a long second.

Underwater voices. Felicia looked worried.

It was being taken toward a sink.

Doesn't she have to cry? Heather asked.

He, I think, Felicia said.

Why isn't he crying?

He doesn't have the strength yet, Felicia said.

236. EACH OF THEIR MOTHERS WORE HOSPITAL WRISTBANDS,
    NOT TOE TAGS, TO IDENTIFY THEM IN CASE THEY GOT LOST
    OR MIXED UP AMONG THE JAZZ.   *Felicia*
    March 14, 1995. 4:40 a.m.
    3 lb, 8 oz.

237. LONG DISTANCE   *Oliver*

After. But not immediately. Oliver called the ex-wife and Hendrix answered.

Did Heather have the baby yet? Hendrix asked.

That's why I'm calling. Put your mother on the phone.

Boy or girl?

Boy, Oliver said. Hendrix, this is long distance.

Is Army there? Can I talk to Army?

238. FOR THE ANTS   *Hendrix*

The baby was born with a lot of dark, straight hair.

239. UNTIL WE FIGURE OUT WHAT HEATHER IS GOING TO DO   *Oliver*

The ex-wife was angry that Oliver expected her to have been there.

Am I supposed to just know that she went into labour? she asked.

Nobody's blaming you.

You said that I should be there—

You should.

Yet you didn't tell me. How? By teleporter? I just twinkle my nose and magically appear?

Are you and Hendrix coming or not?

God knows the stress you put the girl through to have the baby all by herself so early.

Yes, I threw her down the stairs and the baby—

Wouldn't surprise me.

Are you coming or not?

Let me speak to Heather.

Oliver gave Heather the phone and went to stand with Felicia near the window. He knew the ex would not come. He didn't want her around. He had this situation under control. But he wanted her to declare to everybody that she had no maternal instincts whatsoever.

Isn't that what you would have done? Oliver asked Felicia.

Felicia cleared her throat.

I mean, any half-decent woman.

I wouldn't send my child away in that condition.

Oliver accepted that. Then he expressed to Felicia that this was typical behaviour from the ex-wife. Talked a good game, but when it was time to act, except for the preparation of various salads for family picnics, she was nowhere to be found.

They let you make a long-distance call? Felicia asked. In my time—

You're missing the point.

240. NAMED   *Army*

Later in the morning, to make an entrance into Heather's recovery room, Army pretended to hold a baby while beatboxing Chariots of Fire and running in slow motion. He announced, They've got Chariot on display in the baby room.

What? Oliver woke up.

The baby. Nobody was naming the baby, so. His name's Chariot. Strong Bible name.

Chariot's not a name, Oliver said.

It's in the Bible.

You didn't write that down on the birth certificate? Felicia asked.

They said I couldn't, Army said. Army launched his hand into the air like a plane. You get it? He's gonna fly over this thing.

Chariot, Heather said.

241. 2 KINGS 2:11   *Army*

And it came to pass, as they still went on, and talked, that, behold,
there appeared a chariot of fire, and horses of fire, and parted them
both asunder; and Elijah went up by a whirlwind into heaven.

242. I'M GONNA RIDE IN THE CHARIOT   *Heather*

He went up to heaven in a chariot, Army finished explaining.

So that means the baby, Oliver began,

Chariot. He has a name now.

will die.

No, Army said. Elijah didn't die.

Translated, Felicia yawned out. She had laid her head on Heather's bed. Like Enoch.

But, Oliver said, he went up to heaven, which still means that he—

Chariot.

Chariot, Heather confirmed, and when she said the name a second time, she couldn't entertain the thought of the child's death anymore.

Chariot, Oliver said, gets taken away.

Read your Bible, Mr. O. Nobody dies. I mean, Elijah doesn't. He gets in the tricked-out chariot and is like, Peace out, to everybody then he blasts off to heaven to live forever. That's like Bible 201.

243. MAYBE IT, CHARIOT, COULD SLEEP FOR A LONG TIME   *Oliver*

No one wanted the baby to die. It was premature, so tiny and yawny and unaware of its dramatic history that it aroused tenderness in Heather and Felicia and Army.

But Oliver felt like a thirteenth godmother among them. He couldn't shake the feeling that life would be easier (for who?) if the baby died (for everyone).

244. IN THE MORNING, LORD   *Oliver*

We can name the baby Elijah if you want, Oliver said. Not Chariot.

I kind of like *Chariot*, Heather said.

Think of him in school, Oliver said. It was the first time he had imagined the baby as a child, with an oversized knapsack heading up the stairs of Heather's old elementary school.

Call him whatever you want, Felicia said to Heather. Where I come from a child does have a proper name and if you want to give him a nickname then you can give him a nickname.

245. OFFICIAL NICKNAME OF THE CHILD FORMERLY KNOWN AS IT   *Army*

Within a week of the child's birth, Army would shorten the name from Chariot to Riot.

246.   *Army*

Two years later, when Army took a vocal jazz course to get three easy GPA-boosting credits, the choir sang, *I'm gonna ride in the chariot in the morning, Lord* for the spring concert. Bunch of white voices shrilling a Negro spiritual.

247. BABIES GROW ON YOU   *Heather*

She didn't want one then but she wanted this one now.

She didn't want anything sucking on her breasts ever again but she imagined Chariot's mouth would be as neutral as her own hand.

248. THE VIDEO WITH THE BLACK MAN AND THE BURNING CROSSES   *Heather*

Papa don't preach
I've been losing sleep.
But I made up my mind
I'm keeping my baby.

249. PAPA DON'T PREACH   *Army*

In one of their several forgettable teenage conversations, Heather argued that Madonna was singing, *I've been losing sleep*, while Army took the position that she was singing, *I'm on losing street*.

Heather's three supporting points were 1) the rhyme with *trouble deep*, 2) the fact that Madonna was losing sleep over worry about her pregnancy, and 3) Madonna's inability to roll over because of her distension.

Army argued that the song had nothing to do with a pregnant Madonna but about keeping her black boyfriend, her *baby* in the song. Her papa was a racist, hence the burning crosses in the background of the video. The papa had put Madonna out on *losing street*.

250. BUT I MADE UP MY MIND   *Heather*

I'm gonna keep my baby.

If he [survives, Oliver was going to say]—

Chariot.

We'll cross that bridge later. We'll see.

Heather was discharged after two days but the baby—Chariot—Chariot stayed in the neonatal intensive care unit. After a few days of the running joke that was their homeschooling effort, Heather and Oliver surrendered to the pull of the hospital and spent hours of their day monitoring his yawns. On most evenings Army and Felicia joined them, and on the weekends Oliver grimly ferried all four of them across the Styx while Felicia recounted horror stories (a woman strangled her children and set them adrift in a fishing boat and when they returned birds had eaten parts of their faces and extremities) and Heather and Army sat in the back combatting the mythic amounts of doom from the adults with a bag of Cocoa Puffs.

I don't see what there is to see. If I say I'm keeping—

Yeah, Mr. O, you don't want the kid to grow up

You jumping ahead of God.

in an orphanage and be all confused. You don't want him clanging his tin cup against the bars of his crib.

We'll see, Oliver said.

251. ENTERTAINING THE POSSIBILITY OF ANOTHER BABY, BRIEFLY   *Felicia*

What if God were indeed telling her that she needed to have another child, that this other child whom she could barely imagine, was floating in outer space with Felicia's mother and Mutter, waiting for Felicia to wash his hair without getting shampoo in his eyes?

252. REGRETS, EDGAR SENDS HIS   *Felicia*

Why the child? Why the child now? Why the child without the ring? Why the child without her?

She didn't love him—either—but she would marry him for the same reason she put ribbons on presents and polished her shoes. She was thorough.

Did she misremember the moment when he gave her a watch and one of Mutter's rings? Wasn't that the promise of a civil marriage before he rushed ahead of himself and got them married in the eyes of heaven?

She never became his wife or his ex-wife. She was not his surrogate or his mistress. Mistresses, at least, were kept in some state of material decency to compensate for their moral indecency. She was never either.

All the same, Felicia would like to walk through the first floor of the Bay and buy a light blue dress with pleats and shoulder pads for church.

In return, she would get him a uterus for his birthday.

253. MAY THE LORD HAVE MERCY ON JUDGMENT DAY, CONSIDERING   *Felicia*

At least she never enjoyed it, the actual act, the it of it.

254. STAB ME WITH A FORK   *Felicia*

She might, *might*, have had another child with Edgar if she didn't have to have, have to have, sex with him.

255. THE IT OF IT   *Felicia*

All right, all right, she enjoyed the two recent times when she should have been at her night class. Okay, three.

256. POP-POP   *Oliver*

All four of them looking through the glass. He stroked the baby's stomach with two fingers. His fingernail was larger than the child's whole hand. The child, Chariot, opened his eyes.

Oliver no longer said *adoption*. He no longer thought of the baby dying. But he was afraid to hope so openly among the others. When they were looking for fuel to stoke their optimism, their faith, he found himself cautiously pulling them back from their own heartruin.

We'll see, he said.

The plan as set down by the ex was for Heather to stay with him for the spring semester and through the summer then she would return with Chariot to Leominster.

The baby fixed his eyes on Oliver and would not let go.

He said, We'll see what happens.

For the next eight weeks, he said that a lot. Even when the baby was home, in a crib in Hendrix's room and Heather was packing her suitcase and sorting out a lie about rehab, Oliver kept saying, We'll see.

THE SEX TALK

Look.
What's this?
A picture.
I got eyes, little man. Of what?
Of us.

+

Guess, guess, guess who.
Is that you?
No, that's Pop-Pop.
Is that you?
No, that's Hendrix. I drew him with hair.
Okay. So this one must be you.
That's you. Don't you recognize yourself?
Hold up. Is that one you near the garage?
No, that's a girl. That's Heather.
Hm. Then this one must be you.
No, that's a girl too. I'm not a girl. That's Mutter.

+

Give it back.
Wait, I haven't found you yet.
I'm the only one left.
This?
That's a tree.

+

Give it back. I'll fix it.
Last guess. Are you this one?
That's an airplane.
Obviously. I mean are you on it?
No. I mean yes. I mean no. Give it.

+

All right. Done. Look again.
You wrote your name.
Now everybody will know which one is me.

The R is backwards.
I wear it backwards.

+

Mutter's my mom, I know, but is Pop-Pop my dad?
Pop-Pop is your Pop-Pop.
My real dad or my biological dad?
Real.
But Logan said Pop-Pop is too old to be my dad. So he must be my grandpa.
Probably.
How probably? How can he be Grandpa and my real dad?
Because he's Pop-Pop.

+

I'm not crying.
I was just kidding. Nobody dropped you from the sky.
Then where did you find me?
In a box in the garage. I'm kidding, I'm kidding, Riot. We didn't find you
anywhere. You were born just like a normal person.
How's that?
You know what, go to Pop-Pop upstairs and ask him that.

+

What happened to Mutter's skin?
Nothing.
She's darker than everybody else. Why did she change it?
She didn't change it. Maybe you changed yours.
Did I? I don't know. Can I change it back to like Mutter?
Try this summer.

+

Logan was—
You got to stop talking to this Logan.
Logan was saying that Mutter wasn't my real mom.
He's an idiot. You can't listen to anything he says.
He knows stuff though.
He eats his hair. You told me that.

Only because it makes it grow back. But, listen, Army. Logan said Mutter can't be my real mom because she's black and I told him, she wasn't black she was brown and then he said he was white and I was white and I said no he was pink but then he said his mom said that Mutter was black and that you were half black, like grey, but I don't even know when was the last time his mother saw Mutter.

+

Let's everybody go around the table and say who their biological mother is.
How about where instead?
Okay, where. I'll go first because I'm easy. Mine is in the movies.

+

Let's everybody go around the table and say what their biological mother is doing right now.
You're obsessed, little Riot.
You go first.
She's staring at Pop-Pop. She's putting her fork down. She's getting up. She's walking to the kitchen. She's trying to get me to stop. She's saying stop. She's flapping.
What else?
She's coming back. She's sitting down. She's giving you some cherry tomatoes.
No! I already ate mine.
Eat two more. We can play but you gotta eat at the same time.
Okay, my turn, my turn. My biological mother is making a movie with a lot of guns and blood and she's doing her own stunts.

+

Mutter, you have to say.
Her parents are dead, Riot.
All four of them?
Yeah.
Are they dead in heaven or on earth?
Heaven.
Still, what are they doing right now?

+

No, no, everybody has a biological mother and a real mother.

Not everybody, Riot. I just gots the one mom and dad.

No, you got two moms and two dads. Everybody's got two. Aren't you supposed to know this? You're like a hundred years older than me.

Don't believe me if you don't want to.

I have two moms and two dads. I don't know about you. You must have been poor.

+

Tell me about her again.

She's an actress. Very beautiful.

How beautiful?

Like smoking. All the men in Hollywood wanted to get with her. It got so bad that she had to move to New York.

+

Tell me again.

She used to act in soap operas and action movies and sometimes do voice-overs on the radio. I think she might have read the news at one point.

Did you know her?

Yeah, before she got famous. I was the one—

Yeah?

I was the one who told her to lend you to us.

Until she finished making movies.

Right.

+

Because she has to be thin in the movies.

You got it, you got it. And they couldn't have a baby on set crying all the time. They don't like babies in Hollywood.

What do they do with them?

You know.

Tell me again.

They put them in wicker baskets and float them into the ocean.

Like Moses.

That's where they got the idea from.

So you and Mutter and Pop-Pop and Heather and Hendrix all saved me.

+

And Dad? My biological dad, not my real dad.

I told you a million times.

Just tell me again.

He's in the army.

The Turkish militia.

See, you know all this already.

And.

And if he finds you, he's going to hold you up by the leg and take his scimitar and cut you in half down the middle.

He's a bad man.

The worst. So we can never

Never, never

let him know where you are.

+

When do you have to give me back?

Come again?

To my biological mom.

Yeah, no, we don't have to give you back anymore.

She doesn't want me?

I never told you that part of the story?

No.

Your biological mom came back for you.

And you didn't give me back?

She was making a movie in Toronto and when it was done, she came back. She was wearing a fox around her shoulders. Real Hollywood. She said, in this deep smoky voice, I'm here for my baby. And Mutter put you in her arms, but then you started screaming. I never saw you scream that much.

And she didn't want me.

No, she wanted you very much. But you didn't want her, see. That's why you were screaming. And she knew that you were happier here so she gave you back to Mutter and Pop-Pop and got on an airplane and went back to New York.

I wouldn't scream if I saw her now.

She also gave them a whole bunch of money to take care of you.

+

What was her name?

You know better than to ask that.

Tell me this time.

I forget.

No! You don't forget.

She had to change her name when she went to Hollywood.

To what?

She has many names. She has her Hollywood name and her New York name.

And her real name?

Her old name, yeah.

Tell me that one.

+

How beautiful?

The most beautiful woman in the movies. If you watch enough, you'll recognize her. She looks just like you.

+

I think you do it just to piss Pop-Pop off.

Do what? What am I doing?

They tried to make me go to rehab.

I said, No, no, no.

It's not funny.

Yes, I been black.

You get to drive away in your car.

But when I come back.

But I have to sit here and listen to him go on and on about Hendrix.

You'll know, know, know.

+

I researched it, Army. When I turn eighteen, I can find out about my biological mother.

You don't care about your birth father?

Fathers are harder to track down. Sometimes they don't even know. It says right here.

Not every biological mother wants to be found.

You don't think she wants to see me?

Don't take this the wrong way, but if she wanted to keep seeing you after she spat you out her body she would have kept you.

Ew.

I'm just telling you how it is.

So I shouldn't bother.

+

I should just forget her?

Not everyone should reproduce.

Forget her then?

Forget her.

I don't know.

Trust me. You're dead to her.

I'm not dead.

To her. And she's dead to you.

Even if she was dead to me, I'm not dead to her.

+

She's gotta think about me sometime.

She doesn't.

How do you know everything all of a sudden?

I'm just tryna save you from getting invested in a woman who could be dead.

I hate you sometimes, you know that?

Truth hurts, bud. I'm only saying this 'cause I love you.

+

No, I'm done. I'm never going to talk about it again.

You don't still believe you're a celebrity kid?

No, but I mean I could be. You don't know.

Because—

Because you found me in a box in the garage.

+

They were having sex. Logan and Miranda.

Wait, wait, they're eleven.

That's what they were doing, I'm telling you.

They were just playing. They didn't even know they were having sex.

I don't know if they knew, but I knew they were having sex.

+

Army, I'm serious. You can't be taking dumps when I'm in here.

This was my bathroom before it was yours.

You're gonna stink up the place.

Well, hurry up and get out of the shower. Oh, it's a big one. How did all that fit up there?

So disgusting.

It's like two feet. You wanna see?

+

Open the window, man.

That done ripped me up.

Open the window.

The door's open.

The window, Army.

Breathe through your mouth.

+

When are you going to get married, Army?

You're not getting the basement.

How long are you going to live here?

As long as I want. If you want the basement, then you get married.

+

She doesn't like me.

You didn't even talk to her.

She's got a boyfriend.

Listen, the first girl I liked had a boyfriend and she pretty much dumped him once we got to talking.

True?

Pretty much.

+

My girlfriend's coming over.
Girlfriend, right.
Almost. So don't be home walking around.
No, I was planning to take a shower.
Shut up.
Maybe flex a little bit in my towel.

+

Don't come in here.
What are you doing?
Give me a minute.
Hurry it up.

+

I'm in the shower. Don't take a piss.
How long do you expect me to wait?
There's another bathroom.
You were fine with this before. You become big man now?
I'm in the shower, Army.
Come on. Everybody knows you're not cleaning the bathtub in there.

+

Why isn't anybody asking me what I want for Christmas?
I don't know if we're doing Christmas this year, little man.

+

My birthday's coming up.
Yeah, we're not doing your birthday this year.
Funny. You have to get me something separate from everybody else. You
can't just put your name on Heather's gift.
I'm getting you stock, Riot. Trust me, it's what you want. You'll thank me.
Get me this.
Another camera?
The old one's crap.
The sale's over though.
That's not my problem. You owe me for last year and Christmas.

+

Mutter said to take me.

I'll drive you but you have to take the bus home.

She said you should see if they could squeeze you in. She wants to know why you didn't make an appointment for the same time.

Cause you don't need to see a doctor for 'roids. It's a little bit a blud. I have massive logs. What?

I don't need the details.

You used to video these pythons all the time.

There's people who like that stuff.

I bet.

+

What's so funny?

I said to the doctor, I think I'm getting my period.

+

You want to see my movie?

Is it another one with Logan's cat?

Yeah, but this one's really good. It already has like twenty-five views.

Watch out, YouTube.

+

Tell me what you think.

It needs more blood.

See, I knew it.

+

You want to see my movie?

Who's the girl?

That's Faye who I was telling you about. She did the pointillism thing that you said looked like she needed to get laid.

She's hot.

Right?

You should have given her a bigger part.

She didn't even want to be in my movie.

+

Well?
Needs more blood.
I don't do blood anymore.
Oh, excuse me, auteur. Let me get you a turtleneck.

+

You want to see my movie?
Send me the link.
I didn't upload it.
Er. Email it to me then.
The file's too big.
Put in on a DVD.

+

Did you watch it?
It was like five hours.
Yeah, awesome, eh. You watched to the end?
Hell, no. Riot. I don't even know where to start. It was just you going in and out of your room. There was no story.
It's a documentary.
It's not a documentary. It's not even reality TV.
It's reality. You're not getting it.
What's there to get? It was you and the camera in your bedroom. Camera was on your dresser the whole time. You didn't edit.
I'm not going to edit it at all.
Speed up the frames or something. At least it'll be funny. Charlie Chaplin it. Damn.
No, no, no. It's supposed to be slow. Slow TV. Like in Norway. The train?

+

Well?
I support you. You know that. I'll produce your first feature. You know that. But these films of you sleeping—
It's Warhol.
If I'm paying to go see a movie,
You're not paying.

I want to see stuff blow up.

I'm outside of Robert McKee plots and Hollywood profit models.

But, like why am I watching you lotion you knees or fold your drawers? Why are you subjecting me to that?

It's poetry.

See. That's the problem.

+

Do you want to be in my movie?

I'm A-list, boy. You can't afford me.

It'll be like old times.

I retired from python videos.

No, I don't do toilet stuff anymore. I took your advice. I'm going to have to make some commercial films to support my art films. You don't have to act. It's a documentary.

About?

It's more like a workout video.

+

Nobody wants to be in my movies.

Because they suck.

I thought you were my biggest supporter. What happened to that?

Lemme finish: they suck / the will to live from anyone watching them.

Ha ha. When I get my Oscar—

When you get your Oscar you can put it on the mantel right next to your mom's.

Why're you on me?

I'm not on you. It's just time, kid.

Hey, at least I'm not thirty-six and living in my parents' basement.

Ey-oh, oh-ey, and I'm not twenty, living in a movie.

PART 4

XXX

PRESENT

Felicia was at the hairdresser's cutting off all her hair when she got the news from Edgar's old secretary, Polly, that he was in the hospital with cancer, a second bout.

I think you should go see him.

Did he tell you that?

No, Polly said. She had gone from secretary to receptionist to administrative assistant to executive administrative assistant, a trajectory similar to Felicia's. Polly went on, He doesn't know I'm calling. But.

I'll try and go. But Felicia didn't know how or when. She was walking through fire herself with hot flashes, her breaking hair, a countless multitude of students expecting her to wave a magic wand over their enrollment issues, and of course Riot's situation. Then Felicia caught the former secretary's innuendo. But what?

I think you should go see him, she repeated. Before he—

When Felicia hung up, she realized that the hairdresser had never stopped talking to her about short hair while she was on the phone.

Trust me, the hairdresser was saying, sometimes you have to start over. It go look real sweet when I finish. You go be like Rihanna. Where have you been all my li-i-i-i-ife?

+ + +

Riot's tribunal for alleged harassment was held one week into the fall semester.

Such humiliation, Felicia had gone around the house saying, that you make me the first case of the year. Not a spot on the leaf them and I call up before grand jury.

There was no point correcting her pronominal use.

The girl's people were on one side of the table and Riot's people were on the other side of the table and the ombudsman—person, man, it was a man—was at the head. They faced each other in perfect symmetry. Father facing father, mother facing mother, Riot facing Unnamable, the ombudsman facing a portrait of someone dead.

He said, I think we're all on the same page in terms of the inappropriateness of Chariot's conduct. Agreed?

Unnamable's side of the table nodded. Riot's side of the table nodded, except for Riot. Felicia tasered him with her elbow and he jiggled his head. The ombudsman made a note to himself and Felicia looked over her reading glasses at Riot.

And we've decided that the offensive video must be taken down immediately. Agreed?

More nodding. Jiggling.

Is it down? The ombudsman asked Riot.

A stupid question because nothing is ever down the way he meant it. It could be down but downloaded and reposted elsewhere under a different name. It could be down from the clear net but coursing through the deep web. It could be gathering a lump in the dark web.

But Riot nodded.

What's at issue today is whether this video—

Videos, the mother said. There was more than one. Photos and videos. She asked her daughter, How many?

I don't know. A lot, Unnamable said. Neither she nor Riot looked at each other.

Five? the ombudsman asked.

Oh, no, no, no, the mother said.

She probably watched every one of them, Riot thought. Enjoyed him to the end. The wench. The wannabe MILF.

Unnamable shrugged one shoulder. Twelve, thirteen.

Riot glanced at her. Her ombré hair used to make her look all glamorous, at least reality-show glamorous, but now it just looked like she needed to dye her roots. What bothered him was that she sat there with her parents, trying not to chew her gum visibly, as if she didn't have her own camera, her own public spaces, her own private parts, her own dirty talk. She was suddenly leader of the prayer meeting.

There's one video in particular that I have in my notes. The ombudsman returned to his previous script: But what's at issue today is whether these videos constitute harassment. Am I correct?

Not exactly, the father said. We're alleging that the actions of Chariot constitute sexual assault.

What was this guy, a lawyer?

You're saying he digitally penetrated her, Oliver said.

That's not what that means, Unnamable said.

Because there's no such thing, Oliver said, looking straight at her.

She looked away. There was a brief silence where they all waited on the ombudsman to steer the conversation but he was busy noting something. Probably *apple + tree*.

There was violation— the mother began.

Of trust, Riot said.

Of Unnamable, the mother finished.

She's not the one on the internet, Riot said. I don't see what the problem is. Elbow taser.

He's not a sex offender for flashing his penis on the internet, Oliver said.

He did more than flash his penis and you know it. He sent unsolicited—

You know how much junk mail I get every day, lady. Oliver was reddening. And I'm not going after every Tom, Dick, and Harry who sends me something.

How would you like to open up your inbox every day and be assaulted by dozens of—

It wasn't dozens

by dozens of unwanted

every day. Puhlease.

sexual images. That's worse than flashing someone, Mr. Soares.

The ombudsman cooled the conversation. On one hand, he said, we have the issue of assault and on the other, though not entirely separate, hand we have the issue of consent.

She consented, Riot said. I was talking to her when I was doing all that stuff.

There's no sound on the video, the ombudsman said.

Yeah, I know but—

You're talking to somebody. That much is clear. Or, at least, you're talking on the video.

Everyone in the room had sought out and watched the video, except perhaps Felicia. Was the ombudsman gay? Were they all avoiding Riot's eyes because he was forever naked to them after they had watched it?

Well, consent is an easy one to solve, Unnamable's father said. He turned to Unnamable and asked, Did you consent?

She shook her head.

Puhlease, Oliver said.

She consented, Riot said.

Unnamable hadn't made eye contact with anybody. She kept her head down.

She was guilty. Or traumatized. Or imagining him naked. But her act was very convincing.

Would you like some water? the ombudsman asked.

Do I have to stay for this? she asked.

If you're finding parts of the conversation difficult, you're free to excuse yourself for a few minutes.

Unnamable promptly left.

Oliver snorted. It's just two kids who did something stupid. We were all there.

I have to stop you there, the father said. One kid did something stupid. Unnamable clicked. That's all she did.

Then she shouldn't have clicked.

Oliver. Felicia pulled on his sleeve.

No, you're making a big stink over two stupid kids messing around on the internet. Do you hear how stupid you sound?

Felicia intervened: What he's saying is that there's no precedent or policy at this college that polices the online sexual behaviour of students.

We do have an online code of conduct, Felicia, the ombudsman said.

Nowhere in that document is there reference to the *sexual* behaviour of students.

There is something, Felicia.

I know the section you're thinking about. It's about viewing pornography or illicit acts at public workstations in the Learning Commons. It's about posting illegal content—I was at that CCC meeting when this proposal came up for approval and it's not in the document, but in the minutes you'll see that they were referring to things like child pornography, not the transmission of private files, of a sexual or nonsexual nature, between two of-age individuals.

That's not how I understood the document, the mother said.

I have it here if you want it to read it.

And calling her bluff, the mother requested it. She should know better than to test Felicia. Felicia had printed and highlighted every relevant document for this case and left it on Riot's desk for him to study before the tribunal. Presently, she opened the rings of her binder, withdrew a dozen pages, and started starring the margins while everyone waited.

Riot scraped back his chair. I'm going to look for [Unnamable].

When [Unnamable]'s ready, she will come back, the ombudsman said.

Then I'm feeling uncomfortable in this conversation. Riot stood up.

Please take a seat.

What? I don't get the same rights?

Sit down, Felicia said.

I want to use the bathroom.

Sit down. Felicia jerked his arm. Her wrist cracked. She starred a few more pages and offered them to the mother but the ombudsman indicated that he'd like to see them. He studied them for a while, engaged in a private conversation with Felicia, pointing to one section, then crossed out her asterisk. When he was satisfied, he slid the papers to the other side of the table then turned his attention to Riot.

Were you responsible for posting the videos?

Yeah, Riot said, then corrected himself. Yes.

Why?

The question seemed to interest Oliver. Explanation time.

I didn't post them like what you're thinking. I uploaded them to Groover so she could get it.

Blank. Remember your market, Army would say.

It's in the heavens.

Blank.

It's cloud based. Like Dropbox. I do this with all my stuff. She got it and she must have shared it or leaked it or somebody else got into my space and posted it on Pornhub.

Who else has access?

Like technically anybody could get access. I mean nothing's secure even with a password.

Did you protect the file with a password?

No, like everybody needs a password to log in and then it's open. I mean, you can choose to password-protect certain files but like most people just leave it unsecured. The front door's locked. I don't have to lock every room in the house. Open access, man. It's a principle. It's not just— and here Riot ran out of steam.

Unnamable returned at this point. She was putting her phone into her pocket.

Better? the ombudsman asked.

She nodded.

Are there files of my daughter—

Our daughter.

our daughter on the internet?

You mean, did she send me stuff?

No. The father slowed his speech. I'm asking if you uploaded any files of [Unnamable] on any porn sites on the internet.

Have you come across any? Riot said.

Chariot, the ombudsman dipped his head. This is a respectful space.

What's the matter with you? Felicia said, her eyebrows in all sorts of astrological signs.

Riot was instantly regretful. Here Felicia was exposing weaknesses in the offensive line of the Brownstone policies so he wouldn't get expelled and lay waste of her employee tuition discount, putting on her best, efficient-secretary voice, and he was taking cheap shots at the lawyer wannabe.

To answer your question, Riot said by way of apology, no, I did not post any videos of [Unnamable] although, yes, she sent me twelve or thirteen.

I don't believe that, the father said.

Which part? the ombudsman asked.

Any of it.

I can show you, Riot said.

If I can be plain, what's of interest to the college here is that in the video I saw, the video that was submitted, Chariot, you appear to be in one of our science labs and wearing a Brownstone sweatshirt for the first part of the video.

Riot knew what was coming. Partway through the video, he takes off the shirt and it sits on the arm of the chair until the end when he uses it to wipe his ejacule from the gas taps.

The ombudsman continued: And that one of the tags for this video on the pornsite I was invited to visit was *college*. The other tags were, he referred to his notes, *solo* and *twink*. So because this action took place on our property, no different from a dorm room, the college, you'll understand, must take into serious consideration our stake in this matter when coming to a disciplinary resolution. If I can be plain, this kind of tarnishing of our image to prospective students and their parents is potentially irrevocable.

The videos are down. Nobody can see them, Oliver said.

Be that as it may, it was a moderately popular video. Am I right? It has been seen.

Over seven thousand hits, the father said.

Which conceivably could mean that half of the students in this school could have watched this video in which you engage in masturbatory activity.

They're not unique, Riot said. Could be one guy clicking seven thousand times.

The ombudsman looked squarely at Riot. The video down, your profile down. We have blocked the site from our servers. Servers, right? The university is investigating the cost of a forensic specialist to remove all traces of the video from the internet. But you understand that we can't have one student costing us so much money.

The father took over for the ombudsman. We are clear about the appropriate action that the college needs to take right now. If it's not resolved at this level, we intend to take this matter to court. The kind of tarnishing of reputation can hardly—

She's not even in the video, Riot said.

The university understands your concerns. We will notify you both in writing.

Can you tell us what the possible outcomes are? Felicia asked so Riot could hear what she had been saying all week.

The ombudsman sat erect. For starters, there could be possible litigation if you decide to pursue the matter, which, naturally, we don't advise. But internally Riot is facing expulsion with a record of the offence on his transcript. Or suspension for the academic year or a semester, depending. Or he could be asked to withdraw from the college.

I withdraw, Riot said.

That's not your decision to make, the ombudsman said.

He doesn't withdraw, Felicia said.

You'll hear from us in writing within two weeks.

+

Later that afternoon (still Monday), Army emerged early from Principles of Business, no textbook, no laptop, not even a pen in hand, and found Riot loafing outside the classroom, waiting for him though not looking for him. He was coiled over his phone like a lanky question mark, waiting for him there—electronically.

Army assumed he wanted a ride. I thought you were going home with Mom.

They went to the hospital. Riot didn't look up. Check your phone.

Sure enough, when Army checked, he found two texts from Riot.

Old boss? Army asked for clarification.

That's what she said.

Army lowered Riot's phone to get his full attention. That's all?

Riot shrugged.

Whatever gene was reserved for bloodline intuition activated itself in that moment, like an agave plant blooming once after forty years then dying. Army knew who his mother had gone to see. He scanned his call history. How could Felicia not tell him this?

The tribunal went fine, Riot said. Thanks for asking.

You remember which hospital?

Toronto somewhere. Riot sighed. St. Xavier.

The rest of the class was emerging and Army steered Riot down the hallway into the washroom. His bladder was becoming middle-aged lately. He wondered how these kids could hold their piss for hours after consuming barrels of energy drinks when he had to piss by the time he swallowed.

At the urinal, Riot sidled up next to him, elbow to elbow. Army glared at him up and down, trying to ward him into the appropriate distance, but Riot's zipper was already down and he was reading the ad in front of him. It was of a drunk girl passed out on the lap of a guy. The vague background suggested a basement party. *If you don't help her, you're helping him,* the slogan read. Riot sighed again and flicked his hair out of his face.

Look, playa, Army said. He intended to make short work of this conversation. Free expression is like your first amendment right.

This is Canada.

You made some videos. Did anybody get hurt?

You can't quote an American document in Canada and expect—

Listen. Answer me. Did anybody get hurt?

Not really. But I was wearing the sweatshirt and—

That's all they cared about, right?

Right. Riot shook himself but Army was barely halfway through his stream.

Now you see why I dropped out of this place, Army said.

I'm going to withdraw, Riot said. I didn't want to come here in the first place. She was— It was messed up. Like the whole meeting, she was trying to save face with her parents. I'm not even all that interested in her. We didn't have sex-sex.

Just digital sex.

Digitally, yeah.

Sad, Army said. Ask her parents if she's still a virgin.

I don't think she was. Is.

She probably doesn't even know.

Silence.

Army looked over his shoulder. Riot had been pining for Faye, a girl he met in high school, for at least two years. Riot met her in Grade 12 Art. Faye did laborious, menial projects like poking paper with pins ten thousand times then shining a light through. She called that one *Outliers*. For their sculpture project, she wrote *Tylenol* on Tic Tacs and built a capsule. She called it *Time Release*. Riot, for his part, had the most technical skill of anyone in the class. Like Faye, he liked his projects to be labour intensive. He painted frames of a popular YouTube video at 30-second intervals. It was called Skip Ad. It was a comment on something. All their work was a comment on something. Army heard the play-by-play almost nightly. In art class, Faye had rested her head on his shoulder and poked dot-holes into her watercolour paper and asked him name by name did he think *x* was hot, scrolling through both genders. Riot washed his paintbrushes and set them to dry and asked her to be in his movies. Pervert, she said. She was fond of that word. In the caf, she sometimes sat with Riot after eating her actual lunch with her actual friends. They shared earbuds and listened to Adele. When Faye pre-emptively extolled the virtues of platonic male-female friendships over the summer, Riot slumped. He refused food and haircuts, and had begun Brownstone sporting a forlorn, poetic, in-need-of-repair look that attracted Unnamable to him during orientation.

You want to make a movie here? Riot asked.

You know where you should be instead of making movies in public bathrooms. Army had encouraged Riot to go to film school in New York. He got into his third choice there. When he got rejected from his first choice, Army drove him to the doors of the institute and told him to walk in there and Al-Pacino them, Al-Pacino them until they were clutching his legs, begging him to grace them with his genius. He lasted between three weeks and three months at his third choice.

Riot sighed a third time.

Not to bring up old wounds, Army said, but you know where you belong, little man, regardless of what they tell you.

The man? I need to stick it to the man?

Army joined Riot at the sinks. He wasn't going to get caught in the ever narrowing gyre of Riot's semantics.

You're only here because of Mutter. I'm only here because— I'm here but I'm not really here. I might look like I'm here, he pointed to the sink, but up here, he tapped his temple, I'm on a yacht swirling a tumbler of Hennessy. I'm not even in the same time zone as all y'all. I'm light years ahead.

I have to shut down my profile.

Then shut it down, Army said. He turned his face side to side and observed himself in the mirror. His sideburns were greying. Are you hearing what I'm saying to you?

Here but not here. Riot pushed his limp hands into the Dyson Airblade dryer.

So you dicked around for a couple of years after high school. Army made eye contact with himself although he was speaking to Riot. Let me break it down for you, little man. You want to make movies. You didn't get into the film school you wanted. You took no for an answer. You came to Brownstone and now they're kicking you out. You think you might be getting what you deserve? You think the universe is trying to tell you something?

The dryer must have garbled Army's spiel, else the force of Riot's denial, or the force of his persistence rather, prevented him from hearing.

I have to take it down, Riot said.

Army wiped his hands on his pants. He was done. You knew that going in.

Not the video, my whole channel.

Change your name. It was the obvious solution, yet Army could see Riot hadn't thought of it.

Right? Riot said. I mean they're so dumb.

Before they parted outside the bathroom, for Army was in the student lot and Riot was to drive Felicia's car home from the faculty and staff lot, turning neither to the right nor the left, Army took Riot's elbow.

That's all she said about the hospital?

Pretty much.

She drove all the way downtown and that's all she told you?

Pop-Pop drove.

Did it sound serious?

Riot shrugged. He took out his phone and illuminated his face. He bore no resemblance to any of the family as far as Army could discern. Army thought he looked like every other skinny white boy his age.

She didn't tell you what was wrong with this guy?

No.

Army let go of Riot's elbow. St. Xavier was forty minutes away, at this hour. He'd go home and change into a collared shirt. Splash on some John Varvatos. Maybe shave down his sideburns so the grey wouldn't show as much. That's how you prepare to meet your maker.

+ + +

The parking lever to the hospital went up. Felicia and Oliver had spent the entire drive from the college prognosticating Riot's academic future and only now did Felicia brief Oliver about Edgar. what are you missing

This man has cancer, she said. I used to work for him yesterday in the seventies. before my mother get admitted So don't say anything stupid. we had to peel the film off an onion and look at it under a microscope

I'll read the *Sun* in the lobby, Oliver said.

Help me find the room, Felicia said. She didn't want to be alone when she visited Edgar. and then you were supposed to draw the cells right She wanted to be seen draw and label with a man.

Edgar was asleep when they entered. His bed was on the side closest to the door. The curtain was drawn back and a black woman lay in the bed near the window. The scene was almost too much for Felicia, the symmetry to the past, the colour of the curtain, the faithful chairs at the bedsides. what did they look like disappointing naturally She was grateful for Oliver's faithful Mastiff presence to tether her: she was not collapsible: she was a professionally dressed academic program manager; she prepared nutritious breakfasts for her household (this was her preferred term for her group though everyone else in the household called themselves a family despite the lack of matrimonial bonds); she was assistant treasurer at church, a former clerk who prepared indisputable chronicles of board meetings. She was not nineteen no and holding back they just look clear even with the dye death.

From behind, Oliver rested his hands on her shoulders, more to shield himself than to support her. He had steered her similarly through a haunted house in Niagara Falls when Army and Riot (or *the children* as Oliver called them despite the lack of matrimonial bonds though, admittedly, he never called them *our children*) forced the two of them to go through. Pawk-pawk-pawk.

Felicia folded her arms through the short straps of her handbag. I did find the nucleus Edgar was hooked up to an IV. Nothing else. but I couldn't find nothing else As she inched toward him, he became exponentially larger, as if he were approaching too. Dolly zoom, Riot taught the household. so what are the parts you were looking for His head I know the parts seemed disproportionately large you tell me for his body. you went to school He had lost a lot of weight. His scalp was covered in white stubble, thinner at the temples so the top jutted forth in an enormous peninsula.

How does he look? Felicia asked when she arrived at Edgre's head. She didn't want to touch anything. The usual feeling in hospitals.

Oliver let go of her shoulders.

She turned to look at him and asked him the same question silently.

Oliver shrugged.

Riot's filth broke lightning across her mind. There and gone.

I only paid for twenty minutes of parking, Oliver said. Finding courage, he bent toward Edgar's face as if testing it for life. Then he walked to the window, nodding at the black woman in the other bed, and tried to spot his car among the others.

For ten minutes, they were like this, Oliver considering everything beyond the window, Felicia considering mostly Edgar well there's the nucleus with brief disturbances of Riot. and the skin He had always been a tight sleeper, Edgar, face laced up into composure. She had only known the membrane him in good health. Ambulatory. A man without explanation. She observed the half-peeled-back lid from his cup of orange juice, the names and of course the mitonaise on the whiteboard mitochondria over his bed that's what we used to call it of the nurse and doctor attending him. She thought, looking at the lines around his mouth, that he hadn't eaten the cryptonaise a proper meal cytoplasm since the late seventies. the ectomorph I believe then there's the plasma of course Army would organize a World I asking about normal cells Vision you sure you went to school campaign to support the soul-starved executives Mutter's doctor said cancer cells have different parts of the world.

Edgar awoke. He frowned. Felicia perceived a series of recognitions: that he was in the hospital, that her face was indeed her face, that it wasn't the seventies.

Felicia, he said. He tried to sit up.

She slipped back into dialect. I hear you was in hospital.

A little dizziness, Edgar said. I got dizzy. I fell. They're observing is all. His eyes stretched to Oliver.

Edgar, this is Oliver, Felicia said. She hoisted Edgar by the armpit why you keep putting your watch on her to help him sit up. She likes having some weight on her wrists wouldn't bracelets explain watches more.

Edgar looked Oliver in the face handcuffs a long while, said nothing, no then turned back to Felicia. but a knife now and then Dizziness. Just some dizziness.

That's not what I hearing.

Horse's mouth, Ender said.

Felicia still didn't believe a word of it. not funny Oliver a boy in my class approached from the window, not just a boy then stood, fidgeting behind her like my lab partner a boy. drank a whole bottle of antifreeze On one hand she wanted to send him out of the room but he didn't die so she could work the truth from Edgar he drank it after drinking rum but on the other she feared apparently there's something in alcohol that prevents the antifreeze from working being worked from killing you right away by Edgar. Ants crawled over her. It was the kind of irritation that Oliver would later claim not to understand even after she revealed the source to him. He was hovering over them. Why couldn't he say something manly to Edgar? people don't realize all the benefits in a shot or two Why was he such a lump of irrelevance?

Edgrr sniffed the remainder of his juice. You cut off your hair.

Monday, she said.

It's like how you used to look, he said. Your sister, remember, burned it off.

Felicia knew Oliver had never heard that story. It thrilled her.

I didn't come here to talk about my hair, she said. How you feeling?

He frowned and swatted the question away.

Is there something you haven't told me?

There are many things I haven't told you. He took a swig of the orange juice. In fact, I'd say I haven't told you the majority of things that can be told.

You know what I mean, Felicia said.

And you know what I mean, he replied. Then he glanced at Oliver and his eyelids flickered almost into an eyeroll. But, no, as I was saying, they're releasing me any time now.

You not in any condition to leave. You have a nurse?

I have everything I need.

The meter's almost up, Oliver said into Felicia's neck.

What do you do? Edgar asked how did you get paired with this nut Oliver loudly and pointedly. we choose our own groups Apart from monitor meters.

Oliver puckered his lips into oh an anus.

Edgar sat fully erect and waited.

Independently wealthy, Oliver said.

He used to teach mathematics, Felicia said. Independently wealthy—what kind of nonsense was that? Sounded like Army. Oliver hadn't worked a real job what you missing in the twenty years she had known nothing him.

Then it was Oliver's turn to pry. You and Felicia worked I serious at—?

My family owns Paperplane, Edgar said. I go in every day and do my thing By the eighties, you know we had outlets in every airport in this country. Even Yellowknife. what thing It's pretty much the same now, I except now I we have stores in every terminal. I hold a long note Plus America it's been years and Europe. And Asia.

Felicia felt she would have known that if it were true and not, say, machismo.

I bought two condos at the beginning of the boom, Oliver said.

Take that ROI and raise it exponentially, Edgar said. I've never bought a condo.

You should have.

The money I dealt with was more—Edgar searched for the word—abstract. Remember, Felicia, you used to call my money *abstract*.

Well, if you need real money, you should have bought a condo.

A building maybe, Edgar said.

Not now. It's too late. Oliver made his anus face, but he was determined not to crack.

I'll keep that in mind.

Edgar, I should head out, Felicia said. The conversation had quickly become very alpha, to her embarrassment via Oliver, who couldn't compete with a fellow ape in a hospital bed, hooked up to an IV. I just saying hello for now.

Edgar let Oliver out of his jaws and returned his attention to Felicia. He swept his eyes, his lashless eyes, up to her face. You ^{you smell like baby powder} haven't aged, he said.

She patted his hand. He ^{what} covered it ^{no comment} with his other hand.

Oliver squirted some sanitizer into his _{you smell like a house on fire} and walked to the door.

Let me pray with you, Felicia said. Oliver, you want to pray, she called out.

I'll meet you at the front, he said.

You don't need to pray, Edgar said.

Nonsense. She rearranged their hands, cupping his in hers, the way she used to with Army ^{like baby powder} when she taught him how to pray. Lord in heaven. We come before you this day to thank you for the many blessings that you have poured out upon your saints. We thank you that Edgar can be alive and well in this hospital bed, able to praise you from among the land of the living. Father, you know the condition of his health, you who have given life and breath and strength, you who numbered the hair on our heads, dear Jesus. Now we ask you to intervene in Edgar's life and grant him full healing, touch him with your mighty hand, that he might rise up to call you blessed and to see you in your kingdom when all the saints will gather and sing Hosanna unto your name. We pray for the woman in the bed next to him, that you may grant her healing mercies as well. Forgive us where we have erred in thought, word, or deed. All these things we pray, in the mighty name of Jesus. Amen.

Amen, the woman in the next bed moaned.

Edgar was staring at Felicia when she opened her eyes.

You should close your eyes, Felicia told him. And say *Amen* after people pray.

Amen, he said. If I give you the money, you think you could buy me a pack of cigarettes?

+

Felicia and Oliver fought in the car.

I explicitly asked you not to say anything stupid.

And I didn't, Oliver said. I never do. He was confused because this man, about whom he had been lied to, by the way, not that he was using that for ammunition, though he had every right to be angry but no, he would take the high road, because this man had been openly hostile without the slightest provocation from Oliver. What did I say?

Everything you said was stupid.

Lock and load, baby.

You used to work for him, eh? This was when you were a stewardess or building orphanages in Africa?

Busted.

I used to work for him when I just come to Canada.

This wouldn't be the same Edgar Gross who was secretly married to Sophie Fortin and all sorts of women?

I don't know anything about that.

You know exactly what—

I don't know. He's dying of cancer and you trying to dredge up— Sickening, Oliver, just sickening.

What's sickening is—

What's sickening is, Felicia took over, how you could be sitting at home all day and have no idea the kind of nasty things Riot doing on the internet.

Oliver realized he had lost again. In retreat, he found himself taking contrary positions spitefully, not logically. I'm not home all day.

Where you does go?

A black girl loosened the strap of her bikini. He couldn't say.

+

Yet their feud did not devolve into silence. Felicia had dodged the rifle aimed at her blindfolded face. Oliver had avoided the acid in his.

They began to converge over Riot as they were nearing their exit on the 410.

Neither of them thought the hearing went well. Felicia was almost certain that it would result in suspension, not because the crime was especially egregious, Oliver thought, but because the parents were so indignant, Felicia thought, and because the university didn't want this to reach civil court, Oliver thought, and because it was a sensitive cultural moment regarding assault, Felicia thought, and because, of course, the sweatshirt was the sweatshirt, they agreed. The university didn't want to face their own Duke basketball trial or Dalhousie dentistry publicity nightmare or be hashtagged all over Twitter.

He'll have to sit out the semester, Felicia said.

Or he could transfer out, Oliver said.

You're going to pay full tuition? Felicia didn't mean to accuse Oliver of being cheap but that's how he took the question.

I've always said that I don't have a problem paying full tuition as long as they don't go international. By *they*, he meant Riot and, to a lesser degree, Army.

He supported Heather through two degrees, including an MA at Columbia, and Hendrix through one year at CUNY. In American currency. When the Canadian dollar was used as toilet paper by Americans.

In the meantime he can do some night courses through Continuing Ed, Felicia said.

He can get a job is what he can do, Oliver said and he should have stopped there, but he added, raping the middle class, which set Felicia off again.

+

Army calculated. Felicia's car was parked in the driveway but Oliver's wasn't, meaning Riot was home but Felicia and Oliver were still at the hospital. He might yet surprise them there. The four of them would exchange long, soap-operatic stares before cutting to commercial for household cleaner.

But Felicia was home. Hunched over the stove making soup. He was still getting used to her aggressive undercut. Wasn't short hair supposed to make you look younger?

She asked if he wanted some soup.

How could you not tell me this? he replied.

She stirred the pot. He could see her deciding which course of action to take, ignorance or confession.

Mom?

Because it's minor. He got dizzy. He fell down. That's what he tell me.

Like he broke his hip?

Something like that. She stirred the pot. I don't want you going there. You understand me? Let me be very clear. If you think you going to rise up hot and sweaty now and go down to that hospital, you better change your mind. You not leaving this house tonight.

That Army was thirty-six years old and in possession of his own BMW with three-quarters of a tank of gas made no difference in Felicia's kitchen. He should have gone straight from the college instead of wasting his fragrance on Faye's grandmother who was placed in a nursing home, longterm care facility, pardon, when Faye went to university. He shouldn't say it was a waste of fragrance. He had called Faye from the facility, put her on speakerphone, so she could talk to her grandmother. The woman looked up at Army then back toward the Cantonese voice. She lifted her hand from the arm of her wheelchair tremblingly then lowered it. After that, Army drove to Faye's dorm and banged her. That's where his time went.

Sit down and eat something. Felicia began ladling.

Army stopped her hands roughly. Some soup splashed on his shirt. Felicia patted the damage with a tea towel. But Army stilled her. He wanted her full attention.

Mom. He looked Felicia deep in the eye.

It not going to stain.

Mom, he said again. He wasn't interested in his shirt. He released her hands and made the universal sign for money with his fingertips.

+ +
+

The following day, mid-morning, Army made his way to St. Xavier's Hospital, Health Centre, pardon.

Discharged, the nurse said.

With a broken hip? Army asked.

It's not uncommon.

Army drove to Edgar's house. Through some shrewd detective work when he first got his licence, he had discovered where Edgar lived. He had never stepped on the property. He was forbidden, Felicia had expressed that clearly, to have any contact with Edgar. Ye shall not eat of it, neither shall ye touch it. The closest he had come to setting foot was pulling into the driveway to reverse direction.

But he was grown now. Army knocked on Edgar's door.

There was no answer for a long time, even beyond Army's patience as he calculated how long it would take for a man with a hip replacement to rouse himself from a distant upstairs bedroom, make his way down the stairlift—maybe he installed an elevator—and answer the front door. Army peeked around the side of the house.

He returned to the front door and knocked again. He read a study that people responded more warmly to knocks than to doorbells. He heard. He didn't read.

Army looked in a nearby window. He saw his reflection mostly and dark shapes beyond that. No movement.

He knocked a third time. Well. As he was walking back to his car he heard the door open. Edgar stood in the frame, against the black interior, holding a sock. He was no Hugh Hefner, to be sure, but he had no cane, no walker. He wasn't even holding the door for support.

May I help you with something? Edgar ^{you want to call me something} asked. He looked like ^{call me Schatz} he was just waking up.

No, Boss, Army said and smiled. Turn it on, turn it on, turn it up to the highest wattage.

Well, I'll be damned, Edgar said. Armistice.

You said when I turned eighteen, right?

You're—

Twice the legal age, Army said.

Neither man said _{I not cussing} anything else, ^{it's not cussing} had anything to say. Army was determined to prevent the silence from becoming awkward yet he couldn't mention illness else it would seem like he was stomping the man into the grave.

Nice place, Army said.

Edgar led Army down the long hallway ^{come on} to the kitchen. There was a brown bead curtain with some blue glittering strands separating the hallway from the kitchen. He knew without evidence that his mother had been responsible for that. Edgar made no apology ^{Schatz} for the odour or odorous fog. He tossed the sock on a radiator. The kitchen smelled deep fried, like Faye's.

_{what does it mean} Felicia sent you? Edgar asked.

She wouldn't even tell me, Army said.

There's not much to tell. Edgah smelled a glass, decided it was okay, then poured Bacardi for Army and himself.

In the morning? Army asked.

Edgar gave Army ^{treasure} the bottle to hold. I'm cutting back. I usually have it with juice. He beckoned over his shoulder for Army to follow him back into the hallway and then through the garage into the backyard where they sat on two Adirondack chairs that opened toward a view of Edgar's wooded lot. As I was saying, she visited. She prayed. God, did she pray for me.

Army plunged into intimacy. Boss, ^{it means my treasure} what's happening to you?

Some dizziness.

Boss, Army said again. I wasn't born yesterday.

Edgar looked into his glass then back up at Army. Army knew _{I not calling you} _{that} this moment. Ignorance or confession. He opened his eyes a little wider. There was a study about pupils and trust.

Cancer, Edgar confessed. Stage four.

Army tried to recall how many stages there were. Four seemed to be the maximum. But six sounded right as well. Stage six cancer. He wanted to check his phone.

Then both of their mothers were dying in the background. Edgar told Army about the visit from the oncologist that morning before he was discharged, the visit from Felicia the evening before. About a friend with whom he used to play basketball who died of cancer of the balls.

Prostate cancer, Army said.

Something like that.

He told Army about the harassment allegations decades ago, his aversion to nurses ever since a few of them tried to extort him. About Mutter. _{darling would be the} _{better translation} He pointed toward a spot but made no reference to the graves. About _{I definitely not calling you that} the days, the length of days, the mercy of shortening fall days.

Army told Edrag about starting school again at thirty-six, about his various businesses, his procurement of a truck with a belly, his moving company with Oliver's stockiest, hairiest, sweatiest nephews that had him travelling all over the GTA, the province, the country, the globe, about his girlfriend whom he suspected wanted to break up with him now that she was back in university, third year, with all the fresh testosterone.

> Forget her, Edgar said.
> I should just forget her?
> Not everyone should reproduce.
> Forget her then?
> Forget her.
> I don't know.
> Trust me. You're dead to her.
> I'm not dead.
> To her. And she's dead to you.
> Even if she was dead to me, I'm not dead to her.

Bit complicated, Army said. He explained that it used to be his familial duty _{why not} to pick up Riot and his girlfriend, Faye, from high school on the nights _{it's} _{totally innocent} that they stayed late to work on the tech crew for the musical. Faye was from Hong Kong and her English was inflected with British curls. She'd only been in the country since middle school—she, her mother, and the grandmother, who was confined to a wheelchair. They might have been fleeing the father. Anyway, Riot made Army drive her home. She lived a few streets over in any case, in a triple-garage house.

I see where this is going, Edgar said.

Right? To Army it was obvious. You don't put meat in a cage with a lion and expect it to stay there.

My philosophy exactly.

Army paused. I'm the meat in that analogy. She had sex it's not *lover* in her eyes. Positively dripping. Like her eyes were watering with sex I leave my biology textbook at school is how bad she wanted it. She was trying to be all I hope nobody don't take it sophisticated and I'm, to her, like an older distinguished man. That's my Beamer out front.

I saw, Edgar said. German.

Represent. Army continued, She started getting into the car before Riot and sitting in my line of vision. She started I mean looping her fingers in my hair, I understand leaning between the seats so I could see down her shirt and stuff. I mean, the general distrust that your gender has toward mine what teenaged girl wants to watch six-hour movies of the art room, which is what Riot was trying to inflict on her?

Gracious, Edgar said.

Believe you me, I tried to hook her up with Riot. I asked her who she was going to formal with. She said all the boys were gay. I said, What about Riot? She said that would be like going with his brother, er, my brother.

Freudian.

Yeah, then she asked me who I went with. Went with or slept with? I asked her. Know what I'm sayin'. Then I see Riot coming in the rearview mirror.

Slouching toward Bethlehem.

What?

It's a poem. The Bard.

At that point, but I assure you that I am not a teenager trying to put his arm around you Army recovered a sensitivity that you're not to the situation: he had been talking to his father, quite inappropriately, not his boys, as Felicia liked to remind him. He withheld the rest of the story thank you that ended, more or less, with Army pulling Faye by the hand into an unfurnished condo. On the hardwood. Overlooking Lake Ontario. The occasional roar of a muffler way below. In one of her two-car garages. Her grandmother was hard of hearing. Sneaking around the summer before she started university. Then off and on for a couple of years. They found ways to open the black door.

But Army had to keep talking so he told Edgar about the investment condos he "and" Oliver bought. He told him about his latest business venture, Canafries. He imagined a commercial that echoed the climax of *Life Is Beautiful*, only with a series of awkward kisses then a voice-over: We may not kiss like the French. But we sizzle. Canafries. Canada's French Fry. He predicted expansion in Quebec to a poutine kit like those ready-made salad kits. Army went so far as to confess that he hit a pedestrian in America a decade ago and fled the scene. Edfar went to the bathroom at this point. Army was always afraid that someone would find out it was him one day.

When Edgar returned, he asked, Who's this Oliver?

You want Mom's explanation or mine?

Either. Both.

She'd say he's not her husband. Not legally, but you can't command me to call you something I don't want to call you not even common-law. They sleep in separate bedrooms. But he uses her bathroom. She wouldn't call him her partner because it sounds gay. He used to be our landlord.

I remember, Edgar said. Mr. O.

Right. He's not her friend. Actually, she doesn't even like him I'll leave it on the table then most of the time. But they've got an agreement between them. Some kind of commitment. So I'd say that—Army found it difficult—he's Pop-Pop to her Mutter.

She calls herself you may call me *Schatz* if you so choose *Mutter?*

Yeah, it's like almost-mother. That's what my brother calls her. Riot. I just told you about him.

He wasn't your— Edgar began then changed course. How did he become your brother all of a sudden?

It just happened. Army shrugged. People fall into other people's arms, you know.

+

It was mid-afternoon how do you feel by the time Army was ready about dogs to leave. He had missed his class.

No one stays with you? he asked.

Fine, fine. The exasperated wave of filthy hand. Are you okay to drive?

Army nodded if I could stone every last one of them I would and walked down the aggregate path, paused, and turned back.

You forget something?

Army shook his head. Why had he turned back? He said, I wanted to say it was nice seeing you.

Edgar appeared moved. Hurry up and get home. You have a teen drama to work out.

Army took the path with fresh alacrity I was thinking of getting one and waved don't ever and smiled several times or an ostrich over his shoulder. But, again, maybe I will get one before he could get to his car, he turned around and took long strides up the path to the door.

No, Boss, it's not right, it's not right, he said. I can't just leave you here alone.

Army mentally ran through his house. Oliver and Felicia had steadily upgraded it over the last twenty years but structurally the backsplit was still a two-family home, staggered into six levels, connected by short staircases. The lower half had its own kitchen and dining area in the basement, stairs, a living room that led to the garage, stairs, two bedrooms and a bathroom, black door, then stairs to Oliver's section which was stacked similarly on Felicia's.

I got room at my place, Army continued. I mean, it's not huge like this but you can have pretty much the whole downstairs. We can talk brand strategy for Canafries. You know anyone on *Dragons' Den?* I'm gone on the road a lot when I'm a bit older but I mean, I'll be around that's what Mutter used to say if I know you're there.

That's very kind, Edgar said.

I'm not saying it to be kind, Army said. I'm not even asking you. I'm telling you that I'm not leaving you here alone.

Edgar said something but Army missed it as he was stepping into the house. Army took Edgar's wallet from the dining table. His keys. Couldn't find his phone.

Where's your cell?

Infested.

It took Army a moment to get it then he overlaughed at the joke, boggled his head. That's rich. Infested. He strode toward the car.

Edgar didn't follow. He began, Army this is very kind but—

Army interrupted him by twisting his face into impatient concern. how old you waiting to be Come, he said.

Edgar Methuselah didn't move.

Army walked back and held his elbow. Come.

Edgar pushed his feet into his shoes and walked away from his house.

+ +
+

It was a record. Eight days into the semester, Riot had been suspended.

He received the letter from the disciplinary committee (consisting of just the ombudsman, as far as he could tell) at home the day after the tribunal, which suggested to Riot that his case was decided, typed, and mailed before the tribunal was staged. Riot opened the envelope and read the letter on the porch, right by the mailbox. The ombudsman could have saved himself the effort of composition and typed him a large *X*, 900-point font. Riot debated destroying the suspension notice, pretending that he had never received it, continuing to show up to class as usual, but he imagined a scene from a Tom Cruise movie where sirens would go off and campus security in black ninja-like outfits would descend from the roof by rope, ordering him to step away from the classroom with his hands behind his head. And, of course, Mutter probably already knew the verdict.

He didn't want to go to Brownstone anyway. He just wanted to make budget-less, profitless movies (Are you even related to me? Army would say if he heard that) that were untainted by genre or celebrity and hailed as "groundbreaking" and "challenging." His jerk-off videos, notwithstanding.

Riot dropped the letter on the couch. He turned on the TV, which was left on a home-reno show that was climaxing. Decision made? Decision made. And. Are you going to love it? Or will you list it?

+

Army's room reminded Edgar of his office after the company shifted to literal and symbolic transparency. Everything that could be open ^{so you're legal} in the room was already open: each drawer of his chest was open _{of course I'm legal} to varying degrees, his closet was open, the side-table drawer was open, the pockets of his pants were turned inside out, his deodorant was uncapped. Freud was tenting his fingers under his chin: issues with closure.

On the dresser, behind several bottles of cologne, was the wooden carving of Army's name that Edstr had sent him. ^{I'm just asking} What year was wood?

I have the other things somewhere, Army said. Not the candy, _{you can't just look at people and assume} obviously. Or the shoelaces. And I might have sold _{they illegal} the Bulls jersey. But I got the crystal fish _{because they not German} somewhere and those— what were they?—beads in a sack from Vegas.

Edgar snorted.

You should have dinner with me and my girlfriend tonight.

Another time, Edgar said. He just wanted a nap.

But you can't say she's my girlfriend.

Not tonight. He yawned.

Army looked confused. ^{just a question} I mean ^{because I know a guy} unless it's just the three of us, then sure. Also, don't mention her torso

Why would—

or anything about her body, really. She's sensitive. If she's wearing ^{if you need help} a babydoll dress over jeans, just compliment her and move on. But you don't want to say that it gives her the illusion of a waistline or that it makes her legs look longer. Trust me on that. Army swiped some clothes from one side of the bed. She's not so much hot ^{I mean my business is airports more or less} as she is young. But don't tell her I said that.

Edgar reclined against the headboard ^{I don't need no help} and closed his eyes ^{you can keep that card} while Army pecked at his keyboard to wake up his computer.

Did I tell you I manage talent? Army asked.

Edgar didn't know what talent was. I need a quick nap.

I have a few clients. I'll show you the website. When you wake up, not now. I just secured a gig for Mr. O.

Ten percent for you, Edblr said.

It used to be, Army said. He doesn't do it for the money ^{thank you very much} anyway. Your pillow's flat.

Did I tell you he used to play in the subway? Rosedale. I got him a permit and stuff. But then there was an incident. Some girls were shouting at him from the other side of the platform, like calling him Meatloaf, washed-up, and he was trying to ignore them because he thought they'd get on the next train—Edgar ^{I have a flight tomorrow} was sliding through Denmark—but they kept on insulting him for like ten minutes, singing along but changing the lyrics, and he was getting more and more pissed—rosé ^{are you legal} in Chateau Lake Louise—and somebody pressed the emergency notification when he started heading to the girls like the Hulk with his—and here Edgar slid into sleep.

+

Riot took the GO bus to Yorkdale then the subway to St. Patrick Station and walked from there to the Toronto Coach Terminal. He had some clothes in a backpack, his laptop with editing software, two cameras, his passport, and granola bars. Those were the essentials to launch the early career portion of his Wikipedia biography as Chariot Soares, director.

He hadn't been to New York since quitting film school last fall. Oliver was more disappointed that he wouldn't get a partial refund for the semester than he was by Riot's failure. It wasn't really a film school in any case, just a program at an institute. Riot quit during the third week in September and, under Army's advice, pocketed the money from Oliver until American Thanksgiving under the auspices of paying tuition. Felicia hated the cramped New York apartment Riot shared with Heather. She said she lived in a room once and she couldn't understand why he would want to live like a refugee when he could stay home and go to Brownstone.

Riot bought a ticket for the 9:15 night bus, round trip to avoid suspicion at the border, and a bottle of water for the hours until departure:

+

Felicia drove home from work on autopilot. But when she landed she had to check whether she had pulled into the right driveway. Oliver's truck was gone, the garage was open and—had she conjured him?—there was Edgar, standing upright (somehow she assumed he couldn't) with a comforter I take it you're a puritan of some sort around his shoulders, smoking. He was not Christian terminally ill. She had yes fallen you sound like you scorning me for a ruse. He had opened a bear trap yesterday and hidden behind a tree. He had slaughtered Army and Riot. He had bought the house and was asking her to leave the keys in the mailbox.

She got out of her Mazda and looked both ways as if crossing a street.

You visiting me now? she said.

He took a deep drag until his cheeks practically touched each other on the inside. He could take an infuriatingly long time you misread me to respond I'm Christian myself when he was what smoking.

Army, he said conceal your shock then sputtered coughs.

The devil I mean what denomination in that boy. After she had explicitly. She would draw a belt and whip him. Gone to the hospital. Explicitly told him. Hold him by the wrist and whip his tail.

He's upstairs, is he? Felicia said.

Edgar nodded. He wore the mysterious pensive expression of Lutheran smokers. She made an exaggerated display of swatting smoke do you pray out of her face.

Edgar finished coughing, pulled up phlegm and spat into the grate at the base of the driveway. His eyes watered now and again from the effort. He sucked on the cigarette.

Felicia took it from his mouth. But what was she going to do with it? It wasn't stub enough not for things to throw away. One thing Felicia was not was wasteful. Edsir withdrew another cigarette from a pack, lit it, and resumed why else would I pray as if he didn't even notice.

Through what labyrinth of lies did he end up here? Who saw? Did the neighbours think it was Oliver's brother spitting all over the place? When was Army that your sins be forgiven thee taking him home? How could Army bring him here to see where she was living? She scanned the inside of the house mentally. What to do with a perfectly good cigarette? She finally threw it down.

Nice house, Edgar said. I like the doorknobs.

If ^I suppose^ I knew you were coming, she said without finishing. The driveway needed sealing. The garage needed purging. The shrubs needed shaping.

I'm going to cut the charade, Felicia, Edgar said. I wasn't in the hospital for the sniffles.

You was in the oncology ward, Edgar. I not schupid. I just didn't want to embarrass you is all. I don't know why you think you could fool people.

I had cancer.

Had or have? Felicia asked.

Had. Have. Had. Have.

You need to stop smoking. She lunged to take the new cigarette out of his mouth you does read your Bible but ^I don't take it as a book one must read continuously^ he twisted his head like a horse and held it stiffly in profile and so no she didn't dare.

He faced her slowly. I cut back.

Cut completely.

Of his own accord, he stubbed the cigarette against a wall you does go to church and smelled his fingers. As I was saying, ^not every week^ they got most of it.

She said how often nothing. She was waiting excluding Christmas and Easter to see whether he was still a boldfaced liar or not.

During surgery.

One more chance she was giving him.

About ^I mean they know me there^ a year ago.

You mean to tell me you cancer-free right now ^I used to take Mutter^ and was lying when she was able in the hospital bed yesterday for no reason.

I was dizzy, Edgar said.

You was dizzy, right.

I get sleepy lots. Maybe an hour after I wake up, three four times a year then I fall about that asleep again.

Why is only now you telling me this? Felicia frowned deeply. That is your problem from eternity. You does give people information too late. If I did know, I would have tell you about this place in Pennsylvania that does do all natural remedies. The naturopath did a program at church and he said that rum does bore holes in your lungs and sometimes they never fix themselves. That's the warm feeling you getting.

I tried all that the first time.

What did you try?

Edgar ignored ^{that's the church where Mutter's service will be} the question. He said, Cancer is cancer. You think some green juice and prayer are going to save _{nobody} _{going to die} me?

Not if you keep smoking, not if you unbelieving.

Well, Edgar said. He drew another cigarette from the package _{is better if you say} _{that is the church where you plan to get married} then put it back. ^{I prefer what I said} Nice house, he said again.

Felicia heard his superiority.

I forgot my medication. Could you tell Army I forgot my medication?

+

Felicia found Army at the linen closet, selecting a sheet and pillowcases. Some of Oliver's clothes were folded on the floor beside him.

What on earth is going through your head, Army?

You saw Boss?

What you bringing that man here for?

He needed a place to stay.

The man have a house the size of Buckingham Palace. He don't need nowhere to stay.

He can't stay there alone.

Says who?

Says human decency.

You mistaken if you think this man go be living under my roof, Felicia said. You mistaken big time.

Army dropped the bedding on the floor.

He is not staying here, Felicia said. He's not going to die in my house.

That's the point, Army said. He selected two towels. Do we have any Pine-Sol?

Felicia felt blood ticking in her neck. Army only cleaned the bathroom under threat of eviction and now he was Molly Maid for Edgar?

Listen, he can stay and eat with us this evening. You talk to Oliver? And then I want you to take him home.

We'll see.

I am telling you, Army.

We'll see.

You don't know how I worked my life out and now you go bring he here to freeload off me in he dying hour.

Two floors beneath them, Felicia heard the basement door open.

Army lowered his voice, I got this, Mom. Chill. He's my responsibility. You and Oliver won't even know.

Felicia fiercewhispered, You are not trained to take care of anybody, Armistice! You can barely manage yourself. He forget he medication. You going to drive back to Toronto to get his medication?

I'll get it tomorrow.

Medication don't work like that, Army. Take this man back to his house tonight.

Army was already sorting pajamas for Edwas, she saw. He picked up Oliver's folded clothes from the floor beside him. Felicia snatched them out of his hand.

Use your own clothes, she said.

Army shrugged, as if Felicia had, in fact, given him a good idea. He left Oliver's clothes in a pile between them and went downstairs with the sheet, towels, soap.

Felicia straightened the mess he'd made and shut the linen closet firmly by its crystal doorknob.

Then she turned her head and spotted the letter, the familiar Brownstone logo, down the stairs, on the arm of the couch.

+

As Riot was boarding the coach that night, he finally took Felicia's call. He had avoided all previous calls from familiar numbers until he was sure he was sure he was beyond retrieval.

Felicia was shouting about the suspension notice. Riot had to turn down the volume of his phone. He kept his answers brief so the other passengers wouldn't assume he was talking to his mother. She asked him to speak up. He told her he couldn't talk now.

Well, I can talk, Felicia said.

He let her. She could have been talking about omega-3 fatty acids for all he cared. Her planet was distant and unrelated to his. He had an armrest. No charging station? He tucked his bottle of water into the mesh seat pocket in front of him.

Between Felicia's sentences, he tried to squeeze in, I gotta go. Okay. I gotta go. I gotta, I gotta, listen, I gotta go. Bye. Buh-buh-bye. I gotta go. Buh, okay, bye. As Army would say, Stay on message.

Oliver called immediately.

What is this? Oliver said.

Riot pinched the bridge of his nose. Surely Pop-Pop realized that he was not visible over the phone. You found the letter?

Get home this minute.

I'm spending the night somewhere.

Where?

Somewhere.

Somewhere where? Nobody authorized you to go anywhere. People have been trying to reach you. Then, a few seconds later, in a quieter voice, as if he had secreted himself from Felicia's presence and was now engaging in a secret deal, Oliver said, You're breaking her heart, meaning Mutter's, meaning his own, meaning Heather had gone missing before he was even born. I'm coming to pick you up.

I really can't talk. Seriously.

Explain to me where you are that you can't talk.

Nowhere.

Nowhere where?

I'll call you in the morning or something.

The seat next to Riot's was empty. When he was in middle school, a man on a Greyhound along the Trans-Canada Highway beheaded a fellow passenger. Felicia used to repeat versions of that story whenever he wanted to take the bus somewhere. Riot looked behind him. A history-major-looking girl. Sketchy people farther back. Old people at the front. He set his phone on the sill and began recording.

+

Meanwhile, Army was having dinner with Faye, at her request but not her expense. He had motormouthed about Edgar through his quarter-chicken meal, overriding her attempts to share her puerile dramas, and as he was entering his debit information, she retaliated, in front the waitress.

You're going to break up with me right when I have cancer? Army asked. Older women, like around twenty-five, usually got tired of him a month into their relationship but Faye had at least a few more weeks of love in her.

You don't have cancer, Faye said.

I'm dealing with cancer.

So, I should wait?

Well, you can't wait now.

No, if you want me to wait, I'll wait. We can break up after chemo.

That's cold, Faye. Army folded the receipt into his wallet for tax purposes. You don't have reason to be so cold.

+

Oliver was trying to call again.

Seat 33 texted: ?

Upstairs bedroom texted Seat 33: COME HOME NOW!

Seat 33 did not text back.

Downstairs Bedroom texted Booth-in-Swiss-Chalet: Is Chariot with you?

Booth texted Seat 33: Are you supposed to be with me?

Seat 33 texted Booth: No. Ignore.

Booth texted Seat 33: OK

Seat 33 texted Booth: Got suspended for penisgate.

Booth texted Seat 33: Handling a situation. Talk l8r. U ok tho?

Seat 33 texted Booth: Yeah fine. Going to Vegas. 😄

Upstairs Bedroom Texted seat 33: DID YOU HEAR ME CHARIOT? ANSWER.

Seat 33 texted Upstairs Bedroom: Copy.

Booth texted Seat 33: Know your limit play within it.

Upstairs Bedroom texted Seat 33: YOU HAVE ONE HOUR!

Downstairs Bedroom texted Booth: Are you together? Where are you?

+

The morning ^{do you hear that} after Edgar's arrival was the first cold morning of the fall. Oliver approached Felicia accusingly as she was rolling lint from her coat near the basement entrance.

Why is he using my towel? Oliver held up the evidence.

Talk to Army, Felicia said.

Army, Oliver called.

He not home.

Edgar wafted ^{outside the window} into a nearby door frame. The way they were positioned, with Felicia between them and facing Oliver, only the men could see each other. ^{the deaf could hear that} Oliver felt the urge to do something grand yet natural. Give Edwer ^{not the dog} something ^{bloody pot hound} to look at. He leaned forward to kiss Felicia on the cheek, something he did not typically—ever—do. But she jerked her head away and to save face Oliver quickly pretended he was adjusting the collar of her coat. When the door closed behind Felicia, Oliver put his hands on his hips. Edgar unpaused ^{the wind} and floated across the doorway without a word.

+

Riot arrived at Heather's apartment, unannounced, before she left for work. He could hear a whirring inside. She swung open the door with a stankface that he hoped was intended for someone else.

Hey, Runaway, she said.

Pop-Pop called you.

Felicia, Heather said. She frowned at the sound of his voice. Felicia was *convinced* you were already here and I was covering for you. You should answer your phone.

Heather had a sleeve of tribal tattoos, and beyond her shoulder Riot saw a sleeve of books along the wall from the kitchen to the bedroom: anthropology, feminism, critical race theory, Fifty Shades, Zane. She also had a healthy, if outdated, collection of DVDs.

Riot heaved the backpack from his shoulder. For the record, a runaway is, like, an underage kid who leaves home. After eighteen, I can't technically be a runaway.

Fine. Hi, Sexual Terrorist.

Drôle.

A girl he didn't know but had friended during orientation had posted a missive on Riot's Facebook, calling him an online sexual terrorist. Riot was considering deactivating his account.

Heather said, Congratulations on being a landmark case in what could be considered assault. Electrossault? Electrassault?

I didn't assault anybody. And there's no case. They kicked me out. Done.

This stuff has a way of following you.

It's behind me.

Heather continued juicing carrots and kale while Riot unpacked his essentials. He plugged in his laptop and set it on the breakfast bar. The noise from the blender made it unnecessary to talk. He transferred the files from his trip. Dark views from a bus window, the rhythmic pattern of poles, like a music beat, sleeping passengers. On his Facebook, there were a few trickling comments from the sexual terrorist debate, including two terse messages from Army to the coalition of indignant girls who were calling for Riot's castration: *Blow me. Up. Buh-bam!!* and *Shoot all over u.* Mature. Riot clicked away.

Heather set a quarter cup of vegetable juice in front of him as he was scrolling through photographs posted by the small nation that their extended family had become. It was that zone in life, Heather's more than his, where every other week someone they knew was having a baby. Heather was godmother to one of Diane's four children.

Every year he expands, Heather said. No wonder he's broke. She was looking at an album of Army's Neighbourhood Birthday and Labour Day Barbecue that, as of 2008, ended illegally with fireworks, thanks to a few of her pyro cousins and Logan, Riot's childhood friend.

It's his way of—

Giving back to the community. Yeah, yeah.

He did a product relaunch this year for Canafries.

He's been using that barbecue as a taxable expense for years. Heather leaned in, probably to get a better look at Diane's eyebrows. In the photograph, Diane, Felicia, and a girl were spreading a gingham table cloth in the foreground while Army was picking a spring roll off a cousin's husband's plate in the background. Is that Army's girlfriend now?

That's a dude.

No, her. Heather pointed.

That's Faye. You know Faye. Riot sipped his foaming green trial.

That's not Faye. She get implants or something?

That's just one of them— Riot hoisted imaginary breasts.

Push-up bras. You can say *bra*.

Riot turned back to the screen. Another photo. Army was talking to one of their cousins in the background but his eyes were trained on Faye in the foreground. Girlfriend? He recalled how, when Army picked them up, Faye used to get in the car well before he could get everything he needed from his locker and lean back suddenly when he opened the passenger door. There was an audible click as Riot set down his glass of grass.

She's my age, Riot said. But he thought, Of course. No, of course.

Heather shook her head.

What else?

No, not that. She was studying Riot. You just sound different in person. That's all. I'm used to you in simulacrum, seeing you on Facebook or hearing you through my headphones but it's weird to, like, see and hear *you*-you.

Riot shrugged. He had lived with her before. But truthfully, she lost him at *simulacrum*.

Yeah, well, listen, I'm off. Heather dropped her travel cup of slime into a large bag, spun two keys from her keychain and gave them to Riot. These are my only keys, meaning you have to be home before six. Lock both locks.

He was nodding at Heather and at the image of Army draculing Faye—everything plain in front of his face—when he realized that he didn't have a toothbrush to scrub the nasty green taste from his tongue.

+

Oliver wanted to know why his house had become Amnesty International.

It's been a week, he said. He stood in the doorway of the bathroom as Felicia applied mascara. Many of their morning conversations happened here. All this whispering in my own house. All this tiptoeing around nap time.

Her eyes bulged.

This is not a permanent arrangement, he said.

Yet it had all the trappings of permanence. Army had set up Edgar on the basement and ground levels. He assigned the man his own mug, supplied towel service, placed Edgar's toothbrush among his and Riot's, gave him two pairs of Oliver's wool work socks.

I think a week is more than enough time to extend hospitality to a stranger, Oliver said.

He's not a stranger, Felicia said. But I agree with you.

I deserve an explanation as to what's going on.

You want an explanation or you want the truth?

Oliver ignored the question. Felicia said that from time to time when she was feeling righteous. You can't get Army to bring somebody here to live rent free.

Army brought him here on his own.

So what? We don't have to keep him. What is he, a puppy? I'm not a fool, Felicia. Oliver knew who this man was although Felicia would not admit it. He had watched his share of cuckold videos on the internet.

Felicia's wrist made tiny movements as if she were crocheting her lashes.

Everybody's just taking advantage of my good nature.

Since when you have a good nature?

What other man in my situation would allow somebody—what did Heather call them?—the one percent to camp in his house? Cancer or no cancer, I have Riot to think about, he said.

I don't know how, in a week's time, you can't get Riot back in this house.

Me? What's Army doing?

Army's in school.

If it's possible to exhale cynically, Oliver exhaled cynically.

Get on a plane— Felicia began.

I'm handling it. You get Mr. Cancer out of my house.

I'm not fighting you, Oliver. Why you fighting me?

It's your problem.

He's not my problem, Felicia countered.

He's your baggage.

Oliver, put him out if that's what you want to do. Felicia picked some loose mascara from the outside of her eye with her pinky.

Don't guilt me, Oliver said.

No, I serious. If you want him out and you could do it under the eyes of the Almighty then go ahead. I didn't bring him here, though, and I not going to be the one to throw him out.

He's basically trespassing.

Take it up with Army.

Oh, he's studying so hard these days. I couldn't possibly disturb him.

Felicia returned the makeup brush to the case.

Cuckold videos. Was it him or had she applied more makeup today than usual?

+

When Felicia left for work, you were gone long Oliver went down two flights of stairs to the basement and rapped sharply on Edgar's door. Smoke was practically curling from underneath. When he opened the door, there'd be flames and Edwar in a red suit, pointed tail, horns, gripping a pitchfork. There was no answer.

Edgar, Oliver called I went down the side street near the entrance before opening the door.

Edgar was sitting up I don't think that does go anywhere in bed, it doesn't reading a red children's Bible with Felicia's old glasses, and smoking. His shirt, from Army, just garages was deeply unbuttoned. The chemo had eaten his chest hair. Or maybe he was the kind of man that couldn't grow chest hair.

Edgar, Oliver said, I've asked you every day this week not to smoke in my home.

Edgar raised his eyes, the houses aren't so old that whole area of his face, they look old eyebrows everything, they're not from the Bible, they feel old fixed Oliver in his gaze for a moment, they're not then he went back to reading.

If Edgar was going to be contemptuous maybe they've been smoking and disrespectful, Oliver would have no trouble calling him a taxi in twenty minutes.

He said it the way defendants via their lawyers say it around sentencing time.

Explain why you can't smoke outside.

The window's open.

I can smell it all the way upstairs.

Edgar remained mild.

Who's going to clean up after you? There's a garage if you want to smoke. If you're a guest in someone's house, doesn't it, Oliver needed an upper-class word, doesn't it behoove you to be gracious enough not to smoke?

Edgar stubbed the half-finished cigarette into the salsa lid he was using for an ashtray. There, he said. He smiled Bartlebly.

Oliver turned to leave. He took one step there's a great diner down the other way into the hallway I used to have late brunches there when I was in uni before turning around. 2:00 p.m. That's not brunch why I came down here. Edgar's mildness and capitulation had misled him into feeling as if he had achieved a victory. it's breakfast and I know what it is but only women have brunch

Oh?

No.

Edgar turned a thin page of Army's old Bible. Do you know what any of this means?

He was reading it, I was usually with a woman scanning pages, as a man who was inspecting it for something he may have missed earlier in life—time to see what the big deal if you must know was about—rather than searching it we used to go when we woke up with religious zeal or duty.

Edgar, harlotry I've been speaking with Felicia and Army and we've decided that it's time for you to go.

You spoke with Armistice? good French toast Edgar pointed straight to the lie.

There's nothing more they used to make it without eggs we can do eggs are good for you for you they're too here. reproductive Oliver didn't intend to phrase his eviction that way.

Edgar turned a page but they're an integral part of French toast and scanned.

Usually when people ask you something, call it something else then you respond. That's how conversations work.

What was the question?

The man was playing German toast passive-aggressive Haitian toast with him. He was trying to make a monster is that where you're from out of him. incorrect

It wasn't a question so much as a notification, Oliver said. I'll call you a cab. It's been very nice having you.

Edgar began coughing, shrill, dog coughs.

I'm very sorry that you're ill, but if you can't stop smoking, considering your diagnosis, then you need to consider the fact that we have an impressionable—

My cancer's not contagious. Ednar continued coughing. that dog barking driving me mad

Oliver heard the bed in Riot's room creak it's like a yipping directly above them.

I'm not saying it is. I'm saying that there's a child in this house with allergies whose bedroom is just above yours and he can't be inhaling all this second-hand smoke.

Edgar coughed so vociferously you know what that mean that his eyes what watered. you don't know He shook his head, meaning, tell me No child upstairs. Child left you.

Before Edgar could say the words, Army was behind Oliver to the Matlock theme song, ready to defend his client.

Morning, Army said. What's going on?

Could I trouble you for some water? Edgar said to Army, holding somebody go die when you hear a dog barking outside your window out a glass.

Yeah, yeah, I think you have to dream it of course. Army took the glass either way and went to the bathroom.

Get him distilled water, Oliver said to avoid appearing heartless.

Army poured out the water and went to the kitchen.

When he and Edgar were alone again, Oliver said, We can help you get dressed and call a cab or I'm sure Army would be happy to take you back and visit you from time to time if that's what you want out of all this I'm gonna go outside and shoot that dog but you're not going to wedge yourself in my family and—

Oliver stopped when Army came back with the water for Edgar. Army put the water into the man's hands with infinite care. He sat on the bed as Edgar drank.

Jealousy never admits itself. Oliver remembered how Army used to put his feet on Oliver's lap and watch TV. And it has no opposite.

Army pulled the flaps of Edgar's shirt closed.

Whatcha reading, Boss?

Edgar returned the glass to Army and spoke as if Oliver were dismissed. He said, Felicia left it on the nightstand. So it was Felicia sneaking into his room at night and placing chocolate on his pillows and singing Happy Birthday, Mr. President.

It's hard to get past the *begats*, Army said.

I skipped to the end. Edner gave one last clearing cough.

It has pictures if you don't want to read.

I only read the underlined parts. I don't have much time.

You got plenty of time.

Listen to this. It's from—Edgar looked at the top corner of the page—Revelation. And the kings of the earth, ^{which one} who have committed fornication ^{which one what} and lived deliciously with her, shall bewail her, ^{the dog} and lament for her, ^{you still on that} when they shall see the smoke of her burning.

Sounds epic.

Lived ^{which one is going to die} deliciously?

Oliver couldn't stand being deliberately ignored after he had made a clear demand. He said, Army, why don't you help Edgar get dressed?

Why? Army asked.

I missed my last appointment ^{nobody go die} with the oncologist.

You know, we all know you have cancer.

Easy, Army said to Oliver over his shoulder. Go have a coffee.

No, I'm sorry that he has cancer.

Lemme talk to you, ^{don't spare my feelings} real quick. ^{Mutter will} Army stood up.

Lived deliciously, ^{don't say that} lived deliciously, Ender repeated. The smoke of her burning.

You're not going to die, Army said.

I'm sorry that you're going to die ^{well both of them will} if you die, but I can't have you living here.

There, Oliver thought. He said it ^{eventually} in front of Army.

+

Army led Oliver upstairs, sat him in the kitchen, and reheated some coffee in the microwave. All of this should count as management experience. Sick man downstairs, sick man upstairs, brokering peace, negotiating mutually optimal outcomes.

I understand where you're coming from, Oliver. Believe you me, I do.

You can't just bring people here like it's a bed and breakfast.

First, he's not people. Second, he probably owns like seventy bed and breakfases. Third, aren't you called upon to be compassionate?

Don't give me that. Using the Bible as your prop.

Blasphemer, Army said lightly.

This is a man who will take everything and not make a single adjustment for anybody.

Be that as it may, aren't we called upon to give our cloak as well?

You're not talking to Felicia.

Trust me, I'm not feeding you a line. Just give it another couple of days.

Do you intend to make this permanent?

He's clearly not going to be here forever.

He looks strong to me.

Look, we're going to our oncologist on Thursday.

Our?

Empathetic language, man.

Oliver's face was reddening. He was breathing heavily the way he did before explosions.

Listen to me, Army, and listen good. (The microwave beeped.) I want this man out of my house. You're getting drawn into something you can't handle. I. Want. Him. Gone. That's my bottom line. End of story. Final answer. Gone.

Oliver took his mug of coffee and left to wait for *Live with Kelly* and Whoever.

+ ⁺ ⁺

A week after Edgar's arrival, Army took Faye to Edgar's house to help him with some chores, he said. She extolled the virtues of platonic male-female relations. Well this is how friends help friends whose fathers have cancer, he said to her, and she said fine, pulled her hair into a ponytail and came with him. They were pretty much back together. And really he wanted to show her that this showcase and more could be yours if the price is right.

They worked in silence. He held open a plastic garbage bag while she cleaned out the fridge into it. Edgar didn't have much fresh food. Containers of takeout. Various kinds of bread and bagels, a can of tuna open halfway.

As I was saying— Army said.

Stop saying that. You weren't saying anything. Faye tossed the can of tuna into the garbage bag.

Huh?

You can't just randomly begin a sentence with *as I was saying.*

As I was saying, Army said (stay on message), he has no choice but to leave all this for me.

Faye sighed. You don't *know* that, Army.

People like him are pretty much born with generational wills, Army said.

If you say so.

He has an executor, Army said as if it proved something. He poured the liquids into the sink. Cream. Coke. Mango juice. Orange juice.

And, just say, hypothetically, what if you're not heir to the throne?

Then I probate. Legally, I'm entitled to everything as next of kin.

You sound white, Faye said.

It comes and goes, he said. He could see them in a big house like this, he and Faye and two boys. He'd put up a hoop at the front and the neighbours would think the Fresh Prince of Belair had moved in.

The ice cubes in the freezer were dried down. Edgar had frozen dinners, which Army left there, mixed vegetables, shrimp.

Army took a photo of the neat interior of the fridge to show Edgar. He was stoking Edgar's confidence and pride in him.

After finishing the kitchen, Army and Faye took on the living room. They opened the curtains and the windows. Next time he came, he'd wash the curtains. Or were they supposed to be dry-cleaned? The house was deep in smoke smell. Faye wiped down the surfaces, then she posed, holding a can of Pledge and a rag across her chest like a gang sign and mugged as Army took a photo.

There are no pictures of you, she said, lifting picture frames that had been turned face down. FYI.

There were photographs of vintage-looking people—grandmothers, fathers, mothers, rich aristocracy, fur hats, stiff family portraits.

There are no pictures of anyone born this century, Army said.

You weren't born this century, Faye pointed out.

Faye, you know what? Just shut your hole.

She dropped the dusting cloth and climbed the stairs.

Army waited a few moments, lifting the face-down frames, then he went upstairs into the master bedroom. Another dark space. Curtains closed. He opened them, left the sheers closed. Still dim. There was supposed to be a carton of cigarettes on the floor next to the bed. Four-post bed. He emptied the ashtrays. He considered taking some of Edgar's clothes for him, but he liked having Edgar in his clothes. Felicia thought Edgar looked ridiculous in jeans and a sweatshirt. He located a carton of cigarettes in a lower drawer. Those he would take.

Army found Faye coiled internally in another bedroom. The musk was so overpowering, it was almost visible. She was standing in front of a chest of drawers holding the tail of her ponytail over her nose. He took a picture as she looked up.

Everything feels preserved, Army said, kinder.

I need you to say that you love me, Faye said.

She had found her grandmother in this room, Army thought, long white hair over her face, and needed consolation.

He stuck out his bottom lip. I say it to you all the time.

Not to me.

Of course to you.

To everyone else maybe. To your dad, probably a hundred times in the last week.

Army rolled his eyes.

I don't mean now. And I don't care if it's corny or if you think I'm being a little girl. I just need you to say it. Sometimes. Faye nodded to herself. Only to me.

Fine, I—

It doesn't mean anything now. She ended the conversation abruptly by pulling open the top drawer. Look.

So you tell me to say something then when I say it you don't want to hear it.

There's a woman's jewellery in here, Faye said.

The top drawer of a chest was converted into a jewellery holder with velvet at the base of the drawer. Necklaces, rings, bracelets, all tangled with each other. Earrings scattered.

Is he married? Faye asked.

Army shook his head. I mean, that's not how women store their bling. He paused. You think he is?

Maybe not married. But, well, unless he's wearing it himself—

Army gripped his forearms. So there was a woman in Endhr's life, a woman who had returned his jewellery after she ended the relationship and he dumped it upstairs because he knew she came and went. She was an Italian soprano, an elegant woman with short grey hair that she brushed vigorously with a bone-handled brush in front of a vanity wearing a silk nightgown while he took off his cufflinks. They spoke German to each other. They had been apart for the last two years. She didn't know he had cancer. Army's wattage dimmed. What was he doing caring for a man who had been living with a soprano for the last thirty years of his life?

Let's mow the lawn and get out, Faye said.

Not today, Army said. Seeing the jewellery had sapped his energy. He ran his fingers through the tangle. It was old jewellery, wealthy-European-heirloom jewellery.

Take whatever you want, Army said.

I'm not doing that.

Army picked out a ring. From the back it looked like a single gold band but at the front it appeared anthropomorphic, one arm swooped upward and the other downward to grip a clear stone, a diamond, Army was sure. Maybe a blood diamond. His whole body was fizzing with Pop Rocks. He took Faye's right hand. The ring was too big for her. She removed it and placed it in the drawer. Army reclaimed it and put it in his pocket. To have appraised.

Mrs. Gross, he said.

Don't do this, Army.

Play along, he said.

I don't want to be Mrs. Gross.

Mrs. Shaw then. How do you like your new house?

What's old is new again.

He retrieved the key from his pocket. He should make a copy. That would be responsible. He should in case something happened to Edgar, and he needed (to say you love me) to get into the house in a hurry. Yes.

+ +
+

After Heather left for her light administrative job without title or benefits, Riot took his camera and went out filming, same thing he'd been doing since he arrived.

Day 16 of project Day, he said into the camera then he set it down on a table in a coffeeshop and let it record the interactions of the barista. Riot would need a job soon. Maybe he could parlay his experience at Shoppers Drug Mart into—oh, no work permit. Every day, the same thought. But he was white. They could work something out. He got his ninety minutes of footage there.

Day 16B: Subway, he said into the camera. He used to ride the train from Inwood down to 59th Street–Columbus Circle then transfer to line 1 and ride north again up to 207th Street. He would hold the camera on his knee, facing the seat in front of him. This footage tended to be mostly crotches and feet. The point was you could tell a lot about people if you didn't just watch their faces. For budget reasons, he now sat outside the entrance on the sidewalk, recording the shoes of people entering and leaving. He also made some spare change this way.

Day 16C, he said into the camera when he got tired of that. He recorded himself making and eating lunch in Heather's apartment. Today, the couple upstairs was not fighting but he already had enough footage for their inevitable domestic violence trial.

Day 16D, he said. Riot recorded himself turning pages of *Vogue*. Every day he tried to put a medium inside of another medium. Today it was *Vogue*. His Grade 11 English teacher (Faye and Army, really?) waxed wet over the play-within-a-play part of *A Midsummer Night's Dream*. Riot remembered the impact of the play on his teacher and not much else. There was an ass and a girl named Titania, or Titty for short.

Day 16E: nap. As stated. See Warhol. He wasn't sure about this Day project. Too much action. The night project he shot in high school was so much cleaner. He recorded the moon for an hour each night of the month. It was hard to tell the nights apart so he spliced one second of sun between the nights. He called it *joy cometh in the morning* after he heard Mutter quoting the psalm while talking to someone on the phone.

Day 16F, he said. Let's check on the ants. Heather kept an ant farm on the balcony in memory of Hendrix. How are my boys? It was probably the best footage of the day to that point—a line of, an army of ants (that was the correct collective noun), working an assembly line. By then it was evening. This project was interrupted by

Day 16G: phone call.

What's your plan exactly? Oliver asked.

To make movies.

You tried that for two years after high school and how did that turn out, Scorsese?

I'm a different person now.

Oliver explained that Felicia was still working to get him back in school on a part-time basis, that is, under a different status. A loophole, she thought. He'd be four courses short at the end of the academic year, but he could make those up in the summer.

Great, Riot said.

Today you're getting on a bus, Oliver said.

I'm not coming back.

You listen to me. Get yourself on a bus—

Pop-Pop, I'm sorry, I'm not—

Then Oliver insisted he put Heather on the phone. She wasn't home.

Riot said, She's doing makeup for a—

Then the truth hit Riot.

+

Less than a month after Faye's grandmother was put in the home, she died.

Of what?

In the nursing home, longterm care facility, pardon, they said it was natural causes. In the hospital, they said a viral infection that was going around.

Before she died, Army told Riot, they—

Who?

The nursing home people called to say she was being admitted into hospital. Of course, they're not going to let her die there.

People die in homes all the time, Riot said.

Still, it's bad for business.

Whenever Riot thought of the grandmother, he recalled a hunched, feather-haired woman, walking down the street in a walker then back up again. No one at her side. Saturday mornings.

So I guess you're coming back for the funeral, Army said.

Sometimes Riot would send Faye a photograph of the grandmother when she neared their window. Pop-Pop always wanted to know what he was looking at. He used to call him a cat because he loved himself a good window.

Was Heather around when you guys adopted me? Riot asked.

Maybe, Army said. She might have been in Massachusetts. Why?

Just asking.

You making an investigative, Sarah-Polley doc?

I don't work in genre.

Right, right. Anyhow, Faye's grandmother's funeral's in like two days. You know Asians. Chop-chop.

At the end of the summer, he wondered what felt odd in the view along the street. Not the neighbours coiling up their hoses or the new city garbage, recycling and compost bins. It was absence. He hadn't seen the grandmother walking a few weeks before they put her in the care facility.

Hello? Joke. Do you laugh anymore? And you should call her. I ran into her somewhere and she said she hasn't heard from you in, like, a week.

+

Army sent Riot up-to-the-minute texts during the funeral as if he were missing game seven of the NBA championship. Army wanted to sit at the front, near the family, but he had to sit with Felicia and Oliver, his family. That didn't make it into the texts. Mourning family or feuding family? Mourning or feuding? Felicia wanted Oliver to wear a jacket but he said he was not going to squeeze himself into the black velvet one and she said she wouldn't be seen next to a man without a jacket at a funeral. Army sat between them, absorbing radiation.

+ + +

The video of Riot surfaced again on Pornhub, under *bushy teen solo action*. Oliver was just minding his own heterosexual business, clicking through pages of teen girls in the uppermost bedroom away from Felicia and Edgar and, well, Army was out somewhere, when he came across the dead animal of Riot's pubic hair.

He had to go to The Mansion to wash his eyes out with women.

On the way he called Riot several times. No answer. He called Heather.

Put him on, he said.

He's not here, Heather said.

Lies. Lies. She got that from her mother.

I'll tell him you called.

Tell him he needs to call me immediately.

He's having some problems with his phone, I think.

Tell him his video is all over the internet again and I want it removed tonight. Oliver pulled a slip of paper from his pocket and proceeded to read the address of the video, with all its *utf-8&%* gibberish, while driving. Did you get it?

I'll tell him you called.

Heather, whose side are you on? Oliver asked. Usually she was on the side of the woman but in the absence of a woman where did her loyalties fall? She had degrees in Women's Studies (housed in the English department) and Sociology and had written her cross-disciplinary thesis project on the circulation of female bodies in Victorian literature. Felicia read it but Oliver couldn't get through the first few pages.

Look, the video's going to spread. ^{as I was saying} There's no stopping it. Even if he threatens whoever posted it to take it down, it'll show up again somewhere else. You have no aesthetic distance from it because he's family but maybe you could engage it as a site for *Einfühlung*.

English.

I mean that conquest or defeat are not your only options. The fact that the dissemination of an object is beyond your control does not mean that your vita, your viability, is contingent on its regulation.

What are you talking about, Heather? He was lost in the parking lot of The Mansion.

I'm saying—

Tell him I want the video down now! Oliver hung up.

Nothing had changed ^{what was I saying} about The Mansion in the last eighteen years, which was one reason Oliver still patronized it. It had not acquired airs. Same furniture, gold railing, steel pole. What more was necessary? The girls were a little older than the ones at the new club, Up and Down, in an industrial park toward the airport, and the men overplayed their enjoyment of these could-have-been wives back when the men were in their thirties. Truth be told, he preferred the waitresses to the girls; they were pretty but had small flaws, a little older, frizzy bangs, a little wing in the upper arm, freckled and sunburnt cleavage.

Of all possible stock performances, the girl on stage was doing a Japanese school-girl routine although she was neither Japanese nor a school _{we were talking} _{about cells} girl. She was too athletic, too tan, too thick in the thighs. Her wig looked Egyptian. Her uniform was inaccurate too, based on Oliver's knowledge of the genre. At least, _{no after that} get the facts right. Don't these girls research?

Oliver tried to swallow the cider that was placed in front of him but his throat was blocked by a hairball. It was only his second time seeing the video. The white adolescent male body. The strange sunken line under his pecs where his body slouched in the chair. The half-formed face that knew only ejaculation but not orgasm. Why would a man even make a video like that? Why couldn't he stumble upon videos of Unnamable? The digital women Riot's age were thin but soft and small-chested and large-nippled and wore their hair in pigtails and kept their panties on for a long time and they talked to you. They said stupid things that made him certain that he could also teach them a thing or two about life, about finding the hypotenuse of a triangle, about Japan, about letting strangers into your house. O, Mr. O, what are you doing?

The Japanese girl was replaced by a librarian then by a video-game character of some sort then by the non-Japanese Japanese girl who was now a nurse, no, a doctor—she had a stethoscope that she used to floss between her legs.

Oliver and Army brought _{onion cells} snuck _{mitosis} charmed _{meiosis} the owner into letting Riot into The Mansion on his seventeenth birthday. Riot pretended to be on his phone but one of the girls flagged him and security came over and told him no recording.

Can't you just watch and enjoy? Army had said.

But what about later? Riot replied.

Oliver managed to swallow. Too much time, _{are you sure} too much time. That boy had too much time on his hands. He needed the discipline of hard work. Oliver would find Riot a more labour-intensive job, even if it was minimum wage in a warehouse assembling buckles. Or he could train him to lay hardwood and install tile. Riot and Army could be Property Brothers. What he did not want was for Riot to be at home at thirty-six, contributing nothing to the GDP of the household, as Army would say without a whiff of irony, eating a box of cereal a week and laundering one sock at a time in the hot water superload setting.

Some cider dribbled from his lip onto his shirt. He looked down at his belly. He was still wearing the white shirt from Faye's grandmother's funeral. His face grew hot. He wasn't as tall or as slim as Edgar. Mendel But he didn't have cancer either. are you sure Pricked by thousands of hot needles. His eyes. It was the only funeral Oliver had attended since Hendrix's.

+

There were already two people in the kitchen at breakfast on the weekend when Edgar shuffled in and kissed Felicia on the cheek.

What do you drink in this house? Edgar asked.

We don't drink in this house.

It's for the pain, he said.

Drinking is not going to do anything for you or the pain. She had arranged his breakfast in courses. First a bowl of assorted berries for its antioxidant properties and to help with constipation. Where does it hurt?

Everywhere.

You can't drink with medication. Are you trying to—

Edgar gripped his lips between his teeth as he was lowering himself into a seat.

Felicia peered into the bowl of berries as a reason to look away. She knew it was Mendel what would happen. trust me He would ask Army. Army would buy rum (to Felicia all alcohol was rum) and pour it into his Cokes and coffees. They would think they were keeping a secret from her. She would act as if she knew nothing. Let everybody (go around the table and say) win.

When the flash of pain had passed he was German you know Eggar asked, Was it you probably or Army who was telling me about licensing homeless people somewhere?

Yeah, back home, the government want all the vagrants to register with their county. They found one of them he did something with something washed up mice on the beach.

Really?

And it took the police dogs months to identify him we were talking about the dog and notify the family.

Terrible. I see them all the time on the grates outside the subway.

Yeah it stopped and there was a whole public outcry.

Hello? Oliver said. He was there dead the whole time, tapping his fork on his plate for the egg course.

Wait, Felicia said. Back to Edgar: It's utter nonsense though. pea plants Vagrant registration. Mendel right

Hilarious, Edgar said without laughing. Next thing, they'll charge them for licences.

Oliver got up in a huff to make himself an omelette, though what he really wanted was Felicia's stuffed French omelette.

Good morning, Oliver, Edgar said.

Oliver tried to glare at Felicia but she would not meet his eyes. Then the three of them busied themselves separately for a few minutes: it's called hybridization Edgar dominant with his berries, Felicia with slicing sweet peppers, and recessive traits Oliver with his cracked eggs and bruised feelings.

Edgar held a berry out to Oliver to make a point. He squeezed it between his thumb and index finger like he was making a reference to penis size. right right Army says you play music right for money in the subway. True?

And as Oliver was going to blast him, Egger's face screwed up in a wave of pain and Felicia dropped the knife and fanned him with a pizza flyer.

+

Heather was right. I used to know mitosis and meiosis The video spread like the back of my hand from Pornhub to XVideos to Xtube and then to XNXX.

There were excited, over-punctuated comments in English, Spanish and Portuguese, all of which Oliver could understand. They were written using the limited vocabulary of porn by men whom Oliver wanted did you now to castrate with scissors.

+

Edgar examined the object like the back of my hand in his hand. It was about the size of a pack of cigarettes, cool, white on one side, black on the other, and already covered in fingerprints.

It's my old Galaxy, Army said. He was working his way up to an important conversation with Edgar about the jewellery he found at his house. But that could only happen once he and Edgar were securely attached.

I know what it is, Edgar said. He tapped the screen as he had seen all those kids in skinny jeans do. He wasn't Amish. He double-tapped it. Or a Luddite. He swiped. Or a caveman. He held it up to his ear. Or a dinosaur. Finally he shook it. He had opposable thumbs.

Boss, you gotta turn it on. Army pinched the phone and it illuminated. The lockscreen had an image of a dandelion mitosis is when against a blue background. no meiosis is when I factory reset it for you.

Army walked him around the phone. Volume rocker here. Headphone jack up top. Front camera. Mic. Speaker grill. Power ^{when the cell splits} on the side. Charger port down here. Home screen button. Rear camera. SIM card and battery are inside the case. But you don't need to open it.

I have something for you, Edgar said.

Later.

Army put the phone back in Edgar's hands.

He continued, ^{and you have twins} Date, time, weather. You can click the mic icon here to Google search. ^{oh it's coming back to me} Apps here. Internet, texts, contacts. This one is how you make a call. Play store, if you want to buy more apps. Email. I'll set that up for you later. I can synch up your calendar too.

Edgar was already overwhelmed and exhausted. How do you go back ^{with meiosis you get fraternal twins} to the dandelion?

I can change that.

You don't have to.

Army squeezed next to Edgar on the basement couch. Their temples touched. The screen reflected ^{and with mitosis you get identical} their faces.

Your first selfie, Army said.

And last, Erger said. (But, in fact, he would take photos of himself daily and scroll through them on the couch.)

As he changed the wallpaper to the selfie (condition Edgar into seeing them together), Army smushed his forehead ^{and how do you get Siamese} against Edgar's ear.

Better, he said. Personalized.

Edgar agreed.

This is all you need to know. ^{that's mitonaise} On. ^{mitochondria} Army pushed the side button. ^{I think in German it's *mitonaise*} You never need to turn it off.

Edgar elbowed Army's body away from him but Army stayed close. He read about the importance of skin-to-skin contact between parents and babies in *Psychology Today.*

Army continued, When you want to call me, press the receiver here, then you see my name there. Just press it. That's all.

And to hang up?

It'll be a red receiver. But you don't need to hang up.

+

Now that Edgar had a phone, Army could go back to being the Godfather, disappearing for days at a time, don't ask me about my business. No one saw him until

Felicia, always a light sleeper, heard the furtive rustling of a nocturnal quadruped do you speak German in Riot's room late one night. She removed the earbud from her ears and went to investigate.

Army was on his knees, spreche ich Deutsch digging through a storage container of course under his bed.

You are supposed to be taking care of him, Army. Not me, Felicia said in the loud whisper that the household had adopted I went to kindergarten in Germany since Edgar's arrival. Edgar was sleeping in which Germany Army's room one floor down.

I am.

Buying him a phone

It's my old phone.

is not taking care of him. Who's paying for that plan? You don't have money to waste.

Isn't the life more than flesh and the body more than raiment?

Felicia never quite knew how to respond when Army used her own Bible against her. She just wanted him to walk the dog and make sure it had clean water and toss a tennis ball around once in a while.

I understand where you're coming from, Army said. Believe me, I do.

Don't give me that, Army. That language.

I take full responsibility. He was on autopilot.

Oncology 9 a.m. write up big on the calendar, Felicia said. We been using the calendar since time immemorial.

Indeed. Indeed, Army said. He was still searching it was more like kinderuniversity through the storage container. But what I regret most, *most*—and here he looked up with his irresistible self—is that I have breached your trust and I will do everything in my power to, to, you know.

Felicia sat on Riot's bed an absurd ridiculous preschool where they read us Dostoevsky and began refolding the clothes he was tossing out. Army pulled a second container from under the bed.

The doctor give him a month.

Army stopped. He looked up from his confused self.

One to three months, Felicia confessed.

Army *The Double* went back to searching I didn't know it was Dostoevsky at the time as if the extended time frame dismissed all worry.

You hear me?

I heard you.

And?

And, I mean, of course, it's not the news that anyone wants to hear but, you know, what is man, dust to dust, ashes to ashes, and three months is like eternity if—and who's to say that he's not going to defy the odds and be all Lance Armstrong, Tour de France. I used to have a magnifying glass.

Felicia wondered whether her son that's no reason to cut off your parts them was on drugs. It was not the first time. Occasionally he did seem possessed by a mechanical demon. The matter-of-fact tone, the torrent of words they taught us to talk with our eyes closed in the absence of feeling.

I mean just 'cause someone says you have three months, I mean if I told you that you had three months to live would you believe me? So all I'm saying is you need to stop trying to kill Boss off.

Boy, Felicia couldn't whisper anymore. I is the one here while you running to and fro throughout the earth.

I understand where you're— Army began but just then he found one of the things he was looking for. He stood up with a ring between his fingers and held it to the light.

Where you get that? Felicia asked.

You remember that magnifying glass with the light built in? He tried to slip the ring into his pocket, but Felicia grabbed his wrist and took it from him.

Felicia had recognized the ring. Take it back, she said.

He's got like a whole drawer of—

Take it back, her mouth said. First thing tomorrow morning. But her body grabbed the ring in a fist and left the room.

+

Tomorrow morning came.

What's the matter with you? Army asked Oliver.

Nothing was bothering Oliver. The first thing that was not bothering Oliver was Riot's continued absence that left him bobbing in a house of sharks. That a kid could cross the border in this day and age and go to one of the most dangerous cities in the world because he was accused of digitally assaulting some elusive snivelling girl never crossed his mind. The second thing that was not bothering him was that everyone on the planet was watching a porn video of a dead animal in a science lab while terrorists were in their own corner of the internet planning to blow themselves up on crowded buses.

The third thing that was not bothering him as he opened a Coke Zero and walked back to the upstairs living room to watch *The Price Is Right* was the chainsmoker in the garage, scattering butts all over his property who, you want to know how mitosis and meiosis does really work at breakfast, not really no kissed Felicia on the cheek again.

She turned her cheek up for it, Oliver thought. He was right there, scraping some egg from his plate into the garbage and in waltzed Don Juan, sprinkling kisses all over the damn place.

I hear you, Army said. He cupped a hand to his mouth and tested his breath. I feel you. Not to change the subject, but did Mom leave anything for me?

No. you sure He paused only for a second before continuing his rant: I've never seen anything like it.

He's German, Army explained. The boy had an answer for everything lately. Self-righteous I'm good as hell.

Oliver: He might be a Nazi in his heart it might come in handy one day but that doesn't mean he's German. If he's German then I'm Ronaldo.

I thought Ronaldo was Brazilian.

He's Portuguese. Oliver whacked him.

That's the Old World in him, Army said.

I'm Old World but I don't—

Look, I'm not here to debate who's Older World, Army said. He kisses me sometimes. It's like being kissed by a muffler.

By a chimney.

But I'm culturally sensitive, you know. I wouldn't make Holocaust jokes, by the way, Army said.

He hadn't intended to. Self-righteous as hell, Oliver thought again.

It might do you good to kiss more people, Army said then went searching for Schindler.

Oliver was not bothered by this last matter when in my life would I ever need to know that involving Felicia and Cassanova. He just felt it was very your loss very inappropriate. That's all.

+

Army searched Felicia's room. No ring. No note. He collected his keys and prepared to bounce. Maybe he could have the ring appraised by showing the jeweller a photo.

Edgar was in the garage, smoking among what was left of Oliver's divorce rubble. He didn't look like I'm getting tired he had one to three months left.

Edgar nodded at him.

How was the oncologist? Army asked.

Edgar shrugged sleep then and blew out some smoke.

It was too early in the morning you sleep for charm so Army came out with it directly: Boss, what's your plan?

Edgar smoked for a while, I'm not the one who's tired a frown passed through his face, sleep then floated no over the sea. He asked, My exit strategy?

Generally speaking.

I don't plan to fight, if that's what you mean. That's for those, he planted the cigarette in his mouth and drew a ribbon on his chest. Breast-cancer women. He removed the cigarette and gazed out into the suburbs.

My plan is to lie down and let the lawn go to seed.

Army folded his arms what's the time and faced the same direction as Ergar.

When we moved here, he said, Mr. O had the garage packed full it's okay of his divorce I'll read my book pile o' rubble.

Edgar did I throw my watch in the river said you yourself give it to your mother nothing.

It would have to be the direct route right again: Boss, I'm not a gold-digger, you know me, but what are you going to do with all your stuff?

Edgar shrugged.

You want me to start selling some of the furniture? Army asked. Kijiji? Craigslist? *Antiques Roadshow?* Some of that stuff she likes to have weight on her is probably worth a lot.

Nothing's for sale.

Well, you already tell me that what about the jewellery?

You found jewellery?

In one of the upstairs rooms. Live or die, you're not going to wear that stuff, right?

A long pause I've always wanted to throw something in a river before any response.

Army prompted again, Right?

That's what stones are for Mutter's jewellery, he said.

Good answer, not the same good answer. He pushed further. How about the rest of your assets?

The rest? her ashes maybe The liquid stuff, you know.

He flicked the remainder of his cigarette bury the woman properly into the grate. Oliver had complained about the butts everywhere and Army's response was to quote Sir Mix-a-Lot: You other brothers can't deny that when a girl walks in with an itty-bitty waist and a round thing in your face you get sprung.

Edgar faced Army, she's your mother looked him in the eye and said, It's all taken care of.

Bad dog, Army thought. Bad dog. If it was all taken care of before he came on the scene with this outburst of hospitality, nay, love, then throw your own ashes in a river he must have people better suited to caring for him in his dying hour. That secretary, maybe. Would it be rude to ask exactly how much Edgar was worth?

But Army kept his composure. Charity? he asked.

Do you have a favourite one?

Cancer research, Army said. Heart and Stroke Foundation. He meant them both sarcastically but Edgar expressed no umbrage.

I'll keep that in mind.

Army could have wept. He felt like he was eleven again. How could Edgar pour his wealth in that case down the toilet why wait for ashes of cancer research?

He upped his sarcasm, Make sure you leave me a mixtape.

+

By that evening, Army had recovered. He found a solution to charity.

He couldn't find Edgar in the three most common areas: garage, basement couch, or Army's bedroom. He wasn't in the bathroom either. Army swung open the door to Felicia's room and surprised Eegar, surprised himself too.

What're you doing in here? Army asked. He knew Felicia was secretly reading the Fifty Shades series.

The long pause keep me awake before keep me awake the answer. you does read a lot of books or what He was sitting on a stool in front of Felicia's vanity. Looking, he said.

He held up the ring. I do

Army chose not to explain. I mean He felt himself I used to becoming gentler. before this job He was interrupting something, I read that book you're reading some thatch of light *Great Expectations* in a secret garden.

I was calling you, Army said.

I didn't know how to answer, the whole thing Edgar said. just English people yammering

You gotta swipe to the green receiver. I can show you. He held out his hand for the phone, but Edgar was not interested.

I was thinking, Army said. Here came his solution: You should set up your own foundation. Like Bill and Melinda Gates.

I'm more of a Warren Buffett man myself, Edgar said.

Well, that's kind of automatic.

I mean, actively. He's not leaving anything behind the whole book yammering for anybody.

Eleven again, _{how does it end then} eleven again.

It's his gift, Edgar said.

Yeah, I get that about privilege, Army said. ^{bitterly} But if it was me, I'd cut up that pie while I was alive so I could see how— ^{if I remember correctly} For example, Faye's mother is planning to give her and her brother a downpayment on a house when they're ready.

I wouldn't put my money in real estate at this point, not up front at least. If you invest the same money—

I know all that, Boss. _{you could save me the trouble} I'm just saying.

I know what you're saying. ^{take the trouble} It's indelicate.

I don't mean it to be, what, indelicate, but it's a reality. I'm taking care of you—

Because? The truth.

Because I want to.

Because you think I'm your fairy godmother. Edgar paused a long time, _{some parts are slow} meaning ^{well it has to piss you off to be art} he considered what he said next. When I saw you, I thought my death had come for me.

Damage control mode. _{is that so} Army saw all of his work crumbling. Believe me, ^{I wanted to major in English} he began, ^{but you know} I know how this might appear. But he couldn't finish the thought so he started again, ^{Vater wouldn't let me} Believe me, Boss, I know what you might be thinking.

I was thinking, Eeger said. I was thinking it may be time, time for me to go home.

Army was going to say something like, This is your home now, but Edgar held up a finger.

Let's cut the charade, he said. I'll be out of your hair by the morning.

+ +
+

When Felicia went to work the next day, Edgar was standing motionless facing the shower nozzle, Oliver was pointing through the floor and whispering to her about his water bill, Army was sleeping on his back in Riot's bed, and Riot still was not home.

But when Felicia came home, no one was there. She was almost never home alone, certainly not since Edgar's arrival. Oliver, for his part, hadn't worked in over twenty years. Evening came. ^{Vater kept an old car in a storage garage for over fifteen years} She ate and watched CNN. ^{never fixed it} Then night. _{we had one too where I come from} She read some *Fifty Shades of Grey* in her bedroom. _{no wheels on the thing} Then deep night. She placed her one phone call to Army.

Yeah, we're on our way, he said.

It's getting late. I hope you put a proper coat on him.

We'll be there by morning. We're taking turns.

There was a rush of sound and another voice in the background.

Morning? Where you going?

New York.

With who?

Oliver.

When did you decide this?

It's Felicia, Army said.

Don't call me Felicia. Who you calling Felicia?

There was a crumpling sound as Army passed the headphone and mic to Oliver.

Oliver: I spoke with Riot and he knows that he's at the end of—

You kick out Edgar before you leave? Felicia asked.

Edgar's gone, Oliver said to Army.

Army in the background: Yeah, well.

Riot's not answering his phone because he knows I'm about to bring down the rain.

Army laughed in the background. Tell 'em, Stone Cold!

It's time some order was restored in my house. Children hopping the border, old men showing up, thinking they can just live off me, smoke in my carpet, and I have to bend over and take it. Uh-uh-uh.

You go, girl! Army said.

They sounded drunk to Felicia. And—hard to verify—they sounded like they were speeding.

Toll's coming up, Army said in the background.

They negotiated the amount of change needed while Felicia tried to clarify exactly what had happened to Edgar. From the decisiveness in Oliver's mouth, she deduced that Oliver threw out Eeeer after breakfast, locked the door on him while he was out smoking, and Edgar walked to the mall without a coat, got a cab we did play in it from outside the Asian supermarket, and went home. but in the evenings Then feeling his new power, Oliver terrorized well Riot all you could see was the car rocking hither and yon on the phone until the boy wouldn't answer, and threw some dollars and promises at Army so he would accompany him to New York.

You happy with yourself, Oliver? Felicia asked.

You told me to do it.

Then they fought and when they were done fighting, rocking she was dressed.

+

Edgar's eyes were red not from sorrow or sleeplessness—from smoke and possibly whiskey—but when Felicia met him at his door, he was neither smoking nor drinking. His hands were empty. How long his arms were. The length of a life.

Felicia said, Your phone just ringing out and I wanted to make sure—

Telemarketers. There was a silence ^{as I was saying} the length of an arm ^{when I was in uni} before Edgar said, ^{there was a girl on the floor} ^{one of your brunch girls} ^{no she was on the floor below mine} I didn't tell you? I went to Turks and Caicos.

When would you have told me that? Felicia had only been standing there for seconds ^{and she used to sing very loud} or decades. ^{it took me weeks to go down there and talk to Sophie}

White beaches. This was years ago. Landing in Providenciales, for a minute you think the plane's going to crash into the ocean. I thought of you.

I'm not from there, Edgar.

Anyway, as I was saying, ^{because her singing wasn't unpleasant} that's the place to die. ^{just loud} If dying is something you want to do.

Look, Felicia said, Oliver can be very forceful when he ready.

There were no lights on ^{right and it wasn't a song so much as it was three notes} in the house. When the motion sensor failed ^{the same three notes} to detect any motion, ^{do you know a song that goes *ooh-ooh-ooh*} the porch light went off with a soft snap.

Eeeee gripped his forearms across his stomach. If you_{ooh-ooh ooh} want to die happy. Happily.

You're correcting me ^{no} now?

Tru^{ooh-ooh-ooh}e. Her whole life he had never corrected her grammar, even during the time when her first Canadian teacher screwed up her face and pretended not to understand *I Love You Just the Way You Are* the dialect of her small unrecognized island.

Felicia heaved a Riot-sized sigh. ^{that came out later} Get your things together ^{it could be any song} and let's go, she said. _{maybe it's hers}

+

You look like a tramp.

Pops, Riot said.

Nice to see you too, Heather said.

Oliver eyed her sleeve of tattoos. He was becoming more conservative ^{I used to go out a lot} as he aged. You go to the gym?

Do you? Heather replied.

Oliver clapped his hands sharply at Riot. Chop, chop.

I toldjou. I'm not go*wing* anywhere! where

Let him figure out out his life, Heather said.

He can figure it out out in Brampton. Dump your stuff in a bag because we're out outta out places here first thing in the morning.

It's already morning, Riot said.

Put that smart ass to good use and get packing.

You can't make him go back to school, Dad. Heather tried to mediate the intervention.

Oliver sized her up.

That's between him and Felicia, Oliver said. If it was up to me, Oliver turned back to Riot, you'd be full time at Shoppers Drug Mart and paying rent. Or Canadian Tire. Choose ye this day.

Riot bowed his head and sat on Heather's couch as Oliver outlined a life-plan for him then he reclined on the couch and closed his eyes. When he was little, Felicia read him *Harry Potter and the Philosopher's Stone.* He believed he had arrived in the family magically.

No, he could not explain to Pop-Pop the importance of making films I'll take you to the movies that no one wanted to watch when terrorists were hurling trucks into crowds like missiles. He could not explain why why he could no longer live in a house where food was free and showers endless and how his parents were both good to him to get your mind off things and killing him. Clichéd but true. Except to say there was no I not allowed to date nutrition for his soul. He wasn't talking about God. There was no one who would sit with him on a train through Norway, says who only in his company. Maybe she not dead when he was a child they would. They all used to place him in the sweet centre of their lives.

Don't mind me. Army wiped his hands on his thighs it won't be a date and cut from the bathroom, through the window, anymore than this is a date to the fire escape.

+

Two days, what do you want to see three days it doesn't matter passed.

Army was still where in New York I not from anywhere when it came time for Edgar's next oncology appointment. no I mean where do you live Edgar walked with unusual Regent Park effort. where Felicia took the morning off. what's Regent Park The public housing appointment was east of here tragicomic: grim news but with bouts of laughter between Edgar and the doctor. In the weeks he had been at the house, I not from there Edgar had never laughed, so the sound made Felicia feel both in-adequate (why doesn't he laugh at home) and intimate (you don't know the real

Eeeee). The doctor increased Edgar's dosage of morphine pills ^{Mutter always says} ^{low-rise apartments look like Auschwitz} and asked him ^{was she in Auschwitz} whether he wanted to continue ^{not Auschwitz no} the other medication. ^{but you know she's Polish.}

What's the point? ^{she only speaks German now} Edgar said. ^{even when Vater met her}

Your call, the doctor said.

Felicia was going to report him ^{she would try} for malpractice. She wanted to ask him about pau d'arco, trumpet leaves, which she heard was good for cancer. But, Your call? What kind of quackery ^{and pretend like she was} was ^{German} that?

The men stood up ^{who wouldn't} and shook ^{if is a matter of life and death} hands. Felicia studied the prescription ^{if she knew I was telling you this} so that she would not have to shake the doctor's. ^{she'd kill me}

+

They were like two opposing walls across a dirty alley.

I'm not going anywhere, Riot said.

We're not leaving without you, Oliver said. We can tie you up ^{so your father marry} ^{she} and put you in the trunk or you can walk out of here on your own.

I'm not leaving, Riot said. Stay on message. ^{he married somebody} Stay on message. ^{she's a total forgery} Stay on message.

Army, you hear that, Oliver said. News release. He said he's not leaving.

I'm not.

We'll see.

+

When Felicia called in the evenings, she spent more time listening to Oliver and Riot in the background ^{you shouldn't talk like that about your mother} than talking to either of them or to Heather or Army. The disputants held the phone to their ears but really they were performing to her, becoming more and more recalcitrant.

You've missed so much class, Army, Felicia said. You need to come back.

I'm brokering a deal, ^{why not} he said. ^{it's true}

In the background: I don't care. I'm not going back with you.

Then it looks like we're all moving to New York.

Leave them to work it out, Felicia said. You need to be back here, Army.

But he couldn't hear what she was really saying.

In the background, she heard Oliver's smooth baritone begin, Start spreading the news.

+

A ^{total} week ^{forgery} passed.

Finally, Heather ^{of a woman} had had enough. Four people in her one-bedroom apartment. The pressure on the narrow drains of her toilet. Army's chatter about Wall Street. Riot's screencentrism. Oliver's criticism.

If she could locate her breaking point in one precise moment, it was when her father threw himself down on the couch beside her and ripped a fart and didn't tint red whatsoever. It was like a threat uttered directly at her: I'm moving here forever.

She spoke ^{that's no way to speak about the woman who birthed you} privately to Riot, took him to breakfast at the coffeeshop he liked, treated him like an adult (that's all he wanted anyway, not to be coerced like a calf through an electric gate).

He sensed something was up, because he got to the point first.

You want me out, he said.

You know you're welcome here any time. *You* are.

Then what's the problem?

They are.

So throw them out.

They're not leaving here without you.

That's not— That doesn't have to be true. You can tell 'em that this is my home now.

Is it?

He reddened. For one more week then. Until I finish my film. I won't be any trouble.

She almost changed her mind. She wanted to say, You can stay forever. Only in therapy had she disclosed that she had had a child in high school who was being raised as her brother. The therapist said, That's not as uncommon as you think. But that wasn't the heart of Heather's problem. The heart lay somewhere between how Felicia became *Mutter* and her father became *Pop-Pop*, and how Riot didn't automatically *know* who she was when she first arrived for the summers, per the divorce agreement, and how he used to take Felicia's hand or Army's and was wary of her for days. She could barely touch him. She had problems with how they kept his hair. Felicia didn't cut it for three years out of superstition then all the haircuts Army gave him made him look like a convict. At thirteen, he started growing frighteningly tall and his T-shirts got short and he started moving in the languid, apathetic, hands-in-pockets way that skinny male bodies move. By the time he got into his late teens, she couldn't bear to visit that house. Fortunately, she only had two weeks of vacation.

I can't, Riot. Why don't you go back, sort things out at home, then come visit next summer?

I'll be in summer school. They'll make me.

Riot twirled his cup. And suddenly they were in a McDonald's from the nineties, eating Egg McMuffins.

Listen, kiddo, she's my mother she said. but she's not herself I'm all for the Knausgårdian struggle of your film project. But you got to get these people out of my apartment before I shoot them in the face.

Riot was silent.

Heather waited. He lived as a slow motion replay of someone else's life, didn't he? She felt like she was always waiting for him to grow up and become himself, not Hendrix at seven or Army at fourteen, and hopefully not like Skinnyboy in his twenties or like her father after that. All the ages of men were occupied by her memory of men.

Riot looked her in the eyes for a few seconds. Who's my dad? he asked. Then his nerve failed and he looked down at the lid of his coffee cup.

The precision of the question. There were certain subjects that could not be discussed with certain people in their family. One could not talk about Hendrix with her father (although he had been publicly discussed in the American newspapers). While not strictly off limits, she avoided asking Army about his debt. She no longer lent him money and Army no longer asked her. And crowning the list of subjects to avoid was the circumstances around Riot's birth. The silence or fabrications were intended to protect him and to protect her. Heather could keep her life in front of her without the obstruction of (a child in) her past.

You know we don't have that information, Riot.

You do.

Heather shrugged one shoulder in a believe-what-you-want gesture. She drank some of her kale smoothie.

I was thinking about Faye, Heather said. In the photo.

She's not my girlfriend.

She's Army's.

Do you think I'm ugly? Immediately, Riot appeared embarrassed at having asked the question. Objectively, he continued. Was I an ugly baby?

I don't know that there's anything objective about beauty, Heather said.

Thanks.

Adorno might disagree. Or maybe not. I mean, you're not a monster, Riot.

Wow.

You're fine, Heather said. But we were talking about Faye. Have the two of you—

I said she's not my girlfriend. We're not having crazy sex. Then he added with sententious weight, Or digital sex.

Sex in itself is not a problem. Forbidding it is just another way of regulating the female body.

I'm a dude.

I know, I know that, Riot. What I'm trying to say is that you, is that *one* should respect a woman's decision to be with whoever she wants, that you can't make someone do what you want them to do. You're probably feeling all sorts of things. Jealousy.

I'm not jealous.

Or anger.

I'm not.

You can't just contradict everything I say. What are you feeling?

Riot returned to the question. I want to know who's my dad, Heather.

He held her eyes until she looked away.

Heather put on her client voice. I am feeling like you are trying to pin me against a wall and mug me.

You sound like Mutter.

Whenever he called Felicia *Mutter*, Heather sensed that an identity was taken from her that she could never reclaim. It must be how decolonized islanders felt once their colonizers left.

I'm sorry to be the one to tell you this, Heather said, but there's no talk-show reunificiation narrative in your future.

I'm not asking for that. I just want to know who he was.

I don't know, Riot. I don't know. Heather could not bring herself to say, Your father raped me when I was sixteen. How would that be a just and generous inheritance to leave Riot? If he didn't know, there was a chance he wouldn't grow into him.

You must, Riot said.

Again, I am feeling a violation of my—

Come on, Heather.

If you could leave your subject-position for a while, consider from the other side what it means to give up your colonies even if they were never yours to begin with.

She resisted the potentially destabilizing effect of truth on her relationship with Riot. She didn't want to be his mother. A mother at some point, maybe. But not his, not now.

For the last time, I don't know, Heather said. She took a sip of her smoothie. But I imagine, he was nothing like you.

She swallowed painfully.

+

Their last night. it's cold Heather, on the fire escape, smoking.

Cold put this on out here, Army said.

It's my Gulag, Heather said.

Army took a drag from her cigarette then you'll be cold and gave it back to her. The stress, she said. I was fine it's not cold until you guys showed up.

He still thinks you're going to run off with Kurt Cobain.

Army's phone vibrated. you're not cold but it is cold He smiled, texted a blur, paused, texted some more.

That your little Lolita? Heather asked. Army didn't have a wrinkle on his face, sang froid not a liverspot on his hands. He looked like a taller version of four-teen. Despite her education anything under 20 is cold and some years of therapy, she could not suppress the comparison serious to her own softening body. No amount of green shakes or Fitbit data seemed to stay her destiny—that of a short, fat, divorced woman with a floral couch and professionally manicured nails. For now, she could pass as a petite, curvy, unmarried woman with a Craigslist couch and clean nails, but her mother was gaining on her.

Army slid his slim phone into the slit of his pocket. My what now?

Your underage sex princess, Heather said, barbing the sentence.

She could see him struggling with whether to deny his girlfriend or boast.

Wish I could find myself one of them old-money princesses, he said. Yeah, some young, fine, Brazilian, guitar-booty princess who be all like, *Ohh, obrigado, senhor.*

You realize that your sexuality—

My sexuality, yes. He Trumped his lower lip. where I come from you'd be burning up Tell me about my sexuality.

Your sexuality was arrested in high school somewhere. That's why you prey on girls half your age. are you from hell

That's your diagnosis?

I accept insurance.

It's not that I like hot girls, most of which—

Of whom.

are under thirty.

You're thirty-six.

I'm thirty-sexy, Army said and shimmied his shoulders.

Heather didn't have sex after the assault you know both we mothers in critical condition and you invoking hell until her first year in university. He was in her pardon Women's Studies class. She thought he was gay but it turned out he was just poetic. She could have slept with him I forget my biology book earlier. In his room, which she preferred because she could always leave, they'd make out and she'd put her hand on his chest time after time to see if he would stop and he did. Time after time. Stop. lighten up Even with his zipper down, get serious he stopped. He sat up, put his hands on his lap, and nodded imperceptibly. Vibrated really. She thought he might make a good longterm partner. Together okay fine they could train dogs to wait at their heels before entering intersections. Around American Thanksgiving, he got passive-aggressive at her *no*, sulky, I can be serious the white-boy entitlement to the world. They were together until the end of the semester, what are your ambitions then she had to get out of the toxic stultifying nausea do you want to talk about that of his presence. He had about four ideas although most people are just duplicates of other people in his head that he kept repeating. and the people who are truly themselves They popped around his head like lottery balls in an air-mix machine. By the end of their relationship, he never withdrew a ball for her, but he did for company. With her, he became very casual. He had sex as if he were urinating. are those alcoholics you see in parks In any event, they were currently Facebook talk to one friends. you'll see

Riot's seriously broken up, she said. About you that's your ambition then and the dead-mother girl.

Grandmother, Army corrected.

Whatever.

Faye.

Heather explained the photograph, the silence, the what-if questions when she came home, the Aspergery projects, including videos of two Asian girls leaving their apartment and walking up the street, every day, every day.

I'm not with her. You think— Army pointed to the phone in his pocket or to his penis.

I think you're in denial what's yours about a lot of things.

For instance?

For instance, maybe a nurse you think time stopped I don't mind blood when you were eighteen. You think you're more successful than you are. You realize living in your parents' basement at thirty-six is the epitome of failure in our culture? All you need is to play guitar.

Army looked into the distant lights. I used to like bandaging people when we played nurse. She opened her mouth to apologize.

I told you that I got Oliver's permit unrevoked? Army asked. He can play in the subway again.

Watch out, Ed Sheeran. How many times can he sing Pine Cone?

Well, his set's more old school but I feel you, I feel you, the singer-songwriter thing.

He only does covers, Heather said.

He only does covers, Army confirmed. Apart from Pine Cone.

Heather was quiet didn't you play doctor for a while. Army took a drag of the cigarette then threw it off the balcony.

After I came back home, we played nurse Heather said, you said the worst thing anybody has ever said to me.

Impossible. Army held his wrists.

You remember?

Army shook his head.

Why did you let him rape you? Heather said. You remember now?

I was, like, twelve, Heather.

Fourteen. And you were standing just like that we didn't have a boy to play with when I came home.

Like what?

Heather locked her wrists over her belly.

+

The passenger seat texted Faye, We got im.

Faye texted the backseat, Another dream bites the dust?

The backseat didn't text back.

Faye texted the backseat, I'm Team Riot on this one.

The backseat didn't text back.

Faye texted the passenger seat, He's not texting back. Sleeping?

The passenger seat texted Faye, No.

Faye texted the backseat, Just so you know.

The backseat texted Faye, You mean Team Army. 🖕

Faye texted the passenger seat, Did you tell him something?

The passenger seat texted Faye, ??

Faye sent the passenger seat a screenshot of the backseat's text.

The passenger seat turned around.

The backseat texted Faye, You know he's 36.

Faye texted that blasted hound back again the passenger seat, How old are you?

The passenger seat texted Faye, A gentleman never reals [sic] his age

Faye texted the passenger seat, Answer me.

The backseat texted Faye, Just cause he's in college doesn't mean he's young. You know he failed out before right?

The passenger seat texted Faye, Driving now. Talk later.

The backseat texted Faye, You know he's never had a gf longer than like 2 days right?

Faye didn't reply.

The backseat texted Faye, You know you only sneaked around because he prolly has 3 or 4 girls right now right?

Faye didn't reply.

The backseat texted Faye, Just so you know.

Faye texted the passenger seat, You're 36!!!

The passenger seat turned around.

Faye: You're a perv!!

Passenger seat: Chill.

Faye: I never shd got back with u! Done wit u! maybe I'll get a dog when she dies Don't call me don't trext me don't fvook me! [sic]

Passenger seat: Pause your menopause.

Faye: Pause YOUR menopause!! SEX OFF ENDER!!!

Passenger seat: Talk when I back… Misunderstanding.

Faye: I hope you crash!!!!!!!

+

Army was fourteen, in the garage, holding an envelope and making a speech, only he was thirty-six, in the food court of the Eaton Centre, lowering a tray of bagels and coffee, trying to get Faye to admire him again, to adore him, to look at his lips as he spoke.

He began, Remember when you and me took that roadtrip up north and you told me you'd never been happier? You had that blue handkerchief over your head and the parachute skirt. Never been happier is what you said.

No smile. you didn't think about marriage Faye leaned back.

So I'm a bit older when you was hacking up your body than you thought. It's not the end not to have children of the world.

It's the lie.

I wouldn't call it a lie.

I'm calling it a lie.

It never came up.

You went around acting ^{did I think about it} like you and Riot were twins.

If you ^{do I think about it} had asked, I would have been willing—

How old are you?

Listen. I apologize if I misled you. Army uncapped one lid of coffee ^{I didn't think about it} and set it before Faye. He blew over the top gently. But you were Riot's friend, ^{no} hot friend, if I may say so myself, and I had no intention of— Because if there's one thing I've learned from business it's ethics. And you got with me. I mean, that's the way it happened.

Right, well, I'm ungetting with you.

I didn't mean that. I apologize.

She looked down.

Army clasped his forearms. Reconciliation would require truth.

I'm thirty-six. I've started college four times, mostly for the money. I don't have any savings, per se. I'm overleveraged. If this Canafries business doesn't work out, I'm going to file for bankruptcy. I've never been with anyone more than half a year. So, you understand. Riot hates me. Heather thinks I'm a joke. Oliver wants me to pay rent. My dad's giving all his money to charity. And Mom, she thinks I'm doomed to get shot by the police for driving my Beamer. So. There.

Faye took her hands off ^{you should have} the table ^{why's that} and rested them in her lap. She and Army sat, facing each other, slumped, with an orange tray between them.

You're not a joke, Faye said.

Marry me.

She pulled her hair over her shoulder. Is that all it takes?

I'm not even kidding, Faye. He hadn't planned a proposal. He didn't walk with a ring in his pocket but his instincts, which had never, almost never, led him wrong in business, flashed him arrows and green lights. City Hall was across the street. He was tingling. He would pack up her belongings from her dorm and they'd move into one of the condos. After evicting the tenants. He'd get a Bay Street job somehow. Wear tailored suits and sunglasses. She'd get him a leather satchel for Christmas. He'd get her Louboutin pumps.

She rolled her eyes. ^{you have grossly reduced your chances of having a family} But she had rolled her eyes. Amber alert.

Army took his keys from his pocket and unspooled the keys. He extended the silver ring toward Faye.

Wrong, she said.

It's temporary. Until.

No, I mean— I think I've eliminated my chances

Until I can get a real one. Until death do we part. He had to keep talking ^{quite} frankly until he could sense the victory. We can go and choose one. I can leave the car key on there to sweeten the pot.

No, I mean, that's not how men propose.

Army sprung up then went down on one knee, then both, as he would at church, key chain still extended to Faye.

She made him wait a long time. It began to feel like penance.

I'm thinking, she said.

Can you walk and think at the same time?

On the counter of the service desk at City Hall, Army tapped his credit card to pay the fee for the marriage licence.

+ +
+

Edgar kept complaining about pain, despite the morphine.

Give it time, Felicia said.

How much time do I have? EeEee replied.

From work, Felicia called the quack, expecting to pick up a stronger prescription on her way home, but the secretary gave her a hard time about power of attorney and when she insisted she speak to the doctor, who knew she was the primary caregiver, how many mixed couples you know he said that he could not legally take Felicia's word.

So Felicia plenty went home at lunch, put Edgar Indian and Black in her car, drove to the office of the worst doctor ever, as Riot Chinese and Indian would say, so he, the doctor, could hear from Edgar's Spanish and everybody own mouth about the inefficacy of morphine.

The doctor spoke to Edgar directly, not to Felicia.

We could admit you.

Edgar shook his head.

I could give you liquid morphine.

How's that different from the pills?

It works a little faster—twenty, thirty minutes before you feel an effect—but it doesn't last as long. There's no liquid long-acting preparation.

What works faster?

Subcutaneous. You couldn't administer that yourself, the doctor said. Remember, Edgar, you're not taking morphine in response to pain. By then, it's too late. Stay on schedule.

He is, Felicia said. He's having breakthrough pain. We checked the internet.

The doctor continued speaking to Edgar. We could set you up with an IV.

No good, Edgar said. I need to be free to smoke outside.

You're not going to be smoking outside, Edgar, Felicia said. in uni I used to know a couple It almost brought tears she was black and he was white to her eyes.

Free to smoke inside then, he said to the doctor. No cords and wires is not news you broadcasting and what have you.

Felicia used the lull only she was the whitest black woman I ever met in the conversation and he was into everything black to make a declaration soul music to the doctor. I'd like you to note the talk and to tell your staff that I am authorized to make decisions picked out his hair into a little afro about Edgar's care.

The doctor looked at Edgar. Is that right?

Edgar shrugged.

Felicia exhaled sharply. Even now, you want news he would not affirm her. She was about to tell the doctor to admit EeEeE to Palliative. where I come from one of them mixed race couple did get in a fight and the man hack up she body and put it in a suitcase. She would wash everybody was asking for the wife and he acting like he don't know her hands clean of him.

It's not that I don't trust her, Edgar said.

Then what? Felicia said. lo and behold when they put two and two together the police find the man in khaki short pants planting lemon seeds behind he brother house as if nothing didn't happen Because clearly you don't understand the strain you putting me under.

Edgar spoke to the doctor, attempting to twinkle: It's that she'll try to keep me around too long.

It was like neither man understood the gravity of the situation. Quips and cracks and all that levity in the face of his death—simply appalling.

Can't blame the old girl for trying, the doctor said.

Felicia despised him.

Edgar looked like he wanted to smoke immediately and therefore needed to speed up the conversation. As I was saying, what's the strongest thing you have?

That depends on dosage but we use fentanyl in—

Give me that.

You can't just request your medication, Felicia said. She recalled countless ask-your-doctor-if-maycausedeath-is-right-for-you commercials.

Fentanyl it is, EEEEE said. I don't want to feel anything.

Fentanyl it was. Edgar would begin with short-acting tablets for the first day while waiting for the patch to kick in.

+

While waiting ^{for such a young girl} for a new fentanyl patch to blanket the pain, Edgar confessed to Army, privately, that he was most afraid ^{you have a penchant for the macabre} of losing his ability to smoke. He said it as if smoking were a sense. Army searched for *fentanyl and nicotine patch*. No contraindications. He went out and bought nicotine patches. He applied one to Edgar's right flank.

Give me another, Eeeer said. For the other lung.

So Army did.

And Edgar said, Atta boy, or, That's my boy. It was unclear which but the syllables returned Edgar to Army's confidence. He squeezed I just telling you what I does hear the package of the nicotine patches gratefully. See, Heather, people could be proud of him. When he returned from New York, Army had been glad to see Eeger back at home. In front of Riot, he made a show of asking Edgar about his medication ^{try listening to some music} and holding the pill bottles up to the light. He intended to impress Riot back into loving him.

I got married, Army told Edgar. It was a half-truth. He and Faye had a marriage licence but only an appointment for the actual marriage service.

Edgar turned his head to face Army directly. His eyes shone. He blinked rapidly.

Let me take a picture of yo_{ooh-ooh-ooh}u, Army said.

+

as I was saying Felicia she's Polish instructed the men to move Hendrix's twin bed downstairs and to move the couch upstairs, she had to be German all this so Edgar you can't fault her for surviving could have a proper bed.

Why doesn't he just stay ^{during the war} in Hendrix's room?

To answer ^{fine} that question truthfully ^{but not her whole life} would begin a fight with Oliver, who, Felicia knew, didn't want Eager ^{never spoke a word of Polish at home} dying in anyone's room, especially not Hendrix's. They still called it Hendrix's room although he hadn't lived there since childhood and ^{never talked about her parents} hadn't lived in years.

The stairs, she said. Too many stairs.

Oliver flipped the mattress upright and Army and Riot began dismantling the bed. They fell into silent contemplation most people life is just a set of horror stories while unscrewing the headboard from the frame. It was an old frame from Ikea. Army twisted the Allen key near the headboard. He didn't look at either Oliver or Felicia.

I don't think we can take care of him anymore, Army said into his work.

Oliver had delicious satisfaction on his face. You brought him here.

We'll do what we can. Life and death are in the hands—

He needs stronger pain medication. I feel like we're killing him. Army did not look Felicia in the eye.

You should have thought of that a month ago.

We not killing nobody, Felicia said. Don't damage the wall. She placed a T-shirt on the edge between the headboard and the wall.

All four of them heard Edgar groan ^{no} lightly downstairs ^{when we were little} as if God was no longer breathing into him but blowing lightly atop a bottle.

I'm calling an ambulance, ^{she said that her parents were gobbled up by eagles} Oliver said.

You don't just call an ambulance without an emergency. What had gotten into them all? It's not— It's not ^{but she said it smiling} transportation. ^{you know}

He can't die in the basement, Mom.

Be sensible, Oliver said.

He needs ^{I wish my father did tell me something like that} to die among people, Army said.

I'm people, Felicia said. I don't know ^{what did he tell you} what you consider yourselves.

He means a hospice, Oliver said.

^{the truth} Or something, Army said. Witnesses, I mean. Other people need to see him die ^{more or less} among us.

Think of the responsibility, Oliver said. You want someone accusing you down the line of—

We could record it, Riot said out of nowhere.

+ +
+ .

On her way to work, Felicia was in the centre lane of three, heading south on the 410, behind an SUV, thinking that everyone these days was tinting their windows so dark, she couldn't see inside, wasn't that illegal, thinking that the formal appeal process for Riot could wrap up by the end of the semester if she pressed the ombudsman's assistant, that she would peek into Army's Blackboard, Brownstone's course management system, to see if he had been submitting assignments, thinking that Christmas would soon be here, that she would not be the one to sort through Edgar's things, she would not step into his house again because he had refused to cooperate yesterday when she asked him what he wanted, what kind of arrangements, and he said don't worry about it with the same cavalier evasion he had when she first visited him in the hospital. It's taken care of, he said. He would not tell her important things yet she would learn that he had told Army those very same things casually.

She was thinking that matrix of thought when suddenly she couldn't breathe. She was aggrieved, she thought, with Edgar's inability to trust her, his withholding of information as a kind of power over her, she would not sort through his dusty china at her age, no more cleaning up after people.

The tinted-window SUV was still in front of her. She was getting hot, although the high was only going to be four degrees, well below the fall seasonal average.

She lowered I noticed something a long time ago the window what and lowered the world has enough the volume what of the news radio. She tried to pull the car into the right lane but no one was letting her in. Reports just in of a woman being. suffering She reached for her handbag, no for her phone, not suffering and was going to call Army or Oliver, Oliver or Army, children let me in, who would be better, when the whole world got slapped away and she called out, Jesus.

+

Both of their mothers were dying in the hospital.

+

Army was listed first in the emergency contact information inside Felicia's purse but Oliver arrived at the hospital first. The doctor told Oliver that it was spontaneous, Felicia's heart attack. Spontaneous Coronary Artery Dissection. SCAD.

But Oliver knew it was not spontaneous. It was Riot's desertion. that's not funny It was the last week of Edgar's groaning I'm not trying to be funny from downstairs, sending Felicia through the house sleepless and into work in the morning like a ghost. In the morning her face looked full of coffee, inflamed. She came home as soon as she could and tried to feed Edgar soup for an hour. It was pathetic, how she let a man wreck her life to his dying day.

If it wasn't for Oliver and the roof he provided for her, what would she have? surely you don't mean it A thirty-six-year-old deadweight of a son.

When Army arrived, holding his elbows, Oliver's explanation of SCAD was: Her heart exploded on the highway.

+

you're confusing me with someone else   with the Father Abraham sort of man who   you ever spend Christmas alone me you never you look like a man who does spend Christmas alone

+

Riot woke at noon and noticed the voicemail and text alert icons but did not open them. Instead, he went downstairs to check on the video or on Edgar. Same thing in his mind. At first he thought Eegrr was snoring on the exhalation portion of his breath but when he actually looked at Ergrr, not via the screen, he realized that the sound was of whimpering, a vestige of groaning, of agony that had exhausted its expression.

Riot wasn't sure that Egrrr could swallow the old morphine or fentanyl pills. He retrieved the secret—secret only to Felicia—stash of Bacardi from the divorce rubble in the garage, poured some into the cap and held it to Errgr's mouth. The whimpering softened. you will regret it Repeat. when you dying alone Repeat. you will regret it He lit a cigarette and put it to the man's mouth as he has seen Army do. Since coming back from New York, Army had started smoking for Errrr. It was mostly second-hand service, as he called it, but he would occasionally hold the cigarette to Error's lips, careful not to let the ash fall on his face.

Only then, sitting on Hendrix's former twin bed and holding a cigarette to Error's mouth, did Riot feel his own body—a wetness through his socks. Someone had knocked over the strawberry meal replacement drink. He would have to check the video.

+

Home texted hospital: SCAD?!
  Hospital texted home: Sudden corinary [sic] accident disease.
  Home texted hospital: I know what it means. And? Doctor says?
  Hospital texted home: Stable.
  Home texted hospital: Meaning?
  Hospital texted home: Nothing.
  Home texted hospital: Can you come get me?
  Hospital texted home: Don't leave Boss who says I will alone. I say
  At this point, Chariot Soares placed a phone call to Armistice Gross.

+ +
+

They swapped positions, Army and Riot. Riot took Army's car to the hospital and Army sat on the floor next to Rrrrr's bed, as he had for nights, until I mean what is death but mandatory sterilization it so much more than that same with menopause is okay if you frighten for your mother I'm not you don't have to rationalize I'm just saying what exactly are you saying I'm saying I'm waiting that I hope you have yourself until two girls and a boy Edgar finally quit smoking.

+

But Edgar would die twice more after that. Three days later for Army and Riot at the foot of Felicia's bed. And once again for Army who watched the last ninety minutes next to Felicia's head, the section where men removed the body and Army stuffed the sheets into a garbage bag and approached the camera, his crotch growing larger and larger as he did, to turn it off.

+

Riot and Army began watching the video together from two chairs in Felicia's hospital room. They began so that the time in the video corresponded exactly to the time in real life. Riot said it was to aid the illusion that they were living two days at once, that they were in a divine state of past, present, and virtual all at once, to which Army rolled his eyes and removed his gum.

Army couldn't watch all the footage in one stretch, for boredom, not sensitivity, so he sometimes went for what he called *spins* around the hospital or neighbourhood or internet.

I'm not pausing it, Riot said.

No, you go ahead.

You're leaving at your own risk.

Little man, it's not childbirth in the Dark Ages, Army said. Text me when something—it was obvious he wanted to say something good—happens.

Riot doffed an imaginary hat.

But before it happens, Army said.

Riot's love for slow Norwegian TV had built up his endurance. In principle and practice, pausing long videos was disrespectful to the work. Indigenous people didn't interrupt their elders. A viewer's needs, which were more often than not conveniences, were secondary to the primacy of the work's right to be. He wrote something like in his application essay to his first-choice film school. He might have written something like, *primacy of the work's unfolding Dasein.* And they still didn't take him.

+

Mind the cord, Oliver said to the nurse.

+

Faye said they needed to talk but Army knew no good ever came out of needing to talk.

Did you hear me?

You realize both my parents just died, like within days of each other? You do realize that, right?

When did your mom—

Like any minute now.

Long tender pause. So she's not—

She's not going to make it. He began rolling up his sleeves as if that were necessary to get into the meat of the phone call.

That's not the same, Army. And I'm not saying we have to talk now.

Yeah, let's wait for her to die first.

Goodness, Army, what do you want from me? All I said was—

I'm not stopping you. If you want to talk, come down here and talk. As my wife—

I'm not your wife.

Legally, as my wife, don't you think you should maybe pretend to be supportive?

As part of my secret girlfriend duties.

Timing, Faye. Timing.

+

It might appear that nothing was happening on screen. Rrror *der Schmerz* she used to say is lying on his back, clamped tight in a blanket by his arms. It would appear as nothing, *das Leid* until one found one's breath *der Kummer* synching to his, his sleep tugging one underwater. Eventually the background *die Qual* softens. The pitch of the fridge, for instance, is much higher than Riot imagined. The cars and buses passing outside sound like waves. There is also a steady dog whistle in the house that nearly overwhelmed Riot's attention. He spent a long time trying to identify the source of *so starke Schmerzen* the sound until he realized that it did not originate in the video but in the hospital room. He looked up at Felicia—stable, stay stable—and quickly looked away.

+

Faye's on her way, Army announced to Riot when he returned from a spin.

Riot unplugged his laptop and gathered himself to leave.

Come on. Don't do that, Army said.

Army was trying to be courteous, to give people foreknowledge, something Felicia had been trying to teach him for years, but what was the point? He had tried to explain to Riot, She came on to me, she came on to me, and Riot had said, Whatever, intending both *I don't believe you* and *I don't care*. Army was tired of Riot's wounded feelings. What about his feelings? How had he failed at everything? Let's work on one set of feelings at a time. Yours? No, yours.

Don't walk away from me, Army said.

+

Faye's coat had fur around the collar that made her seem leonine.

How is she?

Look, Army said.

Faye sat beside him. She looked between Felicia and the side of Army's face several times but said nothing. She had never known Army to be quiet.

When she finally thought to ask him how he was, he told her a story instead.

+

The source of the dog whistle was not in the hospital room, as Riot previously thought, nor in the Tim Hortons where he removed himself to avoid Faye. It was coming from inside of him.

+

Army told Faye that he had finally cornered a senior buyer at the Delish corporate office and set up a product demo for his French-fry line, a project that had been in the works for about a year. The buyer said he'd give Army and his partner ten minutes and would come to a decision right away. Just prepare the fries and let the product speak for itself. He practically put his arm around Army's shoulder to warn him against entrepreneurs who thought they could sell him sugar in a cat-shaped pink box, exact words, taking Army into his confidence, saying, I know you're not like them but really meaning, Don't be like them. So Army and his partner went down to Delish headquarters with a few frozen packages of fries, thinking that in the twenty-five minutes it took to bake the fries, they'd have the chance to conventionally pitch the product. Army would do most of the talking and his partner would be the hype man, but the secretary directed them to the company break room, which was stocked to the heavens with every conceivable edible product, and told them that the buyer and team would need everything ready at 12:30 as if Army and his partner were caterers. They came in on time, the senior buyer, and some folks clutching coffee mugs but no work implements, folks who looked like they were recruited in the hallway and knew each other but didn't really display the cohesion of people who worked together on a team. And as Army was reaching for the tray of fries with the oven mitt from Felicia's kitchen, it occurred to him that the purpose of the product demo at 12:30 p.m. with this crew was to provide its members with lunch. That was all. Lunch and a free sample to take home and chuck on their granite countertops.

So if I was neglecting you, Army said and lowered his head. So if you felt for some reason I was neglecting you.

+

Stable.

+

The longest Riot had gone watching a screen with only the briefest of shuteyes was a video he found of a girllikehim's (that was her YouTube moniker) trip from her house in Halifax to her hostel in Auckland, which included lengthy layovers in PHL, LAX, and SYD to a total of forty-two hours. He wrote the girllikehim afterward. And she responded. So he responded. She really was like him, only older. And she responded to that response. And so on until he learned that she had a boyfriend and suddenly it seemed pointless to continue.

+

Faye told Army that when she first moved to Canada she used to throw her noodles in the toilet at lunchtime although she wanted to eat them.

My father used to feed me worms, she said. I don't remember much about him. My mother said it wasn't worms.

What then?

She said it was a snake.

+

In the video, Army says *so starke Schmerzen* to an unconscious Edgar, I went to the meeting with proof of product insurance, with sales numbers from a mom-and-pop grocery store. I had to render them as percentages because the manager doesn't order tons and every time I go in there he has them stocked below eye-level. I'll have to talk to him again. I had my laptop. I had a projector. I had the website updated with a couple of new testimonials. I had handouts about the company, growth the last thing my mother say to me in the morning forecasts, the marketing plan, printed up business cards.

Error breathes.

I'm rethinking your jingle idea, Boss. I thought it was whack. But I could lose all the kissing in the commercial and go old-school. Kid hears, Army sings now, Canafries, see the smile, kid walks into the kitchen, humming the jingle, mother picks up the jingle, mother remembers it before she gone and drop down on the white lady floor next time she's in the grocery store. Conversion right there.

+

For Riot, the slow entertainment movement gave him the same pleasure as those spot-the-difference drawings in the ethnic newspaper Felicia brought home from time to time. Only he wasn't identifying differences between two static and, under casual inspection, identical drawings but differences between one moment of time and the next. In the video of Edgar, was try your best Riot spent minutes watching the minutes of the LED clock change at night until he finetuned his internal clock to predict exactly how long a minute lasted. He got to be so good at predicting the time that he'd say, Now, under his breath and the time would change within two seconds. Or he spent time watching a shadow form and lengthen. He heard footsteps upstairs. He heard Oliver shuffling in the garage. He heard soak the rice pot toilets flush, doors close elsewhere in the house, mysterious sounds with no source, just and try your best with it the house groaning. All of these were major points of deliberation. Why did Oliver keep letting the screen door bang upstairs?

+

In the video, Felicia says, I should check on her Turn that thing off.

Still in the video, Riot says, It's off.

Go and eat, she tells Riot in the video.

I'm good.

I'm not asking you, she says in the video.

Riot rises up his lanky frame from his director's chair near the camera and leaves the room.

When he goes, Felicia looks at the camera long. There's no red pinhead of light as she'd expect from cameras in her day. Then she turns back to Error. She inspects him, she's stable checks to see if he's dry, checks the adhesion of his fentanyl patch, sniffs his armpit while she's there. Then she closes her eyes and soundlessly prays, only her lips move, while resting a hand on his forehead.

She leaves the room.

A few minutes later, she returns with a straw in a strawberry flavoured meal replacement drink. She rouses him and tries to get him to drink it. He groans. She insists he take one sip. She places the straw in his mouth _{you turn doctor} and he frowns in what could be interpreted as _{don't use that word on me} displeasure. One sip, she says. His embouchure contracts. One more, she says. Contracts. She wipes his mouth with the hood from his sweatshirt, Army's, Brownstone's. She quickly screws on the cap of the bottle and places it on the side table with a straw.

She leaves the room.

Upstairs you can hear her getting ready. There is a conversation with Oliver where their voices are heard but not their words.

Half an hour later, she returns to Edgar in the basement, this time she's dressed for work in the very clothes she was wearing when she arrived ^{it's the} ^{medical term} at the hospital. With her hand on his skull and her thumb hanging into his face, she explains that she's going to work and she'll be back early, that one of the children will give him a snack and then lunch and when she's back she'll make him some soup for dinner. Soup. Would he like that? He nods.

Then she, like, presses his forehead with her thumb ^{I believe} and exits into the garage for the last time, _{death is stable too} possibly ever.

+

Army told Faye that he saw Felicia one day when she couldn't see him. She was crossing, waiting for the light. He was in the comfort of his car, behind dark windows. She hesitated until all the cars had stopped. He saw her. How much taller than her he was. How each part of her was a decision, to wait or to go, to trust the cars or her instinct, her coat, her shoes (she shopped a long time for those boots), her bag. And now she forgot about them. She was not his mother then but Felicia, thinking about whatever she did, the street, some administrative task certainly, some worry. It seemed to Army an especially adult thought, one he had never had before, one he was sure no one else had. No one else took note of her. She'd die and disappear. Never thought of by strangers. Like the vague deaths of an earthquake. His mother was one of ordinary billions. A depreciating asset. As she waited to cross at the other intersection and he drove away, she became fractionally smaller. One of six billion, then seven, then seven and a half.

+

Oliver stayed away from the basement during the final days of Edgar's life. He stayed outside of the house as much as possible, raking, bagging, laying down fertilizer for the winter. He washed the shovels, rolled snow tires from one spot in the garage to the other, pruned evergreens, removed the tomato risers. He listened to his tinnitus. He did whatever he could to avoid facing Edgar on Hendrix's bed.

He did whatever he could to avoid a patch of dirt where Hendrix (long stint with crystal meth, costly rehab that Oliver paid for, joined the army) cared for ants. He, Oliver, was caught between places he didn't want to be, pushed away from the house (survived a roadside bomb) and pushed away from parts of the yard (captured, recorded) and pushed away from the hospital (executed naked in a dusty country). So why so much *Sturm und Drang* over one death when, to use a neutral example, 70,000 died in Sichuan? Over two deaths when 250,000 died when the tide suddenly disappeared? Over three deaths?

+

Faye told Army that when she first moved to Canada everybody said she was Chinese although she preferred to say that she was from Hong Kong. She avoided saying certain words that made her sound Chinese. Tachnowogy.

I sounded like Tweety, she said, reclining. But in the car, you used to listen to me like you were deaf.

See, I listen.

My grandmother said that after we left him my father clipped the lobes off his ears and cut off part of his tongue. They found him facedown on the *fānzhuō* where we used to eat dinner.

Dead? Army asked

Oh, that can't kill you.

If that don't kill you, I don't know what can.

Blood, Faye said.

I thought you said he drowned in a pool.

He did.

+

Without pausing the video, Riot left the hospital Tim Hortons so you planning to fly and leave Mutter alone and went upstairs where he found a comfortable seat in a waiting area.

For a man who had little attachment to living, who spent his time on earth like a tourist, just checking out what this consciousness thing was about, Error took a long time to die. To be exact, Riot collected thirty-seven hours of footage.

During the first day of recording, Army kept close watch of Edgar, making actor-like gestures of grief, the ER doctor-head-shake, the knuckle to the mouth, the sigh, the constantly revised announcement, ^{I don't think she'll last the night} I don't think he's going to make it to the afternoon, to the evening, to the night, to the morning. He had an audience in mind, because he said it to the camera in the absence of others.

Then sometime during the first night, _{even more reason to stay} all that play acting stopped and Army sat on the floor next to the bed, knees up, elbows balanced on knees, forehead lowered on the bridge of his forearms, that is, with his face hidden from the camera and pulled snot back into his nose, wiped his face with his wrist from time to time, and sighed wetly when he was done.

+

When I was in high school, I had a barbershop in the garage, Army told Faye. Then I sold burgers for a while. Then I had a gym. Then a love service.

A love service?

Matchmaking, sort of. It didn't pan out. Then Army catalogued selected failures: he screened bags in the airport, he delivered pizzas, he ran a pyramid scheme with Oliver's nephew, the graphic design business, retail, retail, restaurant, retail, the talent management stuff, retail, food truck, retail, retail. Now there's the moving company with Oliver's truck and burliest nephews, the rentals that barely break even—I owe Oliver a bunch of money. There was the house-flip thing when the market softened a bit. French fries. Quit, fired for giving away pizzas, collapsed, on pause, fired for repeated tardiness, quit, fired for overcharging customers, quit, one client, fired for repeated tardiness, lawsuit pending, quit, fired for using customers' credit card information.

I don't want to wrap people's furniture in skins forever, he said.

You know what your problem is?

Access to opportunity. I can't close. The sun in my feathers. No capital. Hucksters.

道高一尺,魔高一丈. Dào gāo yā chǐ, mó gāo yī zhàng.

Ninety-nine problems, Army said as if he hadn't heard. Too many, too many. What I'm saying, Faye, is, Don't make me fail again.

+

She told him that when she first moved to Canada she had a standard school-girl haircut, hair to her chin, severe bangs, and she sat in a group with two white girls.

And still sometimes when I'm looking down in lecture and I see the couples, I wonder.

In the background, Felicia breathed.

Faye continued, Do I have to be blonde—

No, of course not.

To be considered, Faye trailed off then reset the question: Do I have to be blonde to be a woman?

+

No change.

+

When Faye left, Army went to check on Riot but really to have a quick ciggy. He couldn't find him in the shopping or food districts of the hospital.

Text: Where u at

Text: Maternity

Text: What u doing in mat

Text: Watching

Is she gone? Riot asked as Army approached.

Army thought he meant Faye but then corrected when he saw Riot about to pause the video. No, Mom's still there.

She's not my mom, Riot said.

Army sat close and they watched the video alongside Army's commentary. The parts he most enjoyed were the ones where someone was on screen.

Technically, someone's always on screen, Riot said.

I mean someone else, Army said.

+

It wasn't until the third day of viewing, at the foot of Felicia's bed, that they got to the moment of Edgar's death. what time you flying Riot woke Army for it. On the recording eight and in life nine it was early afternoon.

Riot is gone to the hospital. Army is sitting on the floor in front of Hendrix's bed with his head tilted back on the edge of the mattress, looking up at the ceiling, and cupping his elbows.

What were you thinking? Riot asked.

Army shook his head. He was thinking, you should sleep Do you think I could be a pallbearer? I'll sleep on the plane Does his father have six friends or living relatives? He was thinking, Mom, let's say Dad died.

His phone vibrates. Army looks at it, frowns, and puts it aside. He throws his head back I thought you say you was a pilot against the mattress.

Who was that? Riot asked.

Army shook his head. [I said no such thing] Notification, he said.

Like, a like? Riot asked.

Yeah, Army said. He couldn't explain [but you does work for an airline company] that it was, in fact, a text without [as you would say] getting into the whole [incorrect] story. Faye had cancelled the marriage ceremony.

A few moments later, [I didn't just imagine everything] in the video, Army thumbtypes [you does work in the airport] into his phone.

What were you searching for?

I wasn't searching. I was texting.

Who?

A partner.

About?

Okay, Barbara Walters. Mind your business, [I work for my family] Army said. Then he relented after more video passed. He said, About money.

Army had paid for the marriage licence with his credit card. Faye paid to book the service with cash. It was non-refundable. She wanted her money back from Army as well.

+

Then Error has a revival. He speaks. [by the way] It seems that he [it's pronounced *Mutter*] might survive. But it is delirium. He does not know where he is, Edgar.

Army repeats his name, Armistice, Armistice, Armistice, until it becomes a mantra but it does little to quell Edgar's confusion. So Army says, Felicia, Felicia's house, and Edgar frowns. Then he asks for [*Mutter*] Mutter. [try again] And Army says, [*Mutter*] in exaggerated syllables, Fe-li-cia.

+

Predictably, his breathing is irregular. He'd shore up energy for a long inhalation then make it stretch as long as possible until the next one. He has the breathing control [cover your mouth] of a good swimmer, smoker, or meditator. He keeps his eyes closed most of the time but he seems conscious under there. It is only by his mouth that the viewer can tell whether he is sleeping or not. Slack for sleep. Closed for awake.

He is generally silent but sometimes he chatters, mutters things in English and German, while Army makes I'm-listening noises in his throat. His face jerks into a smile, breakthrough smiles instead of breakthrough pain, like a baby at a mother's face. He asks for cigarettes and Army lights one for him. He holds the pack in his grip at his side.

Point of confusion. Once when he bursts the surface of delirium to try to communicate with Army (because his words were mostly for himself at that point though by being spoken, they seem tossed out to retrieve a response), he spends a long time searching for the right word. It is a German word, *Das* something and the rest sound like a sneeze, is that how you sneeze *das Taschentuch.* bless you (In the hospital room, an audio Google search for the word kept telling him to try again.) *Das das* with the *d* weak so Army believes he is asking for *mas,* gesundheit more. gesundheit And he is patting himself on the face it hurts when he says if I keep it in it, hurts near his mouth, so Army thinks he is asking for another cigarette or water but he refuses them both. He says, Han hand, and tries to cough so Army puts his hand on his forehead and that seems to comfort him or be close enough to whatever he was asking for.

+

Felicia by contrast could not say anything. She lay near the hospital window modelling a good death, taking her certificate from a small unrecognized island with her.

+

The final time he breaks into delirium, as I was saying he is saying, As I was saying, a long stream of it, As I was saying, as I was, as I was saying as I was saying as I was saying, an attempt at clearing his throat, as I as I as I as I was you wasn't saying nothing

+

He died the way a tourist might float inside a donut with a drink in one hand and a straw hat low over his eyes and drift toward the edge of an infinity pool.

+

Felicia was unconscious but still she seemed absolutely unmoved by the video's climax. There should have been a single, fat, glycerine tear. She looked like she might wake partway through a long flight when she heard the snack cart approaching, turn to the stranger next to her, and ask, Which Germany?

+

At Hendrix's funeral, purely ceremonial, Oliver overheard Felicia telling the story of Hendrix's death to a perfect stranger as if it were just another in her catalogue of stories.

And Army, as consolation to Heather, had said, It's how he'd want to go.

+

I have something for you, Edgar had said when Army first gave him the Galaxy. Here's a number. He gave Army a thistle-coloured card with embossed silver letters. Bill Luther. Lawyer.

He's a friend?

Something like that.

Army got his phone to begin dialling Bill Luther, Lawyer.

Not now. Edgar put his hand on Army's to stop him. When I go, call him. He'll take care of everything. Do not resuscitate, funeral home, Bill has instructions for everything.

On the video, Army makes a phone call. He is pinching the bridge of his nose and pacing back and forth in front of Edgar's body.

After the phone call, Army takes his finger and lifts Edgar's jaw closed.

Army was disturbed that Oliver stayed away from Felicia's room. He probably couldn't handle another death: Not *another*. Hers.

+

Make me a copy, Army said to Riot. I don't want the whole thing. Just the last couple of hours.

I can put the whole thing up on my site.

Don't do that.

You can access it from anywhere that way, Riot said. Riot already had posted the video.

Don't.

I don't see what the—

Riot, he's not porn.

+ +

There were voices coming from the summer, voices without words. There was something in her nose. And animals. There was a hill outside, she knew there'd be as soon as she opened her eyes, a hill and a standpipe and water to carry in a yellow bucket. Hair. She needed to touch her hair. A girl with her hair in a messy ponytail. Where were her hands? They were burned off. She turned back to see them in the waving gallery. Hurry. The handle of her suitcase. Greeting cards as decoration. In the back row of the choir. A black novel where the pages smelled like carpet. Her mother eaten by red ants. Her blouse melting in the fire behind the house. Smoke. Her voice on fire. Smoke. Polar bears on floes in his eyes. His forearms bare. A dark garage. Another garage. A dark garage. On top of his car. In a room with a seal, clapping his flippers. Standing in reeds on the Nile. Could you watch him tomorrow night? A typewriter. The bus stop. Red airplane tails. Her seal came home with an ungloved hand holding a Mother's Day card. A man holding a hose. A girl with her hair in a messy ponytail. A needle in the back. Red bank book. The couch. An Ikea bed. On a bus in the night with no food in his bag, no proper coat. Work in the morning. The prescription counter. Work this morning. A colourful Ferris wheel. Light.

What you looking at? Her voice was burned off.

You.

What was she holding in her hands to make them so heavy? Her movements were four times slower than usual. She was shaking was shaking was shaking was shaking her head. With the slightest tilt of a head, she pointed she pointed she pointed she pointed to Riot.

Riot looked alarmed. He eyed Army, who unclasped his forearms, and slowly lowered the lid of the laptop.

Mutter, Riot said, approaching her side.

Felicia turned her head to the window. Away from the two of them.

But they raced forward like speedboats.

You feeling all right? Riot asked.

You want the TV on? Turn on the TV, little man.

Army ate your Jell-O.

It was like a bright light before you blacked out, right? Hark the voice of Jesus calling. You know you should have been in like four accidents before the car stopped.

I had them turn up the heat so you don't catch pneumonia but if you're too hot I can have them lower it.

Did you hear me and Faye talking all night?

Can you stop dropping Faye into every conversation?

He started taking photos of you when you were slobbering, tube up your nose, but I wasn't having it.

I didn't.

I made him erase every last one.

Felicia said, Let me see.

Honest to God, I didn't, Mutter.

It exhausted Felicia to listen to them. They had regressed in the hours she had been sleeping. She was certain she would have to be at work in a few hours, not in a hospital gown.

Call Brownstone.

They know.

They've known since last week.

What day is it? Felicia asked. It felt like the next day but she couldn't remember next to what.

Tuesday.

Days had passed apparently. She became focused on practicalities. Who'd you talk to?

Don't worry about that. They know.

And the ombudsman?

I'm not going to show, Riot said.

Felicia shook her head.

I mean, I'll cancel it.

No, you're going, Felicia said.

Riot began to protest, but Army stopped him.

No one had to tell Felicia that Edgar had died. She knew by how they avoided it with irrelevant chatter.

Did you call his family? she asked.

No answer.

Take my address book.

I handled it, Mom. I'm meeting with his lawyer. Army pointed his finger comparatively between himself and Riot. Same day as Riot's thing.

Felicia studied Army for a while then began to smile. You called Jerry? Her eyes watered from soundless laughter then closed.

+

Play it, she said when she woke up again. They were treating her like she was a delicate flower.

No one moved for a while then Army set the laptop on the tray. But when Felicia turned her face to the window again, Riot closed the file.

Play it, Felicia repeated.

You looked away so I thought—

Play it. But she didn't want it so close. She said, Over there, meaning the empty bed beside her. She wanted it running, even if she didn't see all of it. She wanted it parallel to her, not over her. Then the voices became high and childlike and summery again and she couldn't make out the words with her eyes closed.

She woke up and he was with her and he was with him and they were they.

+

He was going to make Riot an anaconda video for old times' sake.

At first he thought that his phone had some dead pixels. But when Ahme looked into the toilet bowl itself, there was some blood, like flakes of red pepper, in his stool.

+ +
+

Army was called into the lawyer's office.

Riot was called into the ombudsman's office.

I understand Edgar Gross was a relative, the lawyer said.

My father, Army said. Not a sixth cousin by marriage.

We have received additional complaints, the ombudsman said.

I can't control everything, Riot said.

The lawyer backtracked. First of all, I'm sorry for your loss.

Army wanted to know if Edgar had in fact left him millions. He apologized for the snark. Grief, he said.

The ombudsman leaned forward. It's important that you know we're turning this matter over to our legal department. You're twenty.

Riot thought of Adele. *19. 21. 25.*

I won't take up too much of your time. I do need a few signatures from you. The estate of Edgar Gross has made a donation in your name to charity.

Swell, Army said and flashed a shiny fifties smile. He placed his hands on the arms of his chair to sit up.

To be clear, Brownstone's lawyer does not represent you or any other party connected with this incident. I advise you to retain a lawyer of your own should litigation follow.

They were trying to shut down a public relations nightmare. No father would send their daughter to a school plastered over the news for scandal.

And, the lawyer reached into a manila envelope and produced Army's old phone, he left you this.

He couldn't even leave him a new phone. Just return his old one.

The ombudsman cleared his throat.

What about the house?

That's the other thing.

Already Army planned to sell it, sell everything in it, cash out, buy three preconstruction condos, invest the rest. Oh, he'd have to do a market analysis like he used to. He'd rent an office downtown and—

He left the house for Felicia Shaw.

But relieved when he got out of that office. Relieved. Riot. Relieved.

In his car, Army turned on his old phone. It turned out Edgar had bought a lot of music. He must have had someone help him. There were playlists for Army, for Edgar, and for Felicia.

The lawyer said, You were probably expecting more.

ACKNOWLEDGEMENTS

Thanks to the Calgary Distinguished Writers Program at the University of Calgary for a year, an office, a community, a view, all of which played a part in the completion of this novel. Thanks to the Al Purdy A-Frame. Thanks to the Banff Centre for a Leighton Residency that emboldened me to discard 25,000 words and rewrite better ones. I am also grateful for my colleagues and students at the University of British Columbia.

Phanuel Antwi, Jane Munro, Larissa Lai, Robyn Read and David Chariandy asked to read drafts of *Reproduction* and I wouldn't let them. Thanks for trying. Nothing stopping you now.

Thanks to Eddie Parker for naming Edgar and for saving a character's life. Thanks to Florian Gassner for German, to Harry Ludwigsen for German, Germans and German families. Thanks to Caitlynn Cummings and Shazia Hafiz Ramji for minding the details. Thanks to the other writers who were writing books alongside me: Myronn Hardy, Larissa Lai, Nick Sousanis, Lauren Carter, Jane Munro, Jane Hilberry—or music, Reiko Yamada.

Thanks to folks for intellectual and creative company or for conversations that set new standards of honesty: Christian Olbey, Basil Chiasson, Blaine Newton, Leslie Greentree, Shyam Selvadurai, Evelyn Lau, Benjamin Voisin, Nancy Kang, Phanuel Antwi again, Phanuel Antwi again.

Thanks to Judy Wark for a year. Thanks to Courtney Gustafson and Patrick Cuff for a November, to Ted Slingerland for afternoons of tennis after mornings of editing, to Richard Bedell for countless shifts, to Jean Claude for Saturdays, to Ragne Pajo for weekly recurring hours, to Zack Hobler for a dawn we wandered Toronto, to my family for ever since.

Thanks to my fearless, persistent, straight-talking agent, Denise Bukowski. Thanks to Random House Canada, particularly Sarah Jackson and my editor, Anne Collins—perceptive, precise, always right from her vantage somewhere in the futureland of every novel's potential. After six years of somewhat secretive writing, I thank you for instantly understanding.

And to everyone who asked, When are you going to get a haircut? the answer is, When I finish *Reproduction*.

IAN WILLIAMS is the author of *Personals*, shortlisted for the Griffin Poetry Prize and the Robert Kroetsch Poetry Book Award; *Not Anyone's Anything*, winner of the Danuta Gleed Literary Award for the best first collection of short fiction in Canada; and *You Know Who You Are*, a finalist for the ReLit Prize for poetry. He was named as one of ten Canadian writers to watch by CBC. He completed his Ph.D. in English at the University of Toronto and is currently a professor of poetry in the Creative Writing program at the University of British Columbia.